E.R. PUNSHON
MYSTERY OF MR. JESSOP

Ernest Robertson Punshon was born in London in 1872.

At the age of fourteen he started life in an office. His employers soon informed him that he would never make a really satisfactory clerk, and he, agreeing, spent the next few years wandering about Canada and the United States, endeavouring without great success to earn a living in any occupation that offered. Returning home by way of working a passage on a cattle boat, he began to write. He contributed to many magazines and periodicals, wrote plays, and published nearly fifty novels, among which his detective stories proved the most popular and enduring.

He died in 1956.

Also by E.R. Punshon

Information Received
Death Among The Sunbathers
Crossword Mystery
Mystery Villa
Death of A Beauty Queen
Death Comes to Cambers
The Bath Mysteries
The Dusky Hour
Dictator's Way

E.R. PUNSHON

MYSTERY OF MR. JESSOP

With an introduction
by Curtis Evans

DEAN STREET PRESS

Published by Dean Street Press 2015

Copyright © 1937 E.R. Punshon

Introduction Copyright © 2015 Curtis Evans

All Rights Reserved

Published by licence, issued under the UK Orphan Works
Licensing Scheme

First published in 1937 by Victor Gollancz

Cover by DSP

ISBN 978 1 911095 38 5

www.deanstreetpress.co.uk

INTRODUCTION

Although E.R. Punshon had a spotty publication record in the United States, where between 1933 and 1938 only six of his first ten Bobby Owen detective novels were picked up by American publishers (overall, merely twelve of the thirty-five novels in the Bobby Owen series, just over a third, ever appeared in hardcover in the US, a major reason for the rarity of these books on the collectors' market today), he was one of the most popular authors of classical detective fiction in Great Britain, where his novels were published by the noted firm Victor Gollancz. In the 1930s he became a member of the Detection Club and his books were favorites of his club colleagues Dorothy L. Sayers and Milward Kennedy, in the Thirties successive mystery reviewers for the influential *Sunday Times*.

Also numbering among Punshon's English readership was the beloved humorist P.G. Wodehouse, a great fan of detective and thriller fiction (see William A.S. Sarjeant's 1987 *The Mystery Fancier* article "P.G. Wodehouse as Reader of Crime Stories.") In Wodehouse's 1938 novel *The Code of the Woosters*, we find that Bertie Wooster himself is a Punshon devotee. In the novel Bertie divulges that he, like many another Thirties mystery fan, relishes curling up with a good crime tale: "A cheerful fire was burning in the grate, and to while away the time I pulled the armchair up and got out the mystery story I had brought with me from

London. As my researches in it had already shown me, it was a particularly good one, full of crisp clues and meaty murders, and I was soon absorbed." Bertie's later reference to this mystery story leaves no doubt that the tale is Punshon's *Mystery of Mr. Jessop*, published in England the previous year. Tasked with discovering where Stephanie "Stiffy" Byng may have hidden a small, brown, leather-covered notebook, purloined from Gussie Fink-Nottle, Bertie finds inspiration from the pages of *Jessop* (page 151 of the Gollancz edition, to be exact), quoting a Scotland Yard superintendent's pronouncement concerning the whereabouts of "every woman's favorite hiding-place".

As the admiring Bertie Wooster attests, *Mystery of Mr. Jessop* indeed offers detective fiction fans a rich repast of satisfying mystery. Like *Crime at Guildford* (1935) and *Proceed with Caution* (1937), contemporary mysteries by Punshon's Detection Club colleagues Freeman Wills Crofts and John Rhode (Cecil John Charles Street), Punshon's intensively plot-driven *Mystery of Mr. Jessop* concerns nefarious criminal activities, including murder, implicating a prominent firm of jewelers. The novel opens with a police raid in progress on The Towers, the Victorian villa residence of Timothy Thomas ("T.T.") Mullins, a notorious stolen goods receiver. (The Towers is located in the imaginary London borough of Brush Hill, a neighborhood that plays a prominent role in two previous Bobby Owen mysteries, *Mystery Villa* and *Death of a Beauty Queen*.) The raid, in which Bobby is participating, is led by Scotland Yard's Superintendent Ulyett, Bobby's former mentor Superintendent Mitchell, last mentioned (briefly) in *Death Comes to Cambers* (1935), evidently having retired. The Yard has been informed that a fabulous diamond necklace consigned by its owner, American film siren Fay Fellows (star of the Hollywood hits *Rich Man's Baby* and *Millionaire's Sweetie*), to a London firm of jewelers, Jessop & Jacks, in order that its sale may be arranged, has instead gone missing; and it is suspected that T. T. Mullins is on the verge of receiving the pilfered sparklers at The Towers. The raid quickly devolves into a fiasco, however. No fabulous diamonds are found at The Towers, but instead the body of a man, only just shot dead; and this dead man is Mr. Jessop, a partner in Jessop & Jacks and the very individual who informed the police that Fay Fellows' necklace had been stolen.

This unexpected turn of events plunges Bobby and Superintendent Ulyett into a baffling brouhaha of double enigmas: who snaffled the diamond necklace and who snuffed out Mr. Jessop? The Yard investigation uncovers a goodly number of suspects for both crimes, starting with the smarmily mendacious T.T. Mullins himself. Punshon's plot is intricately developed, with, as that noted mystery fancier Bertie Wooster indicated, a series of enticingly crisp material clues (including a copy of an illustrated weekly, some missing pages of Saturday football results, a wealthy American's monogrammed cigars and the torn tip of a rubber glove), and should appeal greatly to puzzle enthusiasts; yet there also is much of interest in Punshon's writing and his characters. As Milward Kennedy noted in his review of *Jessop* in the *Sunday Times*, the events in the novel are "related with the drily humorous touch which we expect from E.R. Punshon, and with his accustomed skill in portraiture." Once again Punshon includes some fine touches of social satire, especially after the haughty Duke of Westhaven and his baubles-bedazzled wife enter the case. Superintendent Ulyett, an ardent Tory, is so deferent to the aristocracy's prerogatives, as he imagines them, that he is rather at a loss over how to handle a murder case involving a duke and duchess. Consequently he delegates these august personages to Bobby, whom, he has heard, comes from the top drawer himself (word gets round about these things), even though Bobby protests that his uncle, Lord Hirlpool, is "only an earl" and "practically bankrupt" at that. Some of the novel's most amusing exchanges on class and politics take place between the conservative superintendent and his more iconoclastic sergeant:

> "This duke and duchess seem mixed up in it, too, but of course they're above suspicion. Thank God," said Ulyett piously, "we aren't Bolsheviks yet at Scotland Yard."
>
> "No, sir," agreed Bobby. "Perhaps we shall be, though, after another election or two."

Punshon portrays the topical subject of the rise of fascism and communism in Thirties England through a character who over the course of the novel migrates from the one ideology to the other before finally becoming disaffected with both, suggesting that in the author's view there was a fundamental interchangeability between these illiberal totalitarian political faiths:

"….The fact is, I've had enough of that sort of thing: fed up I am. I've really made up my mind to chuck politics."

"Sound man," approved Bobby.

"I shall vote," declared Higson, "for each lot in turn, so as to give 'em all a chance."

"That's the spirit," said Bobby. "Makes the British Constitution the envy of the world."

"After all," said Higson thoughtfully, "when it comes to kicking the other fellow's ribs in, which is all these Fascists and Reds think about—well, a gorilla could beat 'em both at that game, couldn't he?"

Bobby looked at Higson admiringly.

"….You're right. Funny thing that in the fourth decade of the twentieth century the gorilla should be an accepted ideal."

Modern readers of *Mystery of Mr. Jessop* can reflect, if they are so minded, on just how much the world has changed in the second decade of the twenty-first century; or they can simply enjoy what is a cracking good mystery. As Milward Kennedy put it, E.R. Punshon "has once again supplied us with a puzzle which is also a first-rate story."

Curtis Evans

CHAPTER I

THE FURNITURE VAN

Along Chesters Street, which runs its full length by the west side of Lonesome Fields Common, the furniture van lumbered clumsily on its slow way. On its roof, an old-fashioned mangle with heavy wooden rollers wobbled dangerously, restrained only by a loosely tied rope from toppling over into the street. Next to it a horsehair sofa, such as our fathers and our mothers loved, held up its four legs into the air, as if in dumb protest against the cruelty of fate that had driven it from the place of honour in the drawing-room to a doubtful perch on a van roof, without so much as even a shred of cover against the lightly falling rain that was turning this dull London Saturday evening into a misty night. On the tail-board balanced a sickly looking aspidistra, apparently nearly forgotten during the loading of the van and then hurriedly gathered up at the last moment but not thought worthy of the re-opening of the van. By its side sat a burly person enveloped in an enormous green baize apron, a sack drawn over his head to protect him from the drizzle. He was smoking a short clay pipe, and he stared out into vacancy with the blank indifference of a man for whom, between the jobs of packing and unpacking, life held little of interest.

Evidently a family whose roots went back into the dim Victorian past effecting a change of residence.

The street was not well lighted, and the falling rain, the mist drifting in from the common, the oncoming night, threw a dim veil around, through which the few passers-by, the big old-fashioned houses each standing aloof in its own grounds, an occasional stray passing vehicle, all loomed up, vaguely indistinct, as though half proclaiming, half withdrawing, the testimony of their presence. With many of the inhabitants this bad lighting of their street was a perennial grievance, but somehow repeated complaints to the borough council produced no effect. Improvement was always promised but never carried out. There seemed mysterious opposing influences, a kind of " hidden hand " operating in the background. Rumour said that this was because some of the youthful inhabitants of the borough, including some whose parents were influential councillors, found the obscurity prevailing in the long, straight street resulted in their being able to use it for trying out their motor-cycles and their sports cars with less risk of possible complainants seeing their registration numbers.

Probably that explanation was worth little. Motor-cycles seemed to go banging up and down this street with no unusual frequency. Another, perhaps more likely, theory—since, after all, the saying that " money talks " is as valid for borough councils as for other bodies and persons—points out that Chesters Street has very sadly come down in the world. Its big early Victorian houses, all with unnecessary basements, all planned on the assumption that domestic help would remain cheap and frequent, all void of such conveniences as a hot-water supply or central heating, boasting at best but one bathroom, and that generally tucked away in a dark and inconvenient corner, as something not quite proper, were now either vacant or let off at the rate of a family a floor, with no restriction upon lodgers. An additional disadvantage, too, was that, abutting, as they did at the rear, on the common, they afforded many facilities to the enterprising burglar. It used at one time to be a local joke among the police that no London burglar considered himself out of his apprenticeship till he had broken into at least three Chesters Street houses.

De Montfort House, for example, past which the furniture van was now slowly lumbering, had at one time been occupied by a well-known financier, whose magnificent garden-parties had been the talk of London, had indeed transferred to themselves in their heyday all the glamour and the prestige of Mayfair, then in the height of its glory before sacrilegious hands had been laid even upon Park Lane itself. Since the financier's arrest and trial, and sentence to a term of penal servitude, the house had remained empty, and even the notice-board " To be Let or Sold," whereon the man in the green baize apron turned now a lack-lustre and indifferent eye, seemed to have given up hope as, half obliterated by wind and rain, it drooped sadly and unsteadily earthwards.

The next house, The Towers, was an exception to the general air of shabby depression pervading the street. For many years it had been occupied by a prosperous City man who had been born there, who had hoped to die there, but whose family, by long, persistent effort, aided by a timely burglary or two, had finally succeeded in uprooting him to what was at that time the novelty of a block of West End flats. After having remained empty for some years, it had been let to, and was still occupied by, a Mr. Timothy Thomas Mullins. Mr. Mullins was not much known in the neighbourhood. It seemed he liked privacy. He took no part in the life of the borough; but, then, few of the residents in London suburbs do interest themselves in local affairs. He described himself as " Import and Export Agent "; it was understood he had an office in the City, though no one knew exactly where, and certainly his attendance at it seemed somewhat irregular. At any rate, he appeared to be very comfortably off. The house had a prosperous air. The grounds, between one and two acres in extent, were well kept up, especially in the front of the house, which stood well back from the road, wherefrom it was further screened by what could almost be called a labyrinth of trees and shrubs, planned, planted, and maintained by a well-known firm of landscape gardeners. Inmates of the house might well have thought themselves living in the heart of the country, with what looked like the outskirts of a forest before them and the open expanse of the common behind; and incautious visitors, following the broad gravelled path that seemed to lead from the entrance-gate to the house, were apt to find themselves conducted to what once had been the stable yard and was now only a vacant space before the garage. Such visitors had often to retrace their steps to the inconspicuous turning screened by a hawthorn copse that did in fact lead to the front entrance. Mr. Mullins always thought it a good joke when his visitors were caught into making this blunder, and for his part, if he wanted to proceed on foot to the street, he took a short cut from a side-door through a gap in the hawthorn copse to the path used by tradespeople and others on their way to the back premises.

At the rear of the house, too, the garden was well looked after, and, even in this time of early autumn, was still gay with flowers. The lawn was such a lovely expanse of velvety green as only the British Isles can show, and on each side of it ran two paved, sheltered alleys, bordered by trellis-work, on which grew climbing roses and other plants trained on cross-pieces between the borders of trellis-work, so that in summer the alleys were completely covered in by a green growing roofery. But many people have little private fads, and, though Mr. Mullins spent money freely on his garden and saw that it was always beautifully kept, he appeared to grudge even the smallest sum for the repair of the fence running between his domain and the common. Not even occasional trespassing by children and others, flower stealing, raids on the gooseberry-bushes, and so on, could induce him to have the many gaps in the fence attended to. Sometimes he talked about having a wall put up to replace it, and he had even gone so far as to obtain an estimate of the probable cost. But the project remained in abeyance. Apparently Mr. Mullins hesitated at the expense of erecting a wall and yet did not wish to spend anything on a fence he contemplated replacing.

Exactly opposite The Towers there opened, from Chesters Street, West Lane, as it was called—originally, no doubt, a country lane between common and village, but now a wide street, lined at the end near the common by smart little villas that further on changed gradually to shops, and then, at the corner of the first cross-street, blossomed into two magnificent public-houses, facing each other across the Lane. Naturally, at a third of the four corners stood the natural companion of flourishing public-houses, an equally flourishing pawnbroker's shop. Only a short distance further on was the chief shopping-centre of the district, with the local tube station. As the lane ran due west, the setting sun, when visible, shone down it full upon The Towers, and along it now drove a big old-fashioned car no second-hand dealer would have given more than a five-pound note for, if as much. In spite of its age, it was travelling at fully the thirty-mile speed-limit. Perhaps because of its age, its steering or its brakes may not have been in perfect order. At any rate, at the corner of West Lane and Chesters Street it blundered full into the furniture van, damaging itself pretty badly, apparently; less so the van.

The van driver jumped down and expressed himself with fluency and vigour. He seemed, indeed, to be thoroughly enjoying such a chance for self-expression. The two men in the car that had done the mischief got down too, and looked dejectedly at the damage done, and commented to each other on the impossibility of moving car or van. The man in the green baize apron alighted from the tail-board and came up to join the others and to look on in his uninterested way. Miraculously, as though rising from the earth or falling from the heavens, for there had been no sign of them before, two policemen appeared. One, in the uniform of a sergeant, said it was a bad smash, and such was a disgrace, and, if he had his way, six months' hard was what all concerned would be the better for. His companion, a constable, produced an enormous pocket-book and began to write with slow diligence. A motor-cyclist sped by—built-up area or not, he was doing a clear forty mile an hour, but he seemed to care nothing for the presence of the two policemen.

" What ho ! she bumps," he cried, " she bumps," and so sped on, forty m.p.h. again, police or no police.

Through the gate admitting to The Towers drive emerged Mr. Mullins, a short, fat, smiling man with pale blue eyes, a big bald head, and quick and secret movements, so that unless you watched him closely you were never quite sure of what he had been doing last, or what he would be doing next.

" Dear, dear," he said, his somewhat high-pitched voice full of solicitude, " another accident ? Really, the roads these days—intolerable."

He made clicking sounds of sympathy with his tongue. Behind him was another man, tall, fair, elegant, well-dressed, languid in manner, drawling in speech. The carefully patterned tie he wore suggested the old school, though it was a little hard to be quite sure which one. A fine signet-ring, probably bearing the family crest, showed on the hand that held a cigarette as he observed disdainfully :

" Another of these jay-walkers, probably."

He had not come into the road, but was still within

The Towers grounds, leaning easily on the big five-barred gate at the entrance to the drive. He yawned, evidently bored by the scene, and Mr. Mullins began to walk round the van.

"The only thing to do," he observed to the world at large, "is to unload—lighten the van—unload."

Suddenly, swiftly, dexterously, unexpectedly, he swung open the van doors, heedless of the fate of the aspidistra that he knocked from the tail-board into the road, and began to haul and pull vigorously at the furniture within.

"Here, I say," shouted the sergeant, beginning to run towards him.

"Unload—only thing—lighten van," persisted Mr. Mullins, dragging out a chair, a fender, and a small table. "Good God," he screamed at the top of his voice, "there's men in there."

The sergeant said something unprintable, unreportable, altogether shocking. He also took Mr. Mullins by the coat-collar, and, none too gently, jerked him back. But Mr. Mullins made no attempt to resent this rough handling. He said, with every appearance of extreme astonishment:

"Why, it's my old pal Superintendent Ulyett been and gone and got himself demoted to sergeant again. Oh, Superintendent Ulyett, Superintendent Ulyett, whatever have you been a-doing of?"

Superintendent Ulyett again said something unprintable, unreportable, shocking.

"You must have been heard using such words, that's what it was, I'll bet a monkey," declared Mr. Mullins, shaking a reproachful head. "Bad example to junior ranks." Then he looked at the constable with the note-book and fairly reeled against the van, as though under the shock of even further and greater surprise. "Sergeant Bobby Owen, if my eyes don't deceive me," he moaned. "The most promising and thickest-headed of the younger

C.I.D. men reduced to the ranks, sent back to the uniform branch. This moves me to tears," he said, and produced accordingly a very large, very white silk handkerchief.

" Anyhow," said Detective-Sergeant Bobby Owen to himself, prudently preferring not to make aloud a remark his superior officer might have failed at this crisis fully to appreciate, " anyhow, they've got it in writing I said a blessed old stunt like a furniture van, that was old before the war "—he said this as another generation would have said " Before the flood "—" would never come off against the smartest receiver in London—that's old T. T. Mullins."

From the van emerged in solemn, sad procession five full-sized members of the C.I.D., headed by Inspector Ferris, all looking somewhat sheepish, none making any response to the cordial greeting extended by name to each by Mr. T. T. Mullins, whose memory for faces was as remarkable as were other of his gifts and qualities.

" Splendid to see what good pals you fellows are in the C.I.D.," he said. " One of you moves because of the rent he owes and won't pay, and the rest of you hurry along to help with the family heirlooms. Touching, I call it," declared Mr. Mullins enthusiastically, " even if some careless bloke has knocked over great-grandma's own pet plant pot."

He shook his head sadly at the overturned aspidistra pot that had scattered plant and mould into the gutter. He began to busy himself gathering up plant and pot, and pushing them into the van. The police officers stood round in a circle, big men all, the least of them a head taller than he was, all regarding him with a nice mingling of reluctant admiration and intense yearning to slay him on the spot. And the smile with which he regarded them would have done credit to an angel at the gate welcoming a lost sinner home at last.

From the man leaning on the gate at the entrance to

The Towers drive came a loud, sudden laugh, harsh, less elegant than might have been expected from such a very elegant exterior. As abruptly as it had been uttered it ceased, and, turning quickly, the laugher disappeared up the drive towards the house, walking with a long, swift, easy stride that took him out of sight almost immediately.

"Getting wet, most likely," observed T. T. Mullins, watching him go. "Something amused him though. I wonder what? Business friend of mine—Augustus Percy Wynne. Augustus Percy because such is his nature, as his loving parents knew; Wynne for the same reason. Nice chap. Wanted me to go in with him on some South African deal—De Beers and diamonds and that sort of thing. Too risky for me. I prefer local loans to—er—diamonds. Getting old, I suppose."

He shook his head again with an air of deep self-pity, and his remarks seemed somehow to increase the general depression. Superintendent Ulyett glared at his companions as if selecting one or all of them for instant dismissal. What he was really thinking of was the interview due to take place next morning between himself and an Assistant Commissioner known to possess a caustic tongue.

"I suppose," said Mr. Mullins timidly, "I couldn't persuade you gentlemen to come in and have a glass of something comforting? Do you good after standing about in this horrid damp mist. November fog before its time. Of course, if you can spare a minute, I mean?"

"We can," said Ulyett briefly; "and, if you want to know, T. T., and would like to see it, I've a search-warrant in my pocket."

"Now, isn't that just too wonderful?" cried T. T., beaming with apparent delight. "Extraordinary how things turn out. Wouldn't happen once in a million years, your search-warrant and my invitation coming together. Talk about coincidences," said T. T., lost in admiration.

Ulyett grunted, and made a move in the direction of the house. T. T. trotted ahead to open for him the gate of the drive. Pausing in the opening, he turned to murmur once again his pleasure over the unexpected arrival of his visitors.

" You shan't one of you go out of the house," he declared firmly, " till you've tasted my cocoa—the best in London, if I say it myself."

Ulyett grunted again. His appetite for cocoa was limited. Some of the others, overhearing what T. T. said, looked more depressed than ever. T. T. continued to survey them with gentle, coy benevolence. The man in the green baize apron he had not had time to discard, though his eyes had lost their dull, lack-lustre expression—had grown, indeed, keen and alert instead—said to Bobby:

" Do you know what it's all about ? I got pulled in the moment I came on duty, and they've had me sitting on that blessed tail-board ever since, without a chance to say a word to anyone."

" Swagger diamond necklace," Bobby explained. "Quite No. 1 in diamond necklaces—runs to a hundred thousand or so. Belongs to Miss Fay Fellows, the film star. She's not such a favourite as she was, and, as her income has dropped to something under a million a week, she's been trying to sell. Jessop & Jacks, the Mayfair Square jewellers, had it in hand, and they rang up in an awful sweat this afternoon to say they were afraid it had been pinched. But they wouldn't give any details, so our people said they couldn't do anything, and Jessop said they must avoid scandal, and big people were implicated, but would we stand by and be ready ? Of course, we said we were always ready, but they muts tell us more if they wanted us to take action, and then they rang off. Next thing was what seemed a sure-fire tip that T. T. was going to be offered the biggest ever in sparklers this evening somewhere round eight or nine o'clock. Looked like a chance to score—to ring up Jessop & Jacks and say, " Oh, by the way, we've got that necklace of yours," and have them eating out of our hand ever after. Jewellers get to know a lot that's going on, and can give useful tips at times if they want to. So we were packed off to see what we could do, and Ulyett came along himself because he's jolly keen on roping in T. T. if possible. The idea was to surround the house and rush it before there was time to spot us, and get the thing away or hidden. But a furniture van is too old a stunt for a wary bird like T. T."

The other nodded agreement, and from the direction of the house came suddenly, sharp and loud and ominous on the still night air, the sound of two pistol shots in quick succession.

CHAPTER II

IDENTIFIED

Short, round, and fat T. T. Mullins might be, but no champion of the hurdles or the track could have been swifter in response to that startling summons from the house.

" The diamonds, diamonds," he screamed, and ran, his little fat legs carrying him along at an astonishing speed, so that he was almost out of sight round the curve in the drive before the echo of those two shots had died into the evening quiet.

Also, whether by chance or calculation, he had, as he started to run, swung back with violence the gate he had been holding open, so that it and burly Superintendent Ulyett came into somewhat violent contact.

For perhaps some five or six seconds there was delay as the swung-to gate and the breathless superintendent blocked the road. Then the gate was hurled back, and all of them went pelting up the drive. But, though five or six seconds does not sound much, an astonishing amount of ground can be covered in that time, and the start T. T. had secured enabled him to reach the turning by the hawthorns and dodge round it unperceived, and so by the side-path direct to the garden door, while Ulyett, not as young now as on the day when he joined the force but in first-class training and keen to show he was still good for a bit of a run, headed the race straight down the deceptively straight remainder of the drive to the dead end of the open space before the garage. Two or three of the others, however, including Bobby, turned off by the hawthorn bushes, though they in their turn missed the path to the side-door. But in this way they reached the front entrance a minute or two before the arrival of the superintendent and those who had followed him.

" No answer, sir," said to him Bobby, who had been beating a loud tattoo with the knocker. " Do we break in ? Lawson says the window's not bolted."

" Only wants lifting, sir," said Lawson, who was the man in the green baize apron. " I've tried it."

" Surround the house first," Ulyett ordered, giving brief directions. " See no one gets away." But before anything could be done the door opened abruptly and T. T. himself appeared—a changed T. T., though, no longer brisk, pert, and confident as any little cock sparrow, but pale and shaken to the depths of his being.

" It's murder, " he stammered breathlessly, " murder. Some bloke I never saw—lying dead there in the study— dead—and I don't know who he is or where he came from."

" Get the house surrounded; see if our chaps are at the back; hold anyone you see," Ulyett repeated, speaking this time to Inspector Ferris, who, nearly the last to arrive, had now joined them. " Then report to me. Owen, come with me. Whereabouts ? " he added to T. T.

Mopping his face with his handkerchief, showing himself profoundly and deeply moved, T. T. led the way across the hall. Though his reputation was that of being the cleverest receiver in London, though during the last quarter of a century he had been kept fairly constantly under close police watch, though he had been arrested half a dozen times—always celebrating his release for lack of " sufficient evidence " by a liberal donation to the police orphanage— though his house had been searched from top to bottom at least as often, not one single conviction had ever been registered against him—except one for leaving his car unattended in the High Street, an incident accepted on both sides as the best of jokes. Nor were his the ways of violence. An extraordinary nerve, a presence of mind and readiness of wit of the highest order, he had often shown he possessed, but, in addition, a certain bodily timidity. Any scene or suggestion of violence he was always careful to avoid, and if any of the rougher elements with whom he sometimes dealt ever tried to take advantage of this weakness, they were fairly certain to find themselves very soon in the hands of the police as a result of " information received " so full and complete as to ensure a good long term of imprisonment. Even then, it would be a very extreme and unusual case if the convicted man's dependants did not receive a weekly allowance during his absence. It was T. T.'s boast that none who worked for him were ever refused help; with the odd contradictoriness of human nature, he took more interest in, and showed greater thought for, his humbler associates than did many a " big business " man proud of his reputation and high standards of integrity. True, T. T. always took care to secure for himself the lion's share of the loot, but, then, the " big business " man is equally firm about that.

From the hall, furnished as every good Victorian hall was furnished fifty years ago, a small room—the study, it was called—opened on the south side, the whole of the rest of the southern side of the house being occupied by the seldom-used drawing-room. The study, too, was furnished with good solid old-fashioned mahogany furniture, including a big writing-table in the middle of the room, two arm-chairs before the fireplace in which a small coal fire burned, a side-table on which stood cigars, cigarettes, soda-water, an empty, or nearly empty, bottle of whisky, and glasses. In one corner stood also a big iron safe of antique appearance, its door ajar. Between it and the wide-open window lay the body of a man, supine, the blood oozing from two wounds in the chest. On the right of the body, at a little distance, lay a small automatic pistol and a half-smoked cigar.

" Never saw him before. Never set eyes on him till now," T. T. stammered, still mopping at his brow. " Dead, isn't he ? My God, who did it, and what for ? "

He went across to the fireplace and pressed the bell-knob, then collapsed into the nearest chair, still mopping his face and muttering to himself. Bobby knelt down by the prostrate man, and, taking his hand, tried to feel his pulse. But it was evident it was too late for anything to be done. Already the glazing eyes, the pinched face, told how near was the end. But the touch of Bobby's hand seemed to revive the dying man a moment. He made an effort to rally his strength. He said loudly:

" The duke—duchess—knew . . ."

His voice ceased. He breathed twice very deeply and was still. Bobby looked up gravely at the superintendent, who said :

" Yes, he's gone. . . . What did he mean ? "

" Oh, my God, my God, my God," muttered T. T., and pressed the bell violently again.

Ulyett gave him a long, hard, calculating look. Certainly all T. T.'s record was against the idea of his being the murderer, but this was his house, his room, and one never knows. He had, of course, not been on the spot when the actual shots were fired, but such things as mechanical traps are not altogether unknown. Ulyett decided T. T. would have to be very closely questioned, but that could wait. On the table by the empty whisky bottle was a telephone. He picked up the instrument and, getting through to the local police station, told them to send a doctor at once and then to communicate with headquarters for further help to be sent. He put the instrument down again and said to T. T., still angrily pressing the bell:

" What's that for ? What do you want ? "

" Brandy," T. T. told him. " I need it. Why the hell don't they answer? I'll sack the lot." Without looking at the body, he made a shuddering gesture towards it. " Who is it ? How did he come here ? Who did it ? "

His teeth were chattering; he seemed so much on the verge of collapse that Bobby, thinking he really needed some stimulant, looked at the whisky bottle.

" It's empty," he remarked.

" It's always nearly empty when any of the boys are coming," T. T. muttered. " Doesn't do to give them too much."

" What boys were they ? " Ulyett asked sharply.

" Only Wynne. You saw him," T. T. answered.

" Where is he ? " Ulyett asked.

" I don't know—cleared out most like," T. T. answered. " You don't think he did it ? " he asked, with a kind of muffled yell. " He wouldn't. Why should he ? Who is it, anyway ? " He leaned forward once more and kept his finger on the bell. " Can't they hear ? " he demanded.

" Who else is in the house ? " Ulyett asked.

" Mrs. Nixon, the housekeeper, and the maids—two of them. Unless they're out."

" Do they know what's happened ? "

" They heard. Couldn't help," T. T. answered. " When I got in, they were in the hall, Mrs. Nixon and both maids— at least, I'm sure of Mrs. Nixon; I think the maids were with her; one anyhow. You can ask her; she'll know. I called out to them, I think. I said: ' What is it ? What's up ? ' I don't think they answered—scared out of their lives. Now they're having hysterics in the kitchen, most likely. I'll sack them if they don't come," he added, jabbing at the bell again.

A sound of footsteps and of voices in the hall became audible. Bobby went to the door. An elderly woman was hovering at a distance near a door opening from behind the stairs. Behind her hesitated a pale-faced girl in cap and apron, who emitted a faint squeal at the sight of Bobby. The elderly woman said quaveringly:

" There's a man at the back—he says he's a policeman."

" We are police officers," Bobby confirmed. " Your master wants some brandy. Are you Mrs. Nixon ? "

The elderly woman nodded.

" That's right," she said, with more confidence, as if reassured by the fact that her name was known. " What's happened ? There was   shots," she concluded in a whisper.

" Yes, there's been an accident—or something else," Bobby answered. " The doctor's been sent for. Get the brandy and then wait in the kitchen. There's nothing for you to get alarmed about, but the superintendent will want to ask you some questions."

The girl behind emitted yet another squeal at this, and vanished precipitately. Mrs. Nixon said:

" We heard shots—that's all. Mr. Mullins came."

" Well, get that brandy," Bobby said, and went back into the study.

The local police had just rung up to say that a doctor was on his way, and that Scotland Yard had been communicated with and was sending help. T. T. was still sitting back in his chair, apparently in a state of collapse. Ulyett, standing in the middle of the room, was looking carefully all round.

" That's what it was done with," he said, pointing to the small automatic on the floor. " Don't touch it till ' Fingerprints ' has had a go. Not that it'll be much good. See what's caught in the trigger guard ? "

Bobby bent down to look.

" Finger torn off a rubber glove," he said.

" Means gloves were worn," Ulyett remarked, " means there won't be any prints." He added to T. T., pointing to the half-smoked cigar on the floor. "That yours?"

T. T. roused himself sufficiently to shake his head.

"Not mine," he said. "We had cigarettes, Wynne and me; his they were—Bulgars; he always smokes 'em. Look in the ash-tray."

A glance at the indicated ash-tray confirmed this and then a tap at the door announced the arrival of the brandy. As Mrs. Nixon firmly declined to enter the room, Bobby took the tray from her and put it down near T. T., who helped himself liberally, and with the stimulant recovered a little of his poise and confidence.

"Well, who is it?" he said. "What's he doing here? Who did it? Nice thing, find a fellow shot dead in your own house."

Bobby was bending over the half-smoked cigar still lying in the same place, for nothing yet had been touched. He said:

"There's an initial or monogram or something on it, nearly burnt away."

"Yes, I noticed that. May be useful," Ulyett agreed. To T. T. he said: "Doesn't that help you—nobody you know who smokes cigars like that? Looks like the expensive sort. Sure you've no idea who it is?"

"Never saw him before; don't know him from Adam," T. T. insisted. "Isn't there anything to show in his pockets?"

"Not that I can find," answered Bobby, who had made a hurried and necessarily superficial search. "Money, keys, cigarette-case, fountain-pen—nothing else much; no papers except that," he added, showing a copy of a smart weekly illustrated, *The Upper Ten*, well known for the excellence of its photographs of prominent social personalities.

"Anything missing from the room?" Ulyett asked. "The safe's open."

" It wasn't before," declared T. T. " That blighter must have opened it, or someone. There was nothing in it; there never is. I only keep it there for show; half the time it isn't locked. I don't believe it was to-night."

Ulyett received this statement with a grunt, though he knew it was more or less accurate. T. T. was not the man to keep anything of real value in anything so obvious as that safe, which was, besides, of cheap and old-fashioned manufacture, so that there would never have been any great difficulty in opening it. He crossed over to the window, from which he had become aware of a current of cold air. It was wide open.

" What about this ? " he asked. " Was it open before ? "

" Good God, no—a night like this ! " exclaimed T. T. " He must have got in that way. I wondered why the room was so damn cold. Shut it, can't you ? "

" Have to wait a bit," Ulyett answered. " Mustn't get messing things about yet a while."

T. T. helped himself to more brandy, muttering something about " silly rot " and " catching cold." Ulyett noted with approval how freely he was drinking, and hoped that soon he would become more talkative. But in fact the shock to T. T. had been too great for the spirit to take much effect. The door opened and Inspector Ferris appeared.

" Sergeant Oldfield, in charge of party posted at rear of house," he reported formally, " states he closed immediately on hearing apparent pistol shots. No one seen in vicinity of house, but is of opinion there was time for persons implicated to escape either direct by common or by garden of next-door unoccupied house, especially in view of poor visibility. He——" Ferris paused, stared, gaped at the dead man, whom only now did he see clearly, forgot to be official and became human. " That's Jessop," he cried. " Mr. Jessop, the jeweller, him who said he had had the necklace pinched."

CHAPTER III

THE FAY FELLOWS NECKLACE

IT WAS AN ANNOUNCEMENT sufficiently surprising to them all. More than surprising, indeed, it seemed to T. T., who gaped at Ferris with open eyes and mouth. Bewilderedly he blurted out:

" What ? Nonsense ! Are you sure ? "

" Know him quite well," asserted Ferris. " It's him all right."

Ulyett turned to Bobby.

" Get their 'phone number and ring them up," he said. " There ought to be someone there—a caretaker or someone. Tell me when you get through." To T. T. he said: " Now, Mullins, what do you know about this ? "

" Nothing," asserted T. T. with vigour. " Murder's not my line. You know yourself I was talking to you at the time."

" Yes, I know that much," agreed Ulyett, in no way relaxing the fixed and questioning gaze with which he was regarding the other. " Tell me some more," he invited.

" Nothing to tell," T. T. persisted. He helped himself again to the brandy. " I need it," he apologised. " Wynne and I were having a business talk together. That's all."

" Who is Wynne ? " Ulyett demanded.

" Don't know much about him," T. T. answered. " Pleasant, chatty fellow; seems to know his way about; gave me a good tip about gold-mine shares once. I didn't take it. Wished I had afterwards. It would have been worth money. The other day he said he had an A1 deal on he would like to talk to me about. I told him to come along any time he liked, and he turned up this evening."

" How long have you known him ? How did you meet him first ? "

" Oh, a year or two," T. T. answered. " I don't know exactly. I had seen him two or three times before we spoke—at some night-club or another, I think. Or else just when I was having a drink somewhere. I can't say exactly. We just got into a kind of nodding acquaintance, seeing each other round places, and then we got talking. That's all. I understood he was in business in the City, but I don't know; I never asked. He always seemed to be well off; talked about his car—a Silver Phantom—and a country cottage he said he had. I don't know where, so don't ask me."

" Where will be the best place to pick him up ? "

" You'll just have to look out for him round about the West End, I suppose. It won't be difficult for you, with your organisation. Why," declared T. T., to whom the brandy had restored much of his old perky self-confidence, " I always say if a stray cat knew Super Ulyett was after it, it might just as well go along at once and say : ' Here I am, super.' Save a heap of trouble in the end."

Ulyett grunted, in no way placated by this compliment.

" What was the business you were talking about ? " he asked.

" We hadn't got that far," explained T. T. ; " just general talk about markets and so on. He was telling me about a good deal he had brought off in—in tapioca," said T. T. thoughtfully, " or was it semolina ? Anyway, right in the middle of it we heard the smash outside, and we thought we ought to see if anyone was hurt and if we could help. Luckily there wasn't, but you could have knocked me down with a feather when I opened that van and there were men inside—men ! Such a shock as I never had before in all my born days."

" You called out something about diamonds."

" No, did I, though ? " exclaimed T. T., apparently much surprised.

" You did. The moment you heard the shots."

" Oh, yes, I remember now," agreed T. T. " Yes, so I did. Wynne had shown me a packet of loose diamonds— two or three hundred pounds' worth. Small stones, but quite good. Asked me if I would like to buy."

" Where did he get them ? "

" Very first thing I asked him," asserted T. T. virtuously. " Can't be too careful about that sort of thing. But it was all right. Straight as a die. He had a receipt from a Hatton Garden firm."

" Name ? "

T. T. appeared to be searching his memory.

" Was it—— ? " He named one of the best known of the Hatton Garden dealers. " No, I think it was——" He named another. " No, I couldn't be sure," he said with the utmost frankness. " I didn't notice particularly, because I meant to take a note and check up with the firm if I went through with the deal, and, if I didn't, then it was no matter. And first thing I thought when I heard the shots was that someone had broken in and pinched 'em. So of course I ran."

" Was that why you slammed the drive gate on me the way you did, holding us all up ? " demanded Ulyett.

" Did I ? " asked T. T. innocently. " I didn't know. I just got excited—lost my head a bit, I suppose. We aren't all like you fellows, cool as cucumbers no matter what it is. I did notice," he added reflectively, " you were all a bit slow coming along. I know I wished some of you were there when I got inside and heard the maids screaming. But even then I never dreamed it was—murder," he said with a note of horror in his voice that sounded genuine enough.

" Want me to believe," asked Ulyett, " you left a packet of diamonds worth two or three hundred pounds loose on the table ? "

" Wynne may have put them back in his pocket," T. T. answered. " I couldn't say. Didn't notice. When I heard those pistol shots I made sure someone had pinched them. But I don't know. You must ask Wynne."

" Where is he ? "

" Gone off home, if you ask me; felt he had to get away and get over the shock. Nervous, sensitive sort of chap, Wynne. Even before this, he was upset; all in a twitter, nervy, when that van turned out full of life-sized police instead of harmless wooden furniture. Such a contrast; such a surprise; so different every way."

" If they were Wynne's diamonds," growled Ulyett, vaguely aware of lurking, subtle satire in T. T.'s remarks, " what were you worrying about ? "

" I had made up my mind to have them, you see. Now there's a good deal gone west. I could have made a good profit on that little packet. Any good asking the Yard for compensation ? "

" Try it," Ulyett advised briefly. " Then what you say is that there were loose diamonds worth two or three hundred pounds on the table here when you and Wynne left the room ? "

" I'm not swearing to it," protested T. T. earnestly. " Wynne may have put them in his pocket. I don't think he did, but I'm not sure. I don't much suppose either of us thought of them at the moment. We heard the smash outside, and we thought perhaps there was some other poor devil got killed in another accident and it was up to us to see if we could help. Humanity—that's more than diamonds isn't it ? "

" Cut it out about the humanity," Ulyett ordered. " You knew all right. I suppose you had runners out on the watch ? "

" Well now, super," T. T. asked reproachfully, " did you really think you were going to get away with a dodge like a furniture van, that new-born babes know all about without being told ? I'm not saying, mind you, that if any kind, thoughtful friend of mine did happen to see a furniture van coming this way late on a Saturday night—a Saturday night—he mightn't just happen to mention it if he was ringing me. He wouldn't think it worth ringing special for, of course, but he might mention it if ringing about something else."

Ulyett went a little red. He was not, indeed, very proud of the furniture van idea ; but, then, time had been so short, there had been no chance to think out anything better. He tried another line of approach.

" Have you any idea," he asked, " what Mr. Jessop meant when he said something that sounded like ' duke ' or ' duchess ' just before he died ? "

T. T. looked at him sideways, and for a second or two hesitated—so short and slight a hesitation, indeed, it was only to be noticed by contrast with the glib and easy readiness of his previous replies. He said :

" Some friend or relative most likely he was thinking of— someone called Marmaduke, perhaps. Or it might be a nickname. One of his business pals, perhaps."

" Ever heard of Miss Fay Fellows ? " Ulyett demanded.

" The film star ? I should say I had," responded T. T., glib and enthusiastic again. " Best of the whole boiling, I say. There's some say she's not as good as she was. Take it from me, she's better."

" Ever hear of her diamond necklace ? "

" No. Never. Has she a diamond necklace ? What about it ? "

" Supposed to be the finest in existence. Been plenty of gossip pars in the papers about it."

" In *The Times* ? " asked T. T. innocently. " I never noticed them. *The Times* is my paper, you know."

" It would be," agreed Ulyett. " Tells about the movements of people likely to own trifles worth picking up. Anyhow, Miss Fellows has been trying to sell. Mr. Jessop's firm had it in hand, trying to place it for her. Now he's here, murdered—and you and your friend Wynne were talking about diamonds, and diamonds were the first thing you thought of. Does that suggest anything to you ? "

" You mean," said T. T. slowly, " you think perhaps Mr. Jessop brought the necklace here to show me, in the hope that I could find him a buyer, and that some crook followed him and shot him and got away with the necklace ? It's possible, of course, but it doesn't seem likely to me. Of course, I might have found a buyer or got up a syndicate to speculate in buying it. That's all right, but I can't think he would have brought it along without warning me first. Still, he might have thought it safer to let no one know. Some of those in that line think the ordinary post is better than a registered parcel, that only draws attention to itself. Yes, you may be right."

" I didn't mean anything of the sort," Ulyett growled.

" You don't think Wynne had it, do you ? " T. T. asked incredulously. " Of course, I don't know. I didn't search his pockets. But it doesn't seem likely. Now, does it ? Would any man with a stolen necklace in his pocket worth goodness knows how much go strolling off to watch a motor accident that stank of fake a mile away ? I ask you."

Ulyett made no answer. He turned to stare again at the dead body on the floor.

" He must have known something to bring him here," he muttered. " Only what—how much ? " He turned fiercely upon Mullins. " You listen to me, T. T." he said.

" If you've got that necklace, you may as well turn it up. We're going over this place soon with a comb, and if it's here we're bound to get it."

" Speaking," said T. T. earnestly, " as one gentleman to another, you've got it wrong. There's nothing under this roof that there oughtn't to be." He added reproachfully, " Think I'm a fool ? "

" Well, what was Jessop doing here ? " demanded Ulyett.

" Beats me," said T. T.

" Who did him in ? " Ulyett asked again. " T. T., this is a hanging matter, remember."

T. T. helped himself to the brandy again.

" Super," he said, " I know no more about it than you do."

Bobby, who in an effort to ring up the Mayfair Square premises had been struggling with the telephone all this time, turned round and said:

" I can't get through, sir. I don't think there can be anyone there."

" Must be a caretaker or someone," Ulyett declared, plainly intimating that he thought it was entirely Bobby's fault if there wasn't. " Can't leave the place empty. Better get along yourself and see. Get in touch with anyone you can find and bring 'em in—to-night if possible; first thing in the morning at latest. I wonder if this poor chap had any family ? A shock for them. Get a move on, Owen."

" Very good, sir," said Bobby, though this was a severe and unexpected blow, for he badly wanted to remain on the spot to take his share in investigations that would probably continue far into the night.

However, orders are orders and must be obeyed, and now from outside came the sound of approaching cars to tell of the coming of the doctor who had been sent for, and of the help Scotland Yard had been asked to provide.

" There's just one thing, sir," Bobby said as he was going.

" About that monogram on the cigar stump. It looks to me like one I've seen before, though there's not enough left to be sure."

" Saw where ? " demanded Ulyett.

" You remember, sir," Bobby said, " about a fortnight ago the Duke of Westhaven complained that his flat in Park Lane had been entered—he has the whole top floor of one of the buildings there. There is a private lift, but access by stairs as well, in case of fire. I was sent to investigate. There was evidence the flat had been entered—the burglar alarm over the door at the top of the stairs had been disconnected and the servants were sure the furniture and so on had been moved. But there wasn't a thing missing, and there seemed nothing to be done about it."

" Well ? " snapped Ulyett.

" I saw the duke himself, sir," Bobby went on, " and an American gentleman was there—a Mr. Patterson, a New York banker, I understood. Mr. Patterson gave me one of his cigars—said he was so interested to meet a Yard man : seem to think a lot of us over there."

" Got the cigar ? " demanded Ulyett.

" Well, sir, I smoked it," admitted Bobby apologetically.

Ulyett's manner indicated he had expected no better, but that a really intelligent officer . . .

" Mr. Patterson," continued Bobby hastily, " said he had his cigars specially made for him in his own factory in Cuba, and I noticed his monogram was on them—A. T. P. What's left on the stump on the floor there looks very like it."

" Well, now, think of that," interposed T. T. " But these American millionaires—you can never trust them."

" Mr. Patterson sailed for New York a week ago," Bobby said. " He's there now."

" Then it must have been the duke," cried T. T. " Going up in the world, we are—dukes and millionaires and all."

Cj

" Duke of Westhaven," repeated Ulyett, and stared suspiciously at T. T. " What do you know about him ? " he demanded.

" Only what you read in the papers—never even set eyes on the bloke in my life," T. T. answered. " Proper pals we should have been if we had ever met, but somehow no one's ever thought of introducing us. I suppose he's the kind could buy diamond necklaces by the dozen if he wanted to, though they always say he's too mean to buy anything except at Woolworth's. You don't think he had arranged to meet that poor devil here that's got shot ? "

" Do you ? " asked Ulyett. " Better come clean, T. T. You're in this, and the best way for you to get out again is to tell the truth."

" That's right. That's what I've always found," declared T. T. He paused. He looked straight at Ulyett, and with more appearance of sincerity than his manner often showed, he repeated: " Super, this thing has me beat just the way it has you."

CHAPTER IV

MAYFAIR SQUARE

NOT TOO PLEASED at the errand assigned him, Bobby took the tube from the local station to the West End. From the Green Park station a walk of two or three hundred yards brought him to Mayfair Square, once the central habitation of the rank and wealth of England, now divided between flats, offices, and shops, the flats being chiefly remarkable for their rents, the offices for their total lack of all conveniences, and the shops for the prices they charged, but all alike sharing in the prestige and the glory the name of Mayfair Square was still able to bestow. Even yet it managed somehow to convey an air of aristocratic repose, dignity, and calm, in spite of the hooting clamour of the taxis and the cars charging across it, in spite of the big gambling-party in progress in one of the flats or of the " bottle party " being held in another, with two large-size retired heavy-weight pugilists in attendance to make sure that all drunks were removed quietly and promptly and unostentatiously, without any risk of attracting the attention of the police; in spite, too, of the group assembled in one of the basements to test and experience the delights of an entirely new " dope," or of the select assembly gathered in what was a beauty parlour reception saloon by day to witness there such a film as would have delighted the Tiberius of whom we read in the pages of Tacitus, or, again, even of the small flat on a top floor where two or three optimistic foreign gentlemen were laying careful plans for the swift abolition of the British Empire, with special attention to leaving over stray bits to be picked up by any odd dictator on the make.

" Has not the greatest and wisest of British newspapers admitted that their enfeebled country is faced with defeat and disaster if it continues to oppose our great leader's will ? " one of them was demanding passionately of his applauding, convinced, and enthusiastic auditors, of whom the first was an elderly Arab visiting England on the strength of the substantial sum for which he had sold his property in Palestine to a grasping Jew, and not without hopes of getting the land back for nothing in order to sell it again to some other grasping Jew. He answered for the East when the Moment came; as the second of those present, an eager Bengal law student, answered for India, from which country he had landed the week before; as the third and last of them, an earnest, solemn, elderly Irishman from Cork, answered for the rest of the world. He it was who long before had invented that splendid slogan, " Ourselves Alone," which now by its own force and value has spread from Ireland all across the world till to-day, like the cross the Emperor Constantine saw on the eve of battle, it hangs above the universal struggle with the message written around in letters of fire : " In this sign, perish."

Of some of these various parties, groups, assemblies, Bobby had some slight knowledge. He rather hoped that he would one day be one of the party to raid that private film show, and of course the solemn, elderly Irishman's reports were read at Scotland Yard, whither a photographic copy was always dispatched by his group leader in return for a small but regular remuneration. But with them he had no concern to-night, and soon he identified the fine old house now occupied by the firm of Jessop, Jacks & Co., Court jewellers, established in the year of the accession of her late gracious Majesty, Queen Victoria, whose declaration at that moment, " I will be good," now causes Chelsea and Bloomsbury to rock with in-extinguishable laughter. Though the interior had been largely remodelled, outwardly the house remained much as when built in the time of good Queen Anne by a merchant of the City of London who had just made a fortune through buying up all the available supplies of pepper and then releasing them again at an increase of price so small it was hardly noticeable, except, indeed, by those of a mean and grudging disposition. Even the iron extinguishers on each side of the finely proportioned front door were still in place, nor indeed was there much to show the building was now a shop—except that during the day the front door was always open and a uniformed commissionaire always on duty, and that at times there would appear in the discreetly curtained window some such article of rare and precious jewellery as, for example, the famous Fay Fellows necklace itself.

The ground floor was occupied by the showrooms—luxuriously fitted up, nothing in them so vulgar as a counter—and the private rooms of the partners. On the first floor were the offices of the manager, Mr. Wright, and the staff, and one special showroom reserved for more important transactions, and, occasionally, for clients wishing to do a deal by stealth and most unwilling to blush to find it fame—as, for example, when there arose some question of disposing of family jewels without troublesome and pedantic heirs having a chance to make unnecessary fusses.

This, indeed, was the apartment in which Miss Fay Fellows had shown to the enraptured eyes of the firm her magnificent necklace she had purchased in the days when the mere lifting of her eyebrows shook Hollywood to its depths, when a regular clause in her contracts stipulated that at least a million dollars had to be spent on any picture in which she was to appear, when no palpitating director had ever known until she had actually signed whether she might not ask for another ten thousand dollars a week he knew he would have to concede if she made the demand.

But now things were different, as they so often are. She had even been asked to call on a director instead of being able to regard it as mere routine to keep the fellow waiting an hour or two while she finished her grape-fruit—true, he had apologised, but it was a sign, even a portent—and the public had shown a disgraceful tendency to flock in less enthusiastic and embarrassing numbers than usual to her last two or three pictures. So she had decided that diamonds were a little vulgar, and, one or two firms in Paris and New York having ridiculously refused to give her its full value of £100,000, the sum she had herself paid for it, she had come incognito to London—she always preferred to travel incognito, as she found it attracted so much more attention—and, the sale still hanging fire, had left it with Messrs. Jessop & Jacks for them to dispose of at the best figure available over the reserve of £50,000.

" And, in the present state of the market, lucky to get as much," Mr. Jacks had declared gloomily, though Mr. Jessop's views were slightly more optimistic.

The basement of the building, where once had been the kitchen and domestic offices, and below them the wine and coal and other cellars, had been transformed into a strong-room in concrete and steel, fitted up with a door in armour plate that after business hours could only be opened by three keys, one each in the possession of Mr. Jessop and of Mr. Jacks, and one in that of their manager. On the second floor were the workrooms, and storerooms for articles of small value, and above them again were the attics, converted to serve as living-rooms for the caretaker, who was also the magnificent commissionaire of business hours, and whose wife presided over, and even assisted in, the labours of the charwomen responsible for the cleaning and tidying of the premises.

No caretaker or charwoman answered, however, the

summons Bobby beat upon the front door, using for that purpose a knocker that was a remarkably fine piece of eighteenth-century ironwork, though that was not a fact Bobby was in any mood to notice. There was a bell, too, that he rang with equal vigour and equal lack of success, and he was turning away to find a call-box wherefrom to ring up Scotland Yard, report his failure to obtain a reply, and ask for the further instruction he was gloomily certain would condemn him to sit on the doorstep till someone did arrive, even though that were not till the following Monday morning, when by good luck the constable on the beat came by, and, seeing another uniform man where none was to be expected, came across to investigate.

Bobby introduced himself, explained his presence, learnt that a caretaker did live on the premises, that his name was Kendrick, and that on Saturday nights he and his wife always went to visit relatives from whose house they did not return till late; but by good luck the constable knew that Mr. Jessop's new secretary occupied a one-room flat in a block not far away.

" Kendrick told me about her," the constable explained. " Quite swanky about it he was—young lady name of Hilda May come to them straight from being secretary to a duchess, no less."

" What's the joke ? " asked Bobby, for the constable was smiling broadly.

" Well, it's funny," he said. " Bit of a coincidence, but I've just been pulling in the young fellow that took her job with the duchess—found him trying to climb a lamp-post to get a light for his cigarette. Fair soaked he was; been getting it at the Cut and Come Again; been sitting there soaking all evening, he said, and wanted to take me in for a drink. Of course, the Cut and Come Again lot swore they hadn't seen him all day—pretty thick, even for them, when I had seen him myself coming out of their place."

"Like them; like their cheek," agreed Bobby, for the Cut and Come Again was a club that balanced more delicately upon the edge of the unlawful than ever did a world financier upon the narrow line between the legal and the swindle.

Their chief line of defence, when challenged, was always bland denial, always expressed in the form of a " Don't quite remember," for there's no crime in a feeble memory, and failure to identify the man you served with a drink not two minutes past may be due to that exceptionally bad sight, hearing, memory, from which all the staff of the Cut and Come Again suffered—though, fortunately, only intermittently. But there was nothing crude about the Cut and Come Again. If they there defied the law, they did so not blatantly, but with a subdued and subtle insolence— Bobby was indeed surprised to hear that anything so crude as a drunken member had been permitted to appear in visible form anywhere near their premises. Generally drunken members were either made so drunk they passed into peaceful slumber, or else were swifty conveyed by a back way into another street, where they could be as noisy as they wished.

" They didn't half like it, either—him making that row right in front of their place," the uniform man went on. " He hadn't any coat or hat or umbrella. Soaked through he was; it was raining hard just then. But they wouldn't turn his things up, though they must have had them all right. Rather let him get soaked some more than admit he had been there. Said he never wore a hat, and must have got his raincoat pinched or something."

" How did you know who he was ? " Bobby asked.

" He told me," grinned the policeman. " Told me he worked for a duchess, and she wouldn't stand having one of her staff run in. Luckily a cruising car came along, and he went with them like a lamb—seemed to sober up sudden. Perhaps they'll just drop him where he lives and not bother charging him."

" Did he say who the duchess is ? " Bobby asked.

" Westhaven," the other answered. " I expect Miss May got the push so he could have the job instead—he's one of those high lookers you don't often see off the pictures. Just like a picture himself—curly hair and teeth like an ad. for tooth-powder; just the sort these old dames fall for. He said he had been on the films, but jealousy had done him down. Told me a lot, he did; he must have taken in enough liquor to float the *Queen Mary*, and I will say he's enough to make any female heart work overtime."

" Doesn't sound as though the duchess has made a good exchange as far as work is concerned," remarked Bobby.

An odd coincidence that, after his recognition of the monogram on the half-smoked cigar by the dead man's side as that of someone who was a friend of the duke's, now the name of the duchess should crop up in this entirely incidental fashion. No more than a coincidence, of course, but Bobby's experience in the police force had given him a certain distrust of coincidence.

He thanked the other for his information, said what a help it was when the man on the beat kept his eyes and ears open and he would say as much in his report, and so went on to the block of flats near by, where Miss Hilda May occupied one of those modern and up-to-date cupboards so many young people of to-day mistake for a home.

The building was not far, and he was soon there, but it was midnight now, and the porter regarded Bobby's uniform with distrust. He implied that unless it was cars, which of course all even—even specially—tip-top swells, are liable to, the reputation, standing, and social importance of all tenants of the building made visits from the police as unnecessary as unwelcome, and, more likely than not, if there were any trouble, it would be the sack for him, the office being like that. So, if Bobby wouldn't mind going away and returning when the office was open and the responsibility theirs, he would be much obliged. And Bobby explained there was nothing he himself would like better, but his own " office " was even more autocratic and insistent than the porter's, police business would never wait, and would the porter kindly get out of the way—unless, indeed, he wanted the trouble he feared to take place then and there. He added an assurance that only an address was wanted, though wanted immediately, even at the cost of knocking some out of bed and disturbing the beauty sleep of others, and so was finally allowed to speed upward in an automatic lift that conveyed him to the top floor, where proximity to the heavens reduced the rents by £20 a year.

Miss May's flat was situated at the very end of the corridor on which Bobby emerged. He was a little afraid he might, as the porter had suggested, find its tenant retired for the night, but was reassured, as he drew near, by seeing that the door was open an inch or two. Then it opened more widely, and there appeared a tall, good-looking, fair-haired young man with flushed cheeks and untidy hair, as if an agitated hand had recently been run through it. He was looking back into the room he had just left, so that, his head being turned away and his attention occupied, he remained unaware of Bobby. He said loudly and angrily:

" I tell you I mean it—by the Lord, I do—so you needn't think I don't."

There was an emphasis of passion and of feeling in his voice that made Bobby wonder what it was he meant with such intention, and then, coming nearer, he was able to see within the flat through the open door, and was aware there of a tall girl, sedately dancing.

It was an odd sight, and Bobby stood still to watch it. He was no amateur of dancing, but no one could fail to perceive the grace and harmony of her movements, or how utterly she was absorbed in what she did, so that all knowledge of place and time had passed from her. To and fro she swayed, every movement of head and limbs and body in perfect unison, forming, as it were, a process to some significance onlookers felt but did not know. It was as though she wove a spell that opened paths hitherto unseen and undreamed of, and still she danced gravely on, and still the young man watched her, and Bobby also, silent and intent, behind.

She had kicked off her shoes, and now on the points of her toes, now with both feet changing so swiftly the eye could hardly follow them, she continued in the same almost solemn rhythm, about which there was no suggestion of abandonment or excitement—so, in a way, purposed and controlled did it seem, so like the working out of some propounded problem. The flat was small, tiny even: there was the furniture, too, further to confine and limit; and yet in that narrow space in which she moved—and moved without changing her actual position by more than an inch or two—she conveyed most strangely the impression of boundless expanse, as though no walls nor anything held it apart from the universal whole.

Puzzled and bewildered, Bobby continued to stare in silence, forgetting for the time his errand. The fair-haired young man, too, remained intent, at gaze, though with evident in his manner a kind of grudging anger, as if he would have stopped her if he dared. Then suddenly— it was some movement of the young man's that revealed him to her—she caught sight of Bobby, and on the instant stopped, and in that instant changed, so that mystery and wonder fled from her and she stood there like a little frightened child.

" Oh, Denis, look," she gasped. " Oh, Denis, have you done it ? Have you ? "

The young man she called Denis turned quickly, and

when he saw Bobby the flush faded from his cheek, a startled look that might have been terror sprang into his eyes, he swung round again quickly and banged to the door of the flat behind him. Then, standing defiantly before it:

" What do you want ? " he demanded.

Evidently the sight of Bobby's uniform had startled and alarmed them both more than was to be expected from those whose consciences are perfectly clear, even though some surprise at the sight of a policeman there at that time of night was natural enough. And what, Bobby wondered, had the girl dancer meant by her sudden startled exclamation: " Oh, Denis, have you done it ? " And why was he standing on guard before her door with that air of mingled hostility and fear ?

" I think Miss Hilda May lives here, doesn't she ? " Bobby asked.

" You can't see her now," the other answered. " It's too late. Come along in the morning if you want to."

" Police business can't wait," Bobby told him briefly. " Please move. I want to knock."

" Not at this time of night," the young man repeated obstinately. " You've no right to worry people so late. Come back in the morning if you like."

" I've told you——" began Bobby, losing patience, when the other said triumphantly, as if he had just remembered a handy ace of trumps to play:

" Where's your warrant ? Have you got a warrant ? "

" Good Lord," exclaimed Bobby crossly, " do you think I want a warrant to speak to people ? And what business is it of yours ? And does it strike you that obstructing a police officer is a serious matter ? And," added Bobby slowly, " makes him wonder what reason there is."

It was a shot that told. The young man looked disconcerted. The door behind him opened abruptly and the girl herself appeared.

CHAPTER V

MODERN FLATLET

ONCE MORE SHE HAD CHANGED. No longer, as she stood there, did she resemble the priestess gravely serving an unknown altar, no longer had she her air of a small and frightened child. She had changed all that, and now bore herself simply as a brisk and confident young business woman of to-day. She said to Bobby:

" You wanted to see me ? "

" You are Miss Hilda May, on the staff of Jessop & Jacks ? " Bobby asked.

" Yes," she answered. She stood back a little to allow him to enter. " You had better come in," she said. " There'll be complaints if we talk here."

" Thank you," Bobby said, moving forward to accept her invitation; but when the young man showed some signs of following him he said: " I shan't keep you long, Miss May, but, as it concerns your firm, we had better be alone."

" Very well," she answered. " You had better go home, Denis. It's late enough."

" I'll wait," he answered, scowling. " How do we know this chap really is a policeman ? He may be after the Fellows necklace or something."

Bobby swung round on him.

" What do you know about the Fellows necklace ? " he demanded.

" Well, everyone knows old Jessop's working overtime to sell it," Denis retorted.

" Come inside, please. I don't want complaints about talking out here," Hilda interposed—but a little, Bobby thought, as if she wanted to cut short the conversation for reasons of her own.

Denis turned away and walked off down the corridor, and Hilda pushed the door to, Bobby having to come further inside to allow it to close. It was a tiny vestibule in which they stood now, one not more than a square yard or so in extent, and with two tall, narrow cupboards at one side, one for hats and cloaks and the other for brooms and brushes, though each so small the plural did not seem the appropriate number to use. Opposite was another door, admitting to the main apartment, into which Hilda now led the way.

" Sit down," she said to him. " Well, what is it ? "

With some hesitation, for he was not quite sure that it would not collapse under his weight, Bobby lowered himself into the chair she indicated, and, under pretence of not quite knowing what to do with his helmet, gave about him one of those quick, searching, intent glances by which he had trained himself to observe and memorise every detail of his surroundings, no matter how apparently trivial or unimportant it might seem.

The room had a pleasant and attractive look, and considerable pains must have been taken with the colour-scheme, to tone wherewith even the flowers in the vases on the table, before the window, on a corner bracket, had evidently been carefully chosen. To the masculine eye there was perhaps a lack of really comfortable-looking chairs, but there were many cushions and pouffes, on one of which, ingeniously shaped like a pig, Hilda had now seated herself. Altogether a very feminine apartment, Bobby thought, with its many photographs and knick-knacks—on the mantelshelf stood a perfect Zoo in tiny models of animals, ranging from expensive things in bronze to others in papier maché, bought probably at sixpenny stores—and its general appeal to the æsthetic sense rather than to any mere vulgar ideal of comfort. But, then, ideas of comfort are relative, and Hilda May's idea of it was to sit on the floor with her legs tucked under her and her head against a chair she seldom thought of using as a seat, just as her idea of a really satisfying meal was a soft boiled egg, followed by a plentiful supply of cream buns and éclairs.

At one side of the room, curtains, matching perfectly those before the windows, and making, with the table cover, a delicate harmony too subtle for Bobby's imperfect colour sense to appreciate, veiled a recess he guessed contained a divan bed. The table cover, however, he did notice for its beauty. It was really an Indian shawl with a lovely golden thread running through the pattern. Owing to two small accidental burns it had suffered, it had been relegated from its status of evening wrap to its present use, the two small, neatly darned holes being less noticeable so. Two doors admitted to what were probably, Bobby supposed, a bathroom and a kitchenette, and he noticed on a wall bracket what at first he thought was a real cat, till a second glance showed him it was manufactured from some soft black furry material that with the aid of a well-modelled head gave it quite a life-like appearance.

" Well ? " Hilda asked again.

Bobby decided to keep his helmet on his knee and transferred his attention to her. Sitting there, a little stiffly, she no longer made that impression of extreme grace and ease of bearing she had given before. Gone, too, was the suggestion of a radiant brightness her movements in the dance had seemed somehow to convey. Now she looked merely a somewhat heavily built, hefty young woman, a little awkward somehow, though probably one who would do well on the links or the tennis-courts. Before, Bobby had hardly been conscious of her looks, so much had they seemed subordinate to the unknown message hidden in the lovely harmony of her movements. But now it struck him that if anything she was almost plain, or at any rate with no pretensions to unusual good looks. The lower part of her face was much too heavy, with a wide mouth and large square chin contrasting with the small nose and low forehead. Her hair was dressed in the conventional permanent wave style, the only conventional thing about her, and her complexion, too, was dark, and apparently less laid over with cosmetics than is usually the case to-day. But her eyes were really fine; large, dark, and shining with a kind of inner light, though so carefully hidden beneath heavy, drooping lids they were seldom clearly seen. It was a mannerism, partly natural, partly acquired from a conviction, strengthened by experience, that their brilliance made them unsuitable for business hours. The general impression that she made upon Bobby, as indeed was often the case with others, was that of a personality of doubtful and yet perhaps tremendous potentialities. And another conviction that stole into Bobby's mind was that she was afraid. He thought her hands were pressed together a little too closely, her eyes hidden a little too carefully, as if she did not wish to be seen what it might be they showed. Nor had her voice, he thought, been quite steady when she uttered that last " Well."

" You are employed by Messrs. Jessop & Jacks," he said slowly. " Can you give me Mr. Jacks's private address ? I have been to Mayfair Square, but I couldn't get an answer."

She got up slowly; and now she was standing he was impressed again by her height and build, and also he still noticed a certain heaviness, almost awkwardness of manner, that in her dancing had seemed to fall from her like a cast-off garment. He had the impression, too, that his question had come to her as a relief, as if she had feared something else. Stretching out a long, white, well-formed arm that showed, too, a ripple of muscle beneath the skin, she took down the life-like cat from the wall bracket and showed it had served as a cover for a telephone. Lifting the instrument, she dialled a number and said presently:

" Miss May speaking—Hilda May, Mr. Jessop's secretary. There's a policeman here. He wants Mr. Jacks. No, he has not said why. He says he can't make anyone hear at Mayfair Square." She listened a moment, and then turned to Bobby. " Is it important ? " she asked. " Can't it wait till morning, or till Monday ? "

" I am afraid not," Bobby answered.

" He says not," Hilda repeated over the 'phone, and, after listening a minute or two, turned again to Bobby. " Mr. and Mrs. Jacks are out. They went to the cinema and they were going on to play bridge. They didn't say where—to friends. Mr. Jacks said they might be late. They aren't likely to be long now, though. Is there any message ? "

" No, except that I must see Mr. Jacks as soon as possible. Will you say I am coming on at once, and, if Mr. Jacks gets in first, will he please expect me and will he wait up for me. What is the address ? "

Hilda gave it—a house in a Bayswater square. She had passed on his message, and now put down the instrument. Bobby said to her:

" Was Mr. Jessop a married man ? Had he children, relatives ? "

" He is a widower," Hilda answered. " He has a service flat—Bloomsbury. There's one daughter, I think. She lives in Australia. I don't know of any other relatives. I expect there are some. I don't know. Why ? Has there been an accident ? Or—— ? "

" Or—what ? " Bobby asked.

" Or what is it ? " she completed her sentence quickly, but not, Bobby fancied, as she had originally intended. " What do you want Mr. Jacks for ? At this time . . . asking about—relatives," she concluded, a little breathlessly.

Dj

" Mr. Jessop has been shot," Bobby told her then.

" Shot ? " she repeated, and, oddly, his first impression was that this word brought her overwhelming relief. But then her expression changed as she seemed to realise more clearly what was implied. " Shot ? " she repeated. " You don't mean . . . not on purpose . . . not—killed ? Not—murdered ? "

Bobby made an affirmative gesture. He was watching her closely. He saw that she had gone very pale, and she turned a little away, as if to steady herself with one hand against the wall, and also, he thought, to escape to some degree his gaze.

" It's that necklace, that awful necklace," she muttered.

" You mean the Fay Fellows necklace ? " Bobby asked.

" We've been trying to sell it," she answered. " To different people—the Duchess of Westhaven and others. I showed it her. Was it that ? Had he it with him ? Where did it happen ? "

" At a house in Brush Hill."

" Brush Hill ? Where's that ? Had he the necklace . . . ? "

" We know nothing at present," Bobby said. " Nothing more than that a man has been found shot and identified as Mr. Jessop. If there is anything you can tell us anything you can suggest . . . ? "

She shook her head.

" Do you mean . . . he's—dead ? " she asked again, as if unable or unwilling to believe it.

" Can I use your 'phone ? " Bobby asked.

She did not answer, and, taking her assent for granted, he lifted it and rang up first the Yard to report himself and then Mr. T. T. Mullins's number, to get in touch with Ulyett and report what he had done.

He explained that he intended to go on to Mr. Jacks's address to wait for that gentleman's return, and was told to do so and to bring him on to Mullins's house, where the investigation was still in full progress.

" Found nothing of any interest, though," the voice at

the other end of the wire said. " Hope Jacks can give us a line to follow."

" I am 'phoning from the flat of Mr. Jessop's secretary, Miss Hilda May," Bobby continued. " Shall I ask her to come with us ? "

The distant voice asked one or two questions and then decided it was hardly necessary to trouble the young lady that night. If there was anything she knew likely to be immediately useful she could tell Sergeant Owen what it was. Anything else could wait till morning, when perhaps she would be kind enough to answer a few questions. Bobby also asked if one of the police cruising cars could be instructed to pick him up and take him to Bayswater, and was told decidedly not. They were all far too busy trying to pick up Mr. Percy Augustus Wynne. It was also intimated that he was expected to get to Bayswater just as quickly as if a car could be spared for him, and that the fact that by this time all normal means of communication had stopped was immaterial. His business was to get there, not to talk about it.

Bobby, well used to being told to make bricks without straw, sighed, hung up the receiver, and, by way of taking a chance, hinted that if Miss May had a car, and could lend it to him, he would be greatly obliged. Hilda let the suggestion drift by her unheeded. She seemed absorbed in her own thoughts, from which, however, she awoke abruptly when Bobby said :

" You said you showed the Duchess of Westhaven the Fellows necklace. Was that while you were her secretary ? "

" No. Afterwards," she said. " How did you know I was with her ? "

" We get to know things," he answered vaguely, not willing to expose the communicative Kendrick to the risk of a rebuke for gossiping. " Do you smoke ? "

He offered her his cigarette-case as he spoke, but she shook her head.

" Not now," she said, depriving him of the chance he had wished for to notice how steady was her hand, for there was still something about her, about her attitude, about her silence even, that troubled him a little, and that he felt he did not understand.

" Have you been long with Mr. Jessop ? " he asked. " You came to him direct from the duchess ? Were you with her long ? "

" Three years," she answered. " It was my second job. I have been six months with Mr. Jessop. I came to them when the duchess sacked me."

" Oh," said Bobby, a little taken aback at this plain way of putting it. " There was some disagreement, I suppose ? "

" Denis," she answered briefly.

" Denis ? " he repeated, not understanding.

" The boy outside, if he's still there and hasn't pushed off home," she explained. " I had better see, perhaps. You'll want to ask him questions too, perhaps ? I suppose the police always do. You see, Denis wanted me to marry him. The duchess didn't. So she sacked me."

" Is Mr.—Denis ? "

" His name's Chenery."

" But had the duchess any right to say anything about it ? "

" He's one of the family. He may be the duke himself some day. It's not likely, but it's possible."

" May I take it, then, you are engaged ? "

" You may not, nor shall we be. I've told him so again to-night. Denis hasn't a penny, and, even if he ever does inherit, it won't be for years and years. The one before him is an invalid who can't possibly have children but may live as long as Denis." She paused, hesitated. " You may as well know," she said. " I suppose you'll be going on asking questions, and there'll be plenty ready to tell you. Denis may be a duke some day, and I'm a bastard."

CHAPTER VI

BACKGROUND

Bᴏʙʙʏ ᴡᴀs ᴜsᴇᴅ ᴛᴏ ᴍᴀɴʏ ᴋɪɴᴅs of language. Once, in his uniform days, he had assisted in the arrest of a lady who, born in Liverpool between Scotland Road and the docks, had graduated in Chicago, and returned to polish and perfect her style in Soho night-clubs. Nevertheless, this calm application by Hilda to herself of a word against the use of which a certain prejudice still exists, did startle him a little. It was, of course, an example of what nowadays it is thought profound to call a " defence re-action," but, all the same, a somewhat extreme example.

" Oh, yes. Yes," he said, for the moment at a loss.

Hilda seemed to think no other remark was necessary. But her feet began to sketch a movement, and he was aware of an impression that but for his presence she might again be seeking refuge for her spirit in that grave and solitary dance he had already seen her practising.

" I had better be getting on to Mr. Jacks," he said, rising from his chair. " That is, if there is nothing else you can tell me. It would be after you left her employment that you showed the Fellows necklace to the duchess ? "

" After she sacked me," Hilda corrected.

" Was there any prospect of her buying it ? "

" She wanted to badly enough. But she knew the duke would never let her."

" Have there been any other negotiations ? "

This time there was a momentary hesitation—very slight,

but sufficient to emphasise her failure, Bobby had noticed, to answer directly his last question.

" I don't know all the firm's business," she said then. " I was only Mr. Jessop's typist. I showed her the necklace and she loved it. No one could help; it's the loveliest thing. That's all I can say."

" Mr. Jacks would know, I suppose ? "

" You must ask him," she replied again with hesitation, so that he was certain there was something she either knew or suspected, something that she was keeping back. " I've told you all I know about that part of it," she went on, with more assurance in her tone. " The duke saw it, too. At Mayfair Square. He turned up one day and wanted to see it. I can't imagine why—diamond necklaces aren't his line; not unless he saw a chance to buy it cheap and sell it for twice as much somewhere else. Sixpenny pearl necklets at Woolworth's are more his idea. Naturally he faded away as soon as he knew the price. The firm was quite bucked, though; they didn't know him as well as I did. I told them there wasn't an earthly, but I think they still hoped."

" I see," said Bobby thoughtfully. There could, of course, be no connection, but it was odd how continually references to the duke and to the duchess kept turning up. There was that odd business of the half-smoked cigar, too, with the monogram of the duke's New York friend, Mr. Patterson. He went on : " You said your engagement with the duchess was not your first ? "

" I was with a firm in the City before," she answered. She gave their name—well-known ship-owners. " Then I was asked if I would like to go to the duchess as her secretary. It was Lord Harrowby who got the chance for me."

" Lord Harrowby ? " Bobby repeated; for the name was that of a peer equally well known in political and in sporting circles.

He thought to himself that this somewhat puzzling young woman appeared to have a wide acquaintance in the aristocracy. She saw his surprise, and explained:

" He is my "—she hesitated—" my father's brother."

" Your uncle ? "

" No," she said. She looked at him steadily. It was almost the first time he had seen her eyes, the first time he had realised their depth, their brilliance, a quality in them of hidden passion that might mean many things. " The law does not allow that," she said. " For the law I do not exist. I am outside the law."

He gave her a quick and doubtful glance, for this was a phrase, it seemed to him, of many implications.

" Hardly that," he said.

" The family have been very kind," she went on. " My mother died when I was born. My father died soon after. His brother succeeded him. He did what he felt was his duty. He paid for my education. He had me sent to a good school. He would have paid for me to go to college. He would have given me an allowance. He promised a settlement if I ever got married. But I wanted to know who I was. I found out. Then I preferred to be independent. The lawyers said I was a fool. That was my business. I expect Lord Harrowby was very relieved. He said he admired my spirit. Really, he has been very decent. I ought to be grateful. Every year regularly his lawyers write to say I am to remember that if I want any reasonable help, money, or advice, they are always at my disposal. I never have, but when people know that, it makes them careful."

Bobby half wondered if this was meant as a warning to himself and to the police in general, though he did not much think so.

" Do people know ? " he asked.

" They do at the business," she said slowly. " One of the girls there, Grace Ellison, got to know. She's a dear, but she can't help talking. The duchess knew, too, of course. It was through Lord Harrowby that the duchess offered me a job. Then—Denis happened. So she sacked me. Naturally."

" Was it through Lord Harrowby, too, that you went to Mr. Jessop ? "

" No, it wasn't," she answered, with a swift emphasis that showed how much her fierce and lonely spirit resented any hint of dependence upon others. " Mr. Jessop knew of me. The duchess has a passion for jewellery. I think jewels are the only things she really loves. She has no children. Her jewels might be them. But she likes to make a change sometimes. She sells some and buys others. She understands jewels, and often she makes quite good bargains."

" Has she had dealings with Mr. Jessop ? "

" Not directly. She always goes to a firm in Bond Street. I think Mr. Jessop would have liked to get in touch with her. I suppose every firm wanted to, and didn't see why the Bond Street people should have all her business."

" But she kept to them ? "

" Yes, always. Only I think that is really why Mr. Jessop offered me a job when he knew I was leaving the duchess. He had sold stuff to her and bought from her, too, but only through the Bond Street people. I met him two or three times when deals were being settled. I told him I was leaving, and he said he wanted a secretary and why not come to him. I think now he hoped to get in touch through me with her. What he said was he wanted someone who knew people, and through being with the duchess so long I have got to know lots of important people, and a good deal about them. It isn't only cooks and housemaids who like gossip. There's hardly a character in London I haven't heard torn to pieces. Part of my job with Mr. Jessop is to go about as much as possible wearing jewellery we want to sell. It was an idea of his. I was to be a kind of travelling show-case, a mannequin in jewellery. At first people used to get awfully excited when they saw a girl they had known as a typist appearing at a first night or somewhere—a smart restaurant perhaps or a charity ball—wearing a row of pearls worth hundreds of pounds or diamond rings you could see sparkling all across the room. They are getting to know now, but at first all the little dears scented a first-class scandal. They simply came buzzing round. It was awfully funny how disappointed they were when they found the pearls and the rings were for sale, and they had to pretend to be interested all the same and let me book an appointment for them. I'm not allowed actually to sell or to let the things out of my possession, but I quote prices and say what wonderful bargains they are, and arrange times for the things to be seen and so on. It's been quite a success. I rather like it. Denis hates it."

"Why ? "

" He sells motor-cars himself, or tries to, so I don't see it's any worse for me to sell jewellery. He says it's dangerous. I suppose he thinks I may be kidnapped or something. I can take care of myself, and there's not a scrap of danger if I'm careful. I don't go to night-clubs wearing the big lines, you know—only wrist-watches and small stuff we are offering at double ordinary prices."

" Have you shown the Fay Fellows necklace in that way ? "

" No. I think I should draw the line at wearing a thing like that in public. I have gone to a first night wearing £20,000 worth of stuff. But that's my record, and there was a private detective watching, and our own car to take me to and from Mayfair Square. Up to five figures' worth I don't mind, but over—well, I want precautions."

" But you showed the Fellows necklace to the duchess ? "

" Yes, but not wearing it. I took it in a brown paper parcel to show her by appointment. After the duke's visit,

Mr. Jessop got it firmly into his head she was sure to buy. Everyone knows how she loves jewellery. I told him there wasn't an earthly. She hadn't the money herself, and I knew the duke would never rise to it."

" It's worth £100,000, isn't it ? "

" The reserve price Miss Fellows put on is £50,000. That more or less represents the break-up value. Miss Fellows paid £100,000, but it was an extravagant figure even for that time. I expect partly it was a publicity figure; she got advertising value out of it. Now she wants a quick sale. Even as a break-up, it would take a long time to realise that figure—markets are slow enough still, in spite of the revival they talk about. You understand this is strictly confidential. I am only telling you because of what has happened to Mr. Jessop, and I suppose you ought to know exactly how things are. Our lowest price officially is £65,000. We still hope for that much, but we would take a lot less for a quick sale."

" But at present you are standing out for £65,000 ? "

" Well, if we get that much our commission will be good and Miss Fellows will be exceedingly pleased."

" Thank you," Bobby said. " It's a great help in an investigation if people explain how things stand—often prevents great waste of time. I'm sure my superiors will be grateful to you, too, for your help. Now, may I ask you a straight question ? Have you told me all you know ? "

" I think so, yes."

" All you suspect ? "

The question evidently took her unawares. Again she hesitated, though for so short a time it would have been perceptible only to someone, like Bobby, on the watch.

" Yes, of course, certainly," she said then. " Besides, I don't suspect anything "; and the thought came into Bobby's mind that she lied with difficulty.

But he felt it was no good pressing her further now.

Further and closer questioning would be for his superiors if they thought it advisable. Besides, time for reflection might make her inclined to be more open—and more time, too, might provide surer ground on which to base a further interrogation.

They were still standing facing each other, and it was easy to see that she was lost in deep and troubled thought. Quite suddenly her feet began to move; she lifted her arms slightly; there came again upon her that strange grace and lightness of bearing she had shown before, as if somehow she lifted herself from the solid ground into the air. Bobby thought for a moment that she was going to begin dancing once more, and possibly it was the involuntary astonishment in his eyes that made her remember and stop.

" I'm so sorry," she said. " Ever since I was a child somehow I have always danced my thoughts."

" Do you dance in public ? " he asked.

The question seemed to surprise her.

" Do you pray in public ? " she countered.

A little disconcerted, he did not answer. He understood vaguely that for her the dance was the way whereby she could put herself in unison with that Real which lies behind all Appearance, as is for others prayer, or contemplation, or even action—or sometimes, for a time, drink or drugs. She began to move towards the door.

" Denis will be wondering what's up. He'll be doing something violent soon if we aren't careful," she said. " That is, if he's still there, poor lamb."

She opened the door admitting into the tiny vestibule and then the outer door. Over her shoulder Bobby saw that Denis Chenery was still there, leaning against the corridor wall opposite, his arms folded and with a very grim and resolute expression that suggested he was holding himself in a restraint that might not last too long.

" Denis," she said to him, " Mr. Jessop has been murdered."

" I thought there was something like that," he observed coolly.

" You can tell him all about it," she said to Bobby, who had followed her. " Good night, Denis."

She went back into the flat, and Bobby had a vision of her making again in solitude the dance her vehicle of thought and contemplation. Denis said to Bobby:

" Know who did it ? "

" We have certain information," Bobby answered cautiously. " You knew Mr. Jessop ? "

" I've only seen the blighter once. Quite enough, too."

" You didn't like him ? "

" I didn't like the job he gave Miss May. Might have landed her in a hell of a hole. She might have got murdered herself. I didn't think he was straight."

" Why ? "

" I just didn't think so, that's all. Too fond of keeping things to himself. I knew he had been showing stuff to the Duchess of Westhaven on the q.t.—trying to lead her on. Hilda didn't know that, but I did. If he's got himself done in, as likely as not it was because he was up to something."

Bobby thought that quite probable. But something else Denis had said interested him more.

" Do you know what it was he had been showing the duchess ? " he asked.

" Oh, that swagger necklace of theirs; thought he could let her in for buying it. Of course, she hadn't the coin, and the duke wasn't likely to spring it."

" How was it you knew ? "

" Charley Dickson told me—the bounder that took on Miss May's job. He seemed to think it very funny. He said Jessop had been at Hastley Court the day of a big garden spree there was there, and at their London flat as well, only on the strict q.t. Struck me that meant Jessop was up to funny work of some sort.''

" Did you tell Miss May ? "

Denis shook his head.

" No good," he said. " Besides, I didn't know. It might have been O.K. My idea was Jessop was trying to plant the necklace on her without the duke knowing."

Bobby thought the idea possible, though he did not see exactly where it led. Nor could he afford to spend any more time just then asking questions more or less at random. At any rate, he had now in his mind some idea of the background against which the victim had moved, and at the moment it was more important—or so his superiors would probably think—to get in touch with Mr. Jacks as soon as possible. If Mr. Jacks arrived home before Bobby got there, and rang up Scotland Yard to ask why he was being inquired for, Bobby would certainly be asked to explain his delay in reaching Bayswater. Besides, it was really the business of his superiors to decide the lines interrogations should follow, and Denis, moving towards the automatic lift, remarked:

" Someone will be making a row if we stand gassing here."

Bobby, following him, said:

" I must get on to let Mr. Jacks know what's happened. But you might give me your card. I expect our people will want to see if there's anything more you can tell them."

" Don't suppose there is," Denis remarked, but produced his card accordingly, and the lift conveyed them downwards to the street.

CHAPTER VII

MR. JACKS IS AFRAID

As Bobby had known to be the case before, the bark of headquarters proved worse than its bite, and a cruising police car had been told to look out for him. It picked him up accordingly soon after he left Hilda May's flat, its occupants in a very discontented mood.

" Orders to look out for a bird called Wynne," one of them grumbled, " and they give us a description to fit half London. Seem to think there'll be a label, ' Wynne—wanted,' on his back. Murder case, isn't it ? And what are you got up like that for ? Gone back to uniform for keeps ? "

Bobby explained briefly the circumstances, and how his uniform was the outcome of a not very brilliant plan to get near the watchful T. T. Mullins without rousing his suspicions, filled in as best he could from the brief glimpse he had had of him the scanty description supplied of Wynne, and then relapsed into silence, for his long interview with Hilda had left him in a very worried and doubtful frame of mind.

He had a troubling memory, for instance, of that expression she had used when she had spoken of herself as " outside the law," a phrase, as it seemed to him, of so many implications.

She had spoken, too, of Denis Chenery as if she had a certain fear of his " violence " of temperament, as if she were not sure how far his self-control was to be trusted.

And he, on his part, had spoken of the dead man with what was plainly a deeply felt anger and resentment.

Then, too, it appeared that Denis was in an extremely difficult social position—a probable heir to great possessions who yet was not likely to enter into his inheritance for many years; who might, indeed, never do so. Bobby thought it a cruel situation for any young man, and one likely to affect any character except the strongest. Of course, it could and should have been alleviated by some sort of recognition and allowance made by the present holder of the title and estates of Westhaven, but that, Bobby gathered, had not been done, and, in fact, the general reputation of his grace of Westhaven did not suggest that any idea of the kind was likely to occur to him.

Nor did Bobby forget the further complication that, in spite of Hilda's denial of any engagement, the two young people were evidently on terms of intimate friendship, and that it was this friendship that had cost Hilda her post. Even if their graces of Westhaven saw no necessity to supply a possible heir with any allowance, at least they considered themselves entitled to interfere with his matrimonial plans. Unjust, of course, and injustice, it has been said, makes even wise men mad. Certainly, then, the movements of the two young people that night would have to be carefully investigated, for it was a possibility to be considered that the knowledge Hilda undoubtedly, and Denis most probably, possessed of the Fay Fellows necklace, and the interest taken in it by duke and duchess, had suggested to Denis at least a means of alleviating the difficulties of his position.

Then, in addition, what had Hilda meant by her uncompleted exclamation: " Oh, Denis, have you—— ? "

Had he—what ?

Bobby did not much like the looks of the answer that presented itself to his mind. Though he did not phrase it in so many words, the psychological situation seemed to him charged with too many explosive elements to be regarded with any degree of comfort.

" Here you are," said the driver of the car, drawing up before one of those solid, solemn Victorian houses that still give to Bayswater squares their air of immovable respectability. ' Hop out and we'll go look for Wynne—and hope we do."

Bobby paid this jest the expected tribute of a laugh, said " Thank you " for his lift, and then knocked at the door of the house.

He was expected, and the manservant who opened the door relieved him by saying that Mr. Jacks had not yet returned, but was not likely to be much longer. He was not a late gentleman, Bobby was assured. He was given a seat in the hall, and most of the household staff, either not yet retired to bed or risen therefrom for the occasion, surrounded him in an effort to find out what it was all about, his telephone call having plainly caused much excitement.

Bobby resisted these blandishments firmly, and, to his relief, was not long exposed to them, the sound of a car drawing up outside heralding the return of Mr. and Mrs. Jacks, and sending the domestic staff into hasty retirement.

Mr. Jacks was a tall, thin, worried-looking man, his hair quite grey though he was hardly yet middle-aged, with small excited eyes, and very straight thin lips, tightly compressed over a small round chin—an unstable mixture, Bobby fancied, of obstinacy and impulse, a man likely to follow a determined line of conduct with extreme firmness until he swerved from it to follow another quite different line with equal vigour and resolve. A man, too, generally persuaded that his own conclusions must be right; not that that is exceptional.

" Hullo," he exclaimed, the moment he caught sight of Bobby. " Burglars at Mayfair Square again ? "

" Oh, how—dreadful," said from behind him his wife, a small, round, fat, good-tempered-looking woman.

" No, sir——" began Bobby, but Mr. Jacks did not allow him to continue.

" Didn't get in, eh ? You scared them off first ? Very smart, of course, though I suppose it's what we pay rates for."

" It's nothing——" began Bobby, intending to say that his errand had nothing to do with burglary, but again Mr. Jacks interrupted.

" Well, then, if it's nothing, why come bothering at this time of night ? Not that I should mind much if it were something. We're insured up to a couple of thousand, and there's never more than that value outside the strong-room. Puzzle all the burglars going to get in there. Barnes," he added to the manservant, " give the constable a glass of beer, and then we can all get to bed."

" Mr. Jacks," said Bobby firmly, " a man has been found shot, and has been identified as Mr. Jessop, said to be your partner. My orders are to ask you to come with me to identify the body."

Mr. Jacks stared at him, and there came into his eyes a look of sudden terror, of panic almost. Mrs. Jacks screamed, and gave signs of contemplating hysterics or fainting. There was some confusion for a moment or two. Barnes went running for a glass of water; one or two maids appeared from the upstairs landing, where they had probably been listening. Jacks did not seem to notice his wife, or the maids fussing round her. He was evidently holding himself in strict control, and yet his hands were shaking, his whole body, indeed, trembling. He said, as if hoping for a reassurance he yet did not in fact expect:

" Jessop ? It can't be ! Are you sure ? "

Without waiting for an answer, he turned and stared at his wife, with the maids murmuring sympathy and

EJ

proffering help. Bobby wondered if this was because he did not wish his face to be seen. He said over his shoulder:

" It can't be Jessop—must be a mistake."

" If you will come with me to view the body," Bobby said, " you can make sure."

" But what could Jessop be doing at Mayfair Square at this time of night ? "

" It wasn't at Mayfair Square it happened," Bobby answered. " It was at the house of a Mr. Mullins at Brush Hill."

" Brush Hill ? That's beyond Clapham somewhere, isn't it ? Who's Mullins ? A bookmaker, I suppose."

This was said with a bitterness Bobby noticed but did not comment on, though he felt it was a thing to remember, as was also the extreme agitation, more of terror than of surprise, Mr. Jacks had shown. It was almost, Bobby thought, as though hidden fears he entertained had been abruptly verified. But that perhaps was fanciful. He said aloud :

" Our information is that your firm has a very valuable diamond necklace, the property of Miss Fay Fellows, you are trying to effect a sale of ? "

" What about it ? You don't mean . . . it's in our strong-room—the necklace, I mean. Jessop . . . shot . . . who . . . what do you mean about the Fellows necklace ?   . Are you sure it's Jessop ? "

" It is to be sure that we are asking you to establish identification," Bobby repeated.

" Well, then, we had better get along," Jacks said with sudden resolve. " The Fellows necklace—how do you know anything about it ? It's in the strong-room."

" If it is," said Bobby, " the information we received that it had been stolen must be wrong."

" Information—information," Mr. Jacks repeated, stammering a little. He had somehow an air of finding this word alarming. He paused in his resolute march towards front door and waiting car, and with equal determination flung open the door of a small room on the right of the entrance. " Come in here," he said. " Information—what's that mean ? "

Bobby obeyed, but suggested that the sooner they started the better.

" Can we use the car outside ? " he asked. " If not, I can ring up and ask for a police car to be sent. But if that is your car, and available, it would save time to use it. The sooner Mr. Jessop's body can be identified the better. Then, too, you may be able to help us."

" Jessop's body ? " repeated Jacks, and, as though the words had called up a picture he had not before been able to visualise, he became very pale and sat down, trembling violently. Bobby observed him with a close attention. Jacks took out his handkerchief and began to mop his face. He said in a loud, unsteady voice : " The Fellows necklace is in the strong-room. Must be."

" If so, one point will be cleared up," Bobby remarked. " To-morrow is Sunday, but I suppose you have the key ? "

" The thing is worth £100,000," Jacks said, " and it's not insured—except during business hours. After business hours, it's always kept in the strong-room. We have a key each, Jessop and me and Wright—that's our manager; it takes all three keys to open it. You said you had—information ? "

" Mr. Jessop himself—or someone claiming to be him," said Bobby, " rang up this afternoon. I'm not sure of the exact time, but it'll be on record; it was some time early in the afternoon. He said the Fellows necklace had been stolen—the actual expression used was swindled—' swindled out of.' Mr. Jessop—assuming it was him speaking; we had no way of testing that, of course—sounded very excited and was rather incoherent. He had to be told we could do nothing unless he gave us more details. Instead, he rang off. One of our men went round to Mayfair Square to make further inquiries. He couldn't get any answer."

" Closed Saturday afternoon. Probably the caretaker was out," explained Mr. Jacks. " The strong-room is all right, and we don't worry too much about the small stuff."

" The next thing," continued Bobby, "was information from what we thought a reliable source that a man named Mullins we've been watching for years—he's a receiver of stolen goods—had a big deal on about eight or nine to-night. We tried to get in touch with Mr. Jessop again, but failed. It was decided, as the information seemed trustworthy and as we knew a lot about Mullins, to try to find out what was really happening. While we were talking outside the house to Mullins—he had spotted us coming "—said Bobby wryly—" we heard shots. In the house we found Mr. Jessop. He had been shot, and was dying. Mullins swore he had never seen Mr. Jessop before, or heard of the necklace."

Mr. Jacks wiped his face with his handkerchief.

" I don't understand," he muttered. " It's incredible—incredible."

" Yes, sir," agreed Bobby. " It often is. Shall we be getting on ? "

CHAPTER VIII

THE MISSING FOOTBALL PAGES

THEY WERE WELL ON THEIR WAY to Brush Hill, Mr. Jacks driving and Bobby by his side indicating to him the best route to follow, before much more was said. Then Mr. Jacks asked abruptly :

" What makes you think it's Jessop ? "

" The body was identified by one of our officers," Bobby answered. " He seemed quite certain."

" I don't see what Jessop could have been doing there," Jacks muttered, and as nearly as possible swung the car into a street refuge.

" I wonder," said Bobby uneasily, " if you would mind my driving ? You're worried—naturally."

Mr. Jacks relinquished the wheel readily enough.

" If there's been anything crooked——" he muttered. " If there has . . ."

" Any reason to suspect it ? " Bobby asked, settling himself comfortably in the driver's seat.

Mr. Jacks turned and stared moodily at Bobby, his small, excited eyes looking smaller and more excited than ever.

" What was Jessop doing there ? " he countered.

" You can't suggest anything ? "

" This man Mullins, you say he is a receiver of stolen goods ? "

" Yes."

" Well, then," muttered Jacks, and made an odd sort of choking noise in his throat. " Perhaps it isn't Jessop at all," he said, like a man clinging to a hope he knew was none.

Bobby had no authority to question his companion, but there was no harm in encouraging conversation, and often enough a chat reveals more than does any formal interrogation.

" Mr. Jessop," he remarked, " must have had some reason for thinking something was wrong or he wouldn't have rung us up—that is, if it was Mr. Jessop. Anyhow, from the information given us there were stories going round about the Fellows necklace."

" It's in the strong-room," Jacks repeated obstinately, as if reiteration of a statement could persuade the fact to be so. " It must be. None of us had the right to take it out, outside business hours, without letting the others know."

" And during business hours ? " Bobby asked.

" Well, of course, it had to be available if any possible client wanted to see it," Jacks answered.

" Would its presence be checked before the strong-room was closed for the day ? "

" Yes, of course—well, I suppose not always. To-day I left early, and so did Wright; he was going motoring somewhere. Jessop would be responsible for closing the strong-room to-day."

Bobby made no comment. After a time he said :

" You thought Mr. Mullins might be a bookmaker."

" Jessop's interested in racing," Jacks answered. " He always said it was just as well to be able to chat to clients —young fellows who came in to buy presents." Jacks was fidgeting with his collar and tie, as if he found breathing a little difficult. He muttered : " It must be in the strong-room all right. If it isn't, we're done, finished. Ruin," he burst out loudly, and then, to Bobby, very hurriedly : " Of course, I'm quite certain the necklace is there, in our strong-room, perfectly safe."

" When that's established, that will be one line of inquiry closed," agreed Bobby. " I suppose plenty of people knew you had the necklace for sale ? "

" Everyone," Jacks agreed. " There have been paragraphs in the papers for that matter. And we've sounded every likely quarter we could think of."

" Wonderful bit of work, I suppose," Bobby remarked. " Beautifully matched stones, aren't they ? Didn't Miss Fellows wear it in that film everyone raved about—*Rich Man's Baby* ? I think I remember it."

" That was a copy made specially for film work," Jacks explained. " Fine bit of work it was, too—Miss Fellows sold it for fifty or so, I believe, when she had done with it."

" I suppose it wouldn't have done to wear the real thing knocking about the studios," agreed Bobby. " Wasn't the Duchess of Westhaven thinking of buying ? "

" No," answered Jacks. " The duke did make an offer —came to see it one day and made an absurd suggestion; took us for fools, I suppose, or else didn't know it's real value. About a quarter of the break-up value he offered. We did think it might possibly be his way of getting the lowest price quoted. So we sent it round for his wife to see, just in case."

" Nothing happened, I suppose ? "

" No. She wanted it badly enough. We knew that before. She has a craze for jewellery—previously we've done deals with her through her agents, a Bond Street firm; very smart business woman, too. But she hasn't a penny herself. The duke's a millionaire two or three times over, but he keeps a tight hand on the money."

Bobby had been driving as fast as respect for the speed-limit permitted, and as the streets, less encumbered by traffic at night, encouraged. He swung into Chesters Street now, and drew up at The Towers, where, in spite of the late hour, a small crowd still lingered, staring at the constable on duty at the gates he opened to let their car into the drive.

The house was a blaze of light from floor to roof. Behind the uncurtained windows men could be seen moving to and fro. In the grounds others were conducting a search by the light of electric torches. Half a dozen cars or more were drawn up before the entrance—one or two of them Bobby recognised as belonging to journalists, and again he wondered at the speed—unwelcome speed—with which tidings seemed to reach newspaper offices, as though by some kind of instinctive and instantaneous attraction. Another constable was on duty at the open door. Bobby led Jacks past him into the hall and reported his arrival to Superintendent Ulyett, who was busy writing in the dining-room at the big table there.

" The body hasn't been moved yet," Ulyett told Mr. Jacks, " though·the men are waiting to take it to the mortuary." He called in Ferris, and told him to let Mr. Jacks see it and then return. To Bobby he said, when Ferris and Jacks had gone: " Anything to report ? "

Bobby gave a brief account of his activities.

" So Jessop was a betting man, eh ? " observed Ulyett. " ' *Cherchez la femme* ' may be all right in France, but over here ' *Cherchez* the bookmaker ' is a sounder idea."

" Jacks rather gave me the impression," Bobby continued, " that he had been expecting trouble of some sort —Mrs. Jacks, too. Of course, that's only an impression. Also I'm inclined to think the firm's in deep water, but that may be wrong, too. Jacks said something about ' ruin ' and this finishing them. He and Mrs. Jacks were out, the servants couldn't say where. I had to wait till they got home."

" Where had they been ? "

" To the cinema and then on to a friend's for bridge. Mr. Jacks says there's a copy of the Fellows necklace in existence which Miss Fellows used to wear at the studios. I thought that might be worth mentioning, as the telephone message from Jessop used the word ' swindle ' rather than ' robbery.' "

" Yes, that's a point," agreed Ulyett. " Is it in their possession—the imitation, I mean ? "

" I don't think so, sir. Mr. Jacks didn't say so; he said something about Miss Fellows having sold it."

" Have to inquire," observed Ulyett. " Complication if there's a fake knocking about."

" Yes, sir," agreed Bobby. " I found the Mayfair Square premises shut up, but I got Mr. Jacks's address from a Miss Hilda May, who was formerly secretary to the Duchess of Westhaven. Her place has been taken by a Mr. Charles Dickson, who was a film actor at one time and has been run in to-night for being drunk and disorderly near the Cut and Come Again club. He said he had been there all night, but the Cut and Come Again porter denied it."

" He would," said Ulyett bitterly. " If you believed the Cut and Come Again bunch, they never drink anything there but cold tea and lemonade. But does Dickson come into the picture at all ? "

" No, sir, except as successor to Miss May, who seems an unusual young lady. I didn't quite know what to make of her."

" Does she come into the picture ? " demanded Ulyett, with a certain slightly ominous patience.

" She knew about the necklace," Bobby explained, " and had shown it to the Duchess of Westhaven."

" When she was her secretary ? "

" No, sir. Apparently she was sacked because she got friendly with a Mr. Chenery, who is in the line of succession to the dukedom. Mr. Chenery seems to have no means and no allowance. He will probably inherit in due course, but it may not be for many years. I gather those in the succession before him are not likely to have children, but are likely to live long enough."

" The duke's not an old man, is he ? "

" No, sir. The point about Chenery is that he is not the immediate heir, but he is in the direct line, so that he is almost certain to succeed some day, but very likely not till he is quite old. It seems an awkward, even demoralising, position for him. Also Miss May seemed uneasy, as if she was half afraid he might be implicated. I thought it might be as well their movements to-night should be checked, or at any rate that the two of them should be kept in mind. Part of Miss May's work with Jessop & Jacks is to act as a saleswoman. She wears jewellery to attract attention to it; she called herself a mannequin in jewellery. When I got to her flat, Mr. Chenery was there."

" We'll make inquiries," promised Ulyett, writing vigorously.

" Mr. Jacks," Bobby continued, " insists that the necklace must be in the strong-room at Mayfair Square. He says none of them had any right to take it out after business hours without letting the others know. But the strong-room needs three keys to open it. Mr. Jessop had one, Mr. Jacks has the second, and their manager, Mr. Wright, has the third. Unluckily, Mr. Wright is motoring over the week-end, and it may be difficult to get in touch with him before Monday morning, when he is due to return to business. Until then there's no way of telling whether the necklace is actually there or not."

" Like the awkwardness of things," growled Ulyett. " We shall have to work on the assumption that the thing's been pinched and then Monday morning will show it safe and sound and all our work wasted."

But he did not say that as though he much believed it, and then Mr. Jacks came back into the room. He had seen the body and identified it as being certainly that of his partner. Evidently he was much shaken, and Ulyett began to question him in the hope of finding out something to throw light on what had happened, and more especially how Mr. Jessop came to be there, in Mullins's study, without, apparently, the occupier's knowledge or consent.

Bobby would have very much liked to remain for this interview, but he was not asked to stay, and the superintendent had already a shorthand writer who had been taking down a record of the examination to which the inmates of the house had been subjected during Bobby's absence. In the hall Bobby found a colleague, who warned him away from the drawing-room, where various journalists had been safely caged till it could be decided how much or how little to tell them—and where they would at any rate be more or less prevented from finding out for themselves more than they were wanted to know.

No trace, Bobby was informed by this colleague of his, had been found of the supposedly missing necklace.

" We've been over the house with a small-tooth comb," said the colleague, " and not a thing in it but's as innocent as a baby's rattle. They've been trying to search the grounds, too, but that's only a waste of time till it's light. The house-keeper sticks to it no one has been here all evening except Wynne and the paper-boy bringing the *Evening Announcer*. She remembers that, because Mullins is keen on football and wanted to see the results. But she sticks to it she saw no Jessop or anyone else."

" Which means Jessop must have come round by the back," observed Bobby.

" Which means," commented the other, " Mullins wasn't expecting him."

" I wouldn't say that," objected Bobby. " Mullins left his garden fence full of gaps on purpose, so that his pals could slip in and out without being seen—those he expected most were generally those he least wanted seen."

" If it was that," his colleague suggested, " then most likely the whole crowd was up to something crooked together. Jessop brought the necklace along, and Wynne or someone shot him to get it."

" Although Wynne knew we were on the spot ? Besides, there was hardly time—anyhow, only just time—for Wynne to do it. And if it was like that, why did Jessop ring us up to tell us the necklace had been stolen ? "

" Might have been a way of putting us off," suggested the other, and then added : " Here's T. T."

Mullins was, in fact, descending the stairs. He looked very worried and dishevelled, and was chewing an unlighted cigar between his teeth.

" Nice sort of thing to be mixed up in," he grumbled. " Just my luck. Why couldn't the blighter go and get himself shot somewhere else ? What's he got to choose my house for ? I've always kept myself out of that sort of thing. I shall have to move; I shall never feel O.K. here again. Lucky for me I was with you fellows when you heard the shot, or ten to one you would have wanted to pull me in."

" May yet," said the other C.I.D. man, winking at Bobby. " Expect we shall find there was an earlier shot none of us noticed."

" No good trying to pull my leg," retorted T. T. " The gun's there, and only two cartridges fired. Besides, you all know murder's not my line—I hate violence. What have we got brains for ? "

" What indeed ? " murmured Bobby.

" I shall clear out, find another place, move," repeated T. T. " I like it here, but I shall never feel right again after this. I should always be expecting to see that poor devil's ghost. You fellows ought to pile in and help me get out. It's all through you; the least you can do is to help. What's a good firm for removals ? Who did you hire that van from you chaps came in to-night ? "

" Don't know. I wasn't one of that lot," answered the C.I.D. man, who, in fact, had come later on the scene.

" You'll know," suggested T. T., turning to Bobby.

" What's the idea ? " asked Bobby. " Want to send some of your toughs round to bully them for helping us ? "

" Good Lord, no," exclaimed T. T. hastily.

" No idea of offering a tenner for advance information another time ? " Bobby asked again.

" Sergeant," declared T. T. very earnestly, " I never thought of that for one moment; never entered my head. Honest—God's truth. All I want is just to get hold of a good trustworthy firm."

" Plenty of them," said Bobby. " No trouble finding one."

" Oh, well, if you want to be so almighty close," snapped T. T. " I'll bet some of the others won't mind telling."

" I'll pass the word round they're not to," Bobby said calmly. " We don't want any of your pocket gangsters trying to make themselves unpleasant."

" Sergeant," protested T. T., even more earnestly than before, " you've got it wrong. Straight, all I want is the name of a good reliable firm, because I'm not going to stop here after this—not me. And I know if it's a firm you can trust, I can trust them too."

" Yes, but we don't trust you," retorted Bobby.

" Oh, well, it doesn't matter," said T. T., though with an angry emphasis that made it a little difficult for him to get out his words. "I call it childish to be so close about trifles."

He turned away in a great temper, and the other C.I.D. man, who looked a good deal amused, both at T. T.'s insistence and at Bobby's refusal to gratify his curiosity, gave a chuckle and said to Mullins :

" Official reticence—you mustn't mind him, T. T. Comes natural to us fellows; why, we don't give anything away, even where we buy the baby's milk. Comes especially natural to sergeants, particularly when caught young."

Bobby acknowledged the hit with a grin, and the other continued:

" Mustn't bear malice, T. T. Tell us instead how the Arsenal got on—the football *Evening Announcer* special's there, but the results are missing."

Mullins turned very pale; his jaw dropped; he stood aghast, as if for the first time he saw disaster clearly facing him.

" Why, what's the matter ? " the C.I.D. man asked him; and without a word T. T. rushed furiously away.

" Well, now, what's biting him ? " wondered the C.I.D. man, turning bewilderedly to Bobby, who only shook his head in an equally bewildered response.

CHAPTER IX

THE SUMMER-HOUSE DISCOVERY

THEY WERE STILL WONDERING why this demand
for information about the day's football results should have
so startled, thrown into panic even, the generally self-
possessed T. T., when Inspector Ferris joined them.

" Better get some sleep while you can," he said. " Orders
are, every man available to help go through the grounds as
soon as it's light. The necklace isn't in the house, but it may
have been dumped outside somewhere."

" Well, sir, I'm wondering," said the C.I.D. man, who
had been talking to Bobby, " what's the matter with Wynne
having gone off with it ? "

" That would mean he had it in his pocket when he was
standing there while T. T. was talking to us," Ferris
observed doubtfully. " He would want a lot of cheek to do
that, knowing he might be questioned any minute and his
pockets gone through. T. T. would have enough gall, but
not many. Anyhow, T. T. hadn't got it. I made him turn
out his pockets all right."

" Wynne might have rushed back to the house and
grabbed the thing before he cleared off," the C.I.D. man
persisted. " How's this for a guess ? Jessop was crooked,
and meant to swipe the necklace for himself. First step :
rings us up and says it's been stolen. Then he comes on here
to put through a deal with T. T. They get warning we're
on. T. T. and Wynne come out to divert attention while
Jessop does a bunk. But then Wynne sees his chance, rushes

back to the house, pots Jessop, grabs the necklace, and off."

" If it's like that," objected Bobby, " what was Wynne doing here ? T. T. isn't the kind to bring in a third person unless he has to. And why didn't Jessop do a bunk himself if that was the idea ? Besides, was there time ? The shot was fired almost immediately after Wynne started back to the house from where he had been standing at the gate to the drive."

" It could have been done," decided Ferris; " matter of seconds, but it's feasible. No one timed when Wynne walked away, and ' almost immediately ' might mean much longer than you think."

" Yes, sir, there's that," agreed Bobby, " only there are the rubber gloves, too. The murderer was wearing them— there's a thumb torn from one caught on the trigger guard of the pistol used. And in a matter of minutes even the time to pull on rubber gloves would count."

Lawson, of the now discarded green baize apron, had come up and was listening. He said:

" Well, as to that, I had an eye on Wynne, because I thought I knew the bird, though I couldn't quite place him. I'm pretty sure he didn't go straight back to the house; anyhow, there was someone behind those bushes where the drive turns. Looked to me like it was Wynne waiting to see what happened. Then, when we heard the shots, whoever it was cleared off, top speed, but he didn't make for the house, more away to the left."

" You're not sure it was Wynne ? " Ferris asked.

" I thought it was at the time, but I couldn't swear to it," Lawson repeated.

" Knock any case on the head if that came out in evidence, though," Ferris commented, " and the defence would have to be told. Unless we can show some other bird."

" The funny thing is, I'm nearly sure I've seen him somewhere," Lawson said again.

" That's right," Ferris told him. " Expect you have. ' Fingers ' got some dabs in the study, and one lot has been checked up as those of a bird that's been inside twice. Card-sharping and confidence and a bit of bullying, too— one three-year stretch for shooting with intent. Name of Isidore Hill and plenty others as well—Count de Teirney and The MacGregor of that Ilk, whatever he thinks that means. Description seems to answer to Wynne, so it's likely him, unless there's been the Hill bird round here as well, and he and Wynne are twins or something like that."

" Was there anything on the pistol—or the cigar ? " Bobby asked.

" No; cigar half burnt away and the pistol probably handled with gloves on," Ferris answered. " We'll have to check up on the pistol; that may help. Anyhow, Wynne's in the picture. Plenty to ask him when we do pick him up."

" If T. T. was expecting Jessop," Bobby repeated, " what was Wynne doing ? And if Jessop turned up on his own, without being expected—well, what for ? "

" To do a deal on the cross with T. T. ? " suggested Ferris.

" Well, sir, it might be that," agreed Bobby, with the deference mere sergeants owe to the theories of inspectors, " but, with his position in the jewellery trade, Jessop would surely be able to get rid of all the stuff he wanted without bringing in T. T. or anyone else."

Ferris remarked that possibly another reason might have been the necessity for keeping the transaction hidden from partner and staff, and Bobby agreed that was possible, and got leave to return to his lodgings and change from uniform to plain clothes again, though only on the strict understanding that he was back before dawn, since the renewed, more thorough search of the grounds was to start the moment daylight appeared. By the unauthorised use, in the

FJ

face of all regulations, of one of the waiting police-cars, Bobby succeeded in being back not only before dawn, but even in time to get a little sleep on the dining-room hearth-rug, all the available pieces of furniture in that room being already occupied by snoozing colleagues. Upstairs was strictly forbidden—T. T. had not proved hospitably inclined. The drawing-room was occupied by patient reporters, who there sat or slept or smoked or gossiped as inclination was, so that they might be ready when operations began again. The study had been locked up. The breakfast-room was occupied by Mr. Ulyett himself, on whom none dared intrude. And the hall was draughty, and the kitchen, like upstairs, out of bounds, so that there was nothing for it but the floor of the crowded dining-room.

The first sign of light came to most of them as a relief from their uneasy slumbers, and, as the light strengthened, a carefully organised search began. Every inch of ground almost was examined, if not quite with a microscope, at least with very keen and close attention.

The flagged paths that ran from the broken-down fence separating garden from common up to the house were hopeless for footprints, and revealed nothing else of interest, but a print was found in the border by one of the gaps in this fence that corresponded exactly with the shoes worn by Mr. Jessop. Other footprints, less distinct, but fairly certainly made by the same person, were discovered in the ditch on the common side of the fence, so that it seemed proved this was the way whereby Jessop had reached the house.

" Either Jessop had been there before, or someone had told him," was the general verdict.

Then came another discovery, heralded by a shout of triumph, for there, it seemed, was the missing necklace itself, dangling in the middle of a rose-bush on the south side of the house, almost in a line with the study window and not more than twenty yards or so distant. But the triumph and the excitement caused by the discovery soon faded when it quickly became apparent that this was only imitation jewellery—probably the copy made for Miss Fellows to wear on the sets.

T. T., when questioned, was quite open about it.

" Oh, yes," he said. " Gave a fellow a tenner for it two or three weeks back at the Cut and Come Again when I was there one night. Don't know who he was; said he had been in that swell picture of Fay Fellows's—*Rich Man's Baby*, was it ? No, not that one. *Millionaire's Sweetie* I think it was called. Or was it *Big Business Boy's Kiddy* ? Anyhow, he said he bought it in Hollywood when they were getting rid of some old props. I thought it was worth what he asked. It was in that old safe in my study. The murderer must have grabbed it and run, thinking it was genuine, and then he saw it wasn't and dropped it. Probably means he got away through the garden next door. Better ask them there if they heard anything."

His explanation was not much believed, but had to be accepted, and the search continued with unabated energy. No other discovery was made on that, the southern side of the house, but on the north side, at the spot where the path from the entrance to the drive turned towards the house footsteps as of a man running, but from, not to, the house, were plainly visible in the soft, damp mould of a flower-bed, at just about the spot, indeed, where Lawson believed he had seen Wynne waiting. Other prints in a line with these could be traced leading towards the wall dividing the garden of The Towers from that of the unoccupied house next to it. Also on the flower-bed where the footsteps started there was a half-smoked cigarette of the Bulgar brand that apparently Wynne favoured. Ferris shook his head gloomily.

" Looks like letting Wynne out," he said.

" Had the necklace in his pocket all the time," declared Lawson. " Waited to see if we cleared off and it would be safe for him to carry on with T. T. When he heard the shots he cleared out himself as quick as he knew how."

" No proof of all that," Ferris said. " May have been someone else we haven't got track of yet. Nothing to show."

On the hard gravel path the tracks disappeared, but were visible again on a border near the garden wall that was nothing like high enough to offer any obstacle to an active man.

" Got over there, whoever it was," Ferris said, and, when they in their turn climbed over into the next garden, they found clear proof that the fugitive—Wynne or another— had in fact there scaled the wall. They even discovered a burnt match thrown down, as if, feeling himself there in safety, he had stopped for a moment to light another cigarette. On the overgrown lawn before the unoccupied house they lost the tracks, and made, in fact, no great effort to trace them, since it was plain enough that the fugitive had crossed the lawn and so reached the street beyond. But one of the searchers made another and unexpected discovery. In a summer-house, neglected and badly in need of repair, but with its roof still sound, standing not far from the point where the wall had been climbed, he found fresh cigarette-ends—though of a different and cheaper brand— a paper bag that had contained chocolates and that had printed on it the name of a local shop, and a woman's handkerchief without either name, initial, or laundry mark.

But what the significance of these discoveries might be none of them could decide.

Had Wynne—or someone else—had accomplices waiting for him here ? And, if it was Wynne who had made his escape on this, the north side, who was it who had thrown away the imitation necklace on the south side ?

CHAPTER X

FOREIGN CURRENCY

NOT TILL AFTERNOON that Sunday was it decided that everything possible had been accomplished at The Towers. The house and grounds had been thoroughly searched, numberless photographs taken, sketches made, plans prepared, measurements recorded. Plaster casts of the footsteps found on the northern side of the house had been secured, and it had been established that no other tracks or signs of any kind were discoverable elsewhere, save those made by the police themselves and by the victim of the crime. If others had been that night in the house, or in the grounds surrounding it, they had escaped unseen during the confusion following the pistol shots, and probably along those flagged paths that retained no tracks. T. T. had been questioned and re-questioned without further result than a growing conviction that on this occasion, by exception, he was telling the truth when he declared he knew nothing of Jessop, had never seen him before, and that the discovery of his dead body in the study was as great a surprise to himself as it could have been to anyone else.

Then, too, there had been carefully wrapped up, in various containers, the revolver, the half-smoked cigar, the torn-off thumb from a rubber glove, and even such things as the cigarette-ends, the empty paper bag, and the unmarked handkerchief from the tumbledown summer-house of the unoccupied residence next door. These were all clues, and it was impossible to tell which might or might not turn out important or negligible, misleading or significant.

" That handkerchief," declared Ulyett, looking at it doubtfully, " does look a bit as if there were a woman in the picture somewhere. Why," he asked resentfully, " hasn't the thing got a laundry mark? Then we might have a chance to trace it."

All over London, too, and indeed all over the country, a sharp look-out was being kept for Augustus Percy Wynne, also known as Isidore Hill, Count de Teirney, The Mac-Gregor of that Ilk, and probably by other names as well.

" Though he's not likely to use ' The MacGregor of that Ilk ' here," observed Ulyett. " Too many Scots about who might ask him what he thought ' Ilk ' meant."

Another search, too, had been conducted at Mr. Jessop's flat, and there a somewhat curious discovery had been made. In a small safe used for the secure keeping of any article of value Mr. Jessop might have had occasion to bring from the Mayfair Square establishment there was discovered Swiss, French, and Dutch currency to the value of £5,000, mostly in small notes. There was nothing to indicate where it had come from, what it was to be used for, why it was being kept, and, as the notes were generally of small denomination, there would be little hope of tracing any of them. Nor was there anything to connect this private hoard with the Brush Hill tragedy, and it was, of course, easy to imagine fifty perfectly good and proper reasons for which foreign currency might have been required. All the same, the fact seemed a little unusual, even disconcerting, for, after all, few people in England keep large sums in foreign currency. Nor could Mr. Jacks explain it in any way. He knew of no transaction the firm had in hand to account for it. Plainly he, too, found the thing disturbing. And he was equally unable to offer any suggestion as to why Jessop had made his tragic journey to Brush Hill. As for T. T. Mullins, Mr. Jacks had never heard of him. Nor did anything else found in the flat appear to be of any interest, though Ulyett did knit his brows over a slip of paper, discovered with the foreign currency, on which the figures £55,000 had been subtracted from £65,000, and the remainder, £10,000, put down in large and careful figures, as though that simple calculation had a certain significance.

" May mean something," Ulyett decided, " but, if it does, there's no way of telling at present."

Ulyett obtained, too, from Mr. Jacks the name of Jessop's solicitors, and his inquiry whether it was the same firm who acted for the partnership in the affairs of the business received a somewhat sulky " No " for answer.

" Jessop chose to take his private business elsewhere some time ago," Mr. Jacks explained in a tone that suggested this was a grievance of some kind.

" Any reason for that ? " Ulyett asked, quick to notice the hint of resentment in the other's voice.

" He seemed to think there might be some clash between his private interests and those of the firm. He said he preferred to have fully independent, neutral advice. Nonsense, of course. We aren't a limited company. If the firm had gone bankrupt, he would have gone bankrupt, too; nothing private about it."

" Yes, of course," agreed Ulyett, noting silently that this was the first time the word " bankrupt " had been pronounced, for, though " ruin " was a word that had been used before, " ruin " may be more or less a metaphor, but " bankruptcy " has always a realistic, factual flavour.

A decision was arrived at to wait to interview the lawyers until the Monday morning, since to conduct any kind of business on a Sunday in England means endless trouble and delay—and also puts everyone in a bad temper, which has also its importance. The search of Mr. Jessop's flat having terminated, the searchers were withdrawn. A cable was sent to his daughter in Australia—the only close relative, apparently, he possessed—and most of those who had been engaged on the case were sent to their homes to get a little rest before starting again.

Bobby was less fortunate. Before the general exodus from The Towers, he was summoned to Ulyett's presence. He had already sent in a brief note reporting T. T.'s anxiety to know the address of the firm supplying the removal van of which such ineffectual use had been made, and now he found his reticence approved.

" I've told Inspector Ferris to warn the others to hold their tongues," Ulyett said. " We don't want T. T.'s pocket hooligans making trouble for the people we employ, or trying to bribe them to give information next time. T. T.'s got quite a good intelligence service of his own," said Ulyett, musing bitterly on T. T.'s unmasking of their earlier manœuvres and of how the story would soon be whispered all through London's underworld—and overworld, too, for that matter. T. T.'s cry of sham amazement as he banged open the van door—" Why, there's men inside "—was likely, Ulyett knew, to become a general catchword. Probably for months to come the door of no bar, no night-club, in all the town would be opened without the accompanying cry: " Why, there's men inside." Ulyett sighed resignedly. Some day, perhaps, they would get T. T., but not yet. He said suddenly: " T. T.'s talk about moving from here sounds a bit as if he had got the wind up and meant to do a bunk."

" Yes, sir," agreed Bobby thoughtfully. " Perhaps to pick up the Fellows necklace somewhere and get out of the country with it."

Ulyett winced at the suggestion, which he liked the less because it was one that had occurred to himself.

" Can't do anything," he said. " Nothing we can hold

him for. We can trail him, of course, but what's the good of that ? We can warn the Customs, but what's the good of that ? "

" Yes, sir," agreed Bobby sympathetically, fully agreeing with Ulyett's unspoken thought that, after all, the thumb-screw and the rack had their advantages from the point of view of a harassed C.I.D.

" I'm sending most of the others off duty," Ulyett continued, abandoning happy dreams of T. T., boiling lead, and a full and complete account of what the dickens it was had really taken place. " No such luck for me," he added enviously. " I shall have to be at it all day and all night, too, getting out schemes. We'll have to be getting busy, you know. The papers will make a big splash of this affair. Bit of luck for the Government."

" Sir ? " said Bobby, astonished.

" Help to take people's minds off the Abyssinia affair," explained Ulyett. " Everyone wants to forget that. Of course, they all will before the next election, and that's all that really matters, but the sooner they forget, the happier the big hats will be. They don't want people—brooding."

" No, sir," agreed Bobby. " Of course, sir, I'm not a politician."

" I should hope not," said Ulyett, very sternly indeed. " Sorry I can't let you off with the rest, Owen. There's a job I want you for."

" Yes, sir," said Bobby with resignation, for full well had he known this was coming.

" We've got to follow up that half-smoked cigar," Ulyett went on. " T. T. swears he knows nothing about it, and that he and the Wynne bird only smoked cigarettes. So apparently it was either Jessop's or the murderer's. You are sure you're right in thinking the monogram on it is that of the American gentleman you met at the Duke of Westhaven's flat ? "

“ I think so, sir,” answered Bobby. “ It could easily be checked, but I don’t think I’m wrong.”

“ Jessop,” observed Ulyett, looking at the ceiling, “ said something just before he died—something that sounded like ‘ duke,’ didn’t it ? ”

“ Yes, sir,” agreed Bobby.

“ If it was someone we had something against,” continued Ulyett, “ it would be nearly good enough to pull him in on—what with the cigar we can trace to him and dying words as well. But there it is—a duke ! ”

“ Yes, sir,” agreed Bobby.

“ Of course,” mused Ulyett, “ dukes aren’t what once they were, not by a long chalk. And more’s the pity,” added Ulyett, who was a strong Conservative and read the *Morning Post* every morning. “ But still dukes.”

“ Yes, sir,” repeated Bobby, who always felt safe when he could conduct a conversation with superintendents and their like on the grounds of “ Yes, sir.”

“ It’s got to be checked up on all the same,” declared Ulyett. “ No getting away from it, only we’ll have to be tactful—tactful.”

“ Yes, sir,” said Bobby—it was almost mechanical now. Then he added reassuringly, “ It’s not as if there was any serious suspicion.”

“ Exactly,” said Ulyett; “ only dukes and such—touchy, I’ve found.”

Bobby produced his accustomed : “ Yes, sir.”

“ Got one in your own family, haven’t you ? Grandfather or something ? ”

“ Oh, no, sir, not at all, sir,” protested Bobby, stung this time to indignant denial.

“ I thought——” said Ulyett, with a stern don’t-you-try-to-pull-the-wool-over-my-eyes-young-fellow expression.

“ Well, sir,” admitted Bobby, “ I’ve an uncle, but he’s

only an earl; besides, he's practically bankrupt," he added as an extenuating circumstance.

" All tar from the same brush," declared Ulyett, waving excuses aside. " Anyhow, he has seen you before, and I want you to go round there again—alone; less official if there's only one of you. Try to get a list, if possible, of all who might have had one of those cigars. At any rate, find out if Mr. Patterson was free with them. Then try to pump him about the necklace: why he went to see it; if he really contemplated buying it; if there have been any further negotiations; if he's talked about it with anyone; how often the duchess has seen it; how badly she wanted it—anything you can get out of either of them, in fact. Oh, and you might ask him if he can make any suggestion what Jessop meant when he said ' the duke ' just before he died. That'll need tact."

" Yes, sir," said Bobby, this time more uneasily than mechanically.

" And get him to tell you," continued Ulyett, " where he was round about eight or nine o'clock last night. No harm in having a good alibi well established for him, and him being a duke—well, there won't be any trouble about that. Lots of people will know where he was—dining at Buckingham Palace very likely, or something of the sort. Of course, it'll need tact."

Bobby had his note-book out.

" Trace possible possessors of cigars similar to that found near body," he said, " and known to belong to duke's friend now in New York. Inquire as to reason for inspecting Fellows necklace; how often his wife has seen it; was there serious thought of buying it, either on his part or that of duchess, who is known to have been interested. Inquire if he can suggest why Jessop made dying reference to him."

" Putting it like that," observed Ulyett discontentedly, " it sounds almost like a case."

" Yes, sir," agreed Bobby once more.

" But of course, a duke ! "

" Of course, sir," said Bobby.

" You'll need," said Ulyett impressively, " you'll need—tact."

" Yes, sir."

" Of course," mused Ulyett, " if it really began to look like a real case—have to be hushed up, I suppose. Couldn't afford it, with all this Bolshevism about ; wouldn't do at all."

" No, sir," said Bobby, for variety's sake, and was on his way to the door when Ulyett called him back.

" Owen," he said earnestly, " there's one thing you mustn't forget, one thing you'll need more than anything—— "

" Yes, sir," interposed Bobby. " Tact, sir."

" That's right," said Ulyett, relieved. " Glad you realise that, Owen."

But, though he understood, Bobby was more than a trifle uneasy as he departed, for the Duke of Westhaven was a Personage, and knew he was a Personage, and, moreover, had not the reputation of being the most amiable or best-tempered man in the world. And if he chose to take offence at this police questioning—well, that would mean that Bobby would be held to have failed badly in tact.

In the hall he found T. T. looking on with gloomy satisfaction at the final preparations for departure of his uninvited and unwelcome guests.

" I don't see what I've done to have a thing like this happen to me," he complained bitterly. " Look here," he added to Bobby, " I suppose I've got to put up with you police chaps, but what right has all this crowd of journalists nosing round here ? "

" None," said Bobby cheerfully. " They never have."

" Well, why don't you throw them out ? "

" Why should we ? Nothing to do with us. We've no

authority to throw people out of houses. For all we know, they may be friends of yours."

" Friends ? " repeated T. T. wildly. " Friends ? Why, one of them has offered me a thousand for a full confession, only to be used after I'm hanged—£100 down and the rest to my heirs."

" Did you accept ? " asked Bobby interestedly.

T. T. spluttered something fierce and indignant, spluttered it almost as though the rope were already round his neck. Then he said:

" Can I throw them out ? "

" Theoretically, yes. Practically—but anyhow you could try. Why not ? But, even then, there's keeping them out."

" I'll buy a dog," said T. T.

" They'll buy another," said Bobby, " set 'em both fighting, and get a good—er—snappy story for the front page. There's only one way to deal with a newspaper man."

" What's that ? " asked T. T. eagerly.

" Tell him the truth, the whole truth, and nothing but the truth, down to the last little detail," said Bobby, " and then tell him it's confidential."

" Oh, hell ! " said T. T.

" So it is," agreed Bobby; " for them—worse. Talk not of grief till thou hast seen the tears of a journalist told an exclusive in confidence. But you mustn't mind that—serves them right. But I must get off. Any paper shops near here likely to be open ? "

" Lots," answered T. T. " Why ? "

" I want last night's *Evening Announcer*," Bobby explained, " with the football results."

T. T. was too pale with fatigue and worry and lack of sleep for his pallor to increase much, but there came into his pale and startled cold blue eyes a look that was almost murderous, even though murder was not, he said, his " line." With those quick, furtive movements of his, he vanished, passing suddenly through the baize-covered service door behind the stairs. As it closed behind him, Bobby heard his somewhat shrill, high-pitched voice raised in what sounded like a vigorous curse—though aimed at what, or whom, Bobby could not hear, though he could guess.

Thoughtfully Bobby made his way to the tube station, wondering very much to himself what there could be on the football pages of the *Evening Announcer* so disturbing to the usually imperturbable and self-possessed T. T., and what connection there could be between football results and the death of the unfortunate Jessop. In his possession, too, Bobby had that copy of the two-weeks-old *Upper Ten* that had been in Jessop's pocket, but that, disregarded, had got kicked under a chair, whence Bobby had rescued it.

CHAPTER XI

NEWSPAPERS' SECRET

BUT CAREFULLY, MINUTELY, REPEATEDLY, though
Bobby read over and over again every one of the football
pages missing from T. T.'s copy of the *Evening Announcer*,
deeply though he brooded upon the *Upper Ten*, with all its
lovely photographs on paper as shiny as the front of a dress
shirt just back from the laundry, there was nothing he
could find that appeared to have any possible connection
with the recent tragedy or the theft of the Fay Fellows
necklace—if, in fact, that necklace had been stolen, as could
only be known for certain when the strong-room of the
Mayfair Square establishment was opened on Monday
morning.

What, for instance, in this connection could it matter that
the Arsenal had bewilderingly met with defeat from a club
of comparatively humble standing ? The *Upper Ten*, it is
true, had a photograph of the Duchess of Westhaven, in her
characteristically old-fashioned attire, clapping her hands
at the announcement of the victory, in the three o'clock, of
the horse of a friend. But, then, no doubt it was precisely
for that reason—because all the world knew she would be
at those races—that that day had been selected for the
odd affair at the Park Lane flat when unlawful intruders
had apparently been satisfied to sit about and smoke their
cigarettes. Nothing could Bobby find that by any stretch
of the imagination could be supposed to account for the
alarm and agitation a merely casual reference to the missing

pages of the *Evening Announcer* had seemed to cause the usually cool and collected T. T. Nor could he see any reason why Mr. Jessop should have been carrying about with him that old copy of an illustrated society paper. Yet, none the less, Bobby was aware of an uneasy feeling that somehow, somewhere, in some odd way, all that he needed to know lay hidden there.

" Beats me," decided Bobby, as he reached his destination and, folding up the paper, put it in his pocket in the hope that time might bring an explanation. " Sort of thing that needs real brainwork, hard thinking, intuition, brilliant flight of the imagination to sweep you right over seas of doubt and land you on the firm facts with no bother about building logical bridges." Bobby shook his head sadly. " Wish I could do that sort of thing," he thought, " but I jolly well can't. All I can do is dig up a lot of facts and see if any of 'em fit—journeyman of detection, that's all I am."

A little depressed by this conclusion, but reflecting that it's no good longing for gifts denied, Bobby emerged from the tube station to find himself in a world turned liquid. The rain that had been slowly gathering since the previous night's drizzle had now burst into a kind of heavenly cataract. The gutters were overflowing, pedestrians had scattered in all directions, taximen were chuckling. Bobby was able by good luck to pounce on one taxi that had just brought to the tube station a passenger with whom Bobby almost collided as they simultaneously dashed, one for the cab and one for the station. Three other marooned pedestrians were frantically beckoning to the taxi, but Bobby's dash had gained it for him, and, fortunately for his pockets, the block of flats, his destination, was not far, since it was quite certain that " Taxi—to avoid getting wet " was not an item with any chance of scraping through any expense list.

The building was a new one, designed by one of the most eminent architects of the day, probably with the aid of a child's box of bricks, and the whole of the top floor was occupied by the Duke of Westhaven. Changed times, no doubt, from the days when every duke had a town mansion like a young town itself, with a host of servitors to look after it and each other—and even their employers—and a private park around it big enough for a hunting-party. Another sign of changing times was that the rent payable for the flat was itself as much as some ducal revenues of earlier days, though this fact was of less importance to his grace of Westhaven in that much of what he paid as tenant went back into his pocket as landlord.

The flat had its own private lift the porters in the entrance-hall had the strictest orders to see was used by no unauthorised person. There was, of course, also access to the flat both by an interior stair, in case the lifts failed, and by the exterior stair insisted on by the building regulations for use in case of fire. Both these stairs, however, ended, as far as the ducal flat was concerned, in a small square lobby, whose one door, admitting to the flat itself, could only be opened from within, these careful precautions being insisted on to the insurance company as a reason for reducing the premium charged against the risk of burglary or housebreaking.

Bobby, producing his official card, was allowed the use of the lift. But due warning of his approach was conveyed over the house 'phone, and when he stepped out of the lift he found the butler and a footman waiting to receive him, and a maid or two hovering in the background, though this was less a tribute to his social importance than to their own curiosity.

" His grace is engaged at the moment, sergeant," the butler informed Bobby, " but I'll take in your card and I don't suppose he'll be long. Found out anything yet ? "

GJ

" You expect quick work, don't you ? " Bobby remarked.

" Two weeks ago, isn't it ? " retorted the butler, and Bobby realised he was referring to that unexplained incident when the flat, left temporarily unoccupied, had been entered by those odd intruders who, however, had removed nothing and done no damage.

" Oh, about that," Bobby said. " Well, no; besides, there's nothing much we could do even if we knew who it was. Trespass itself isn't punishable; there must be damage done or resistance to an order to go."

" All my eye, I say," interposed the footman, less in awe of the butler than good footmen should be; but, then, the butler owed him for bets made, placed, lost, and not yet settled. " Most likely it was his nibs himself come back for something he didn't want anyone to know about. As I keep telling Mr. Fisher," said the footman to Bobby, with a jerk of his thumb at the butler to indicate that he was Mr. Fisher, " the lift hadn't been used—locked, it was. And the lobby door from the stairs can't be opened from the outside, not without an axe or such."

" No, but it can from the inside," retorted Fisher, evidently going over again a familiar argument, " and a fellow rigged up as a workman could easy climb the fire-escape stair without anyone noticing, get in by the pantry window, and then open the lobby door and let in his pals."

" The pantry window was locked on the inside," insisted the footman.

" Easy to do that before they left by the inside stairs," retorted the butler.

" What should they go to all that trouble for and never touch a thing ? " demanded the footman.

" Must have had some game on," pronounced Fisher. " We'll know some day," he prophesied darkly. " Of course, it's—well, a rum go."

Bobby agreed that it was a rum go—that, indeed, had been the unofficial verdict already rendered at the Yard—and then further discussion was stopped by the appearance of an elderly lady, dressed in a somewhat old-fashioned style, in person short, stout, dignified, and cross, who came abruptly into the hall and said breathlessly:

" Fisher, ring up Mr. Dickson at once and ask him if he will kindly let me know when I may expect him—that is, if it's really not expecting too much to ask for his attendance. Tell him I've been waiting—waiting," repeated the lady rather awfully, " nearly a quarter of an hour."

" Very good, your grace," said the butler as, with as near an approach to a run as the dignity of a portly butler permits, he made for the 'phone.

And at that very moment—the psychological moment if ever moment deserved the epithet—the lift shot up and there emerged a small, slightly built, handsome youth, beautifully dressed, with small, regular features, a tiny moustache, the teeth of a musical comedy actress, hair that would have broken Monsieur Marcel's heart to think how little need it had of him, and really finely shaped and most carefully kept hands he held out towards the elderly lady with a gesture graceful and imploring, and at the same time presenting those exquisite hands for observation and admiration.

" Duchess," he said, in a soft, musical, really agreeable voice, " I'm more than sorry, I'm most awfully sorry, but honestly I can't swim. I never could. I sink like a stone."

" Charles," said the duchess, still awfully, but distinctly less so, " you're a quarter of an hour late, and you know very well I detest being kept waiting."

" The rain," pleaded Charles, in tones to move the hardest heart, " the rain ? No, the flood—not forty days, perhaps, but forty inches—forty feet rather. I had to wait ten minutes for a taxi, and then we were held up in a traffic block."

" You could walk, couldn't you? Hadn't you an umbrella —and your coat? "

" I don't know what you'll think of me, duchess," the young man sighed, his sigh almost a song in itself, " but I've lost it already—left it in a bus or something. Of course, I shall get it back."

" I never heard anything so careless," said the duchess, grown awful again.

She turned and walked, or rather marched, away. The young man made a face at Fisher and followed droopingly, though with about him a kind of aura of confidence that he would soon smile his way back into favour. When they had disappeared, Fisher said to Bobby:

" That's the coat she gave him only last week—wanted him to go somewhere for her. It was raining, and he said he hadn't a coat; said he couldn't afford one—all my eye and Betty Martin, but he gets lots of things out of her like that. She rang up the Stores to send one round same as the duke's just got for himself, ready made being cheapest —she'll be mad at his losing it so soon."

Since this nice-looking young man with the beautiful hands was evidently the new private secretary who had supplanted Hilda May, Bobby was a trifle inclined to suspect that the loss of the new raincoat was a by-product of last night's exuberance that had culminated in the lamp-post-climbing experiment and a visit to the police station. However, that was no business of his, he supposed, and certainly the young, fresh complexion and quick, bright, and alert eyes did not suggest that such excitements were too frequent in Charley Dickson's life. To the butler Bobby said:

" Is the duke likely to be long? It's official business I've come on, you know."

" What his grace will want to know is whether you've caught them that broke in here," Fisher retorted. " Proper vexed about it he was, proper vexed. But I'll see."

He went off accordingly, and came back soon.

" If you'll wait in the library," he said, " his grace will see you in a few minutes. This way."

He led Bobby across the hall into a fair-sized room whose windows afforded a fine view over London. Bobby admired it, and then turned his attention to the books on the shelves, hoping to gather from them some indication of the character of their owner. But they were all library sets of classical authors that not only looked as if they had never been read but had never even been intended for such a purpose. Even a complete set of Jane Austen's works had a stiff and dignified and unapproachable air, as though to chuckle over them in an arm-chair by the fire would be a kind of *lèse-majesté*. As for the *Pickwick Papers*, upright in calf and gilt, it positively scared the reader away; impossible to believe that pompous volume held the jests of Mr. Samuel Weller, the simple friendliness of Mr. Pickwick. " Just furniture," Bobby told himself, and the door opened and there dashed into the room young Mr. Charley Dickson.

" Oh, I say," he gasped, " Fisher's just told me you're police. I say, you haven't come about that binge of mine last night, have you ? "

" Good gracious, no," said Bobby. " Nothing to do with me."

Charley sighed with relief.

" I won't say it's the first time," he declared earnestly, " but it's not often, and it is the first time I've got run in— forty bob or seven days' hard, I suppose, and where the hell the forty bob's coming from, only the good Lord knows. You don't give a chap time, do you ? I say, that's a joke, isn't it ? Just what you do give a chap. I mean to say, has a chap got to pay up on the nail ? "

" That's not for the police to say," Bobby answered, smiling a little at this ingenuous chatter. " The magistrate settles that."

" Well, I'll have to pop something," decided Charley. " Won't be the first time. Have to be the last, though," he said, shaking his head gravely at himself. " Gave me a scare when I heard you were police. What's up ? "

" I have asked to be allowed to see the duke for a few minutes," Bobby answered.

" The old boy been up to something ? " demanded Charley, grinning. " I say, what a lark if we both turn up in the dock together ! Got tight, too, did he ? Was that the trouble Saturday night ? "

" Why ? What trouble ? What do you mean ? " Bobby asked quickly, startled in spite of himself. " What happened Saturday night ? "

" That's what we all want to know," returned Charley, and added, bestowing upon Bobby a most portentous wink : " Especially the old girl."

" You mean the duchess ? "

" I do that," answered Charley. " Wish I knew where hubby was—might do a spot of blackmail. It was somewhere about eight or nine last evening when the American Ambassador rang up—wanted him badly ; some sort of hands-across-the-sea tommy-rot they've got on. Fisher rang up the club. He wasn't there. Rang up every other place they could think of. Couldn't get in touch with him. Came home in the small hours. The old girl waited up for him with the rolling-pin—metaphorical rolling-pin, of course, but just as nasty as the real thing. Scene." Charley grinned again, and made a gesture of which the meaning was not to be mistaken. " At his age, too—the gay old dog ! " he said. " He covers up his tracks jolly well, though. No one even knows who the lady is, except that she must be a real tip-topper. I say, you'll keep all this to yourself, won't you ?

I should get it in the neck if they knew how I had been gassing."

Privately Bobby thought that very probable. Aloud he said:

" The first thing you learn in the police is absolute discretion—subject to duty, of course."

" That's all right, then," said the ingenuous and communicative Charles, and vanished as abruptly as he had appeared.

CHAPTER XII

EXHIBITION OF TACT

Bobby was still wondering whether Charley babbled like this to all comers all the time, or whether his communicativeness was a result of a kind of " hangover " from last night's escapade, of which, however, his clear eyes and healthy skin showed no effects, when the door opened again and there entered the duke himself.

He was a small man, small boned, thin and stooping, with small, distrustful eyes, a generally worried expression, and curious claw-like hands that seemed somehow prominent in his personality, as though expressive of a continuous subconscious desire to grasp and hold. At a first glance he might well have been taken for an uneasy clerk or shopman precariously hanging on to an uncertain post held only at the whim of an employer. But as soon as he spoke or moved he showed in every tone or gesture that unconscious authority, poise, self-assurance, that comes from a universal deference paid since earliest childhood to a great position held by right of birth—and " no damned merit about it," as was once said of the Garter.

For birthright's a fact, but merit only an opinion, an idea, one of the mere imponderables.

In those oddly prominent hands of his the duke held Bobby's card, and even that he held as though he would never let it go again. But it was not that on which Bobby's eyes fastened, nor was it that which gave him the sudden shock and thrill he now experienced as he recognised in the half-smoked cigar the duke also held the exact replica of that found by the side of a murdered man. A mere coincidence, of course, but Bobby had grown to have a passionate hatred for coincidence, and in his thin and precise tones the duke said:

" Sergeant Owen, I see? I think you have been here before. You have been able to get some information at last about that insolent intrusion I mentioned ? "

" Well, sir, it's really another matter I've come about," Bobby answered hesitatingly.

How clearly he remembered the emphasis with which Ulyett had enjoined upon him the necessity for tact, and how exactly the duke looked a man with whom tact— oceans of tact, all the tact that ever was or could be—would be required; and how jolly to be a superintendent, and push off dirty jobs like this upon unfortunate subordinates. Quite clearly Bobby realised that it was because Ulyett had shirked the job himself that it had been passed on to him. The duke, for instance, evidently didn't feel it necessary to " report " or " complain " or " request " or anything like that; he merely " mentioned " a thing, and that, he felt, was enough for all relevant machinery to be set zealously in motion. And that was the man—Personage, rather—he had been landed with the job of putting through a kind of third degree—a ducal third degree that would emphatically need tact.

" It is rather a complicated affair, sir," he said desperately. " It will need a lot of explaining."

" Indeed," said the duke, loftily surprised. " Was it necessary to see me in person ? I should have thought my secretary . . . my lawyers . . . however, as you are here . . ."

He indicated a chair, and set the example by seating himself, choosing an arm-chair for himself but not for Bobby, who now continued slowly:

" It is a serious matter I have to trouble you about, sir,

—a case of murder. We are fortunate in knowing that we can rely upon a gentleman of your position for every possible help."

Tactful Bobby thought this speech, but the duke did not seem to notice.

" Murder," he said, a little as he might have said " Kamchatka " or " Timbuctoo " as something vaguely familiar but unutterably remote. " I am at a loss to conceive . . ." he said stiffly, for, indeed, he was a man from whom tact poured as ineffectively as water from a duck's back. " Utterly at a loss . . ." he repeated.

" Yes, sir, naturally," agreed Bobby. " Your grace knows a firm of jewellers in Mayfair Square—Messrs. Jessop & Jacks ? "

" Extremely worthy—er—tradespeople," conceded the duke, to whom the head of an old-established firm of West End jewellers and a grocer's assistant selling quarter pounds of sugar and cheese in Islington were much of a muchness.

" They have been trying to sell a valuable diamond neck-lace," Bobby went on. " It belongs to a film actress—Miss Fay Fellows. She wants to get rid of it, and she asked Jessop & Jacks to see what they could do. I believe you inspected it yourself, sir, on one occasion, with a view to purchase ? "

" They asked an absurd price," declared the duke, with a touch of irritation in his dry and precise tones, and Bobby, who could not keep his eyes from that half-smoked cigar, saw, too, how the long and claw-like fingers twitched and half closed, as though involuntarily eager, instinctively disposed, to snatch and seize even a mere memory. " I did not consider it for one moment," the duke asserted.

" Last night," Bobby continued, " Mr. Jessop was found shot in a house at Brush Hill. He died almost immediately."

" Jessop ? " repeated the duke. " You mean—Jessop ? "

He seemed really astonished. " Shocking ! Most shocking ! A most respectable man, I always thought. Brush Hill, did you say ? A suburb, no doubt ? How did it happen ? You have arrested the murderer ? "

" No, sir," answered Bobby. " There is nothing yet we can act on. It is because it is thought your grace might be able to give us information . . ."

" I am unable to conceive . ." said the duke coldly. " Is there any possible connection ? "

Bobby had decided by now that tact was about as useful as, to quote Sydney Smith's famous simile, stroking the dome of St. Paul's was likely to please the dean and chapter. He continued :

" By Mr. Jessop's body was a half-smoked cigar, presumably left behind by the murderer. It is believed to be one of those made specially for him, in his own factory, of Mr. Patterson, an American gentleman and a friend of yours, recently staying with you, sir. The cigar seemed to show his monogram."

And, as he said this, Bobby could not for the life of him prevent his eyes from resting on the half-smoked cigar in the duke's hand. Then he looked away again quickly, and that was even worse—not a bit tactful, and just as well he had decided to give up tact. He went on hurriedly, ignoring the startled anger gathering on the ducal brow :

" It was thought your grace might be able to give us the names of any persons likely to be in possession of any of Mr. Patterson's cigars."

The duke paused. It was fully a minute before he replied. Then he said coldly and precisely :

" The inquiry seems to savour of insolence."

" I regret more than I can say," answered Bobby, " that your grace should think so. I am, of course, acting on the instructions of my superior officers. It was felt that a gentleman of your position would be willing in such a case to give every possible assistance, in spite of any inconvenience or annoyance caused."

" I am quite unable to understand," replied the un-placated duke, " why you should come to—Me."

" We understood that Mr. Patterson had close business relations with your grace," Bobby answered. " Our information is that he returned to America last week."

" As a matter of fact," remarked the duke, " he seems to have left the boat at Cherbourg. I understand he was in Paris last week."

" Oh, indeed," Bobby exclaimed, startled, for this, he thought, might mean a good deal.

But then he dismissed the idea as absurd. At any rate, it would be for his superiors to follow up, if they thought fit. So far as was known, Mr. Patterson was a man of high standing in business circles, even if it might be as well to look up his record and make sure that he had stayed in Paris during the week-end. Though sometimes, Bobby reflected again, it does happen that agents are employed who go far beyond their instructions, and it might be too well known in certain circles that Mr. Patterson offered for the necklace a ready market in which few questions would be asked.

So Bobby decided that it would be worth suggesting that some attention should be paid to Mr. Patterson; and, while he was silent, as these thoughts raced through his mind, the duke also was silent, absorbed in his own train of thought.

" I very much doubt," he said at last, " whether the steamship company would refund his fare." Then he seemed to remember Bobby: " I take it, then," he said, " you have nothing more you—er—wish to question me about ? "

How full were those last few words of a dignified and condescending rebuke ! Bobby felt that on hearing them he ought to bow and retire—backward. Instead he said:

"Well, sir, what we specially wanted to know was about Mr. Patterson's cigars. I mean, those he manufactures himself with his monogram on them. We thought you might be able to tell us if he left any of them behind, or if he was in the habit of distributing them freely, and, if so, to whom?"

"To everyone he met, I think," the duke answered. "He insisted on leaving me several boxes. Mr. Patterson is a very keen, experienced business man. He was by no means unaware of the advantage to his cigar factory if it became generally known that its products were smoked by—Me."

"I can quite understand that," murmured Bobby, thinking to himself that his grace of Westhaven was probably also not altogether unaware of the advantage of getting free smokes.

"Mr. Patterson," continued the duke, "offered his cigars freely to all his friends—at the club, everywhere he went. He even consulted me as to the possibility of introducing them into—er—the highest circles, the Very Highest. In that respect I could not assist him, and I believe those particular plans came to nothing. At one or two business conferences held here to discuss matters we were both interested in, he insisted on putting an open box on the table."

He paused, and Bobby realised that all this meant Mr. Patterson had been conducting a very clever advertising campaign by way of what amounted to a liberal distribution of free samples. But that meant the cigars might have found their way almost anywhere, and the significance of the clue seemed to fade into the air.

"I have even seen," continued the duke, dry disapproval in every tone, "Mr. Patterson give a couple to Fisher, my butler. Americans have very often very little sense of what is Due to Themselves. It is no doubt the result of the lack of a true Native Aristocracy."

"Yes, sir," said Bobby. "Very regrettable; very unfortunate," he could not help adding, and was rewarded by what was almost like a passing gleam of approval in the duke's small and troubled eyes. "It means there's a wide circle of casual friends and acquaintances who might have been in possession of these cigars ? "

"Exactly," agreed the duke, and, apparently regretting having given way to so weak a sentiment as a passing moment of approval, he added: "It was, I think, totally unnecessary to insist upon a personal interview to learn that. The information could have been obtained otherwise."

"Yes, sir," agreed Bobby. "More satisfactory, if I may say so, to get information at first hand, and from sources we know can be trusted. When Mr. Jessop was found, immediately after he had been shot, he was still conscious. Just before death occurred, he tried to speak. He could not finish his sentence—he died first—but two words he uttered were ' the duke.' They were distinctly heard."

"Jessop—Jessop said—said that ? " demanded the duke, evidently feeling that so insufferable a liberty was almost beyond the limits of the possible. "There is some mistake," he said. "I do not believe that Jessop—a most respectable man—would ever   . some mistake . . . some misunderstanding on your part . . ." He waved it aside.

"Yes, sir," agreed Bobby, " only there it is. What he said was quite plain. He died almost in the act of speaking. It was impossible to ask what he meant. It was thought there was just a chance your grace might be able to suggest an explanation ? "

"Certainly not," said the duke firmly. "I am not responsible for what you inform me this unfortunate man said when I gather he was not in a condition to know what he was saying—at least, I hope not."

He got to his feet to indicate that the interview was over. Bobby knew it would be tactful to follow his example, rise, apologise, depart. Instead, he remained firmly seated, a proceeding which not only made the duke still more indignant, but entirely baffled him as well, for in a life that centred in convention, that was by it bounded, ruled —was, indeed, convention, as it were, incarnate—he had little idea what to do when convention failed. Bobby went on:

" I am so sorry, sir, but every will-o'-the-wisp has to be followed up in a case like this. We may know it is only a will-o'-the-wisp, but we must follow till we find we are actually in the bog. Our job, sir. And murder is always murder. This murder took place just about half past eight last night."

" Well ? Well, what about it ? " demanded the duke irritably.

" Your grace," said Bobby, with scarce so much as a passing thought to that tact so strongly recommended to him, so utterly abandoned, " was no doubt at dinner at that hour ? "

The duke looked quite bewildered.

" Are you presuming," he asked incredulously, " to inquire into My movements ? "

" Certainly not; we should never dream of such a thing," Bobby assured him. " It is merely that our inquiries would be quite a lot helped if your grace could let us know—in complete confidence, of course . . ."

" I shall do nothing of the sort," thundered the duke— or would have thundered had not his thin voice broken in the middle of the sentence into something more like a squeak. He crossed to the fireplace and pressed the bell. " I am dining with the Prime Minister next week," he said, menace in every syllable.

Bobby had a fleeting moment of sympathy for all Prime

Ministers. Not even at dinner—still, every job has its draw-backs. He said aloud:

" I wish it had been last night." The duke glared. Bobby added: " May I ask, too, if Mr. Jessop's taking the necklace to show the duchess again at Hastley Court didn't mean her grace was still thinking of buying ? "

The door opened and Fisher appeared. The duke was looking both startled and puzzled. Bobby rose to his feet now, but he was not beaten yet.

" Your grace will agree," he said, taking care to speak loudly and clearly, so that the eagerly listening Fisher could hear every word, " that this wish to see the necklace again——"

" That will do, Fisher," interrupted the duke. " I will ring later."

Reluctantly Fisher withdrew, not only dignity making his movements slow. Bobby thought to himself: " Well, perhaps that wasn't tact, but it touched the spot all right." The duke said, when the slowly moving door had finally closed:

" Kindly explain what you mean. She saw it here on one occasion certainly. I remember her mentioning it. A young woman formerly in our employ brought it for her to see. But that is all."

" Our information," said Bobby, " quite unconfirmed, of course, but from a source we have often found trust-worthy, is that Mr. Jessop was asked to take it again to Hastley Court for the duchess to see."

" Nothing of the sort ! Preposterous ! " snapped the duke. " Who told you such nonsense ? "

" We haven't had time yet to find out exactly where it originated—possibly from talk at the Cut and Come Again," answered Bobby, not choosing to mention Charley Dickson's name as yet, or to explain that it was from Denis Chenery he had heard the story. " There is the additional complication, extremely troubling, that Mr. Jessop—or possibly someone in his name—rang up the Yard earlier yesterday and complained that the necklace had been stolen. We don't know, but we think that message came from the Cut and Come Again club."

" Never heard of it," said the duke, as it were abolishing it from existence.

" No, sir, probably not," said Bobby. " Quite well known in some circles. Large membership; good class as a rule, but mixed. A lot of gossip goes on there; they say the night's talk at the Cut and Come Again makes next morning's gossip columns. Some of the gossip is curiously accurate," added Bobby carelessly.

" I believe now I have heard of the place," admitted the duke. " I think I have heard young Dickson—the duchess's secretary—I think I have heard him mention it." He pressed the bell again, and when once more Fisher appeared with a promptitude that suggested he had not been far away, the duke said shortly:

" Find out if Mr. Dickson is here. If he is, tell him I want him. If he is not, find him. If her grace is disengaged, ask her if she can spare me a few minutes."

Fisher retired. The duke turned to Bobby.

" Jessop said the necklace had been stolen ? " he asked. " More likely he sold it and pocketed the money. The fellow was a reckless gambler; ridiculous stakes, in fact. You can never trust a gambler."

HJ

CHAPTER XIII

FILM INTERLUDE

Bobby, a little startled by this remark, that agreed so well with what Mr. Jacks had said, was yet quick to see and seize his opportunity.

" That's exceedingly interesting," he said. " You see, sir, that is just exactly the kind of information that's such a help, and that we hoped your grace might be able to give if we were permitted to ask a few questions."

Bobby was inclined to reach over and pat himself on the back for the tact with which he felt this speech positively purred. But the duke did not seem much affected. He turned his back while Bobby was still speaking and walked across the room to the door.

" Oh, yes, quite so," he said over his shoulder, and then, opening the door: " Fisher ! " he called. " Fisher ! Where is the fellow ? Really, even in one's own house it seems impossible to get proper attention. Oh, there you are, my dear," he added, as the duchess came out of one of the adjoining rooms. " I thought perhaps Fisher hadn't been able to find you. Sorry to trouble you, but someone is here from the police about a very shocking affair. Jessop—you remember him ? Jessop, keeps a jeweller's shop in Mayfair Square; very civil, respectable man. I understand he has been—er—murdered."

" Murdered—Mr. Jessop ? " repeated the duchess. " How dreadful ! Murdered ? Why, I was past the shop only the other day. Was it a burglar ? "

" For some reason," continued the duke, ignoring this question, " the police seem to have got it into their heads that we can tell them something about a necklace Jessop was trying to sell—the one I think I remember your mentioning to me. Belongs, apparently, to one of those film-star actress people one hears so much about, one even meets occasionally. Very valuable thing, I understand. Jessop was asking an absurd price. Was it a burglar ? "

He turned again to Bobby as he spoke. While he had been speaking to the duchess he had carefully kept his back to Bobby, talking to his wife where she was standing in the hall instead of making way for her to come into the room, as would have been more natural. Bobby found himself wondering if this attitude had been deliberate. Then, too, surely it would have been more in accordance with the ducal habits if he had rung for the butler instead of opening the door and calling for him ? And into the duke's generally dry and precise, even expressionless, tones, there seemed now to Bobby to have crept a note of hesitancy and unease. Was it possible, Bobby asked himself, that this apparently deliberate turning of the back, this avoidance of his visitor's gaze, this new note in his voice, were in any way connected with the statement the duke had let slip about Jessop's gambling habits and Bobby's instant response that the information was important ?

But, then, why should it disturb the duke that he should have let slip—Bobby was convinced he had let it slip— this piece of information ?

The idea seemed to Bobby so improbable he was inclined to put it out of his mind, to attribute that turning of the back to mere accident, that new note in the dry, precise voice to his own too vivid imagination. While these thoughts raced through his mind, he found himself answering :

" We hardly know enough as yet, sir, to say anything definite."

" But is it really true ? " the duchess said to him—she had come into the room now as the duke turned from the door. " Poor man—so very dreadful."

" I am afraid it is quite true," Bobby answered. " You will understand, madam, it is necessary to make certain inquiries."

" But why here ? Why should we know anything about it ? " asked the duchess in rather a bewildered voice. " Naturally, if we can help you . . ."

" Any scrap of information may be useful," Bobby repeated once more. " The most apparently irrelevant detail sometimes turns out to mean a lot. His grace has just told me one thing that may be very important."

" Oh—but, no, really," protested the duke hurriedly. " You must not suppose . . . I dare say I'm quite wrong . . . I only intended . . ." He paused, and then continued in a more natural manner: " Gambling is a vice I detest. The moment I know a man bets I know a man it is never safe to trust."

" We often find the same thing," agreed Bobby. " Half the petty thieving that we get reported comes from office-boys stealing the stamp money to go to the dogs with. I am sure my superiors will feel it very important to follow up your grace's information." His grace perceptibly winced, and Bobby was more sure than ever that for some obscure and difficult reason he was uneasy at the thought of possible consequences of what he had said. " Perhaps," Bobby went on, " you wouldn't mind telling us what makes you think Mr. Jessop was a gambler ? If that can be established, it may throw a new light on the whole thing."

" Not at all," snapped the duke. " I only meant I had seen Jessop occasionally on the racecourse and he seemed to be betting freely."

" If your grace could give me the dates and places . . ." Bobby suggested.

" I can do nothing of the sort," retorted the duke angrily. " I don't remember. Why should I ? I was only giving a general private impression—very likely quite wrong. I know nothing about it really. This kind of cross-examination is becoming intolerable."

He glared, he fumed, he bristled, he was evidently extremely angry—and Bobby wondered if this anger was not of that kind which springs from a hidden fear. Wanly he remembered that tact had been enjoined upon him—tact; and here was the duke nearly suffocating with rage. He began to feel the sergeant's stripes he did not wear growing very insecure upon his arm. For the old saying current in the eighteenth century, " Anger of a lord is sentence of death," is even yet not entirely obsolete. He murmured:

" I will report, then, that your grace feels unable to give any further information."

" Do so," said the duke, a little as if monosyllables were all that at the moment he could trust himself to utter. Then, recovering himself, he said more quietly: " I see no reason why it should be mentioned at all."

Bobby was aware of a possibly erroneous impression that something like bribery was hanging in the air. But it was no part of his duty to allow any such unlawful act to develop; an officer of police must be careful, whatever the temptation, never to act as *agent provocateur*. All the same, his impression was strengthened that the duke was really uneasy, really regretted and was alarmed by what he had said. In that case it was probably true, reflected Bobby. But Bobby felt also that he had pressed the point as far as was possible at the moment. Any attempt to continue would only result, he felt, in his being promptly and peremptorily ordered out of the house—a doom he felt was on the very razor-edge of pronouncement.

" I will be careful to say," he murmured deprecatingly, " that your grace is sure it's of no importance."

Fortunately, at this moment the arrival of Charley Dickson made a diversion. And very uneasily and reproachfully the young man looked at Bobby, with the evident intention of reminding him of his promise to say nothing about that Saturday evening " binge," as he had called it. Bobby gave a small, reassuring nod, and the duke, perhaps, like Bobby, glad of the diversion caused by Charley's appearance, said to him quickly:

" Oh, Dickson, I'm told you're a member of some club—the Come and Go Away Again, is it ? "

" Cut and Come Again, sir," interposed Bobby.

" The actual name," said the duke coldly, " is immaterial. I am told, Dickson, that a great deal of gossip goes on there ? "

" Oh, no, sir; none, at least, as far as I know. I never heard any," protested Charley, looking quite shocked. " Of course, I'm not there often. Of course, in any club—well, there's talk. I expect even in the Athenæum——"

" We are not speaking of the Athenæum," remarked still more coldly the duke, with whom it was a sore point that so far that famous club had omitted to elect him.

" I'm perfectly certain," interposed the duchess abruptly, " they talk there just as much as anywhere. I know 'em—bishops and professors; authors, too," she added by way of climax. " They've all got tongues," she said, " and they all like spice."

" Possibly," said the duke, " but the—Cut and Come Away, is it ?—is not, I imagine, a club of the same kind as the Athenæum ? "

He paused for confirmation, which Bobby supplied with a murmured:

" Entirely different."

" Men aren't," pointed out the duchess.

" It seems," continued the duke, " there has been

gossip there about this necklace Jessop's firm was trying to sell—at a most exorbitant price, in my opinion."

" I'm sure I never heard any, sir," Charley protested. " But, then I'm so seldom there," he repeated, looking extremely virtuous—not to say smug.

" They showed it me once when I happened to be at the Mayfair Square shop," the duke continued. " No doubt very valuable thing, but the figure mentioned was quite out of reason. One is used to being asked exorbitant prices," he added with a patient sigh, " but this was really too much. I lost all interest. I think you have seen it, haven't you ? " he added to his wife.

" Miss Fellows wore it at the Film Star Ball a year or two ago," the duchess answered. " I remember noticing it. A wonderful thing," she said, and could not quite prevent such a soft, passionate longing in her voice as others use when they speak of their heart's desire. " She wore it in some of her pictures, too. People often said they went to see it as much as anything."

" There was some idea that you might be induced to purchase it, I think ? " Bobby said to her.

" Certainly not," answered the duchess. " I'm not a film star. I can't afford things like that."

" I understood the firm had it sent specially for your inspection ? " Bobby persisted.

" Oh, that," said the duchess. " Oh, that was just for me to see it. I thought you meant had I asked for it to be sent on approval. It must be six or eight weeks ago Miss May brought it to show me. A lovely thing," she said, and again the note of longing in her voice was very marked.

" I think your grace," Bobby went on, " gave a garden-party at Hastley Court about a month ago ? "

The duchess stared.

" Yes. Why ? " she asked.

" A statement has reached us," said Bobby, " that on

that day Mr. Jessop was present and again produced the necklace to you for your further inspection ? ''

" Good gracious ! " said the duchess. " But that's silly. Who on earth told you that ? Why, my good man, that day I hadn't a moment to myself, much less to spare for looking at necklaces."

" I shall require," said the duke portentously, " to know from what source you receive these utterly preposterous statements. And I consider that this has gone quite far enough. I see no reason to put up with any more of this official—badgering." And Bobby was quite sure a stronger word had been intended. " I shall communicate with your superiors, young man. I shall inform them that I resent it. Resent it," he continued impressively. " Dickson, see that Fisher shows this person out."

Therewith he and the duchess retired with a dignity that was slightly impaired by a certain suggestion of haste in the ducal movements, and Charley bestowed upon Bobby a sympathetic smile.

" Old boy gone in off the deep end," he said. " Good and mad he is. Luckily he don't do much about it as a rule; he feels that his having been annoyed is punishment enough in itself to any bloke who upsets him. What in blazes made you talk about the Cut and Come Again ? You promised not to." And a very reproachful note crept into Charley's voice.

" I only promised not to say anything about you if I could help it," Bobby answered, " and I didn't. But in a case of murder—well, everything's got to give way, even dukes and duchesses. If you get a chance, you might point that out."

" Not me," said Charley frankly. " Don't want to lose my job before I've got to. If the American stunt pans out O.K., I might perhaps—I've got a kind of a half-chance of a job with a film agency out in Hollywood," he explained.

" If I get that, I'll tell the old boy anything you like—and then some. But not before."

It was spoken jestingly and with a laugh, but with a gleam in those soft-looking girlish eyes, with their long lashes and their drooping lids, that made Bobby think this youngster was capable of more than showed on the surface. And with those looks of his—a little on the pretty-pretty side, perhaps, but striking all the same—surely he ought to have a good chance on the films.

" Ever done any film work ? " Bobby asked, on the general principle that the more you knew the more likely you were to know something useful.

Charley looked at him a little queerly.

" Ever hear of *Heavenly Gates* ? " he asked.

" The film ? " Bobby asked. " Rather. Saw it, too. Jolly good. Why ? "

" It was mine," Charley answered.

" Eh ? " said Bobby, very surprised. " You mean you had something to do with it ? I thought it brought in pots of money for everyone concerned ? "

" So it did, except me," Charley answered, a hardness and bitterness in his tone that Bobby felt could be understood. " I didn't write the story, but I found it—bought all rights from the silly ass of an author for £100 down. He jumped for joy to get it, too ; money out of the blue for him. But pretty near all the rest was mine—they shot it just the way I had it worked out."

" But——" began Bobby, and paused.

" Froze me out," Charley explained. " Another gamble gone west. I put every penny I had in it." His soft, almost pretty-pretty look had gone now ; his eyes were fierce and hard, his mouth set in a straight, thin line. " Frozen out," he repeated. " Lesson to me."

The door opened and Fisher appeared as Charley said this.

" His grace seems anxious——" Fisher began.

" For you to throw me out ? " Bobby completed the sentence. " Right-oh. I'll go quietly, though I don't say some of us won't be back before long—not me, though, if I can help it." He nodded to Charley, who, lost in his own dark thoughts, took no notice, and, following Fisher into the hall, he added: " Don't bother about the lift. I'll walk down."

" There's a lot of stairs," Fisher warned him in a surprised tone.

" I expect there are," agreed Bobby. " Nothing like exercise. I might have another look at that outside door, too, just to make sure it can't be opened from without, even with the key."

" It's that sort of patent automatic bolt does that," Fisher explained. He led the way down a passage through the portion of the flat given over to the domestic staff. Safely out of sight and hearing, he allowed his dignity to drop, became more human, and remarked:

" Bit of bad luck for Mr. Dickson about his film."

" I hadn't heard about that; treated him badly, apparently," Bobby remarked.

" Lost his head, that's what it was," Fisher explained. " I heard all about it from a young lady who goes on as an extra sometimes. Had a drop of drink too much, most likely."

" He doesn't look as if he drank," Bobby observed, wondering if this was an oblique reference to the young man's recent lamp-post-climbing exploit.

" He doesn't," answered Fisher. " He knows it don't do for him. But if he gets in a jam, then he has a bit extra to brace him up, and then it goes to his head, not his legs, so he hardly knows what he is doing. Acts anyhow, so to say. If he had just hung on and signed nothing, they couldn't have done a thing. As it was, they had him out in quick sticks."

" Couldn't he have brought an action or something ? " Bobby asked.

" Well," answered Fisher cautiously, " I don't think he dared—been sailing just a bit too near the wind. Handling some of the cash careless like. Nothing wrong, of course, only accountants wouldn't have wanted to pass it. Not that I know anything about it," he added hastily, as if afraid he had said too much; and, evidently wishing to change the subject, he went on: " Our old man in a bit of a paddy, wasn't he ? "

" I had to ask a lot of questions, and he got bored and worried," explained Bobby lightly. " I thought I did enough ' your gracing ' to make the wheels go round, too."

" Used to it," observed Fisher; " not used to being asked questions."

" I suppose that was it," agreed Bobby. " He seems frightfully down on gambling."

" Fad of his," Fisher said. " Much as your place is worth if he knows you've even put half a crown on the dogs. So, of course, none of us do."

" Of course not," agreed Bobby, and winked.

He had often found that a sympathetic wink was curiously effective in promoting confidences, more so even than the standing of a drink, behind which act of generosity all know that more may lurk. But a wink's a friendly, suspicion-disarming, confidence-creating thing, and now Fisher winked back, and forthwith good relations were in being.

" I suppose it's genuine with him," Bobby asked. " He doesn't go in for it himself on the sly, does he ? "

" Not him," declared Fisher with emphasis. " He's that mean the thought of losing half a quid would turn his hair white."

" Doesn't he go a good deal to the races, though ? "

" Only when it's Ascot and such-like and his old woman says it's a social duty," Fisher explained, " and then I expect he's asleep half the time. Talks about it in public, too, spouts about the Evil of Gambling, the Canker of Betting, and all that rot."

" Probably he thinks it's due to his position," Bobby suggested. " After all, a duke's a duke, and his example counts. The American Ambassador rang him up last night, didn't he ? Somewhere about eight or nine, wasn't it ? "

" Nearer nine, I think. Couldn't get in touch with him, though ; the Ambassador had to wait. Can't think where he had got to. Late in, too."

" Good thing the duchess isn't jealous," observed Bobby, laughing.

Fisher laughed, too, genuinely amused.

" Jealous of that dried-up old stick ? " he asked. " Why, I don't believe he could tell a pretty girl from a cold in the head." Unconsciously Fisher straightened himself, smiled, put up a hand to smooth hair of which not one was out of place, very evidently feeling that as much could not be said of him. " Oh, he's not that sort," he said. " Mean as you like, and keen on money as a dog on a juicy bone, and you've got to jump, all of you—the missus, too—when he speaks. But, taking him all round," said Fisher tolerantly, " there's worse."

" The missus ? Oh, the duchess, you mean ? "

" That's right. Proper scared of him, she is, but gets her own way in the end; that's her. He rules her with a rod of iron, as the saying is, but she takes care it's the way she wants to be ruled. Manages him O.K., if you know what I mean. But perhaps you're a married man yourself, and then you will."

" Not me," said Bobby. " No time in our job to think of it."

" You wait," said Fisher darkly ; " you wait."

CHAPTER XIV

DUPLICATE KEYS

At the bottom of the stairs on the first landing he reached, Bobby sat down, though less to rest than in order to think things over quietly, as, too, his preference for the stairs over the lift had been due less to a desire for exercise than to secure an opportunity for his chat with the butler that had turned out so suggestive.

It had confirmed, for instance, the fact that there was some mystery about the duke's movements on the Saturday night, and that his grace's refusal to say where he had been was not merely due to pique and offended dignity, but had some solid reason behind it. Natural, perhaps, that a somewhat lively youngster like Charley Dickson should jump to the conclusion that there was a woman in the explanation. But Fisher evidently thought that highly improbable, and he was an old family servant who might be presumed to know a good deal about his employers, as is the manner of old family servants. But, then, a private secretary, especially a private secretary to the wife, might know things hidden from even the oldest of family servants.

" One thing jolly certain," Bobby decided, thoughtfully lighting a cigarette, " is that his grace will have to be asked some more questions, and they'll have, thank goodness, to turn one of the big pots on the job—the A.C. himself, perhaps," mused Bobby, smiling happily at the thought of the dignified and important Assistant Commissioner interviewing the duke so conscious of his own dignity and importance—a little like the meeting of the irresistible force and the immovable object, Bobby told himself.

Of course, the duke's wish to preserve secrecy about his movements that evening could not possibly have any connection with the necklace or the murder. Still, an investigation is an investigation, and there you are, and no getting away from it.

Another point was, how did the duke know Jessop was a gambler used to risking large sums? And why had he chosen to offer an explanation almost certainly false?

Once more, why had he dwelt so persistently on the exorbitance of the price asked for the necklace, as though that were in some way a personal grievance?

Odd, too, that while it was admitted the duke had been to Mayfair Square to inspect the necklace, and had actually made an offer for it, and that the duchess had had it sent to the Park Lane flat for her inspection there, yet the Hastley Court visit was firmly denied. Yet there seemed no doubt it had been made.

One thing became very clear to Bobby. He would have to draw up his report with extreme care, bringing out all these points and yet avoiding any direct accusation against people of such influence and importance, and of such high social standing. He had no wish to ruin his chance of promotion by getting known to his superiors as the lad who couldn't tell a duke from a crook.

" Tact," he reflected mournfully, " tact, my boy, that's what you want "; and he found himself wondering whether already the telephone was not conveying a stream of acid complaints to Prime Ministers and others of the Great and the Powerful.

" All the same," Bobby concluded finally, as he continued the long, long trail down the stairs to the street, " there's something about the Westhavens, wife and hubby, too, that's got to be dug out, and, if possible, before they start pulling strings to get it hushed up—even though it's inconceivable dukes and duchesses should go in for theft and murder."

But, though he told himself this, none the less he remembered how oddly the duke had dwelt upon the exorbitance of the price demanded, how in the duchess's voice as she had spoken of the necklace had been a soft yearning as of a lover for his mistress, as of an exile for his home.

His thoughts turned again to the minor point of how it was the duke knew that Jessop gambled for large sums. Fisher—that had been a useful little chat—denied that his master went often to the races, and in any case it was not likely the duke would have there noticed, or paid the least attention to, Mr. Jessop's activities, or, indeed, had any opportunity to do so, since there was no reason why duke and jeweller should have seen each other, even though both had been on the same racecourse the same day. That explanation was certainly an afterthought, and, though there seemed no obvious connection with the murder, all the same Bobby felt he would like it cleared up. It struck him that it was believed to be from the Cut and Come Again club that the dead man had rung up to make his agitated complaint about the lost necklace; and it was just possible, though highly improbable, that the duke knew more of the place than he pretended. Gambling went on there for high stakes, as Bobby—and others—knew well enough, and there was just the chance that there the duke had picked up his knowledge.

A forlorn hope, indeed, for the visits of so well known and prominent a personage as the Duke of Westhaven to such a club as the Cut and Come Again were not likely to have passed unnoticed. Still, Bobby decided that a call might be useful; and, anyhow, he would not be sorry for a little delay, and a chance to arrange his thoughts, before returning to the Yard and the difficult task of writing his report.

His way led him by Mayfair Square, and instinct or interest took him by that side of it where was situated the Jessop & Jacks establishment. A car was drawn up in front and the door was open. Bobby went up the steps and entered.

" Is anyone here ? " he called, and there came into the hall a short, broad-shouldered, powerfully built man with what is known as a cauliflower ear and a very scowling, angry appearance. His small eyes, close together under shaggy, overhanging brows, his heavy jowl, a broken tooth that showed prominently when he spoke, his long arms reaching nearly to his knees and terminating in enormous hands, gave him altogether a formidable appearance.

" What do you want ? " he asked Bobby roughly.

Bobby produced his official card.

" I was present when Mr. Jessop's body was found," he said. " I am working on the case. I saw the door open as I passed. Oh, there's Mr. Jacks," he added, as that gentleman emerged from the room on the right.

" Says he's police," said the prize-fighter-looking individual, glaring at Bobby. " Thought he was trying to see what he could pick up."

" The necklace isn't in the strong-room," Mr. Jacks said to Bobby. " Unless we get it back . . ."

" Done in," said the prize-fighter person with a comprehensive sweep of one far-reaching arm. " Offering £5,000 reward for its recovery, but what's the good ? Million to one the thing's in Amsterdam by now, with all the stones being re-cut and re-polished."

" Our manager," Mr. Jacks explained to the slightly bewildered Bobby.

" Money in the firm, too; don't forget that," the other growled. " Three thousand gone down the drain."

" An investment with the firm," Mr. Jacks explained further.

" Worse luck," commented the manager gloomily.

Bobby reflected that anyone less like the manager of a fashionable West End jeweller's business could hardly be imagined.

" You are Mr. Wright ? " he asked, remembering that had been previously mentioned as the name of the firm's manager.

" That's right—Obadiah Wright," answered that gentleman. " Used to call me Bad Wright when I was in the fighting game—joke," he added, still more gloomily. " Meant they thought my right wasn't as good as my left. Rot, of course; my left was my strong suit, but there was nothing wrong with my right. Suppose you never heard my name ? " he added wistfully.

" I'm afraid not," Bobby confessed.

" Ought to have been champ," said Mr. Wright, " only I got a raw deal. The fighting game's like that; you may be as good as the best, but if you get a raw deal you're finished."

" Too bad," agreed Bobby.

" Crooked work," declared Mr. Wright. " Crooked work in this thing too, somewhere. What about this Wynne fellow ? Mr. Jacks says you're looking for him. Where's he come in ? Who is he ? Not that I give a damn if you never find who shot Jessop so long as we get the necklace back."

" We shall get Wynne soon," Bobby answered confidently. " We have a full description; he has been through our hands before."

" If he did in Jessop, he may have the necklace still and it won't have gone abroad yet ? " suggested Wright.

" Possibly not," agreed Bobby. " Until now, we weren't even certain it was actually missing. The Customs have

IJ

been warned to look out for it, but that's routine. I think you were motoring over the week-end, Mr. Wright ? "

" That's right. Got a message at a pub where I stopped. Your people had sent out an S. O. S."

" That would be done at once," said Bobby, who knew it would again be routine to ascertain the number of Mr. Wright's car and then ring up as many heads of provincial police as possible to ask that their men—and the A.A. scouts—should be instructed to look out for it. He added, " You've been able to get your strong-room open without Mr. Jessop's keys ? Or did you find them ? There weren't any in his pockets, and none were found at his flat."

" If they don't turn up, we shall have to have all locks altered," Mr. Jacks said gloomily. " Luckily we had arranged for duplicate keys to be kept at the bank in case any got lost."

" Had to pull out the manager," observed Wright. " Luckily he was in ; has a flat over. Groused about it being Sunday, but we couldn't help that. Duplicate key to the case for the necklace was there, too. Jessop had the only other one."

As he spoke he showed a strongly made case, lined with a thin plate of metal as a precaution against the use of a knife to cut it open, wherein the necklace had been kept. Bobby examined it with interest.

" The necklace was generally kept locked in this ? " he asked.

" Yes, except when a possible customer wanted to see it."

" And Mr. Jessop had the only other key ? "

" That's right. It was he who got the commission from Miss Fellows in the first place. He had the selling end in hand, too."

" When did either of you two gentlemen see it last ? " Bobby asked.

There was some hesitation about answering this, but

finally it proved that neither of them had seen it for three weeks. It was not a thing for which even a probable customer was likely to turn up every day. It had been shown to an American gentleman three weeks previously, but after that apparently had not been disturbed by either Mr. Jacks or the manager. Jessop should certainly have mentioned the fact if he had taken it out to show anyone, but of course he might not have done so for perfectly good reasons—lack of time or opportunity, for instance. And Bobby was interested, when he asked the name of the American gentleman, to learn that it was Mr. Patterson, the Duke of Westhaven's friend from New York. They all seemed, Bobby thought, to have been fluttering round the necklace like moths round a candle, though it was not their wings that had been singed—not so far, at least.

" Have you let them know yet at the Yard ? "

" No; haven't had time. Will there be anyone there ? "

" Always is," said Bobby, " all day and all night, Sundays, holidays, and week-days. I think you ought to go on there at once."

" I suppose so," agreed Mr. Jacks.

" The Duke of Westhaven thought of buying the necklace at one time, didn't he ? " Bobby asked.

" No," snarled Wright, " he thought we might make him a present of it because we loved him so much. He missed his guess."

" But he did come here to have a look at it ? "

" That's right."

" Afterwards you sent it for the duchess to see. Miss May showed it her, I think. Was she alone ? "

" I went with her," answered Wright. " Don't take risks with £100,000. I waited in the entrance-hall while she was showing it."

" Was it Miss May who took it to Hastley Court ? "

" No. That was Jessop. The duchess rang up in a hurry.

We thought, from what she said, hubby might be weakening —we knew she was keen on it herself, as far as that went. We started off as soon as we could get the car out."

" We ? "

" I went, too. Hang it, the thing's worth money."

" Yes, got to be careful," agreed Bobby. " Armed ? "

" We keep a pistol on the premises," Wright answered. " I put it in my pocket any time like taking good stuff to show customers."

" Got a licence, I suppose ? "

" Of course."

" Do you know what make it is ? "

" Smith Webley—·22."

" Ah, yes," said Bobby, remembering that had been the make and calibre of the weapon found by the side of the murdered man. But that was a point for his superiors to follow up. " Did you see the duchess at Hastley Court ? "

" I didn't. I waited in the car. There was some sort of swell party on."

" Didn't it strike you as odd that the duchess should choose a time when she must have been busy with her guests ? "

" That was so we could slip through in the crowd—she didn't want the duke to know," explained Wright. " That's what she told Jessop. She was going to finance the thing herself, and not let on till it was all settled and too late for the duke to do anything but tear his hair. That was her look-out; for all we cared, hubby could tear his hair till he was bald. Once we had got the necklace into her hands and her I.O.U. in ours we were O.K. We knew his starchiness would never face a lawsuit or a scandal. That," said Mr. Wright comfortably, " is where you have the nobs on toast. You and me, we wouldn't give a cuss for being shown up in the Sunday rags, but dukes can't stand for it."

" There's that," agreed Bobby. " But I don't quite see how you managed."

" Why not ? Simple enough. She told us on the 'phone to wait in our car, where all the others were parked—there were dozens of 'em. So we did, and the secretary chap—Dickson he said his name was; secretary or something—came along and fetched Jessop. Jessop came back very bucked. Told me it looked like a deal all right."

" I knew nothing of all this," interposed Mr. Jacks.

" It was entered in the office diary," Wright growled.

" Only ' Fellows necklace shown D. of W. and returned to stock,' " Mr. Jacks said.

" Well, it was no good saying too much before we were sure," Wright answered.

" You brought the necklace back with you ? " Bobby asked.

" That's right. The deal hadn't gone through by a long way; we weren't building on it too much. Our idea was she would have to get round the duke and find the money too. Our terms included prompt payment of at least £5,000 cash, and the rest in instalments."

" What was the total figure to be paid ? "

" Hadn't been settled," answered Wright frankly. " We meant to soak it to her for as much as we dared, but we weren't sure of the limit—there was to be a conference with Mr. Jacks to settle the exact figure. I thought Jessop had said something to you about that," the manager added to Mr. Jacks.

" Not a word; not one word," complained Mr. Jacks.

" Jessop was waiting till he knew for certain, I suppose," observed Wright. " No good gassing till you're sure."

Mr. Jacks looked dissatisfied still, and Bobby could not make up his mind what to think of this story. He remembered how firmly and convincingly the duchess had denied having seen the necklace at Hastley Court—how genuine her dismissal of the story as " silly " had sounded. But, then, some people are wonderfully good liars, especially those who do not think of themselves as liars but merely as economising the truth for some necessary purpose. The duchess might, for example, consider herself justified in concealing from her husband negotiations entered into for the making of a purchase he had not yet approved of.

In any case, Bobby had, he felt, asked quite enough questions. He was risking getting a severe rap over the knuckles for conducting on his own account an examination that he ought to have left to his superiors. He decided, too, that for the present, until the whole business was a little clearer, it would be better to say nothing about the duchess's denial of the Hastley Court visit. That would be for his superiors to follow up, as would also what to Bobby was apparent enough—a lack of trust and harmony between the partners that might or might not have serious implications.

" Did Miss May accompany you to Hastley Court ? " he asked as a final question, and he saw the other two exchange a quick glance.

" No," answered Wright, and added: " Miss May has left us now."

" How's that ? " Bobby asked quickly. " You mean . . . ?"

" Jessop gave her notice a week ago," Wright answered. " It was up yesterday."

" Was there any special reason ? " Bobby asked.

" We don't want to get let in for a libel action," Wright remarked. " I suppose what's said to the police is confidential ? "

" Of course."

" Mr. Jessop got to know she was going about with a fellow we believe to have been behind one or two big thefts, like that one at the Ritz, where a fellow shinned off down the fire-escape with a pocketful of diamond rings sent there on appro—chap of the name of Denis Something, but no one knows anything else about him, except that he's said to be a swell of some sort, well connected. And when Jessop heard that, and found her one day monkeying with his keys—well, he thought she had better go."

Bobby turned to Mr. Jacks.

" You never said anything about that last night," he said.

" Mr. Jacks didn't know," interposed Wright. " Mr. Jessop told me in confidence, but he didn't want anyone else to know. She might have landed us for heavy damages if we hadn't been careful. She has swell friends. Besides, it was only suspicion, nothing in it, perhaps. All the same, Mr. Jessop thought, and so did I, that she had better have notice—only without any fuss, and good references and all that. Nothing actually against her."

" I ought to have been told," Mr. Jacks said darkly. " There's a lot of this I ought to have been told before and I never was."

CHAPTER XV

FORCIBLE ENTRY

Bobby, after he had seen Jacks and Wright depart in their car to Scotland Yard, walked on slowly to the Cut and Come Again club, revolving slowly in his mind as he went this latest piece of information.

Hilda May had known all about the necklace, and would undoubtedly have been a most useful accomplice in any plot to secure possession of it. And there was the coincidence of the name " Denis " that Wright had mentioned, and that was also the first name of young Chenery. Miss May would have to be questioned again, that was clear. He wondered if he ought to ask her to come with him to headquarters. He saw that he had reached the Cut and Come Again, and he decided to ask a few questions there before making up his mind what to do about Hilda.

The Cut and Come Again rented the first and second floors of the fine old house he was looking at. The ground floor and basement were occupied by a restaurant entirely unconnected with the club, though it is true that there seemed somehow a good deal of traffic through a door leading from the rear of the restaurant dining-room to the passage at the back, whence rose the back stairs constructed recently as an additional means of escape in case of fire. But, then, that door led also to the cloakrooms, where the restaurant customers could wash their hands or powder their noses or perform other necessary toilet operations. Nor did the restaurant waiters grumble so much as might have been expected if their customers mysteriously vanished for a time—even for a long time. A police raid on the club —there had been one or two, but none recently—was apt to find the restaurant crowded with guests innocently chatting over glasses of lemonade or barley-water or admiring the surrealist paintings with which the walls were adorned; for the restaurant had quite a name as a centre of surrealist art, and odd-looking people often wandered in just to admire the pictures on exhibition.

On the half-landing was a telephone call-box and a small cloakroom in charge of a former police constable, a Mr. Isaac Finch, who had at one time been much favoured by his superior officers as likely to bring the police boxing championship to their division, but who had afterwards proudly resigned rather than face the indignity of a threatened inquiry into certain entirely personal transactions.

The top floor was a flat in private occupation, though the tenant, Mr. John Smith, was seldom seen, nor did a knock at his door often secure an answer. Occasionally club members wandered up there just to try, but knocking was always vain, though, on the other hand, at times the door would swing open as of its own accord, so that there was no need to knock, and visitors could pass through unheralded and unannounced.

As Bobby approached this intriguing institution there emerged from the ever-open door that gave admission both to the restaurant—on the right—and to the stairway directly in front that led to the club premises, a little thin old woman with a small, shrivelled face, well known to Bobby himself, to the police in general, and in all the more disreputable haunts in town, as Magotty Meg. It was a sobriquet frequently misunderstood and invariably misspelt, for it was in no sense personal, but was due merely to her habit—she was partly of French extraction—of referring to her *magot*, by which she meant her little private store of savings that, with the prudence of her maternal ancestors, she was endeavouring to accumulate so as to be able some day to retire to that little rose-embowered country cottage, at the thought of which she would shed tears on those comparatively rare occasions when she was really drunk. Age had forced her to abandon a profession she had formerly—adorned is hardly the word perhaps—practised lavishly, freely, even generously indeed, and still there was little that went on in the underworld of London that she was not aware of, and wherefrom she did not manage somehow or another to glean for her own use a few ears of ill-gotten corn. In criminal circles she was universally respected, for her silence was that of the brooding pyramids, even though there was hardly a rogue in London against whom she could not have given damning evidence. But what she knew was as inaccessible to the police as the summit of Mount Everest to the aspiring climber. Her *magot*, too, remained comparatively small, since a certain innate generosity of soul prevented her from refusing any demand for assistance. She took, but she gave as well.

" If you're looking for T. T.," she greeted Bobby abruptly, " he isn't there, and if you find him anywhere, tell him I want him."

It was said regally, as by one who had a right to command, and Bobby wondered a little.

" Why ? " he asked, though he knew the question was useless.

" To talk about the weather," she retorted.

" Or diamonds ? " he asked.

" That's it; you've hit it." She beamed on him. " He promised me a diamond bracelet once, and I want to know when I'm to have it."

" I see," said Bobby drily. " Is Wynne at the club ? "

" Who's that ? " she asked, assuming now her expression of bland ignorance police interrogators knew so well.

" The Count de Teirney," Bobby answered.

" Ah," sighed Meg, " I knew a Count de Teirney forty years ago—a lovely man. I remember——"

" Sorry, Meg; haven't time now," interrupted Bobby, for Meg's reminiscences, though both diverting and entirely incredible, were apt to lead far from the subject supposed to be under discussion.

" Perhaps it's his son," mused Meg. " Or even mine," she added thoughtfully; for one of her most embarrassing habits was that of claiming the possible procreation of almost anyone of suitable age—she had even advanced the claim once to a scandalised, indignant, and blushing Assistant Commissioner of Police.

" You've heard about the Jessop murder ? " Bobby asked her.

" It's in the stop press," she said, and gave him a sudden and a different look from her small, beady old eyes. " I don't hold with murder," she said, and walked away, and Bobby told himself it might be as well to remember how she had said that—it might be that if she knew anything, as was entirely probable, since there was so little that she did not know or guess, she might be willing for once to drop her usual impenetrable guard of silence and assumed forgetfulness.

But that would be, Bobby knew well, in her own good time, if at all; and he walked on through the open door and up the stairs leading to the Cut and Come Again premises.

Mr. Finch, in charge of the cloakroom, knew Bobby well enough, and greeted him with a friendly grin.

" Hullo, hullo," he said. " Here's the white hope of the C.I.D. Hope you're off duty or what'll the Home Sec. say ? "

Bobby went white with rage. He had a naturally equable temper, and he had trained himself to keep it in the strictest control, but this reference to the loathsome legend that he was a special friend and favourite of the Home Secretary's was always too much for him. He said between his teeth:

"All right, all right. You wait, Finch, I'll remember that."

There was an energy of anger about him as he spoke that fairly scared Finch, who had meant no more than a little friendly chaff. After all, no night-club porter wishes unnecessarily to antagonise a " busy," even if only because a night raid offers too many opportunities for a clip on the jaw from some unidentifiable but substantial fist.

" No insult or offence intended, mate," he said earnestly, " and hope none such is took."

Bobby took his temper in hand. Even the most deadly insults a policeman must learn to ignore. He said abruptly:

" When was the Duke of Westhaven here last ? "

Finch was one of the readiest and most accomplished liars in the world—made perfect by long practice—but his look of surprise at this question was pretty plainly genuine. Then he rallied.

" Oh, he often looks in," he said. " One of our regulars. Every night almost. Only don't you let on I said so. He calls himself Mr. Smith here. ' Finch, my boy,' he said to me, friendly like, not more than half an hour ago, ' you let on this is my home from home and I'll have your blood. Meanwhile, here's a quid for you.' Jolly little cuss, the duke."

" That was half an hour ago, was it ? " asked Bobby, fully appreciating this reference to the stiff and pedantic duke as a " jolly little cuss," and the suggestion that he, who had the reputation of being the meanest man in town, gave pound notes away so freely.

" There or thereabouts," asserted Finch, and Bobby was convinced by these replies that Finch knew nothing of the duke, and that that maligned peer had never in his life been near the place.

" Heard about the murder of Mr. Jessop ? " Bobby asked. " It's in the stop press this morning."

Finch shook his head.

" Didn't notice it," he said. " Why ? The duke done it ? I thought I noticed a dark, suspicious stain on his left trouser-leg."

" Don't try to be funny," snapped Bobby. " Was Jessop a member ? "

" No," answered Finch. " Visitor sometimes. You'll find his name in the visitors' book."

" Miss Hilda May a member ? "

" Couldn't rightly say," answered Finch. " There's some I know when I see 'em, but not by name. Ask Mr. Dillon. He's secretary. He'll know. He keeps the member list."

" So he does," agreed Bobby, who knew well that list, comprehensive, and, in a very real sense, more than complete. " Mr. Jessop used the 'phone here on Saturday ? "

" Did he ? " countered Finch. " I couldn't say, I'm sure. Anyone can slip in and use the call-box without me knowing. I don't notice; no call to."

" Mr. Dillon in his room ? "

" I'll ask," Finch said, and, using the house 'phone, reported that Mr. Dillon was there and would be happy to see Sergeant Owen.

Bobby went on accordingly to a little room at the top of the stairs, observing with interest, as he passed, the grooves which showed where a light steel netting could be dropped at a second's notice to bar all ingress, so as to prevent, as the authorities had been carefully informed, any attempt by the roughs, who at times infest West End districts, to rush the club premises.

" Keep 'em out until we've time to get you fellows of the police round to protect us," Mr. Dillon had explained blandly. " Everyone knows big money changes hands here sometimes when members settle up the bets they've been making between themselves on any of the big races."

And that big money did change hands at the Cut and Come Again was indeed well known, though not racing was the reason, but baccarat, *chemin de fer*, roulette, poker, and other such devices.

Mr. Dillon, waiting for Bobby at his desk in the small bare room that was his office, was a little wizened elderly Irishman about whose past various picturesque and possibly untrue tales were told. He had a sad and solemn personality, and his almost superhuman ability to absorb whisky without limit or pause was often accounted for by the copious tears over the wrongs of Ireland he was accustomed to shed after beginning his second bottle. How, indeed, could man get drunk when from his eyes moisture poured out in proportion as he poured liquid in by the throat. Curiously enough, when sober—that is, nearly every morning before noon—he never showed a sign of having even heard of Ireland; towards the small hours he could recite in length and in detail every wrong Ireland has suffered since St. Jerome wrote a careless phrase calumniators of the country have interpreted as a suggestion that the saint believed cannibalism was practised there in his day.

He expressed himself as delighted to see Bobby. Any visit from his friends of the C.I.D. afforded him always intense pleasure, a pleasure heightened when his visitor was Sergeant Bobby Owen, who no doubt would now join him in a mouthful of the best. Bobby declined, and Dillon said he knew what slaves the C.I.D. men were to duty, and having absorbed Bobby's share, and his own, of " the best," set himself to work to evade, deny, or profess complete forgetfulness or ignorance of everything Bobby asked. He had to admit that Hilda, Denis Chenery, and Charley Dickson were all members, but protested that none of the three ever visited the club except on the rarest occasions. Of course, members often drifted in and out without his seeing them. Bobby could ask Ted, the barman, if he liked. Ted was pretty sure to see—and serve—any member who did look in. In any case, he, Mr. Dillon, was fairly sure none of the three mentioned had been in the club on the Saturday. Finch and Ted were likely to know if they had been. Wynne was a name entirely unfamiliar to Mr. Dillon. Bobby could look through the members' list and the visitors' book, too, if he liked. As for any gossip about the Fellows necklace having taken place in the club, all Mr. Dillon could say was that he had heard none, and had certainly never heard of the Fellows necklace or of Miss Fay Fellows herself, except vaguely as a film star whose name flared occasionally on placards outside cinemas. But of course Ted might have heard something; members chatted freely both to him and between themselves while indulging in a little refreshment. A reference to the Duke of Westhaven brought a look of such mingled longing and surprise to Mr. Dillon's usually inexpressive countenance that Bobby was again forced to the conclusion that wheresoever it might be that the duke had heard of Jessop's gambling propensities, it was not here.

Another question brought an admission that Mr. T. T. Mullins occasionally visited the club as a friend of one or other member. Apparently he knew several. But the visits were very few and at long intervals. Mr. Dillon did not think he had been there for months, possibly years.

Bobby asked for the members' list, and, looking through it—it was admirably kept, showing the most meticulous observance of all the very strict club rules about the admission of new members—noticed presently with interest the name of the Count de Teirney, his address being given as the Hôtel Magnifique. Bobby took a note of the names of his proposer and seconder, one of whom, Mr. Dillon regretted to say, had now resigned, while the other was at present travelling abroad. To Bobby's request for a description of the Count, Mr. Dillon replied that he didn't think he had ever seen him.

" He hardly ever comes," Mr. Dillon declared.

" Odd thing about your members," Bobby commented. " They all hardly ever come."

" You know, sergeant," protested Dillon mildly, " I resent that. I resent that very much. It's an aspersion on the club. Most of our members are very regular; they look upon it as a second home, but a home free from all the worries and troubles a householder has to put up with."

" Well, if the Count de Teirney turns up here, let us know," Bobby said. " He might be able to give us some information about a man named Wynne we are looking for. Wynne was there shortly before Jessop was shot, and we want to interview him."

" You may depend on us," Mr. Dillon assured him earnestly. " You know that."

" I know all about that," agreed Bobby. " Only, in a case of murder, perhaps you will really help. Murder's a thing I hope you do draw the line at."

But he said this without much hope, for he felt, murder or no murder, Dillon's one idea would be to keep everything connected with the Cut and Come Again as far from the police as possible. He asked a few more questions, and then wandered into the bar-room to have a chat with Ted, whom he found, as he expected, singularly communicative and singularly adroit in avoiding communicating anything of interest or importance. But about the prospects of next week's racing, dogs or horses, Ted was a gushing fountain of information, and in the midst of a highly technical description of the merits of a certain greyhound Bobby interposed :

" Oh, yes, that's the dog Charley Dickson talks about. Dickson hadn't had more than he could carry yesterday, had he ? "

" Mr. Dickson ? Oh, yes, I know him," Ted answered, evidently searching his memory. " Why, he hasn't been round for a month of Sundays."

" He wasn't here yesterday ? " Bobby asked.

Ted shook his head again.

" Don't know when I saw him last," Ted asserted. " Wasn't yesterday, anyhow—or last week, for that matter."

" Funny, then," observed Bobby, " that he was trying to climb a lamp-post just outside here, so as to get a light for his cigarette."

" Was he now ? " grinned Ted. " Must have had a skinful, then. But not here. It happens that way sometimes. Gents get thrown out of pubs, and then they think they'll come here and get served, being members. Don't work, of course, but they try it. Means trouble, though, if they do get here and past Finch. Grateful we are to your chaps if they pick them up on the way."

" Curious," observed Bobby, " that he was seen coming out."

" Out of here ? " asked Ted. " Not him. Out of the door, perhaps, if Finch sent him off. Or maybe out of the restaurant downstairs; may have gone in there for a drink. But I can't remember I ever set eyes on him all day, and that I'll swear to."

Bobby shot in another question about the Duke of Westhaven, and was rewarded by another look of blank surprise, confirming his conviction that wherever the duke had picked up his knowledge that Jessop betted, it was not here. Nor had Ted heard any talk in the club about the Fay Fellows necklace; there might have been, of course, but not that he had heard, or at any rate remembered. But, then, he had his work to attend to, and most of the chatter he heard at the bar went in at one ear and out at the other.

Bobby departed after that, and as he nodded a good-bye
KJ

to Finch he stopped and said suddenly, as if something had just occurred to him:

" I suppose Mr. Dickson was quite sober when he left here last night ? "

" Mr. Dickson ? " Finch repeated. " Member, isn't he ? I expect I should know him if I saw him, but I can't put a face to the name at the moment. But, anyway, if he was here, which he wasn't or I should remember him, he was perfectly sober when he went, because they all were—not a member last night but wasn't as sober as a judge."

" They would be," agreed Bobby.

He went away then, feeling that his visit had not been much of a success. It had produced nothing but a series of denials, though it was a good rule to interpret anything the Cut and Come Again staff said by the rule of contraries. Still, there seemed no special reason why they should so emphatically deny Dickson's presence, if, in fact, he had been there. It was not on their premises he had been discovered. Slowly Bobby walked back to the block of flats where Hilda May lived. He wanted very badly to know what she had to say about her dismissal from the employ of Messrs. Jessop & Jacks she had not mentioned the previous night.

The elevator took him again to the top floor, and when he came near her door he saw that it was an inch or two open. That meant, he supposed, that Miss May was there, but when he drew near he saw that the woodwork of the door by the Yale lock, and on the door-post opposite, showed signs of freshly inflicted damage.

" Looks like forcible entry," he said to himself, a little uneasily, as, pushing the door more widely open, he went in.

The flat was in confusion. Evidently recent intruders had searched it thoroughly. Drawers were open, their contents on the floor. A vase of flowers was on the floor, too, the water it had contained making a small pool. The table-cloth that once had been an Indian shawl he remembered noticing and admiring, seemed to have vanished. As the table was bare now, he guessed it had been jerked off hurriedly, taking the vase of flowers with it. Then he noticed that lying on the floor near by, was a half-smoked cigar, and, when he stooped and looked at it carefully, he saw that it, too, bore the monogram of the American, Mr. Patterson.

Bobby went a little pale as he looked at it. There was something ominous, he thought, about this repetition here of an object found by the body of the murdered man.

He looked quickly and with some dread into the bath-room and the kitchenette. To his relief, there was nothing there, though both rooms had evidently been subjected to the same search. He wondered what else was missing besides the Indian shawl table-cover, and why that had been taken. The search, he thought, had been made hurriedly, and by someone who had not much idea of how to set to work. There were two or three likely places his experienced eye showed him had been overlooked. He took down the 'phone and rang up, first the Yard to report, and then the porter, who arrived promptly and in a state of considerable agitation. He had no idea where Miss May was, had not known whether she was in or out. Why should he ? Probably the office would blame it all on him, but how could he help it ? He had noticed no one suspicious. But he always had plenty to do, and people were always coming in or out without his having much chance of noticing them. If you asked him, his 'phone never stopped for two minutes together all the blessed day. While he was answering it, he had his back to the entrance, and anyone could come in or go out without his seeing them. Nor had he any idea whether anything was missing. How was he to tell ?

" There was an Indian shawl on the table," Bobby remarked. " It doesn't seem to be here now."

The porter knew nothing of Indian shawls. Nor had he any idea where it would be possible to get in touch with Miss May. Tenants didn't tell him where they were going. Why should they ?

Bobby had another look round and then went back into the tiny entrance-lobby. There were two tall, narrow cupboards there, one for brooms and brushes and such other domestic necessities, the other for hats and coats. He opened the first. It had not been disturbed. He opened the second. A body fell out into his arms—the body of a woman, the upper part tightly wrapped round by the missing Indian shawl, the feet tied together with a silk scarf.

CHAPTER XVI

CONSULTATIONS

WITH ALL SPEED Bobby tore off the Indian shawl and
disclosed the inanimate form of Hilda May. To his
relief, she was alive, though her general appearance—the
shallow breathing, the fluttering pulse—suggested that her
condition was not merely due to a fainting fit.

" Had a blow on the head. Concussion, I think," he said,
and thought he could detect a swelling over the left ear.

He had, of course, as a recruit, taken the usual course in
first aid, and he knew enough to prevent the porter, much
to the good man's indignation, from carrying out the not
uncommon and extremely dangerous practice of pouring
brandy as a restorative down the unconscious girl's throat.

" Don't want to finish her off in a fit of choking," he
said. " I don't think she's badly hurt. There doesn't seem
to be any bleeding from the ears or nose." Then he made
the porter still more indignant by refusing to allow her to
be moved to the bed in the alcove in the inner room.
" There's more air where she is," he said. " If you'll open
that window, there'll be a good draught right across where
she's lying. We won't move her till a doctor comes. You
can get some cushions, though, to put under her—but keep
her head down. And some blankets or a coat or something
to keep her warm, and that's all we can do till we get help."

Help arrived soon, first in the person of the doctor
'phoned for. He approved the measures taken, agreed that
the case was one of slight concussion caused by a blow on

the head from behind, and looked grave when Bobby described how he had found her.

" Another hour or so like that—no air, no chance to breathe—ten to one death would have occurred," he said.

Using the 'phone, he summoned ambulance men and arranged for Hilda's removal to hospital, declared that she must have at least twenty-four hours' complete rest, answered Bobby's protest that it was most important to learn from her as soon as possible what had happened by retorting that saving her life was more important still, and that anyhow it was highly improbable she would know or remember anything about it. By way of emphasis he added that any case of concussion, even slight, required at least three weeks' complete rest to allow the brain to recover.

" Easier to shake a brain up than to shake it down again," he said.

Then Superintendent Ulyett appeared with various assistants—not that dignitaries like superintendents often visit forcible entry cases, even when common assault is added, but the suggestion that there might be some con- nection with the Jessop murder was sufficiently plain. The doctor vanished with his patient, grudgingly admitting that if it were really necessary she might just possibly next day be in a state to answer a few questions, provided, of course, some qualified person were present to stop them when necessary.

" Most likely she won't remember a thing," was his final parting shot.

Ulyett and his helpers, left in charge of the flat, pro- ceeded to make of its interior a careful, systematic examina- tion that told them just nothing at all.

There were plenty of fingerprints, of course, but most seemed those of Hilda herself. However, they were all care- fully recorded and classified. An inventory of the contents of the flat was made. Some money, a post office savings bank book, and a few articles of jewellery of some value—amounting in all, perhaps, to about £100—were discovered, so that ordinary robbery hardly seemed the motive.

"Looked nearly everywhere," Ulyett grunted. "Amateurs though—complete amateurs; never thought of the top of the cupboard any experienced crook thinks of at once, because he knows it's every woman's favourite hiding-place. What was it they were after, though? And did they get it—or didn't they?"

No answer being available to these questions, Ulyett turned his attention to the door. It had been forced by the insertion of an instrument of some kind between lock and jamb, and the particular expert who had specialised in forcible entries drew Ulyett's attention to a splinter of wood shaved from the jamb and to a tiny piece of steel he had discovered near it on the floor, with other small broken fragments of wood from the door and the jamb.

" Looks to me," said the expert, "as if a sharp knife with a strong blade had been used—sharp, because of that bit of the jamb shaved off, as if the tool used had slipped; a knife, because this bit of steel looks as if it came from a knife blade; and strong, because it would have to be to force the lock."

" Good," said Ulyett. " It all helps; help us to identify the tool if and when we identify the man, though it won't help us much to do that. Any fingerprints? "

" Only smudges," answered gloomily the other expert whose province that was. " Gloves, of course; always are."

Everything possible having been done, a constable was left in charge until, first, the damaged portions of door and jamb could be cut away for preservation, and, secondly, until the damage so done had been repaired. The porter protested violently, and threatened legal proceedings on the part of " the office," but did not succeed in getting much attention paid to him. Ulyett was serenely confident that the last thing " the office " would desire would be to draw public attention to the fact that burglaries and house-breakings were possible upon their well-guarded premises. Then, back at Scotland Yard, Ulyett took Bobby into his private room, told him he might smoke, set the good example himself, and proceeded to question him closely.

" Taking it, of course," he said, " that this attack on Miss May has some connection with the Jessop case."

" Yes, sir," agreed Bobby.

" Only what ? " demanded Ulyett, and Bobby tried to look as if he were thinking awfully hard, but ventured on no reply.

" Something being looked for," continued Ulyett, " something someone wanted pretty badly—the Fellows necklace by any chance ? "

" If it was that, sir," observed Bobby, " apparently they got it, for it isn't there now. I take it Mr. Jacks and Mr. Wright have reported it missing from the Mayfair Square strong-room ? "

" Yes. I was having a statement taken when you rang up," Ulyett answered. " It's pretty plain Mr. Jacks suspects Jessop was up to something on his own. If that's so, and Jessop had the necklace with him when he was murdered, it explains a lot."

" But not, sir," Bobby ventured to point out, " why Jessop himself rang up earlier to say it had been stolen; or why a man in his position, knowing, presumably, all the ins and outs of the trade, should want to call in the help of a man like T. T. And T. T. certainly didn't know him, or who he was."

" Well, T. T.'s in it somehow," Ulyett remarked. " Complicated sort of business. This duke and duchess seem mixed up in it, too, but of course they're above suspicion. Thank

God," said Ulyett piously, "we aren't Bolsheviks yet at Scotland Yard."

"No, sir," agreed Bobby. "Perhaps we shall be, though, after another election or two."

Ulyett went pale at the thought.

"I should resign," he declared.

"Yes, sir," approved Bobby. "Of course," he added thoughtfully, "they might want an experienced man for Chief Commissioner or something like that."

"Ah," said Ulyett. "Um-m. Yes. There's that. Look here," he said fiercely, "politics are no business of the police."

"No, sir," agreed Bobby. "Of course, sir, I quite agree people like dukes and duchesses are above suspicion—but not beyond proof."

"What's that mean?"

"I don't know."

"Then don't say it," snapped Ulyett. "Of course," he mused, "you coming from the same lot yourself——" Bobby squirmed; references to his unfortunate ancestry that included a—fortunately—impecunious earl as uncle, always made him squirm. "And so," continued Ulyett, "knowing 'em better than most, naturally you respect 'em less."

"Well, sir, I didn't mean it quite like that," Bobby protested, "but I do feel that the duke and duchess aren't being entirely frank with us. I feel they could tell us more than they have. They have some reason, or think they have, though it may have nothing to do with the murder, for keeping quiet. Certainly the duke doesn't want it known where he was about eight or, nine Saturday night."

"Then I suppose we've got to find out," sighed Ulyett. "Got to. Duty. Hell. Nicely we shall burn our fingers poking about in a duke's private affairs. Unless, of course," he added, brightening up, "it's something dirty, but not criminal, we can ignore officially, but put the screws on privately—a woman perhaps ? ''

" So far," Bobby said, " it doesn't seem it's that. Every-one seems to agree he's not that sort."

" You never know," said Ulyett hopefully—and reminiscently.

" Well, sir," said Bobby, " my own feeling is we can wash that out—unless, of course, something else turns up. But it does seem clear he was rather oddly interested in the necklace, and gave the idea he might be a buyer. Miss May states the firm were quite hopeful in spite of what she told them."

" Thought the price too high, didn't he ? " asked Ulyett. " Of course, if he got it for nothing—but that's silly, a duke and all."

" Yes, sir," agreed Bobby. " Another thing is, he knew Jessop was a gambler. It's odd a man in his position should know anything about the private life of a man in Mr. Jessop's."

" There's plenty of gambling goes on at the Cut and Come Again—high stakes, too, even though we've never been able to bring them in."

" I thought of that," Bobby said. "I'm fairly sure the duke has never been near the Cut and Come Again."

" If the duke had somehow got to know something about Jessop," mused Ulyett, " could he have been putting the screws on him to get the price down ? Was T. T. the inter-mediary ? Did something happen while they were discuss-ing it ? Clear as mud, isn't it ? "

" The duchess," Bobby went on, " admits having seen the necklace when Miss May took it to the Park Lane flat, but denies that she ever saw it at Hastley Court. Yet there seems good evidence it was taken there to show her. If she is lying when she says she never saw it there—well, why ? If it was shown to someone else—well, who ? And why didn't Jessop say so ? Why did he let the others, Jacks and Wright, believe he had seen the duchess again ? "

Ulyett was gazing at the ceiling.

" Wright states that Miss May had been dismissed on suspicion of her honesty," he said slowly. " Said to have been associating with someone called Denis said to be a suspected jewel thief. We've no record of any Denis that I know of, though I'll check up on that; and then in the jewellery trade sometimes they know more suspects than we do ourselves. Is it possible this Miss May brought off a masquerade as the duchess ? She would know her way about Hastley Court quite well. In a case like this," he added apologetically, " no suggestion is too wild to consider."

" No, sir," agreed Bobby, " only I don't quite see what the object of such a masquerade could be—and Miss May is about a foot taller than the duchess, and height is one thing you can't very well disguise. And then Jessop brought the necklace away with him."

" Yes," agreed Ulyett, " there's that. She'll have to be checked up on, though. Nearly done in to-day, from what the doctor said. Perhaps when she knows that she may be willing to talk. There must be some connection between the attack on her and the murder. That half-smoked cigar pretty well proves it by itself."

" I did wonder," Bobby said, " if that was left there to make us think so."

" Possible," agreed Ulyett, " only, if it's that way, it must be someone who knows a good deal. Nothing published yet about any cigar. There are a lot of angles to this case—the duke and duchess; this Hilda May girl and her young man; what Jessop was up to; the tension between him and his partner; Wynne. Odds are, it's Wynne we want. We can't be sure how long it was after he turned back to the house before the shot was fired. If he knew

Jessop was there, trying to do a deal with T. T. over the necklace, he would have had time enough at a push. Only, of course, that means T. T. did really know Jessop, and I admit he didn't seem to."

" Also," Bobby added, " Wynne escaped over the wall to the north of the house. The study where Jessop was shot is on the other side, the south side, and the imitation necklace was found there, as if it had been thrown away by the murderer while escaping. He wouldn't want it any more if he had the genuine."

" It might have been thrown through the study window —though it would have been a jolly good throw, and the lie would probably have been different. But one can't be sure of that, and the direction's good enough—line of escape for a fugitive, too, of course. Not much to go on; not enough to clear Wynne, anyhow. There'll be plenty to ask him when we pull him in."

" There's another thing, sir," Bobby continued. " That theory means Wynne double-crossed T. T. No one ever does that with T. T. and gets away with it. If it's that way, we shall be getting plenty of information from T. T. before long."

" No sign of it yet," commented Ulyett. " Apparently he can't talk of anything except moving to a new house after what's happened."

" I shouldn't have thought he was so sensitive as all that," remarked Bobby. " Would you, sir ? "

" No," agreed Ulyett. " Bit of a shock, I suppose. Think better of it, perhaps. Hope he does myself, though. That place where he is, is a sight too convenient. You can get in back way, from the common, or front way, from the street, and on one side there's an empty house with a big deserted garden. And when he has his scouts out like he had the other night, not much chance of anyone getting near without being spotted."

" That's another point, sir," Bobby remarked. " Why

had he his scouts out? He can't have been expecting us, because we only fixed it up on short notice. He only takes precautions like that when he is expecting a raid or has something big on. Looks as if he was expecting either Jessop—but apparently he did not know him—or else Wynne. But that suggests Wynne had the necklace, and how had he got hold of it? There seems no connection— except that in the list of members of the Cut and Come Again there's a Count de Teirney."

" Yes, we've got that," agreed Ulyett, fumbling amidst the mass of papers on his desk. " Seems clear that's Wynne, though he doesn't seem to have been there much. But the whole place seems to have been buzzing with rumours about a big deal T. T. was bringing off. And not only the Cut and Come Again. Half the crooks in London seem to have known T. T. had done it again, though apparently none of them knew details. We haven't got the rumours traced to their source yet, but one story is Wynne had been boasting when a bit over the nine. Only then, again, those stories have been going round several days—we had a hint of them ourselves last Wednesday, I think; anyhow, two or three days before the definite report we got in Saturday we linked up with the Jessop 'phone message. There's another snag— presumably Jessop only missed the necklace on Saturday; and, if it actually was the Fellows necklace Wynne was boasting about, he must have had it in his hands, or been dead sure of getting it, several days before. It'll save a lot of trouble if Wynne has tried to do down T. T., and T. T. comes across with what he knows. We know now the neck- lace is missing; it's as good as certain someone had it at Brush Hill Saturday night, and, if it wasn't for this attack on the Hilda May girl, I should say it was safe betting Wynne has it now. Only this new affair makes it look as if the girl had got hold of it somehow and someone knew. Wynne again, perhaps?"

"Yes, sir," agreed Bobby, "only there's no link as yet between Miss May and Wynne, and it's difficult to fit in T. T. I've been wondering, sir, if there could be anything behind his talking so much about wanting to move?"

"What could there be?"

"And why he seemed worried," Bobby continued, discreetly ignoring this question, "over the football results from the *Evening Announcer* being missing?"

"Good Lord," protested Ulyett, "you don't want to bring football results into it, do you?"

"No, sir," answered Bobby hastily, "not unless they're there already. And I've been wondering about that copy of the *Upper Ten* Mr. Jessop had in his pocket."

"Didn't know there was one," said Ulyett. "Is it listed?"

"Yes, sir, I think so. It got kicked under a chair and left there, so I picked it up. The only thing about it is that there's a snap of the duchess at the races two weeks ago."

"Her again," grunted Ulyett. "Why shouldn't she be at the races?"

"I don't know, sir," answered Bobby, "only it seemed funny Mr. Jessop should have a paper with a snap of her in his pocket. May be nothing in it, of course."

"Don't quite see what there could be," Ulyett remarked, looking rather worried, though. "Gives me the willies the way this blessed duke and duchess keep cropping up. I've been trying to check up on Jacks's story that he was at a cinema as he says; can't do it. He knows all about the programme, but he may have seen it another night. He's got the stubs of the two tickets for stalls he bought, but it doesn't say he was sitting there all evening. He and Mrs. Jacks turned up together at their friend's, but that doesn't prove they came together."

"And Mr. Wright," Bobby asked, "has he anything he can show to confirm his motoring story?"

" I was going into that with him when you rang up about the Hilda May affair," Ulyett answered. " As a matter of fact, he hasn't. He admits it was nearly midnight when he got to his hotel at Winchester. Says he made a long circuit, just for the sake of the trip, without looking or caring much where he was going. Nasty night for motoring. Says that after a week shut up in town he needs a breath of fresh air, rain or no rain. Can't suggest anything by which we can confirm his story."

" I met Magotty Meg leaving the Cut and Come Again," Bobby said. " She's not a member, but she's always in and out there. She's down on the list of staff as housekeeper, though I don't suppose she either housekeeps or draws any pay—except for commission on the pigeons she brings in. It's possible she may know something, for she went out of her way to tell me she didn't hold with murder."

" What she knows," Ulyett sighed, " she won't tell. Never known her come across with anything useful yet. Wynne still seems our best prospect. If we can trace the pistol found near Jessop's body to him, it'll be good enough for an arrest. I don't suppose that thumb torn from a rubber glove will be any good; gloves made away with by now, most likely. There's a report in from the uniform man on a beat at Brush Hill that night may mean something. Says he saw a young fellow running down the Lane about the time of the murder. Didn't notice him much at first—wet night, and he might have been running for a train, or the trams or buses. But when he saw the policeman he slacked up and began to walk, and then dodged down a side-street, and was out of sight in no time. Uniform man thought it a bit suspicious, but not enough to take action on, especially as young fellow wasn't carrying anything. Inquiries made at tube station and from the 'bus and tram men, but no one else seems to have noticed him. May have been our man, but there are plenty don't like policemen looking at them, and, anyhow, not much hope of tracing him. Uniform man didn't even see his face. Also there's a report about the summer-house in the garden of the empty house next to T. T. I've had it gone over pretty thoroughly. Lots of fingerprints, but none we have any record of, nothing useful noted about the cigarette-ends, burnt matches, paper bag that had held chocolates, and so on. One odd thing— several bits of ends of human hair, all different, and all quite small. Looks as if half a dozen girls had been sitting there combing their hair. Don't quite see what to make of that, though, or where it comes in."

CHAPTER XVII

GENERAL QUESTIONS

"Triple problem," Bobby muttered to himself as he walked slowly homewards. " Who killed Jessop ? Who has the Fellows necklace ? Who attacked Hilda May ? "

That the answer to one would be the answer to all he felt fairly confident, and busily his thoughts went to and fro, from duke and duchess to Denis Chenery, from Hilda May to T. T., from the missing Wynne to the Cut and Come Again, from Magotty Meg to Charley Dickson, from Jessop's partner and their manager back to duke and duchess again, and all of it adding up to no more, he told himself ruefully, than just confused noises in the head.

He turned into the street where he lived, and there saw Charley Dickson strolling up and down. Charley, catching sight of him at the same moment, waved a hand and came briskly forward.

" They told me at your place you hadn't got back," he said. " I thought I would wait—even if the Yard never sleeps, I supposed it came home sometimes."

" How did you know where I lived ? " Bobby asked.

" Cut and Come Again," explained Charley. " Not much they don't know there."

" There isn't," agreed Bobby feelingly. " Do you know where they do their big gambling stunt ? I don't mean the John Smith flat upstairs—we know all about that. I mean the place where the extra fat pigeons are plucked."

" Wouldn't be quite cricket to tell if I did, would it ? "

LJ

Charley asked. " As a matter of fact, I don't. Some of the pigeons don't either; just whisked there in closed motors and haven't an idea where it is. I have heard they'll even buy an old house in the suburbs somewhere, use it once or twice, and then sell it again."

" Yes, we know that," Bobby said. " I suppose they can afford to drop a hundred or two on the re-sale if they've made a few thousands on the gambling."

" Wish they would let me in on the racket," said Charley, grinning. " Shouldn't have to worry then about jobs in film agencies in Hollywood or anywhere else. Look here, what's this about Miss May ? "

" Who told you ? " Bobby asked sharply.

" Half over London by now, I should think," retorted Charley. " When I got away from Park Lane, I ran into a pal—Logan; Penny Logan, they call him; decent sort of chap, though Denis Chenery doesn't like him; says he's a wrong 'un. You ought to have seen how they glared at each other—' cut your throat for two pins ' sort of a look on each side."

" One moment," interposed Bobby. " When was this ? "

" Just outside the flats where Miss May lives," Charley answered. " Penny Logan's rooms are in Soho, and so we had to pass there—Penny asked me to come along with him for a drink and a yarn. Chenery was just coming out— of the flats, I mean; in a deuce of a hurry, too. He and Penny looked blue murder at each other, and Chenery went off. I didn't stop long at Penny's—someone rang him up while I was there and wanted him to come along to them, so I cleared out. I went back to look up Miss May— don't see why Chenery should make all the running—and the porter told me there had been a burglary and she had been half murdered. He didn't seem to know much, and the bobby in the flat wouldn't say a word, so I thought I would ask you. Is she badly hurt ? "

" Doctor says she'll be all right soon; only wants to be kept quiet a day or two. No thanks to whoever attacked her, though; she might easily have been killed. What time did you see Mr. Chenery ? "

Charley was a bit vague. He hadn't noticed the time particularly. Presently, however, it was fixed as being about half an hour or so before Bobby's arrival at the flats, and Bobby reflected that the doctor had thought Hilda could not have been where he had found her more than about thirty minutes.

" Did the porter at the flats see you the first time ? " Bobby asked.

" I don't know. Why ? I shouldn't think so. When I've been there he's generally either busy answering the 'phone in that little cubby-hole of his at the back or else he's trying to work out a good double from the racing reports in the paper."

" Do you know why Mr. Chenery and Mr. Logan don't like each other ? "

Charley shrugged his shoulders.

" Chenery runs a small garage; deals in second-hand cars; says Logan tried to do him down. Logan says he didn't, and, anyway, if you can do down a dealer in second-hand cars—well, it's one up to you and that's all there's to it. You haven't told me what happened to Hilda."

" Come in and have a drink," Bobby said, " and I'll tell you."

Charley accepted the invitation—Bobby, indeed, was inclined to think that an invitation to a drink was one the young gentleman seldom refused—and listened with close attention to the story of what had happened.

" Beastly for Hilda," he said. " Lucky you found her in time or she might easily have suffocated. Poor old girl." He seemed genuinely disturbed; even Bobby's offer of a second drink passed him by unheeded—sufficient testimony to his disturbed mind. " Poor old girl," he repeated. " Rotten experience. Suppose she hadn't time to use her gun ? "

" Has she one ? "

" I think so. So have I. Nice fat ·45. Have to if you're private sec. to an old girl who is always wanting you to run round with her blasted crown jewels. I've had to pack off from Hastley Court to Park Lane with twenty thousand pounds' worth of stuff in my pocket, and I expect Miss May had to, too. I know she told me once she had a toy automatic just to make her feel safer. She knows how to use a gun, too."

" Do you know what make it was ? "

" No, I don't think she ever said. Why ? "

" I was just wondering," Bobby answered. " The flat was examined pretty carefully to see if any clue to the burglar could be found, or what was missing. There was no pistol."

" Perhaps the johnny, whoever he was, took it off— thought it more suitable for a burglar than for anyone else," observed Charley.

" I suppose you can't suggest anything—or anyone ? " Bobby asked.

Charley shook his head.

" Can't understand it," he said, frowning heavily. " Can't have been an ordinary burglary if nothing was taken. You say the flat had been turned upside down as if something was being looked for ? Do you think the chap who shot poor old Jessop can have thought he might have left the Fellows necklace in her charge and was looking for it ? It's Sunday, and all the banks and usual places are shut up. Jessop might have left it with her with the idea that no one would think of her having it."

" It's an idea," Bobby admitted, " but it assumes that the murderer didn't get it."

" Well, he wouldn't, would he ? " Charley asked.

" Jessop wouldn't have it in his pocket when he was calling on a chap like T. T., would he? Everyone knows T. T.'s reputation."

" Well, what was Jessop doing there?"

Charley smiled and winked.

" At T. T.'s?" he asked. " Why shouldn't they have been doing a deal? Jessop bought stuff, didn't he? All jewellers do. And the general idea is that T. T. often had stuff to sell."

" Risky for a respectable firm of jewellers to have dealings with a notorious receiver."

" It's when you're respectable you're safe," retorted Charley, winking again. " Mind, I'm only guessing. I don't know anything really. Only that's what struck me at once."

Bobby was forced to agree that it was a possible though somewhat cynical explanation. But again it implied that Jessop and T. T. knew each other. If that were so, then T. T. was a remarkable actor, for certainly his astonishment had seemed genuine.

But it remained a possible theory that Wynne, T. T., and Jessop had all met in connection with some proposed deal; and that the murder had been committed by some fourth person of whom as yet no trace had been found, and who had escaped with whatever the others had met to bargain over. And that might very probably have been the Fellows necklace, but, then, also it might have been something else.

Charley broke in on Bobby's thoughts with a new question.

" What's this about T. T.'s moving?" he said. " He's going round asking everyone for a really trustworthy firm of removers."

" Well, I suppose," Bobby said cautiously, " it is a bit upsetting to have someone murdered in your house. Might get on your nerves a bit."

" Fat lot T. T. knows about nerves," scoffed Charley. " I'll tell you what struck me at once. He wants to know who you go to at the Yard when you use a van for police purposes, so he can get warning in time. But I expect you have your own, haven't you ? Or else you just ring up one of the big firms ? "

" To tell you the truth," Bobby answered, " I think it'll be a long time before we try that game again, after Saturday's fiasco. Vans are a bit of a sore subject with us just now. I wouldn't mention them to any of our people for a year or two, if I were you."

Charley laughed, and asked if it was as bad as that, and Bobby said it was even worse, and Charley said wouldn't the van-driver give the show away, and Bobby said he had been sworn to secrecy on crossed knives and a bottle of red ink, and Charley laughed again and said he was sorry if he had been trying to butt in on official secrets, and Bobby said it wasn't that at all and would Charley have another drink ?

Charley accepted, and then got up to go.

" But I'm afraid you do think I've been nosy," he said. " Because I notice you didn't say whether it was your own van or one of the big shops or what ? I didn't mean, you know. Only I did wonder what T. T. was so keen on moving for all at once."

" Oh, just that, I suppose," said Bobby vaguely, and as he was opening the door for his visitor he paused. " By the way," he said, " had you any special reason for wanting to see Miss May ? "

" No, nothing special," Charley answered, a little hurriedly. " I just thought I might ask her to come out somewhere for a spot of dinner." He added gloomily : " I don't suppose it would have been any good, it's all that Chenery blighter ; now she's got a down on me."

" How's that ? " Bobby asked.

" Well, I suppose I've got her job," Charley admitted. " Had no idea, though; thought she was quitting on her own. Won't catch me stopping, if I get half a chance to clear. The old girl's not such a bad sort really, but she does keep you on the jump, Sundays and all."

" I suppose she was really keen on the Fellows necklace?"

" Dreamed of it," asserted Charley, " but she hadn't the coin and she knew hubby wouldn't come down, so what was the good? Jessop did his best to hook her, you know. Took it down to Hastley Court once to show her."

" I suppose there's no doubt of that," Bobby asked. " You arranged for Jessop to see her, didn't you ? "

" No; never knew a thing about it till afterwards," Charley asserted. " Too busy for one thing. Any idea what a poor devil of a private secretary has to do when there's a big show on ? But Colonel Edwardes was there, and he knows Jessop and happened to catch sight of him, and wondered what he was up to. When he told me, I guessed at once it was the Fellows necklace again. Only on the q.t. Wouldn't have done to let hubby know; he would have gone in off the deep end if he had known she was still playing about with the thing after he had turned it down."

He repeated that he had known nothing of the jewellers' visit till later, accepted without comment Bobby's explanation of his questioning that it was necessary to check up Mr. Jessop's movements in the fullest detail, and returned to his grievance of Miss May's displeasure.

" Wouldn't do her any good if I chucked the job," he complained. " She'll come round in time, but Chenery's making all the running just now, blast him ! Thank the Lord, his garage will have to buck up a whole lot before he'll be able to marry."

" Doing badly, is it ? "

" May be sold up any minute almost—at least, that's what Penny Logan told me."

" Bit prejudiced, perhaps ? "

" There's that," agreed Charley, " but I've heard from other people he's in pretty low water. He may come in for the title some day, but not for half a century or so. No one will take half a century as good security."

" I suppose not," said Bobby, and Charley departed, and Bobby went back and sat down at his typewriter, feeling that his chat had given him quite a remarkable amount of useful information, though how it all hung together was more than he could see for the present.

Slowly he typed:

QUESTIONS

A.   DUKE AND DUCHESS OF WESTHAVEN

AA. DUKE OF WESTHAVEN

1. Why was duke interested in Fellows necklace, and why did he keep harping on the price, as if it were a personal grievance or disappointment ?
   (Theory that he intended it as a present to his wife apparently untenable.)

2. Where was he at the relevant time Saturday night ?

3. How did he know Jessop gambled ?

AB.   DUCHESS OF WESTHAVEN

1. Is she telling the truth when she says she didn't see the necklace at Hastley Court ?

2. If she is, what happened there ?

3. If she is lying, why ?

4. Was she seriously thinking of buying ?

Purely hypothetical questions :

1. Are dukes and duchesses necessarily above suspicion? If so, why ?

2. If a person dreams of a thing, how far will that person go to get possession of it ?

General observations:

1. Dukes are kittle cattle.
2. Bobby, my boy, mind you don't make a damn fool of yourself.

B. MAGOTTY MEG

1. Why did she go out of her way to say she didn't hold with murder?

C. WYNNE

1. Had he the time to commit the murder?
2. Had he the nerve when he knew police were at hand?
3. Where is he?
4. What was he doing at T. T.'s?
5. Has he got the necklace?

D. T. T. MULLINS

1. Is it a fact Jessop was a complete stranger to him?
2. Why does he keep talking about moving?
3. Why did the disappearance of the football pages of the *Evening Announcer* scare him?

E. DENIS CHENERY

1. Is he identical with the " Denis " Mr. Wright says he knows of as mixed up in jewel thefts?
2. Is it pure coincidence he was leaving the flats where Miss May lives about the time of the attack on her?
3. Is it true he is pressed for money?
4. Is it possible he and Hilda May have been associated to secure the necklace?
5. Where was he at the relevant time Saturday night?

F. HILDA MAY

1. Are there real grounds for the doubts her employers seem to have entertained of her honesty?

2. Why didn't she say she had left Jessop and was consequently out of a job ?

3. Was the necklace concealed in her flat, and is that why she was attacked ? If so, by whom ?

G.   MESSRS. JESSOP, JACKS & Co., Mayfair Square, Jewellers.

GA. JESSOP

1. What was he doing at T. T.'s ?

2. Was he a gambler ?

3. Why was there £5,000 in foreign currency at his flat, and where did it come from ?

GB. JACKS

1. Was he at the cinema, as stated, at the relevant time ?

GC. WRIGHT

1. Was he motoring at the relevant time ?

General query :

1. What were the actual relations between the partners and between them, and each of them, and their manager ?

General observations :

1. Firm in low water financially.

2. No one but Jessop had seen the necklace for two or three weeks.

3. Check up on Wright's history as boxer, and secure impressions of his fingerprints to see if they are on record.

H.   SUMMER-HOUSE AND OCCUPANTS (unknown)

1. Were they accomplices of Wynne ? Friends of Jessop ? T. T.'s scouts ? Unknowns after the necklace on their own account ? Unknowns having nothing to do with what happened ?

2. How the mischief to find out who they were ?

J.   **MR. PATTERSON**

  1. Check up on story he was seen in Paris after ostensibly leaving for New York.

  2. Is there anything in the fact that his special cigars were left both in T. T.'s place and in Miss May's flat ?

General note:

Patterson seems to have had an eye on the necklace. Query: Was it more than an eye ?

K.   **CHARLEY DICKSON**

  1. Check his statement he was too busy the day of the fête at Hastley Court to have had any time for making arrangements with Jessop.

  2. See if Wright can identify him. If not, who was it introduced himself to Wright and Jessop as the duchess's secretary, giving Dickson's name ?

  3. Dickson lost his raincoat Saturday night. Is there anything in that ? If so, what ? He had been drinking, by report of constable on beat. If he left it at any pub near, that would show where he actually got his drink if the Cut and Come people are telling the truth in saying it wasn't there. (N.B. Cut and Come staff seldom tell the truth.)

  4. Apparently sound alibi for the forcible entry to the Hilda May flat, but check up with Mr. Logan for this.

L.   UNKNOWN YOUNG MAN noticed by Brush Hill constable, and considered by him to have behaved suspiciously

  1. Does he come in ?

  2. If so, where ?

M.   **GENERAL CLUES**

MA. *Evening Announcer* with football results missing.

1. Why?

2. What became of missing pages?

MB. Copy of *Upper Ten* two weeks old, with snap of duchess.

1. Why had Jessop this in his pocket?

MC. Automatic pistol found near Jessop's body.

1. Jessop and Jacks possess one of same make and calibre. Had they another, similar, and, if so, did Jessop take it with him to Brush Hill?

2. Miss May said by Dickson to have an automatic in her possession. None found in flat. Check up on this when she can be questioned.

MD. Fragment of steel, probably from knife blade.

1. Whose knife?

ME. Thumb of rubber glove caught on trigger of pistol.

1. What chance of finding the glove?

Having typed this last sentence, Bobby put the machine away, and, getting out the copy of the *Upper Ten* found at Brush Hill, he brooded over it so long that presently, hypnotised by that long succession of photographs of super-smart women on super-shiny paper, he fell asleep. So he put the paper away and went discontentedly to bed.

CHAPTER XVIII

SIDE-LINE

Monday morning saw all the usual routine of a Scotland Yard inquiry in full spate. Every detail was being checked, so that the smallest discrepancy, the tiniest point left unexplained, might be carefully and fully examined and reported on. Every police force throughout the country was on the look-out for the missing Wynne; special attention was being given to tracing the history of the pistol found by the murdered man's side from the moment it left its factory of origin. Ulyett himself visited Jessop's lawyers and had a long conversation with them, from which it appeared that his affairs were certainly embarrassed, though to what extent the lawyers did not know. But he had consulted them about raising a loan, and they had been obliged to point out that the security he had to offer was not very satisfactory, especially as he did not wish to give any details of the Mayfair Square business, beyond his personal statement that it was exceedingly prosperous. The loan was, he had explained, to be entirely private to himself; he did not even wish his business associates to know of it; and so there the negotiations had come to an end.

At all ports, too, a sharp look-out was being kept, and every dealer in precious stones all over the country, all over Europe indeed, was already on the look-out for the Fay Fellows necklace, or for loose stones that might have come from it had it been broken up. And Inspector Ferris was

down in the Hastley Court district, his errand there to confirm Charley Dickson's statement that Colonel Edwardes,
who lived near by, had seen and recognised Jessop on the
day of the garden fête, and that Charley himself had been
so busy, and so much in public view, as to have had no
opportunity for arranging private meetings between Jessop
and the duchess—or anyone else, for that matter.

On both points Charley's story received most satisfactory
confirmation. Colonel Edwardes remembered distinctly
having seen Mr. Jessop, whom he knew quite well, having
wondered whether he was there as a guest or on business,
since the duchess's love of jewellery and fondness for little
deals in it were well known, and having mentioned the
incident to Charley when he happened to meet him a day
or two later at the Cut and Come Again, of which club
Colonel Edwardes was also a member—though, as he was
careful to explain, he, like all the other members, hardly
ever went there. By chance also it came out in the course
of the chat with Ferris that he had seen Charley in the
club on the Saturday evening. He had dropped in for a
few minutes before going on to dine with a friend at
Wimbledon, and he remembered having seen Charley there.

" The young ass," said the colonel smilingly, " had been
having more than he could carry comfortably. I told him
so, and he said he was fed up with everything and he was
going to get jolly well soaked, if it took him all evening.
I told the people there they oughtn't to serve him, and
they said they wouldn't."

That seemed also conclusive proof that the Cut and Come
Again staff had not been telling the truth when they denied
Charley's presence that evening, but, then, that didn't
matter much, as anyhow no one ever believed anything
they said until it had been fully confirmed.

Other inquiries Ferris made seemed to prove a general
agreement that on the occasion of the Hastley Court fête

Charley had in fact been in evidence the whole afternoon till the last guest had departed, and long afterwards as well, though it also came out that the hostess herself had retired from the scene once or twice for brief intervals, for a respite from perpetual hand-shaking. It seemed probable, too, though not quite certain, that one of these intervals had been about the time when Mr. Jessop had arrived. But it was clear that, immediately before, during, and after the duchess's brief absence, Charley had been specially busy over some dispute or confusion caused by a threat of a shortage in the supply of strawberry ices.

Apparently too, even to Hollywood itself the news had been cabled, and there Miss Fay Fellows was dividing her time between fits of passionate weeping (see photographs in every paper, magazine, and journal in the whole wide world), granting interviews between sobs to newspaper men, and sending imperative cables to various official personages, insisting on the instant recovery of her necklace, or, in default, a demand for full compensation from the British Government. Also she instructed her agent to demand that her salary should be immediately put back to its former level.

" Big publicity," she said to him, " and the best sort, because there's not even any possible smell of fake about it. Knocks even a pathetic divorce from a brutal husband."

" Yes, it's fine; just all honey, cream, and jam," agreed the agent, who once himself had nearly been a poet before he decided to become rich instead.

The Yard was busy, also, following up all the usual false trails presented to it by circumstance and by too zealous members of the public. Bobby, sent to check a story that a man answering Wynne's description had been seen examining a diamond necklace in a café at Hammersmith, soon found that the only foundation for it was that two girls there had been trying on in turn a string of beads one of them had just bought at a sixpenny bazaar; found, too, that this left him with a little time to spare, and availed himself of it for an investigation of his own—a side-line, so to say, he had received permission to follow up.

" It is just possible," Ulyett had admitted, " that those bits of ends of hair of different kinds reported in the summer-house may point to a hairdresser's assistant having been there, but that's pretty wide, isn't it ? "

Bobby agreed that it was, but thought there was a chance, and now, according to instructions, reported at Brush Hill police station and there was given the name of the con-stable who had mentioned the incident of the young man in a hurry with an apparent dislike to being looked at by policemen. The constable in question was a married man, but lived quite close, so Bobby went along to his home, and there found him, since he did not go on duty again till two, spending a placid and domestic hour helping his wife peel the potatoes for dinner. He remembered the incident perfectly, but thought it was now cleared up.

" Young chap of the name of Young—Nolly Young—we've had an eye on for some time," he explained. " He's been in trouble once or twice for pinching bicycles, and now he seems to have taken to snatching women's bags and purses in crowds. Makes a speciality of Fascist meet-ings, because there's generally a row and a chance to pick up something. He lives in Makin Street, the turning out of West Lane by the Red Lion, and when he saw I saw him he just dodged in home. Must have; the street was empty, and there wasn't anywhere else he could have gone. You can take it from me the artful young dodger wanted me to see him, so I should think he was safe at home and out of mischief, while really he just slipped out again by the back door and off to a Fascist meeting there was that night to see what he could pick up. Sort of establishing an alibi beforehand, if you see what I mean."

" Yes, I see the idea," Bobby agreed. " They do play

that kind of trick sometimes; you have to look out for it. You didn't actually recognise him, though?"

"No; didn't give me a chance to see his face, but it must have been him because of his getting out of sight so quick."

"What about the pub?" Bobby asked. "Couldn't he have slipped in there?"

"Not without crossing the road, and then I should have seen him," answered the other. "Bound to."

"Seems O.K., but we had better check up on his movements perhaps," said Bobby, and thanked his informant, and then went back to the police station and left a message asking the local C.I.D. inspector to do this, if he agreed that it was worth while.

Then he went out again and found the sweet shop of which the name was on the paper bag discovered with the bits of ends of hair in the summer-house of the unoccupied residence next door to The Towers.

There Bobby explained who he was; and, when the awe and excitement two youthful and giggling assistants experienced at this announcement had subsided, went on to say he was trying to trace a customer who might have bought chocolates from them on Saturday night.

"We're that busy Saturday nights," said one assistant.

"There isn't so much as time to look at who you're serving," confirmed the other.

"There's some we know, if you can tell us his name," said the first.

"Or what he looks like," added the second. "Is it a man or a girl?"

"His name and what he looks like are what I'm trying to get at," explained Bobby, "only I think most likely it's a girl I want to find."

They waited expectantly, trustfully; a little bewilderedly, too.

MJ

" You see, we've a lot of customers; nip in and out, they do," said the first assistant.

" Some of them," said the second meditatively, " are that funny, you wouldn't believe."

" When they're boys, that cheeky," added the first, not without appreciation.

" When it's girls," continued the second, a little bitter now, " watching all the time to see it's full weight, and if you don't give under now and then—well, where are you when it comes to stocktaking ? "

" That's right," agreed her colleague.

Bobby produced his paper bag.

" Nothing about that you can recognise, I suppose ? " he asked.

" Is it—fingerprints ? " asked one with a little gasp.

" Are there—blood-stains ? " inquired the other, with her eyes open to the very widest.

However, further questioning established that " dozens and dozens " of customers had gone away with exactly similar bags on the Saturday night.

" Quarter of cream chocs, cheap line," was the expert verdict finally pronounced.

" One of your customers a young lady employed at a hairdresser's ? " Bobby asked.

But they had no knowledge of any such customer.

Bobby thanked them and retired. It had been a long shot, and it had failed, as was the well-established nature of long shots. No great likelihood that the assistants in the confectioner's should have known the occupation of any one customer, but it had been worth trying. Now another trail must be followed. A directory had given him the names of various hairdressing establishments in the neighbourhood, and he set himself to visit them all in rotation, asking for a young lady assistant whose name he thought might be Jones, but he wasn't sure. She had been seen buying chocolates in a shop he named on Saturday night, and she might be in a position to give him some information he needed if he could find her, though of course nothing to do with her personally. At the first two or three shops he visited he had no luck. Many of the assistants bought chocolates at times, but none, it seemed, at that special shop mentioned, last Saturday night.

" It's a pretty slim chance, anyway," Bobby told himself, as he retired from one of these unsuccessful visits. " Nothing to show the girl bought them herself, for one thing, except that a boy would most likely have bought better quality, or a half-pound box perhaps—and those bits of hair found are hardly real proof that she worked in a hairdresser's."

However, at the next shop the luck turned. The manageress was inclined to be chatty. She admitted frankly that it was a relief to see a man when you had nothing in but ladies all day long, all fussing about their hair they would never leave alone, and a good thing, too, or where would her living be? And perhaps the gentleman meant Irene, who spent half her wages on chocolates because she said she had to have something to take the smell of hair oil away, and whose way home took her past the confectioner's mentioned. Then, too, Irene had asked to go off early on Saturday to meet her boy friend.

" Saturday's not our busy night," the manageress explained; " the girls want to be out with their boys, and the married ladies have the shopping to do, or else all the family's going to the pictures."

Irene, however, wasn't there that morning. She had sent round word that she had caught cold and would be away a day or two.

" I always tell my girls to stop off if they've a cold," explained the manageress. " Ladies don't like it if assistants are sniffling all the time, or sneezing down their backs. It's all this infection," said the manageress. " Never heard of it when I was young, and now there's nothing else."

Bobby secretly sympathised with the manageress's customers, but murmured vague sympathy, secured Irene's address, expressed his gratitude for the help given, and went on to find Irene herself.

She was in, it appeared, when his knock was answered, but still in bed, suffering from a cold—one she had caught the other night. But she had been meaning to get up for dinner, and, if the gentleman wouldn't mind waiting a little, she would dress at once and come down to see him.

So Bobby said that would be very kind of her, and was shown into a small, stiffly furnished sitting-room, on the walls some very good photographs of the French Riviera, of Monte Carlo, and of the casino there—that " confectioner's masterpiece," as it has been called. Even a post-card album open on the table was full of picture cards from Monaco, including several of the interior of the rooms. Another photograph, in a specially smart frame, showed a young man standing at one of the roulette tables with a croupier's rake in his hand.

CHAPTER XIX

RECOVERED RAINCOAT

THE DOOR OPENED and Irene herself appeared, a small, trim figure with an elaborate coiffure, a nose the redness of which a liberal use of powder served to emphasise rather than to disguise, and two red and watery eyes beneath thin, plucked, pencilled brows. He noticed she was wearing a ring on her engagement finger. Her arrival she heralded by a shattering sneeze, and Bobby hastened to express his sympathy, his apologies for worrying her while she was so unwell, and his assurances that, though he came from the police, his visit had nothing to do with her personally. Only it was just possible she might be able to give some information that would prove helpful. In fact, he let loose such a flow of consoling, reassuring platitude, nicely mingled with a tactful compliment or two, that Miss Irene was soon quite at her ease, and subconsciously began to enjoy this chat with a good-looking, upstanding young man —better fun, anyhow, than lying sneezing alone in bed— and in her turn apologised for her cold and hoped her visitor wasn't afraid of catching it. And Bobby said he wasn't, and the risk of catching cold was the worst of sitting in damp summer-houses in deserted gardens on chilly autumn evenings.

Poor Miss Irene fairly gasped; all her terrors came flooding back; she evidently became, on the spot, convinced that from Bobby's all-seeing eye there was nothing hidden.

" How did you know ? " she asked breathlessly. " Did Bill tell you ? " she demanded, plainly groping for a solution on this side of the miraculous.

" Bill ? " repeated Bobby. " You mean Mr. —— ? "

" Mr. Carton," said the girl, convinced it was useless to attempt to conceal anything when all was evidently already known. She eyed Bobby with a kind of bewildered awe. She got out her handkerchief—or, rather, one of them; prudently she had brought half a dozen—wiped her eyes, and said plaintively: " We weren't doing any harm."

" Of course you weren't," Bobby agreed warmly. " I'm sure I've not said you were; now, have I ? " She looked a little consoled, and he showed her the photograph representing a young man standing by a roulette table with a croupier's rake in his hand. " This is Mr. Carton," he said, risking the guess.

She nodded.

" He's a sort of cousin," she explained, " only not exactly a cousin either."

" Hopes to be something nearer some day, perhaps," suggested Bobby. " Lucky chap."

He looked significantly at the ring on her engagement finger, and she smiled and blushed and then touched the brooch she was wearing—one of three straight horizontal gold bars, crossed by a spray in emeralds and small brilliants.

" He gave me that only the other day," she confided. " It cost seven guineas. I know; it was scratched on the back—the price, I mean."

" Some fellows have all the luck," said Bobby as wistfully as he could manage, and Miss Irene's renewed blush, toss of the head, and other appropriate reactions were ruined by a fresh fit of sneezing. When it was over and she a little recovered, Bobby, grown official again after this softer interlude, went on:

" You have heard a murder was committed that night in the house next door to where you were sitting ? "

" Bill told me," she admitted. " He showed it me in the paper, in the stop press yesterday. Bill said it was nothing to do with us; he thought we had better not say anything unless we had to. Really, there wasn't anything we could say, and Bill's got to go back soon, and if he has to stop on waiting for trials and giving evidence and all that, he may lose his job. Now things are so quiet, they don't want as big a staff as they did before."

" At the Monte Carlo casino ? " Bobby asked. " Has he been there long ? As a croupier, I mean ? "

" Oh, years and years; only, now they're slack, he comes to England in the summer to help his aunt. She has a private boarding-house at Cliftonville, and, of course, summer's the busy time with her."

" Is he there now ? "

" No: he's having a little holiday now the season's over, and it isn't time to go back to Monte. He's staying at the Bloomsbury—the big hotel just behind the British Museum. It's his holiday before he goes back, and they give him special terms at the Bloomsbury because he recommends it to people who are coming to London and don't know where to stay."

" He's not British, then ? " Bobby asked.

" Yes, he is," she answered indignantly, " only his mother was French—only not French exactly; Monaco; it's different; and, anyhow, he couldn't help it. He was born in London, only after his father died his mother went back to her people and he was brought up there. They're all croupiers, and that's how he came to be one. It's quite respectable there."

" Of course it is. Why not ? " said Bobby.

" It's like being in the Civil Service here," she explained.

" I suppose it is," agreed Bobby. " Now will you tell me exactly what you saw on Saturday night ? "

" We didn't see anything really," she insisted between two fresh sneezes, " except a man jumping over the wall."

" When was that ? " Bobby asked.

" Just after we heard the shots. I thought it was a tyre gone somewhere, but Bill said no, it was a pistol. He knows about pistols; he has to have one where he works; all the croupiers don't, but he does, because they trust him."

" That speaks well for him," Bobby remarked. " Do you know what kind of pistol it is ? "

" Ever so small. He showed it me once, and he said it would kill anyone ever so easy. It's automatic; you just press something and it goes on shooting by itself."

" Ah, yes," said Bobby, and remembered it was a small automatic that had been found by the side of the murdered man. Another coincidence he supposed, yet hardly a coincidence, since small automatic pistols are as common as they ought to be rare if Governments, and not private enterprise, controlled their manufacture. He put the memory aside for the moment. " After you heard the shots," he asked, " what happened exactly ? "

" We could hear running and shouting, and a man got over the wall just opposite the summer-house."

" How soon after you heard the shot ? "

" Oh, immediately. There was the shot, and then we heard him running, and then there he was over the wall. And then he just stopped and lighted a cigarette, so we could see him plainly, and he listened a moment and then he ran off across the lawn, and Bill said we had better go too. He said if there was trouble we didn't want to get mixed up in it, and, anyhow, Bill said the man we saw couldn't have been the one who fired, because it was a long way off and we saw him climbing the wall immediately after. Bill thought it might have been fired at him, though. So Bill said we had better go quick, and we did."

"You ought to have given information," Bobby said sternly. "The man you saw may have been an accomplice. You have given us a lot of unnecessary trouble."

Irene dissolved into tears at this, and said it wasn't fair to expect anyone to lose his job, mixing up in things he had nothing to do with; and Bobby, telling himself it was silly to use a stern tone to a girl from whom evidently coaxing was likely to get far more than severity, soothed her by saying he quite understood, and probably there was no harm done, and, at any rate, what she said now was very useful as tending to clear one suspect. So she grew cheerful again, and asked if it was true Miss Fay Fellows's necklace had been stolen.

"Bill was telling me about it," she said. "He's often seen it. He knows her quite well; she used to play at his table. I've only seen it on the pictures in *Rich Man's Baby*. Did you see that? Wasn't it just lovely? Coo-o," she said, forgetting for the moment all else in her memory of that glamorous dream. "Bill says seeing it on the pictures is nothing to seeing it when it's her own self wearing it. I wish I had."

"When was he telling you that?" Bobby asked carelessly.

"Just before we heard the shot and the man jumped over the wall," she answered. "Bill said there was a lot of funny talk going on about it."

"Gossip he had heard, perhaps?" Bobby hinted, but the girl evidently knew no more, and Bobby thought it as well not to attempt to press the point further at the moment, interesting though it seemed.

He contented himself with warning her not to attempt to communicate with Carton, told her that quite possibly neither of them would be required to give evidence, since what they had to say seemed to have little bearing either on the murder or the identity of the murderer. But of course that would depend on the course the investigation took, and certainly they both would be required to make formal statements.

" I take it," he added, " you and Mr. Carton were sitting in the summer-house for shelter and a quiet chat ? "

" That's right," she said. " It was such a beastly evening, and there's nowhere at home you can be quiet, and at the pictures you can't as much as whisper a word to each other now without people calling 'Hush.' We'd been there before. Bill told me about it."

" How did he happen to know ? " Bobby asked, since he thought it odd that a man who was employed at Monte Carlo in the winter, and Cliftonville in the summer, should know of empty residences and deserted summer-houses in Brush Hill.

Miss Irene at first protested she had no idea. Bobby reminded her that the police know everything and find out everything, as witness his knowledge of how she had come to catch such a bad cold. Much impressed, Irene sneezed several times, and then admitted that Mr. Carton not only helped his aunt with her private boarding-house, but also sometimes got temporary jobs as croupier at private parties in London.

" Bill says," she explained, " you can count on the fingers of one hand the people in England who can be croupiers in a fast game and not get most awfully tied up. Bill says you have to know the job from A to Z to be sure the right people get their money and the table gets its. Bill says you wouldn't believe the way some of them try it on. And he says he doesn't know even one man in England who would stand a chance of getting a job at the ' box '—that's the casino," she explained. " It's ever such a lovely place really, like a picture palace or a Lyons Corner House, but they call it the ' box.' When the swells here—real tip-top swells, too, or Bill wouldn't touch it—are getting up a big do, they are glad to have any one like Bill—beg and pray him, they do. Of course, it's all for charity, and he doesn't ask for a fee; only just a cheque afterwards for his expenses and his trouble and time."

" Does that happen often ? " Bobby asked.

" It just depends," she answered, " only now it's not so often big affairs for charity as small private parties. It was one of the big charity do's when he came across the summer-house. They had the do in that big empty house where the summer-house is—the only do there's ever been in Brush Hill. Bill went out at supper-time in the garden for a little fresh air, and he saw the summer-house and remembered it."

" And thought how handy it would be, eh ? " said Bobby, laughing, and Irene blushed, and Bobby asked one or two more questions, though without getting any further information.

The girl seemed to have told him all she knew, and he thanked her again, and, as he was going, asked her how she liked her work, and wasn't it difficult to get rid of bits of hairs after she had been trimming or combing customers' locks, and she said earnestly that it wasn't difficult; it was impossible.

" Bits get everywhere," she said. " I've come home and had a bath and changed all my things, and gone out, and then I've pulled off my gloves and they've been full of bits of hair, or else it's my handkerchief. They—cling," she said. " It's awful."

Bobby sympathised and departed, and from the nearest call-box rang up the Yard and suggested that it might be as well to try to get in touch with Mr. William Carton as soon as possible, if only to find out if his account of the happenings on Saturday night agreed with that given by Miss Irene.

Scotland Yard promised to take action accordingly, grumbled that there were enough suspects on the list already without having to add another, and remarked pessimistically that, anyhow, the stories of Miss Irene and Mr. Carton were sure to agree, because, if their stories were true, coincidence would be natural, and, if false, then co-incidence would be even more certain and settled.

" Better come along and report more fully in person," the Yard concluded.

Bobby, not altogether displeased at this order, for the rain that had been threatening all day was now coming down heavily, made accordingly for the tube station. Alighting at Westminster Bridge station, he walked along the Embankment to headquarters, and met Charley Dickson, who greeted him with a nod.

" Just been round to see your people," he said. " Remembered something I thought they ought to know. They didn't think much of it."

" What is it ? " Bobby asked. " Anything special ? "

" No, only I heard a rumour that a racecourse gang thought T. T. had the necklace, and were planning to repeat your furniture-van stunt with the same firm, Brown & Co., of Crust Lane, in the City, so as to raid T. T.'s place and get the necklace for themselves."

" Funny yarn," said Bobby. " Very funny," he repeated doubtfully.

" That's what your people seemed to think," Charley said, laughing. " Anyhow, I thought they ought to know."

" Yes," agreed Bobby. " Yes. Funniest yarn I've heard for a long time."

Charley was chuckling to himself.

" Quite by accident," he said, " I happened to hear it was the Crust Lane people you went to for your van that night. Of course, I'll keep it to myself if it's a secret."

" Not a secret exactly," Bobby explained; " it's just a

standing order not to give names. Different when people know."

He was wondering to himself, though, how Charley had got hold of the name of a firm with whom, indeed, there had been official dealings in the past, but who, in fact, had not supplied the special van used in the abortive raid on T. T.'s place. And why were so many different people so interested in identifying the owners of the van ? A vague, improbable answer to that question began to form itself vaguely at the back of his mind.

" One up to me, eh ? " Charley went on, watching Bobby closely. " Fluke, of course, but I felt quite bucked to think I had twigged a police secret."

Bobby smiled amiably, and felt quite sure now that all this meant that Charley was trying to get confirmation of his guess. Evidently he wanted very much to know if he had hit upon the right firm, and Bobby had no intention of telling him. To change the subject, he said :

" I see you've got your raincoat back."

" Bit of luck," agreed Charley. " Left it in a 'bus."

" Oh, well," Bobby said, " pretty sure to be all right if it's a 'bus or tram—then it nearly always turns up at Baker Street."

" This was a chap," explained Charley hurriedly, " who had picked it up himself, only he saw my name on it so he fetched it round."

" Good of him," said Bobby. " Luckier still, that was. Chaps who pick things up in buses and keep them, generally keep them for themselves. Was your address on it, too ? "

" Oh, that was on a letter in one of the pockets," Charley answered.

" Luck again," said Bobby, and was going on to ask some more questions, when Charley uttered a sudden cry :

" Why, there's old Logan. Excuse me, I must speak to him."

He rushed off at full speed, apparently pursuing someone into the tube station, and still more thoughtfully Bobby looked after him and walked on to the Yard, where a colleague also engaged on the case said to him beamingly:

" We've pulled in Wynne. Not so bad. He was hanging round West's, the big furniture removal people, trying to get a job apparently."

" Furniture removing ? " asked Bobby incredulously. " Can't imagine Wynne shifting sideboards and pianos, can you ? "

" Oh, just a dodge to help him lie low," answered the other. " Luckily the foreman spotted him from the photo in the *Morning Announcer* and rang us, so we brought him in. Good enough to take into court, I say."

" Well, I don't know," answered Bobby, " but I've got something that, if it's confirmed, seems to clear him of the murder. Of course, he may have the necklace still."

It was Ulyett's opinion, too, when Bobby made his report, that this new evidence seemed at any rate to clear Wynne of the murder.

" If it's like that, we shall have to let him go," the super-intendent said grumblingly, " and like as not he's got the necklace tucked away somewhere, waiting a chance to get rid of it. Wait months, some of these fellows. Anyhow, we shall want him as a witness, so we'll have an excuse for keeping an eye on him. He tells the same tale as T. T. to explain why he was at The Towers. And, of course, swears he never heard of the Fellows necklace, or of Miss Fellows even; says he never goes to the pictures unless it's Shirley Temple. Says she's the sweetest, loveliest kid ever, and seeing her braces him up a treat."

" Does it, though ? " murmured Bobby, interested in this vision of Percy Augustus Wynne, Count de Teirney, etc., returning from watching that sweet child, refreshed and invigorated, to his daily task of finding mugs to swindle.

" Doesn't help us much, though," Ulyett went on, " if we can wash out Wynne as a suspect only to put this Carton bird on the list instead. Carton was on the spot, he has a small automatic, he knew about the necklace, he had heard gossip about it; nothing to show he didn't nip over the wall, do the job, out Jessop, grab the necklace, and off with it. If it's like that, the girl was put there to establish an alibi. Not far off being a case, and it would mean he's got the necklace all the time."

" Yes, sir," agreed Bobby, " only there seems no direct evidence against him."

" We'll see what he has to say for himself," Ulyett remarked. " It oughtn't to be long before he's brought in. The Bloomsbury people thought he would be back there about now."

" Half the crooks and night-clubs in Soho seem to have known T. T. had something big on Saturday night," Bobby remarked. " If Mr. Jessop had heard the gossip, too, perhaps he went to T. T.'s to recover the necklace, not to dispose of it. And if he took someone with him as a kind of bodyguard, then that someone may be the man we want."

" No good guessing," answered Ulyett. " We want facts. Precious few we've got, too."

Bobby said nothing, though to himself he thought there was no shortage of facts; the difficulty was to fit their multitude into some kind of possible pattern. Ulyett went on:

" Another thing. There's no doubt Wynne was boasting early last week about the big job he had pulled off. But apparently it was only on Saturday Jessop got suspicious. If Wynne's ' big job ' meant the Fellows necklace, why did Jessop only show himself uneasy on the Saturday ? Surely the necklace would be a thing missed at once ? "

" Perhaps Wynne only actually secured possession on

Saturday," suggested Bobby. " Before he was only boasting about what he hoped to pull off."

" His sort can generally keep their mouths shut till the job's done," Ulyett remarked. " And they generally keep sober till then, too. Our report says Wynne was badly soaked the night before—Friday night—and only got up about the time Jessop rang us with his yarn. Another thing; young Chenery seems to have vanished."

" Chenery ? Denis Chenery ? "

" Yes. I wanted to know what he had to say about his visit to Miss May's flat Dickson mentioned and you reported. Well, now he's missing. Gone off in a hurry and left no address. Perhaps," said Ulyett gloomily, " he got the necklace Sunday night and has cleared off to the Continent with it. Nothing said to the Customs about keeping a look-out for him."

CHAPTER XX

IDENTIFICATION OF A DUKE

Bᴏʙʙʏ ᴡᴀs sᴛɪʟʟ ʙᴜsʏ writing out his formal report of the day's activities when a message came that he was wanted by Ulyett.

" It's that bird you rang up about," explained the colleague who brought the message. " He's just been brought in. The super thinks, as you dug him up, you had better be there to hear what he has to say, and see how he checks with his young woman."

Bobby, therefore, was ensconced at a side-table, with note-book and pencil all complete, when presently Carton was ushered into the room. He was a neat, dapper, loquacious little man, the pallor of the casino at Monte Carlo overlaid by Margate tan, and was evidently somewhat alarmed by this sudden and imperious demand for his presence at police headquarters.

He showed himself self-possessed, however, and, though Ulyett adopted at first a stern, official tone, he remained calm enough, answering readily and apparently frankly all the questions put to him.

To Ulyett's reproaches, he replied by expressing his great regret at what he now understood was held to be a serious failure in his duty as a citizen in not coming forward earlier and of his own initiative. But he protested he had not thought that what he had to say could possibly be of any assistance or value. The man he and Miss Irene had watched jumping over the garden wall could not possibly

Nᴊ

have fired the shot they had heard. There had not been a sufficient interval of time. But he was sure he could recognise him again. Croupiers were trained to remember faces. On being shown a number of photographs, he picked out Wynne at once.

"He stood still to light a cigarette," Carton explained. "The match showed his face plainly."

Ulyett went on with his questioning, and presently it appeared that the chief reason why Carton had not come forward earlier was that he had not wanted his Cliftonville aunt to know that he had been in Irene's company that evening.

"My aunt," he explained, "is growing old; she has saved money; she may soon wish to retire." He smiled faintly and apologetically. "I suggest it sometimes—oh, sympathetically, of course. She has a good connection; there are possibilities; in my opinion, there is a good thing there. After all, one does not live in France without picking up ideas on hotel-keeping. Well, if she retires, it is possible she may sell out to me at—well, at a nephew's price. But she does not approve of Irene. She has other ideas for me. They are not mine. Once the business is transferred, once it is in my name, then O.K., eh? I get married. But till then one has to be prudent. You understand?"

Ulyett grumbled, and said private interests must not be allowed to clash with public duty. He continued his questions, emphasising his desire to know what information Carton had possessed concerning the Fellows necklace and what exactly he had recently heard concerning it.

"Only gossip; only that Miss Fellows was selling it, and what a haul it would be for anyone to get hold of," protested Carton. "It was only chaff and chatter, mostly at a club I belong to—the Cut and Come Again. It is very well conducted—your rules! One eye always on the clock. At five to, all O.K.; at five past, fine and prison. Curious.

Formidable. I am English, and England is my country; one can live here; here there is money and security. Even the Communists love their neighbours and would not hurt a fly. But it is so like a school for very little children. Rules, regulations, discipline, one does what one is told —no, one does what one tells oneself one ought to do. In France at least one has liberty, one is considered to be grown up and responsible for one's own behaviour. They think there I make fun of them if I say that, should a woman run short of coffee for breakfast, and run out after a certain hour to buy it, then she risks being sent to prison. I tell them, England to make money, France to spend it."

Carton was quite shrewd enough, too, to realise very soon the drift of Ulyett's questions.

"You suspect me?" he said presently. "You think perhaps I left the summer-house, climbed the wall, committed the murder, stole the necklace, returned to Irene? No, no. It is true I talked to Irene about the necklace, and of the gossip I had heard. I even said I suspected there were plans to steal it. Not my affair. Also, a plan is one thing, performance is another. At Monte there are plans innumerable to rob the tables. But they are not performed. I had no idea theft had actually been carried out. I never dreamed there was any connection with the house next door to the garden where Irene and I met sometimes. We only went to the summer-house for shelter, and I never left it till we went away again afterwards. I cannot prove that, I suppose, for, though Irene will tell you the same, you will say that perhaps we had arranged our story before between us. But equally you cannot prove anything against me, for there is nothing to prove."

"I am not saying there is, Mr. Carton," answered Ulyett, "but you were on the spot; you've kept quiet about what you knew; you agree you did know something about the necklace. We're bound to investigate. Have you a pistol ? "

" Certainly not," Carton replied with emphasis.

" Our information," said Ulyett, " is that you have been seen in possession of one."

" I do not know who told you that," Carton answered slowly, " but it is a lie. I have no pistol, and I've never had one."

Ulyett pressed him on the point, but he persisted in denying that he had ever been in possession of a pistol, or, therefore, shown such a thing to anybody, and Ulyett turned to another point.

" How did you happen to know about this summer-house place ? " he asked. " You don't live in Brush Hill."

" No," agreed Carton, " but, after all, in my profession I am known, I am expert. It is not so easy as all that to become a croupier of the first rank. It needs a training; practice, too. When I return to Monte, I have always to take a refresher course—a week or longer in the school—so that they may satisfy themselves I have not gone stale. So if it happens that here a nice little party is arranged, one is often glad to call me in. Naturally, as it is England, such a nice little party is always for charity—after all, in spite of all the rules in England one can do anything if it is for charity."

" Not anything," protested Ulyett, a little hurt. " There are limits."

" I have not noticed them," said Carton seriously. " One can go with a box for money from door to door and it is O.K. if it is just a little for charity and much for—for expenses. So at the parties here I never receive a fee, only a cheque for expenses. I do not mind, for expenses are bigger than a fee. At this party I tell you of, the play was high and fast—higher and faster even than I am used to, and I am no novice. It was one August, and it happened to be fine and warm that evening. It was England, but there was no rain at all. In an interval I went outside to refresh myself in the open air in the garden, and I found the summer-house. It occurred to me at once—well, there it is; Irene's family is large and their house is small. You understand ? "

" Trespassing," observed Ulyett. " Never mind that. Been to many of these parties lately ? "

Carton shook his head.

" There was a certain unpleasantness at one," he explained. " At Monte it happens, too, but there it can be dealt with. Here it became a scandal. In England, a scandal, that is serious. In France, it would be merely a sensation. A sensation is forgotten when it ceases to be a sensation. A scandal remains. So now, for the big parties—finished. The little ones remain. They are more intimate, *chic*, select. But for me less useful. They do not care to pay so large—expenses. The play is not so fast; even an amateur can deal with it. So I go more rarely. Sometimes, it is true, but not often. When there are not to be more than twenty or thirty present, the expert is not so necessary. An amateur can manage—perhaps."

Ulyett pressed for more details, but Carton was reluctant to give them. He suggested that such questions seemed to have little bearing on the investigation of the murder, and Ulyett retorted that that was by no means certain.

" Here's one point," Ulyett said. " Did you ever see Mr. Jessop at any of these affairs ? "

" That I cannot say," Carton answered. " I am not introduced to the guests. I do not know their names unless I happen to hear them. Their faces, yes; those I know. I remember faces. It is part of our profession, part of our training; one must recognise again those who previously have been incorrect." He smiled. " Once I recognised in a personage of the highest rank one of the guests at parties where I had officiated. But I will not give his name. No. Nor will you ask it, for these little affairs are entirely correct.

On that I have informed myself. I paid even, so as to be sure. A lawyer. He put it in writing. It is perfectly correct so long as it remains private, select, *chic*. That is the English common sense. A thing may be quite wrong when it is done coarsely, brutally perhaps, by poor, ignorant people, and quite correct and lawful when it is done with *chic*, with style, by those who understand how to behave. No strangers must be admitted, nothing to eat or drink must be sold. Naturally, it is there. Champagne, whisky, sandwiches, but one does not pay. Also, the play is perfectly O.K. For that I answer with my professional reputation."

" Glad to hear it," said Ulyett. " Who was the swell you say you recognised ? "

" Oh, for that, excuse me. One has one's discretions."

" That's all right," said Ulyett. " Quite all right. Never mind it then. Now——" He produced more photographs, handfuls of them. " We want to know if Mr. Jessop played. It may be a great help to know that. Do you recognise his picture among these ? "

Carton picked it out at once.

" A gentleman who played high, a gentleman it was a pleasure to see at one's table," he said. " But he was not lucky. A courageous player, not a great one. He was obstinate. When the really gifted player finds he is not in the vein, he stops. This gentleman continued."

Ulyett produced some more photographs, none of which Carton knew. But when one of the Duke of Westhaven was put before him, he looked for once a little startled. Then he shook his head with much—too much—vigour.

" Another I have never seen," he said.

" Lying, aren't you ? " asked Ulyett. " Looks bad, lying to the police. No good either. Odds are, we know. That's the Duke of Westhaven, and we have information——"

He left the sentence unfinished, the information not specified, and Carton shrugged his shoulders.

" Oh, well," he said, " if you know ! After all, there is no harm. It is inside the law. But it was not a lie. I do not lie —never. It was professional etiquette. I knew him as Mr. West. It was the name he gave always. I ascertained that. For one day it happened that I saw him in public and I recognised him. A duke. It is something, a duke. Also he is enormously rich, since others have built houses on his land that before was only sand-heaps. But his play—oh, miserable, paltry, of an inconceivable triviality. He would go pale to see the sums the plucky Mr. Jessop risked. It was as though he could not bear it, though the money was not his."

" Mr. West, eh ? Got to remember that," grunted Ulyett.

Then he produced a photograph of Denis Chenery. Carton recognised it, but did not think Denis played much, unless it was at the card-tables.

" With them I have nothing to do," Carton explained with a slight air of contempt. " The little ball runs true, but with cards——" And an expressive shrug of the shoulders concluded the sentence.

Yet another photograph, this time of Charley Dickson, he failed to recognise, and then he was allowed to go, though told he would presently be asked to read over and sign the statement he had just made.

" And that," said Carton resignedly, " puts the hat on my chance of getting the boarding-house of my aunt at a nephew's price."

But Ulyett promised they would do their best to keep any mention of Miss Irene's name becoming public, and so Carton departed, a trifle consoled.

CHAPTER XXI

DISCREPANCY

WHEN CARTON HAD GONE and they were alone together, Ulyett turned doubtfully to Bobby.

" He tells a good straight story," he said, " only for one thing—notice it ? "

" About the pistol ? " Bobby asked.

" Yes. You are sure the girl said he showed it to her ? You said so in your report, didn't you ? "

" Yes, sir," answered Bobby. " I'm quite clear about that."

" Have to look into it," Ulyett repeated. " Wouldn't be the first time what looked like a good, straight, convincing yarn slipped up on some little detail."

" Might be some explanation, sir, I suppose," suggested Bobby.

" Have to look into it," repeated Ulyett. " Check up on his Monte record, too. Mustn't tell them there we suspect him, though, because we don't—yet. Have to put it we want him as a witness and is he trustworthy ? The Clifton-ville end as well. Anyhow, Carton's cleared up one point for us. His story explains how the duke knew Jessop played high."

" Yes, sir," agreed Bobby, " and it may explain, too, where the duke was himself Saturday night, and why he couldn't be found, and why he won't say."

" At one of these private gambling shows, you mean ? "

Ulyett said. " And doesn't want it known. Disapproves of gambling, doesn't he ? "

" Yes, sir. Sponsored that last Anti-Betting Bill," answered Bobby. " It looks as if he is so fascinated by gambling he can't leave it alone; can't quite keep away, though he is too afraid of losing to play much himself. And he tries to even up afterwards by denouncing it."

" Queer tangled-up minds people have, haven't they ? " mused Ulyett. " Now we shall have a nice little job of work trying to dig up what special show his dukeship honoured Saturday night. They keep that sort of thing as dark as possible, though. Lie like fun if there's any inquiry. Quite likely his identity wasn't known either—just went as Mr. West perhaps. You had better have another chat with him, Owen, and see what you can fish out."

" Very good, sir," said Bobby, with an entirely deceptive air of brisk and willing obedience. But desperately, wildly, he searched his mind for some means of evading, dodging, and avoiding, though, of course, with entire propriety, the direct order just received—a difficult feat, certainly, but one in which some juniors achieve, by a kind of innate gift, a very high degree of technical perfection. He said : " If I might make a suggestion, sir, I think the duke is a bit touchy. Didn't quite like it, I thought, that only a sergeant had come to see him. Felt a duke deserved more than a sergeant; felt he didn't care to talk freely to such a very junior rank. I do feel very strongly, sir, that an officer holding really high rank would have a much better chance of success. Someone really important," suggested Bobby negligently. " More on his own level, sir, so to say."

Ulyett looked coldly at Bobby.

" The work of the department can't be messed about just to suit a duke's whims," he said with severity.

" No, sir," agreed Bobby, shocked. " Of course not, sir. Er—or perhaps the Assist. Commish. himself. He could make it a kind of friendly call. So much better, don't you think, sir, if with a touchy gentleman like the duke any inquiry can be kept on a sort of social footing ? "

" Hu-mm, er-r, ah-h," said Ulyett, less coldly this time. A faint movement became perceptible at the corners of his mouth—not a smile; nothing like a smile; just a movement. " I'll put it to him," he said.

" Then I will wait further instructions, sir ? " Bobby asked, and Ulyett nodded.

" Better see Wynne again now," he said. " Got to let him go, I suppose, for the time anyhow, but we'll give him a flea in the ear to take away with him."

Wynne was duly summoned, and, being asked first why he had described himself at the Cut and Come Again as the Count de Teirney, replied with unblushing impudence that the title had been bestowed upon him by the Tsarist Government as a reward for important secret services rendered during the Great War.

" Lie," said Ulyett dispassionately. " What have you done with the Fellows necklace ? "

" Super," said Wynne earnestly, " I won't deceive you. I've made up my mind. A clean breast of it, super, that's me."

" Well ? " said Ulyett, though with no great enthusiasm.

" Super," said Wynne, still more earnestly, " the simple truth is—I've never set eyes on the thing in my life, and never so much as heard of it till now."

Ulyett scowled.

" You mean you have it tucked away somewhere and you think you'll get away with it presently," he said. " Now, Wynne, my lad, you listen to me. We're on you. Mind that. We'll tail you day and night. Once a week, or oftener, we'll find an excuse—easy enough with your record—to bring you in. There won't be a job done in all England but we'll find cause to suspect you. Better come clean, my lad. Play the game with us and we'll play it with you. Turn the necklace up and we'll let you down as lightly as we can. If you don't, I'll see your life isn't worth living. Don't bother to tell me any more lies, but think it over. Kick him out now, Owen."

" Brutality of the police," sighed Wynne. " I'll write to the *Daily Worker* about you, you see if I don't. And me just turning over a new leaf and starting out in straight business to lead an honest life henceforth for evermore."

Ulyett had turned to his papers again, but this was too much for him.

" You ? " he repeated, quite bewildered. " You in straight business ? You—an honest life ? "

" That's right," said Wynne virtuously. " No more crooked work for me. I'm changing. Honest and respectable from now on. That's me. It pays best. Furniture removing —Birmingham. Nice little business there a cousin of mine runs, and he's offered to let me in if I like it and put up some money. But he says I must get some experience first— take a job for three months and get to know the ropes. Seems hard to get a job, though, when you've no experience. Could you give me a reference to some firm you know or deal with here ? Honest, sober, industrious, trustworthy— that sort of thing. Duty of the police to help an old con. make a fresh start. What about it, super ? "

Ulyett stared at him and then made a gesture to Bobby, who touched Wynne gently on the shoulder.

" I don't want to obey orders literally," he said, with a significant gesture of his foot, " but it would be a plea- sure——"

" All right, all right, I'll go," said Wynne, with some haste. At the door he said : " Don't mind, do you, if I ask some of the others for a ref ?   Oh, all right."

He disappeared, and a moment later opened the door again that he had slammed behind him in Bobby's face.

"Super," he said, "I only wish I did know where the damn' thing is."

With that he vanished again, and Bobby, from the doorway, watched him pass down the corridor in the company of the waiting officer whose duty it was to see him safely outside.

To Bobby, Ulyett said:

"Tough lad! Cheek and impudence enough to set up a boat-load of monkeys and then some. He's got the necklace all right."

"Yes, sir," responded Bobby as usual.

"Furniture-removing business indeed," growled Ulyett. "Trying to pull our leg about Saturday."

"Yes, sir," agreed Bobby, more heartily this time. "It reminds me, I met Mr. Dickson just now. He had some wild yarn about a racecourse gang planning to raid T. T.'s for the necklace they think he has hidden at his place."

"Lot of rubbish," growled Ulyett. "T. T.'s place was gone over with a comb, and he wouldn't keep it there, anyhow, when he knows we are watching and might raid him again any moment. Dickson has just been listening to gossip. Of course, he was quite right to come and tell us."

"Yes, sir," agreed Bobby automatically. "Someone had been pulling Dickson's leg—told him a firm in Crust Lane, in the City, was where we got the van from on Saturday."

"Find out who it was and tell him off," said Ulyett. "Leg-pulling's not allowed in Government time."

"Yes, sir," said Bobby as usual, and retired, though his efforts to find out who had been misleading Dickson were without success. The offence was hardly grave, but no one would admit to it, and so Bobby turned his attention to his formal report. That finished, he signed off, and returned home for supper and bed in such a mood of abstraction and deep thought he as nearly as possible got himself run

over by an enormous furniture van making a stately progress through the streets at about four miles an hour.

" Nothing but furniture vans, furniture vans, all the way,
just now," complained Bobby, and the driver was, naturally
enough, most indignant.

" Ain't we big enough and slow enough for a blind cripple
paralysed from birth to keep out of our way ? " he
demanded, and Bobby agreed, and apologised, explaining,
in doing so, that sometimes it was the big things and the
slow that were the most difficult to see. Whereon the driver
expressed an opinion that Bobby was balmy, and Bobby
said anyhow he had cause to be, and so went still more
thoughtfully upon his way.

All that remained of the evening he spent in meditation
and the consumption of tobacco. Next morning, reporting
for duty, he found instructions waiting him to interview
Miss May, stated now to be in a condition to receive visitors.

" Funny lot at that hospital," complained Inspector
Ferris. "Talk as if a bit of a tap on the head was something
nobody had ever hardly seen before. A Dr. Perkins rang
up to say the patient is not to be pressed in any way or
questioned closely, and there's to be no formal statement
taken—too exciting. Strongly recommended that the person interviewing her should be tactful and not a complete
stranger, if possible. Suppose they think we're full up with
all her old friends. And if we don't do just what they say,
they won't be answerable for the consequences. Seem to
think we may drive her off her head. So the super says
you had better take the job on—not," added Ferris sternly,
" on account of tact, which the Duke of Westhaven doesn't
seem to think you've much of, to judge from what we're
hearing confidential like. But, seeing as it was you found
her inside the cupboard, you ought to be like old friends
almost. And mind," concluded Ferris, " you wash your
face and curl your hair first—and don't forget to powder

your nose. Better put on your old school tie, too, if you've got one, or even if you haven't. A good first impression goes a long way with the feminine sex. Why, if it wasn't for my moustache "—he touched it lovingly in all its waxed and pointed perfection—" why, but for that, I might be a free man to-day."

Bobby, having carried out these instructions to the best of his ability—though more in the spirit than in the letter—presented himself at the hospital, and was a little astonished to be told there that he had arrived only just in time, as Miss May was on the point of departure. She was, in fact, only waiting for the taxi she had ordered.

" But I thought," protested Bobby, " we were told— I mean, in a case of concussion . . ."

" Oh," said the nurse to whom he was speaking, " old Peter Perkins been talking to you ? He's got a concussion complex. Miss May had better keep quiet for a day or two still, and so I've told her, and, if she doesn't, she'll know it—dizzy, and pains in the head most likely. But she's practically all right if she's sensible, and three weeks in bed is only Perkins piffle. We can do with her bed, too. So when she insisted on taking her discharge, and threatened to scream the place down if we didn't bring her her clothes, and going to ring up her tame lawyers, too—well, Perkins's instructions or not, we caved in, and glad to. Perkins will rave a bit, and tell everyone he won't be answerable for the consequences; but, then, he never is. He's not answerable for more things than anyone else on the register."

" I can see her before she goes though, can't I ? " Bobby asked.

The nurse thought so, and promised to tell Miss May he was there. He was ushered into a small waiting-room accordingly, and was soon joined by Hilda, looking a little pale but otherwise not much the worse for her adventure.

CHAPTER XXII

HILDA MAY'S STORY

HILDA BEGAN by protesting that she knew nothing and
could tell nothing, though she consented to the taxi she
had ordered being used by someone else who had need of
one at the moment, so that her talk with Bobby might not
be troubled by thoughts of ticking up pennies.

She had been out on Sunday she said, and on her return
to her flat had noticed that the door was open an inch or
two. Her first impression was simply that the lock had failed
to catch. She remembered thinking she must be more careful, pushing the door more widely open, entering, and that
was all she knew, except for a vague, confused impression
of falling and of darkness. She had had no glimpse of her
assailant, and could not even offer a guess at his identity or
his purpose. The next thing she remembered was waking
up in hospital and wondering where she was. She had no
knowledge of her rescue from the lobby cupboard or of
her narrow escape from death by suffocation.

" Was there anything of value in the flat ? " Bobby asked.

" Some jewellery I have, and a little money, and my
post office savings book," she answered, " nothing else, and
I've asked, and they're all safe."

" Would you think it possible," Bobby asked, " that there
might be an idea about that Mr. Jessop had left the missing
Fellows necklace in your charge, and that was what the
thief was after ? "

" Good gracious, no ! Why should they ? " retorted

Hilda, with a very surprised air. " I'm sure Mr. Jessop would never have done anything of the sort." She began to look a little disturbed. " I don't see how anyone could have such an idea," she said.

" We are looking for some explanation," Bobby explained. " It doesn't seem an ordinary case of housebreaking. Your flat had been thoroughly ransacked, turned upside down. Something was being looked for, something badly wanted, and yet not your money or your jewellery."

She was looking very worried now. Her feet began to move in that strange, rhythmic manner that seemed her natural response to difficulty or to danger. She said slowly:

" Well, I don't see what it could be, unless someone did think I had the necklace, and I don't see why anyone should."

" Did you return to your flat because you were expecting Mr. Chenery ? " Bobby asked.

" Oh, no," she answered. " It was his Sunday at the garage—he owns a garage business. One Sunday in four he has to be there himself to let the foreman off."

" He is said to have been seen leaving the flats where you live about the time of the attack on you."

" Oh, that must be a mistake," she answered. " He wouldn't be able to get away."

But Bobby knew there was no mistake; inquiry had produced evidence confirming Charley Dickson's story.

" Do you mind," Bobby went on, " telling me if you are on friendly terms with Mr. Dickson ? "

" He's been making rather a nuisance of himself," she answered, flushing a little, " that's all."

" There's no ill feeling on your part at his having taken your post as secretary to the duchess ? "

" Gracious, no," she answered. " After the frantic row I had with her, of course I had to clear out in a hurry. We were nearly at the eye-scratching stage, I was so furious and so was she. I just bunged out as quick as I could, and the job was there for anyone to take—Mr. Dickson or anyone else. Nothing to do with me."

" I am sorry to ask you private questions," Bobby said, " but they are purely official, you understand. I gather both Mr. Dickson and Mr. Chenery would like to marry you. Is there any chance for either of them ? "

" I shall never marry anyone," declared Hilda with grave emphasis. " That is quite certain. Never." Having registered this unalterable decision, she permitted her solemnity to relax into a smile. " And I don't think Mr. Dickson really wants to," she added, " only I think he seems to feel he ought to make up somehow for having my job. Besides, he never has any money; he's always hard up."

" Or Mr. Chenery ? "

" That, of course, is entirely out of the question, after what the duchess said," explained Hilda with cold dignity.

" Thank you," said Bobby. " Have you any plans for the future ? "

" I shall have to get another job," she answered. " Why ? "

" You are leaving Jessop & Jacks ? " Bobby asked. " I don't think you told me that before, did you ? "

" The other night, you mean ? " she said. " No. Why ? There was no reason to, was there ? "

" I think it was rather important," he answered.

" Why ? You told me Mr. Jessop had been shot, and you asked for Mr. Jacks's address and I told you. I don't quite see what my leaving had to do with it."

" Was there any reason for your leaving ? "

She hesitated for a moment or two.

" Mr. Jessop's dead," she said. " I don't want to talk about it."

" I think I must ask you to be perfectly frank."

" Well, he was getting silly. If you are a girl," she said

OJ

moodily, " you may be in business, but you're a girl just the same and you jolly well can't help it. Some of them don't try, either."

" You mean—— ? "

" You soon get to know the signs," she said. " If you give them the letters to look at, they try to hold your hand. If you make a bloomer, they don't get raggy. Tease you about it instead. Theatre tickets for you and a friend they can't use themselves, and then presently they want to be the friend. Oh, it's quite a technique. You can hold them off for a time, but when it gets too hot, the only thing to do is to go before they turn nasty and you're reported for insubordination, or there's a discrepancy in the petty cash or something like that."

" Mr. Jessop was forcing attentions on you, and to avoid them you made up your mind to leave ? "

" Yes. Sounds silly and prudish, but it's just horrid when a man goes sloppy when you're working for him—especially if he's awfully old, like Mr. Jessop; over sixty. I just couldn't stick it. And it wasn't only that."

" Please go on," Bobby said. " You must remember there has been murder done. Any detail may give us the clue we want."

" I don't see that it can help, and I don't think I ought to now the poor man's dead so dreadfully. And then very likely there's nothing in it, and I was nervy and fancying things. The firm's been losing money for a long time—not so much in trading, but because of all the capital they have locked up. I think they over-bought before the slump set in. Mr. Jessop used to play cards a good deal, too, and I know he often lost a lot."

" We knew that," Bobby said. " Please go on."

" Very likely he never really meant it. He was only joking, perhaps. But I did think he had some idea about selling the Fellows necklace for more than Mr. Jacks or

Miss Fellows knew and keeping the extra for himself."

"Rather risky," Bobby suggested. "Might have got a stiff sentence."

"I thought," Hilda said uncomfortably, "he had an idea that if I helped him it could be done without breaking the law. Only I didn't want to help. It wasn't honest, really. It might have been legal, perhaps. I don't know. And he said no one could possibly find out. He said even if it was —found out, I mean—the only thing that could happen would be his having to leave the firm. And he wouldn't have minded that. They may have to close down soon anyhow."

"I should have thought," Bobby remarked, "they would be able to do a jolly sight more than asking him to get out. I think I should in their place."

"It's only what I—guessed," she continued; "he kept on hinting. I think he was trying to find out what I thought. It frightened me. He was never plain about it; only hints and little jokes. Miss Fellows put a reserve price of £50,000 on her necklace. I think Mr. Jessop was going to say there was a good offer of £55,000 and it had better be accepted. Only the purchaser didn't want his name known and I was to be a kind of dummy, a nominee, to act for him and to receive the necklace when the money was paid. We had Miss Fellows's written authority to accept anything over £50,000, and Mr. Jessop thought Mr. Jacks and Mr. Wright would agree."

"Was Mr. Wright's consent necessary ? I thought he was only the manager ? "

"He has money in the firm—a mortgage or something. I don't think he wanted to be a partner. If a smash came, he thought he would be better off as a creditor than being responsible for the debts. But they had to treat him as a partner because of the money he had put in the business. He might have drawn it out."

" Do you mean Mr. Jessop had a genuine offer of £55,000 ? "

" Yes. But he didn't want to sell on the firm's account, because then the commission due would have gone to the firm—really to the firm's creditors in the end. What I think is that really he had an offer for a very much larger sum—not £55,000, but £65,000."

Bobby gave a low whistle.

" I'm beginning to see," he said. " It might be worked like that. You mean his idea was that the firm was to sell to you, as nominee of someone else, for £55,000, and afterwards Jessop would have sold on his own for £65,000, pocketing the difference ? "

" He thought it would be quite legal to do it like that," Hilda remarked.

" I don't know," said Bobby doubtfully. " Of course, there's a lot of sharp practice you can get away with in Big Business. Jessop's dodge sounds a bit thick, though. Smart, of course."

" He said no one could ever know."

" Why not ? The necklace would turn up somewhere, and then the purchaser would be known."

" Mr. Jessop said not. I thought his idea seemed to be to say that the real purchaser had turned out to be another firm buying from us in order to sell to one of their own clients. Perhaps it wasn't that at all, and I'm just putting two and two together and making five. Anyhow, I didn't want to be mixed up in it, whatever it was."

" Didn't you say anything to Mr. Jacks or Mr. Wright ? "

" No, I couldn't. I didn't know anything really. I hadn't an atom of proof. Besides "—she hesitated—" I suppose I must tell you. Mr. Jessop got in first. He knew I was uncomfortable about the hints he kept dropping. And he saw I didn't mean to fall for his theatre tickets or his dinners, or hold hands." She hesitated again, and went redder still.

" They gave me a very good reference, so there was nothing I could do, but he told both Mr. Jacks and Mr. Wright I wasn't trustworthy."

" Did they say anything to you ? "

" Oh, no. I only knew through Miss Ellison, one of the girls there I was rather pals with. She heard them talking. You see, it was my job to go out at night wearing the firm's jewellery. He told them he had information I was planning to be run away with or kidnapped or something. If I had started accusing him after he had been accusing me—well, it wouldn't have looked too good. And Denis said I must be careful or I might be let in for an action for slander or libel."

" Denis ? Mr. Chenery ? You told him ? "

" I had to tell someone," she said. " I just had to. When you came Saturday night, I think we were both afraid for the moment Mr. Jessop had really said I was stealing things, and you meant to arrest me. I suppose it was rather silly."

Bobby supposed that explained the sense of strain and unease of which he had been aware in both Hilda and Denis that night. He said slowly :

" I dare say Mr. Chenery was very indignant ? "

" Oh, he was furious," she answered. " He wanted to go straight off. He said——"

" Yes ? " prompted Bobby, when she paused.

" Oh, just talk," she answered evasively.

" Threats ? " Bobby asked.

" Oh, in a sort of way. Just for a minute, I was almost afraid." She added slowly : " If you think Denis had any-thing to do with—with the murder—well, he hadn't ; he couldn't have. Just for one moment after you told me about it, I panicked. But then I remembered he couldn't."

" Why ? "

" I was with him all afternoon and evening."

" Could you tell me exactly where ? "

" In his car—he has a garage business, you know. It's a

dreadful struggle to keep it going, but at any rate he always has a car to use."

" Did you call anywhere ? See friends, for instance ? "

" No, we only went for a drive—in the country somewhere. I don't know exactly where."

" Wasn't quite the weather for motoring, was it ? "

" It wasn't so bad when we started, and the paper said it would clear up. It didn't, but we thought we would risk it."

" You stopped somewhere for a meal ? "

" Oh, no. I always take something to eat. It's so much less expensive."

It seemed then, Bobby noted, that, so far as an alibi for Denis Chenery existed, it depended solely on Hilda's testimony. That did not disprove it, of course, but also was hardly conclusive.

" Mr. Chenery said rather violent things about Mr. Jessop," Bobby went on. " Was Mr. Chenery ever armed ? Did he carry a pistol, for instance ? "

" No, never. I'm quite sure of that."

" Mr. Dickson tells me he carries a pistol when he is in charge of the duchess's jewels, and he thinks you used to do the same."

" Oh, I never did," declared Hilda. " I hate the silly things. If you just touch them they go off very likely. I think they're dangerous," she said with grave emphasis.

" So they are," agreed Bobby. He was glancing through his notes, and now, looking up, he said : " There's one point. Have you any idea of the identity of the person for whom you were to act as nominee in the necklace business ? "

" No. Mr. Jessop hinted it was the duchess, but I knew that was nonsense. He was only saying that. She could no more have raised such a lot of money than—than I could."

" I see," said Bobby. " Has Mr. Wright been with the

firm long ? He seems rather rough to be a manager of a swell jeweller's."

" He is very clever with his hands and he knows a lot about jewels," she answered. " He knows their value at once. I didn't like him at all—he's an awful bully. He used to be a prize-fighter, you know. They said in the office he killed a man once when they were fighting. I don't know if it's true. He's really wonderful with his hands. I've seen him do things with a big pocket-knife he uses when anyone else would want all sorts of tools and things. He never had much to do with the selling end, so it didn't matter about his being such a boor. I never liked him, and he just hated me. I believe he really thought I was planning to run away with their beastly stuff."

" Do you mean after Mr. Jessop had been complaining about you ? "

" Before that. He was always suspecting someone. He's got mirrors fixed up so he can watch people without their knowing—the staff as well as customers. I think it's horrid. Of course, some of the customers aren't customers at all, only crooks. But he might trust the firm's own staff; some of them have been there all their lives. Almost the first week I was there I had an awful row with him because a ring was missed and he wanted me searched, and it turned out it had just dropped down in the showcase, if he had only looked before being in such a hurry to be horrid. He did apologise that time. But you always knew he was suspecting you all the time, and I think that's suspicious, too."

" Quite true," agreed Bobby. He began to look through his notes again. " Oh, yes," he said, " there's that I wanted to ask you. Can you say exactly when you saw the Fellows necklace last ? "

She shook her head.

" I'm not sure," she answered. " Not for some time, though. It was kept in the strong-room, and only the partners or Mr. Wright went there. And it was kept in a locked case and only taken out to show special people."

" One thing more," Bobby said. " Did Mr. Jessop seem odd or excited on Saturday? Did you notice anything unusual? "

" Something he saw in a copy of the *Upper Ten* upset him. He was looking at the photographs—it has splendid photographs—and suddenly he gave a sort of yell—not a yell, a sort of funny noise."

" Yes ? " said Bobby.

" I said, ' Oh, what is it ? ' I was quite startled, and he looked awfully funny, but he didn't answer; I don't think he heard. He let the paper drop, and then he picked it up and made a sort of run out of the room."

" Have you any idea what he was looking at ? Or what upset him ? "

" Not the least. I couldn't imagine."

" There was a copy of the *Upper Ten* in the room where he was shot," Bobby remarked thoughtfully. " I looked through it. I remember there was a photograph of the Duchess of Westhaven at the races."

" I don't see why that should upset him," Hilda said.

" I've wondered why till I'm stupid with thinking about it," Bobby said slowly. " You have heard there was a large sum in French and Swiss currency found in his flat. Have you any knowledge of any transaction to account for that ? "

" No. Mr. Wright might know. I don't. If it was in his flat, it would be something private, wouldn't it ? Nothing to do with the business."

" I suppose so " agreed Bobby. " Well, Miss May, thank you very much. You've given some very useful information I'm sure my chiefs will be grateful for."

With that Bobby closed his note-book and devoted himself to securing for her a taxi to take her back to her flat, where, however, he warned her she might find workmen still busy repairing her door.

When he had seen her off, he turned to the hospital porter.

" Pop-shop near here ? " he asked.

The porter looked highly amused.

" Hard up ? " he asked. " Looks bad so early in the week. Week-end natural enough, but at the beginning . . . !"

" That's all right," said Bobby good-humouredly. " I want to buy something this time. A watch."

" Oh, yes," said the porter, giving the required information but all the time looking hard at the watch on Bobby's wrist. " Out of order ? " he suggested.

" Oh, no," Bobby answered. " That's what I want—one that's a bit out of order and needs putting right. I thought a pop-shop would be likelier than a jeweller's."

The porter evidently thought this a good joke, and chuckled over it immensely.

CHAPTER XXIII

THE POCKET-KNIFE

His way back from the pawnbroker's, where he had somewhat astonished the assistant by his careful choice of a watch he was insistent must be out of order, but not too much so, brought Bobby again past the hospital, where talking to the porter was a young man he recognised at once.

" Why, Mr. Chenery," he said. " Luck to run across you like this. We've been trying to get in touch with you."

" I've been in the country," Denis said briefly. " On business. I heard you people had been asking for me. Look here, what's this about Miss May? I heard she was in hospital, but they say she's just gone out."

" She insisted on it," Bobby answered. " My chief wants to ask you about some pointers he thinks you might be able to give him. Do you mind coming along to the Yard now with me ? "

" I must see Miss May first. I want to know what's happened. Afterwards, if you like."

" Police business comes first, if you don't mind," Bobby said. " Delay's dangerous, you know, especially in our job."

There was a brief argument that for a moment grew heated—so heated, indeed, Bobby felt had it not been day, and help within call, the other's reluctance might have expressed itself more by deed than by word.

However, in the end Denis gave way.

" It's a lot of silly rot," he complained. " Just meddling, interfering official thick-headedness."

" Red tape, we call it," said Bobby amiably; " a strangling thing."

" Eh ? " exclaimed Denis, a little startled.

" A strangling thing, I said," Bobby answered. " Red tape, I mean. But there you are. Much as my job is worth to go back and say I met you and you promised to come along presently. Vacancy in the force after that. No need to worry about Miss May either. She'll be all right again in a day or two, and no thanks to whoever laid her out."

" Who was it ? " demanded Denis.

" Haven't an idea in the world—yet," answered Bobby. " There's a motor-'bus somewhere along this way we could take."

" Any objection to a taxi ? "

" Not the least in the world—if you stand it," answered Bobby. " Sergeant's pay don't run to taxis, and sergeants can't wangle taxi fares through expense lists. Only the big hats can do that."

" All right, I'll pay," grumbled Denis.

He hailed a passing taxi, and, once they were installed and the taxi on its way, he said :

" Now, tell me what's up about Miss May ? "

Bobby gave a brief account of what had happened, and asked Denis where he had been on Sunday. Denis explained that it was his day to be in charge at the garage, so as to give the foreman manager a day off, but added that he had left early to go into the country.

" On business," he said. " I had to ring up Wilks—the chap who helps runs the place. Had to promise him a quid extra to come on again. Lucky to find him at home."

" Odd time, Sunday evening, for important business to crop up," Bobby remarked.

" Well it just happened," Denis answered.

" Can you give me particulars ? "

" Don't see why I should. Nothing to do with you or Jessop's murder, or the Fellows necklace, either."

" What were your precise movements when you left the garage ? "

" Hopped into a car with a friend and left," answered Denis. " Why ? I tried to see Miss May first, if that's what you're getting at, but she wasn't in. I had an appointment with her for Monday I wanted to tell her I couldn't keep."

" You didn't see her, then ? Did you leave a message or anything ? "

" No. I thought I would ring her in the morning."

" I take it you found her door locked ? "

" Of course. She wouldn't be likely to leave it open while she was out."

Bobby pressed the point. But Denis was quite clear. The door of the flat was securely shut, and showed no trace of having been interfered with. It was impossible, Denis insisted, he could have failed to notice any signs of forcible entry had any then existed. But about the time he was not sure, not to half an hour one way or the other. He remembered having noticed Charley Dickson with a friend just outside the flats. He had wondered if Dickson, too, were calling on Miss May, but concluded, as he had a friend with him, that was probably not so. He denied having recognised the friend as " Penny " Logan, but admitted he knew Logan slightly, though he showed no sign of any special interest in, or animosity towards, that gentleman.

" I only noticed Dickson had someone with him," he said. " I was in a hurry. I didn't look particularly, and he was on the other side of Dickson. I dare say it was Logan. Does it matter ? "

Bobby said he didn't suppose so, but one never knew. He thought to himself that what did matter was that, so far as the somewhat vague times could be established, then if Dickson's story were true and his watch was accurate, it seemed to follow that Denis had preceded Bobby's call at Miss May's flat by not more than, at the outside, ten minutes. But certainly it must have taken more than ten minutes to force the door, search the flat, carry out the attack on Miss May, and depart. It followed, therefore, that on Dickson's evidence, corroborated to some extent by what Denis said himself, the door must have been in the same condition when Denis arrived as when Bobby himself got there.

It did not, however, seem to occur to Denis—or, if it did so, his manner showed no consciousness of the fact— that his admitted presence on the spot involved him in any suspicion.

" If nothing was taken," he now said thoughtfully, " does that mean the chap was interrupted ? "

" If so, why was no alarm given by whoever interrupted him ? " Bobby asked. " No one calling at the flat after it had been broken into could have failed to notice the door."

" Well, then, what was the idea; if there's nothing missing ? You don't break into places just for fun."

" No," agreed Bobby, " but I did not say nothing was missing. I said nothing we know of, or that Miss May has reported missing."

Denis stared at him, but made no immediate comment. By this time the taxi had reached the Yard, and when Denis had paid the man he turned to Bobby and said :

" You don't mean some fool thought Hilda had the necklace ? "

" We are looking for some explanation of what seems a meaningless sort of business at present," Bobby answered.

" I call it silly," Denis muttered, but without much conviction, and then was silent, as if beginning to be aware of dark waters of suspicion slowly rising about him on every side.

They entered the building together. Bobby reported their arrival, and, possibly as a reward for having brought Denis in, was allowed to be present at a lengthy examination that revealed nothing new, though Denis remained obstinate in his refusal to say what business had taken him out of London, or where he had gone.

" Isn't it wiser to answer questions ? " Ulyett asked in his mildest manner. " Of course, you don't have to."

" Then I won't."

" Leaves us guessing," murmured Ulyett, looking hard at the ceiling, as though guesses were registered there.

" Guess away," said Denis.

" Well, then, for a guess—just a friendly guess, you understand, by way of—well, guessing. Rather fun, guessing games, don't you think ? Miss May and you had it fixed up together to lift the Fellows necklace—she knew all about it, and you want money; got a position to keep up, and may have to file your petition any day almost. Your alibi for Saturday night depends on Miss May's word and her alibi on yours; cancels both out. Miss May took charge of the necklace. She argued it would be safer with her. You thought you would like it yourself; better a whole share than going halves. You had an idea she would be out. You forced the door of her flat, but she came back unexpectedly. You knocked her out, and your business on Sunday night was to put the necklace in a safe hiding-place. How's that for guessing ? "

Denis was on his feet now, breathing heavily. Bobby could quite believe, as he watched him, what had been said of the strength and sudden fury of his passions.

" I'd like," he stammered, " I'd like——"

" Yes, I know you would," said Ulyett amiably, " only you mustn't, you know. Taboo—that's the police. Besides, only guessing, and you asked for it. If people won't answer questions—well, got to guess, haven't we ? "

" I'll see my solicitors," Denis said, still breathing hard, " before I say another word."

" Right," said Ulyett. " Very sensible, too. Know where you are with solicitors. Oh, you won't be leaving London again just now, will you ? No ? That's all right, then. You'll let us know the name of your solicitors, will you ? Or ask them to write ? We shall want to ask them to advise you to make a statement in full—no gaps."

With that, Denis was allowed to depart, and Bobby, after he had turned in the report of his conversation with Hilda, went off to interview Mr. Wright, receiving permission to do so on the strength of some excuse he put forward, to the exact nature of which, fortunately, little attention was paid, since at the moment his own services were not required and in other directions there was much routine work to be got through.

Pleased at having got the permission he wanted without having had to explain in detail an idea his superiors might have thought a little far-fetched, Bobby went off to Mayfair Square and found Mr. Wright in a surly mood, and inclined to be rude to Bobby over the failure of the police to recover the missing necklace.

" Defence protection," murmured Bobby to himself, for he knew how important it is to be up to date with the latest discoveries, the newest thought, and how much more profound it seems to say " defence protection " than to be so hopelessly old-fashioned and behind the times as to quote the ancient saying that attack is the best defence.

" I don't care a hoot who shot Jessop," Wright declared frankly. " Old swine he was. But what's the good of the so-and-so police if they can't recover so-and-so stolen property ? "

" Must give us time," said Bobby amiably, though wondering at all the different adjectives Wright knew.

"And we have to care who did the murder. That comes first."

"It didn't ought," grumbled Wright. "Jessop's dead and done with, but the necklace is still there and still worth a packet—and we are still responsible. May do for the firm if we don't get it back."

"We'll do our best," Bobby promised. "There's one point I'd like to go over again. The first time it was shown the duchess you went to the Park Lane flat with Miss May, but you didn't actually see the duchess yourself, I think?"

"No. I told you. I waited in the entrance-hall. I didn't have much to do with the selling end. Not my job. Take it or leave it and get to hell out of here. That's my line. Jessop's was soap, and lots of it. Jacks the same. Makes me sick."

"The second time it was shown the duchess was at Hastley Court, I think? Some sort of garden-party on, wasn't there?"

"Yes. That's why she rang us up to come along that day, so we could slip in with the crowd. That was so the duke wouldn't be so likely to spot us."

"Had you any difficulty in getting in?"

"Good Lord, no. Wide open to all the world. You just drove up, parked your car in a roped-in enclosure behind the stables, and went and paid your respects to the duke and duchess—or, if you were gate-crashers like us, kept out of their way. I'll bet we weren't the only ones who had left their invitation cards at home. Of course, we kept out of it as much as we could. We waited in the car, in the car park, till she was ready to see us."

"How did you know when that was?"

"Her secretary fellow came along—chap called Dickson. He was long enough, too. I know I had time to finish my cigar."

"Hope it was a good one?"

" As good a smoke as ever I came across—an American gentleman, a Mr. Patterson, gave me a handful from his own factory. Sell at three or four bob each, I believe."

" Got any left ? " asked Bobby carelessly.

" No. Finished the last the other day. Wish I had more of the same sort."

" Perhaps you will find one you had forgotten," observed Bobby, and Wright didn't seem to like the suggestion, and scowled, and said that wasn't likely.

" You were with Mr. Jessop this time when he showed the necklace to the duchess ? "

" Yes. I hung on to it. All right at the flat, when I could sit in the entrance-hall and no other way out, but I wasn't parting with it in a crowd like that. All sorts there that day."

" Was the secretary, Mr. Dickson, present at the interview with the duchess ? "

" No. I never saw him the whole time. When we were waiting in the car, Jessop spotted him and hopped out to speak to him. Then Jessop came back and said the duchess was waiting for us. Dark little hole where she was, too; running no risks of the duke interrupting. Room off a passage leading straight from a side-entrance. She cooed over that necklace like a mother over her baby. No doubt about her wanting it if she could get the money and fix things with the duke."

" Had you ever seen the duchess before ? "

" Not to speak to; once or twice, perhaps, only at a distance. She wasn't a customer of ours; went to a Bond Street firm when she wanted to deal. She tried to get us to leave the necklace with her. Nothing doing. Jessop wanted to, but I stood out for a first cash payment and a written contract. If we had left it with her, it might have got lost or anything, and the duke could have repudiated responsibility. Not good enough. She got all in a twitter

P J

when I mentioned hubby. He wasn't to know anything about it on any account. Jessop was dead sure he had her hooked. I wasn't so sure. She was in too much of a funk about her old man for my liking. I was right, too. We heard nothing more, of course we might have in time. Jessop declared the wait meant nothing."

" There were no other negotiations ? "

" Not with her. Jessop showed it once or twice to other prospects. He said he hoped she would hear we were still offering it. Hurry her up, he thought. All the time he stuck to it she was hooked."

" I want to ask you something important, Mr. Wright," Bobby said. " Are you certain it was the duchess you saw ? "

" Good God ! " said Wright, startled. " Of course ! It was Hastley Court. Who else could it be ? You mean——? "

" We are trying to consider every possibility," Bobby said. " That's all."

" Yes, but, hang it all, it must have been her all right. You mean someone personated her ? But Jessop was there. He knew her. Anyhow, he had seen her before."

" You said it was a dark little cubby-hole, and there is such a thing as creating a resemblance by make-up."

" Yes, yes, but——" protested Wright, obviously disturbed. Then he brightened up. " What for ? " he asked. " She didn't get the necklace. You wouldn't have caught me parting except for cash or good security. And then we shouldn't have cared whether it was her or her cook."

" It was only an idea," Bobby said. " One has to think of everything. I don't say it would clear things up, even if we knew it wasn't the duchess you saw but someone impersonating her. The identity of the murderer, what Mr. Jessop was doing at Brush Hill, what's become of the necklace, who attacked Miss May and why, would all be as big puzzles as ever. Had you heard of the attack on Miss May ? ”

“ Yes. Jacks and I were at the Yard, you remember. You told us to go round to report the necklace was missing.”

“ Oh, yes,” agreed Bobby. “ Funny business about Miss May—no motive, apparently; nothing missing. Thanks very much for what you’ve told me. It must be getting late.” He took a watch from his pocket—his own he usually wore on his wrist he had left in his desk at the Yard. “ Oh, I forgot,” he said; “ it’s not going. Fellow I took it to said it was worn out. Is it, do you think ? ”

He had opened the case, and as he spoke he handed the watch to Wright. The manager looked at it, smiled, took out a big penknife, and on the point of a small blade extracted a piece of fluff.

“ That’s about all that’s wrong with it,” he said.

“ Thanks awfully,” said Bobby. “ I say, what a jolly knife. May I look ? ”

Mr. Wright handed it over quite willingly.

“ Old friend of mine,” he said. “ Don’t forget to give it me back. I showed it to a fellow the other day—Denis Chenery his name is—and he put it in his pocket and went off with it. I only got it back this morning. Excuse me. I think I’m wanted.”

He hurried off, and Bobby, despite the warning received, put the knife in his pocket and went slowly away, thinking deeply.

“ Another problem,” he muttered to himself. “ Why did Wright think he was wanted just then ? Or is that not a problem, but an answer ? ”

CHAPTER XXIV

THE PISTOL TRACED

IT WAS NOT LONG AFTER the submission of Mr. Wright's penknife to the experts before back came a reply identifying with a tiny notch found on the bigger blade the fragment of steel picked up near the forced door of Hilda May's flat.

" So that's that," said Ulyett, " and one thing established. Important, too. Oh, by the way, Owen," he added, " there's a report in from Brush Hill, too. The young chap seen in West Lane there on Saturday, and who disappeared into one of the houses—the pub, I should say—is not the fellow the Brush Hill man thought. That particular chap was seen at the time hanging about a public hall some distance off, where there was to be a Fascist meeting later on. But I don't see it amounts to much, anyway, unless there's some way of identifying the other bloke. And that doesn't seem possible now."

" No, sir," agreed Bobby. " Of course, you never know what turns up in these cases."

" Red herrings, chiefly," growled Ulyett, and passed on his way, for this brief colloquy had taken place in a corridor when Ulyett was passing and had chanced to see Bobby talking to Lawson, the man who, attired in a green baize apron, sat on the tail-board of the van used in the abortive raid on The Towers. Over his shoulder, as he was going, Ulyett said : " Lawson told you about Chenery, I suppose ? "

That was indeed the news Lawson had been eager to impart, for his special share in the investigation had been to help in the tracing of the pistol found near Jessop, and now he had succeeded in proving that it had belonged to Denis Chenery.

" Had a licence for it, too, all as proper and regular as you like," Lawson went on to Bobby. " Got it three years ago when he was managing a small garage in an out-of-the-way spot where there was a gang in the district that had gone on from poaching to car-pinching and highway robbery. Good enough, eh ? "

" Looks like it," agreed Bobby, for this, indeed, seemed clear, definite evidence at last. " Has he been asked about it ? "

" Yes, and let go again after telling three different stories," answered Lawson with deep disgust. " First said he had given it to a friend, then that he had lost it, and then he wouldn't answer any more questions till he had his solicitor there. And then—what do you think then ? " demanded Lawson, with rising indignation.

" What ? " asked Bobby.

" Let him go," said Lawson. " Like that. Opened the door and bowed him out. Ought to have charged him, I say. I know the inspector thought so—Ferris it was; he was there. Said sarcastic like: ' Perhaps you gave it to your sweetheart for a Christmas present ? ' Chenery didn't like that; went all pale; knew that meant no one believed a word he said. I was getting ready to take him downstairs when they let him go—practically cast iron and they let him go."

" Is it cast iron ? " Bobby said, for he was thinking to himself that perhaps that shaft aimed by Ferris with ironic intent had in fact hit the truth; and that possibly it was the fact that Chenery had given the pistol to Hilda with some idea of providing her with protection when she was in charge of the duchess's jewels. Hilda might have mislaid or forgotten it, and so it might—or might not—have got into someone else's hands. Or, for that matter, Denis might have taken it back. At any rate, there seemed to be

more possibilities about its later ownership than Lawson
was apparently prepared to consider.

" Accumulation of evidence," Lawson was saying now.
" One pointer may be wrong, but not half a dozen. He
panicked, too—panicked when he knew we were on to the
pistol being his."

" Enough to make him," agreed Bobby. " He always
kept his head before," he added.

" Another thing," Lawson went on; " you remember we
couldn't find him when we wanted him on Monday, and
he wouldn't say where he was ? Well, he was asked about
that again."

" Did he say this time ? "

" Yes. Said he had been arranging with some big furniture removal people to do some haulage for their vans—
some sort of tractor he lets out on hire."

" Good Lord," Bobby gasped, " more furniture vans !
The case is lousy with 'em."

" Fed up with 'em myself," agreed Lawson. " Couldn't
sit down all Sunday with any comfort, the way I got
bumped about on that blessed tail-board."

" Did Chenery explain why he didn't say so at once ? "
Bobby asked.

" Wanted to know if we thought he really liked our
nosing round every customer he had, asking questions. Said
it was enough to ruin any business, and his wasn't in any
shape to stand much of that sort of thing. Don't you call
it good enough to charge him on ? Direct proof the pistol
used was his and all."

" Nasty look about it," agreed Bobby, " very nasty.
Holes in the picture still, though."

" There always are," retorted Lawson. " Charge your
man as soon as your case looks good, I say, and you'll find
the holes fill up as you go along. Of course, it's plain enough
what they're waiting for—the necklace."

" Shouldn't wonder," agreed Bobby.

" Afraid," said Lawson, " of acting too quickly and losing the blessed thing for good. Keeping off in the hope of spotting where it is. Not regular, I say. Incorrect. We've got the murderer, or as good as. Our duty is to bring him in, whether what the super calls ' precipitate action ' loses the necklace or not."

" You're a precisian, you see."

" Look here," said Lawson, offended, " don't you come Oxford over me."

" My dear chap," protested Bobby, " what's Oxford got to do with precisian ? One of the finest Parisian detectives ever lived."

" Oh, well," said Lawson, mollified.

" What I mean is, there are still points Treasury counsel will want to know how to answer if the defence brought them up. For one thing, what was Jessop doing at T. T.'s ? "

" No good," opined Lawson. " But what's it matter ? He was there all right, wasn't he ? No defence can get away from that, and we don't want to know any more." He paused, smiled, chuckled. " Old T. T.'s fair upset about it all. Shouldn't wonder if it didn't almost scare him into turning honest. He's taken a cottage in the country—going to spend his time growing prize cabbages, he says. Offered me a job helping him move."

" Oh," said Bobby, interested. " Taking it on ? "

" Put him off," answered Lawson. " Don't see why I shouldn't, though. Do you ? Might get to know something useful, you can never tell. If I did, I'd have a good look at the silver ; might identify some of it. He offered a fiver."

" I'm wondering," said Bobby slowly, " where that fits into the picture."

" It doesn't," asserted Lawson, surprised. " Why should it ? "

" I don't know," said Bobby. " I'm wondering."

" Lots of people," Lawson pointed out, " wouldn't care

to go on living in a house where there had been a murder—
natural enough.”

“ Yes, but T. T. isn’t,” Bobby said. “ Any other of our
chaps had the same offer ? ”

Lawson didn’t think so, but from a few inquiries Bobby
made he learnt that T. T. had been hanging continuously
about headquarters, inquiring what progress was being
made towards the discovery of the murderer and urging
greater effort. One or two men expressed the opinion that
he knew more than he pretended, and that it would have
been worth while charging him himself, only for the incon-
testable fact that he had been in the company of the police
at the moment when the shot was fired.

“ Might have worked it by some kind of man-trap
dodge,” suggested one man, “ and if it’s right he didn’t
know Jessop, might have meant it for someone else.”

“ Too many ‘ mights,’ ” said Bobby. “ They’ve no use
for ‘ mights ’ in the Public Prosecutor’s office.”

It also came out that several others of the C.I.D. men
had been asked to help in T. T.’s prospective removal.
Most of them had taken the suggestion as a joke and had
answered accordingly, but all agreed that T. T. seemed more
nervous and agitated than ever they had known him before.

“ Something biting him,” was the general verdict, and
Lawson added to Bobby :

“ Got half an hour to spare ? What about a cup of tea ? ”

“ I could do with it,” said Bobby, “ but duty before tea.
I’ll slip round to——” He named a building near. “ I
know a chap in an office there ; he’ll let me use their ’phone.
If I’m wanted, I’ll be there.”

“ Lots of ’phones here,” suggested someone.

“ Not a blessed one you can use for two minutes without
someone else asking how long you’ll be,” grumbled Bobby.

“ Going to spend all your tea interval ringing up your
girl friends ? ” asked Lawson.

" That's right," answered Bobby. " Only not girl friends; furniture removers—as many as I can get in touch with."

He went off accordingly to put that project into execution, and, after considerably more than the half-hour he had mentioned, was able to establish that T. T. had made many inquiries about the cost of removals, but had proved hard to please. Every estimate submitted had been rejected, and another obtained from another firm. Also Bobby discovered that a man answering to the description of Wynne had been trying to get employment with firms in the furniture removal business, but, curiously enough, never with those firms from whom T. T. had made inquiries.

" Interesting little point," Bobby said to himself, and, returning to the Yard, was informed that his day could be considered finished and he could go home.

Gratefully Bobby obeyed, looking forward to the quiet hour or two he would thus be able to devote to the serious and careful thinking things out that the rush and bustle of the last few days had allowed little time for. Even less time had he had for any attempt to co-ordinate the confused huddle of ascertained fact and construct therefrom the complete and satisfactory picture of events necessary before official action could be taken.

After supper, he got out again his copy of the *Evening Announcer* with the Saturday football results, and the copy of the *Upper Ten* Jessop had had in his pocket with its snap of the Duchess of Westhaven in her characteristically old-fashioned attire.

But, long and late though he brooded over them, he could find in them no revelation, discover in them no gleam of light to throw upon the problems confronting him.

" If it was that photo," Bobby mused, " threw Jessop into the state of panic and excitement Miss May described, why ? Why shouldn't she have been there ? Anyhow, whoever broke into the Park Lane flat must have known the place was empty, and the duke and duchess and the staff all somewhere else."

He had finished supper now, and, lighting a pipe, he sat down in an arm-chair and turned on the wireless to listen to a popular crooner, hoping that his brain, thus reduced to pulp, might, when it returned to normal, be fresh and clear, cleansed from all previous conceptions.

Often before he had found this a good plan when he wished to make an entirely fresh start.

The half-hour elapsed, he turned off the wireless and, getting out his carbon copy of the series of questions and notes he had jotted down previously, he began to go over them again.

And now, taking them with what he had learned that day, one fact began to emerge.

" If anyone did in fact personate the duchess," he thought, " it would be Magotty Meg; she has every qualification, but she wasn't in the whole affair, and that's why she said she didn't hold with murder. Anyhow, it seems pretty clear what became of the necklace."

He began to write a fresh report, and he was reading it over carefully when there entered his landlady with some question about his laundry which had just been returned with the customary additions and subtractions.

" Still worrying about things, Mr. Owen ? " she said. " I'm sure it's a wonder your brain isn't upside down."

" Oh, it is," he assured her, " at least, it is, if mush can be upside down—a nice point that." He paused, and pointed to his now completed report. " I think I'm right about the necklace," he said. " Probably it's been there all the time. But as for the murder, that all depends on what a pawnbroker will have to say."

" I don't know what you're talking about, Mr. Owen," said the landlady severely.

" I don't know that I do myself," said Bobby, " so I'll go to bed."

CHAPTER XXV

FURNITURE VANS

BOBBY was so far trusted at headquarters that he had little difficulty next morning in obtaining the permission he asked over the 'phone to call, before reporting for duty, at that pawnbroker's shop in West Lane, Brush Hill, which stood opposite the Red Lion. He was warned, however, that this permission was to be in no way regarded as any excuse for coming on duty any later than usual, or at any rate than was absolutely necessary. It was intimated quite firmly that detective-sergeants who went wandering off on their own account were expected, all the same, to keep time like anyone else. However, it was also agreed that his full explanation as to why he wanted to go chasing round after odd pawnbrokers' shops could wait till he gave it in person, since headquarters had, after all, something else to do than listen to long rigmaroles over the 'phone.

So Bobby, making an early start, presented himself at the pawnbroker's in West Lane even before the shutters were down. But he met with a disappointment.

" Last Saturday," said the proprietor, a Mr. Weaver, watching his assistants getting ready for the work of the day. " Oh, yes, I remember. I went off early. Had tickets for the Super-Palace Cinema for the wife and family. Good show, too. I left young Higson in charge."

" Can I see him ? " Bobby asked.

" Not got here yet," answered Weaver. " Won't be yet awhile. Can't say when. A friend's running him up from

Bournemouth in his car and as he's a commercial—the friend I mean—they're making calls on the way. Higson got knocked about a bit the other day, and he went to Bournemouth to get over it. No good having a chap behind the counter with two black eyes, a split ear, his mouth cut, and a nose like a pancake. Customers don't like it."

" I expect not," said Bobby. " What happened ? Motor-car ? "

" No, no," answered Mr. Weaver. " Higson's a thoughtful sort of boy, very interested in politics, and he's got to be very keen on Fascism."

" Been arguing it out with some of the Reds ? " suggested Bobby.

" No-o, it wasn't that exactly. The Fascists were having a big meeting Saturday at the public hall, and Higson made up his mind to join up at it."

" Yes ? " said Bobby, slightly puzzled by this preamble.

" Well, you see," explained Mr. Weaver, " it struck him it would be a good way to get himself introduced if he got up and asked some sort of sympathetic question, such as, ' Did Fascism Guarantee to Stamp Sedition in the Mud ? ' or ' Would Fascism Undertake to Abolish Discontent ? '— something to show he believed in them and their ideas."

" But I don't quite see   . " said Bobby, still more puzzled.

" It was a misunderstanding," explained Mr. Weaver. " When he got up to ask his question, the Fascists thought he was a Red trying to heckle."

" Oh," said Bobby. " What happened ? " he asked interested.

" It's Plan 3, Public Meetings," Mr. Weaver told him. " They put it in action at once—Fascism is Action, you know. Action," he repeated admiringly. " Two of them got each one of his legs, so he couldn't get away; two more held his arms, one each, so he couldn't hit back; one punched him in the stomach, so he couldn't cry out; one hit him over the face from behind, so he couldn't see who it was; and three stood in front, so no one else could see what was happening. Then they frog-marched him to the door, face down so that he wouldn't be able to identify any of them, and threw him into the street, and two others who were on duty there kicked him in the ribs till two of the Fascist ambulance came along and took him to hospital—reported him as attacked by Red hooligans. There was a photo in the papers next day—'Red Outrage.' You can say what you like about the Fascists," declared Mr. Weaver, " but they are efficient—prompt and efficient—and that's what England wants—efficiency."

" That's right," agreed Bobby. " So it does."

" The Fascist Way," said Mr. Weaver, " different from the slow old English style."

" So it is," agreed Bobby. " Very different."

" It's why I like the Blackshirts," explained Mr. Weaver. " Efficiency. Action. They don't talk; they—Act."

" They do, don't they ? " Bobby agreed once more.

" Of course," admitted Mr. Weaver, " misunderstandings do happen sometimes."

" Even with the best regulated Fascists," Bobby murmured.

" But it's in a good cause—efficiency," Mr. Weaver reminded him.

" I hope Mr. Higson thinks so," said Bobby, and arranged that as soon as that so unfortunately misunderstood young man arrived he was to be asked to present himself at Scotland Yard.

Thither, too, Bobby now made his way, and, after a long talk with Inspector Ferris, to whom he handed a memo he had prepared, he was presently sent for by the superintendent. To Ulyett's room he accordingly proceeded, and found his chief frowning over the new report, written the previous night, Bobby had submitted that morning.

" You get at it logically enough," Ulyett admitted, " but, all the same, it's rather a long shot."

" Yes, sir," said Bobby, continuing to think that observation the safest to make when talking to superior officers.

" About this young fellow Higson—it's an idea, of course. Coming up by car from Bournemouth, is he ? The sooner we get hold of him the better. Couldn't we stop him on the way ? "

" Wouldn't save much time if we did, sir, would it ? " Bobby asked. " Besides, Mr. Weaver seemed to think they might not come direct; the friend's a commercial traveller, and they have one or two calls to make on the way."

" Oh, well, we'll wait, then," said Ulyett. " You said nothing about why we wanted him ? "

" No, sir. Only that we thought he might be able to help us. I thought it better he should have no preconceived ideas or theories."

" That's right," agreed Ulyett. " If what you suggest so clearly in your notes is correct, his evidence may be vital."

" Yes, sir, it does seem as if the whole case depended on that."

" Anyway, it's pretty clear about the necklace. We ought to have seen that before, only for having to concentrate on the murder—and then, too, thinking that Wynne had it, and that was why he cleared off in such a hurry that night."

" Well, sir," agreed Bobby, " the moment you have time to sit down and think, this furniture removing shows up as a kind of *leit-motiv* running through it all."

" Looked more like pulling our leg," grunted Ulyett.

" Yes, sir," Bobby said. " It seemed like it, and I suppose that put us all off for the time, till it turned out both T. T. and Wynne were making quite such a pile of inquiries. Charley Dickson, too. He's always harping on the same thing. Denis Chenery as well—he was talking about removals, too."

" Assuming you are right," Ulyett went on, " in thinking

T. T. had the infernal cheek to put the necklace in his pocket when he came along to talk to us Saturday night, no doubt he could easily have planted it somewhere inside the van when he pulled the door open and pretended to be so surprised at seeing our men there."

" I feel sure that's how he managed it," Bobby said. " He had his scouts out—he always had when he was expecting to put through a bigger deal than usual. He was expecting someone to come along with the necklace— Wynne, or Jessop, or the unknown murderer perhaps. His scouts warned him about us. T. T. told them to clear off, wrapped the necklace in two pages of his evening paper so its sparkle shouldn't be seen, and strolled off to meet us as calm as you please. But he had a bit of a shock later when it was noticed that those outside pages were missing and he was asked for them. Bit of bad luck for him they were the pages with the football results one of our fellows wanted to know about. Made him nervous. He and Wynne expected to recover the necklace without any difficulty while we were searching the house, or after we had finished. Jessop's murder threw them out of their reckoning. Wynne panicked and made a bolt. T. T. was too upset and scared to think about the necklace, and, anyhow, wouldn't have been allowed to leave the house till the first investigation was over. It was quite on the cards he had engineered the murder somehow. No chance, as he had expected, to slip away and get the necklace back, or even to make a note of the name of the firm supplying the van. You remember, sir, we got it from people who do a lot of hire purchase business and use plain vans. Anyhow, both T. T. and Wynne were too excited, and too scared for that matter, to think about noting details. When they did, the van had gone, and the necklace, too."

" What's become of it ? " Ulyett asked. " Someone found it and pinched it, or has it been thrown away with the rubbish, or is it still there in the van ? "

" My own idea, sir," Bobby said, " would be that T. T. pushed it away in one of those small lockers some vans are fitted up with for holding any small article of value—and generally used by the men for bottles of beer, and bread and cheese, when they're on a long-distance job. The van would be looked at, and swept out most likely, after we sent it back, but it's quite likely, too, no one troubled to look in the lockers they wouldn't expect us to have used. I should think there's a very fair chance the necklace is still there, where T. T. pushed it. And, ever since, he's been trying to find out where the van came from, so as to try to get the necklace back."

Ulyett smiled grimly.

" Over-reached himself for once," he said. " Funny to think of him knowing where the necklace was, but not where the van. came from, and not daring to ask straight out for fear of putting us on. That's why he wanted to move, and wanted us to recommend him a good honest firm we had dealings with ourselves. All the same," Ulyett added, " it did look like a leg-pulling stunt."

" Yes, sir, I think we all thought that at first," Bobby said.

" Better see about the van at once," Ulyett said. " Go yourself. Don't be too quick telling them what it's all about. No good putting temptation in anyone's way. It's possible they may not be sure which particular van they let us have. It was Saturday afternoon, and the foreman in charge may have turned out the first he saw and not made a proper record. You'll have to ask. If the van's there, and the necklace is there too—still there—mind you hang on to it. Take someone with you. You may need help."

" Yes, sir," said Bobby; and, with Lawson for companion, was soon hurrying to the premises of the firm from whom that Saturday the van had been obtained.

There Ulyett's forebodings were at once justified. There was no certainty which van had been used. On Saturday afternoons routine was relaxed. There were consultations.

It might have been Van 11. Van 11 was in the yard. It had not been out since Saturday, and investigation showed it swept clean and empty, with no vestige of any necklace. Or, if it was Van 14, then that had gone to be repainted and repaired. But then it might have been Van 17 or Van 19—Van 17 was on the road somewhere to Scotland. Somewhere near Carlisle, perhaps, now, or maybe further on. Van 19 had gone out that morning with a load to Cheltenham, and the driver had rung up to say he had a further offer to take some heavy stuff somewhere in the Cotswolds.

" Trustworthy man, Stephens—that's the driver," the manager explained. " I told him O.K."

" Whereabouts in the Cotswolds ? " Bobby asked.

The manager didn't know.

" I don't think Stephens said exactly," he answered thoughtfully. " If he did, I didn't notice. One of our most reliable men, Stephens; been with us a good many years. The offer he quoted was good enough. I told him to go ahead and we would expect him back to-morrow."

" Then," said Bobby, " you mean Stephens and your van may be anywhere in the Cotswolds ? "

" I think he said the Cotswolds," said the manager, still doubtful. " Or was it somewhere else ? Perhaps he said he would have to cross the Cotswolds. I didn't notice much— ' destination and distance no object.' That," said the manager proudly, " is our slogan. Stephens knows his way about —and he knows, too, he would be for it if terms and everything weren't O.K. when he reported back. We trusted him; I knew we could."

" Do you know who engaged him in Cheltenham ? " Bobby asked.

The manager was sorry, but he had no idea. He hadn't asked.

" Comes to this," said Bobby bitterly, " the blessed van may be anywhere in all England."

QJ

The manager thought that was probably an exaggeration.

" Must be within a run of Cheltenham," he pointed out. " That's where Stephens rang up from. Funny thing," he added casually, " someone else was inquiring about that van—more of your people, perhaps ? Seemed to know you had had it out Saturday night."

" Who was it ? " asked Bobby, startled.

The manager didn't know. No one he had seen himself. One of the men had answered the inquiry; the foreman; Tonks his name was. Tonks was duly sent for, and on his appearance was able to give full information.

" Knew him at once," he said proudly. " He didn't know I knew him, and of course I said nothing. But I twigged him the moment I spoke to him. He was chairman."

" Chairman ? " repeated Bobby, puzzled.

" Yes. It was a big meeting about the new Betting Bill, and making it stiffer, so me and the missus went."

" Doesn't approve of betting, doesn't Tonks," interposed the manager in a grinning aside.

" Well, it wasn't that so much," admitted Mr. Tonks, grinning in response, " but me and the missus, we pick a horse every week—regular. Takes some picking, too. Then we put a dollar on it—regular. Well, this meeting was to stop that, just like Hitler and them lot stops things, so me and the missus, we went along to heckle like, and ask his ruddy grace whether he didn't ever put a bit on himself."

" His—grace ? " gasped Bobby. " You mean—— ? "

" The Duke of Westhaven," said Mr. Tonks calmly. " It was him in the chair that night, and said no questions would be took, and it was him as was here asking questions himself about that there van. Mind," said Mr. Tonks, " I never let on I knew him; not my place. Besides, it was out of business hours when I saw him that other time. But I spotted him all right, moment I saw him."

CHAPTER XXVI

ALL COTSWOLD BOUND

"I would rather," declared Superintendent Ulyett with restrained passion, " handle dynamite than dukes."

Bobby, returned in haste to the Yard, had there made his report concerning the duke and the van, and from their first sheer, complete bewilderment his superiors had passed to extreme depression and annoyance.

" Dukes," repeated Ulyett morosely, " why can't they keep their noses out of this sort of thing ? Anyway, what does it—Mean ? "

He glared ferociously at Bobby, who, having no idea what to answer, nor the remotest notion what it—Meant, remained discreetly silent.

Then Ulyett brightened up a little.

" Perhaps," he said, clutching at a straw as drowning men will, " perhaps the Assistant Commissioner will want to handle the case himself."

This seemed to Bobby but a slender hope. Ulyett bustled away, however, with a very confident air, and returned presently with an expression of deep gloom that showed only too well his expectations had been disappointed.

" Says he's too busy, and has the fullest confidence in my tact and discretion," said Ulyett, with a resentment so generous a compliment hardly seemed to deserve. " Means he's getting from under in case the roof falls in— as it probably will. All police forces—town and county— to be warned, and asked to look out for the van. Nothing to be said about the duke yet." Ulyett paused here to say on his own account a few things about his grace. " And I'm to go chasing round to try to spot him and twig his little game. Case for a senior officer, the A.C. says, but isn't touching it himself; not him." Ulyett paused again and fixed Bobby with a baleful glare. " You'll come with me, young fellow," he said, " and if the duke means the sack, you'll be for it, too."

" Yes, sir," said Bobby dutifully, but reflecting with inner satisfaction that it would probably be the senior who would get the axe. Odd if a mere sergeant could not dodge away in the shadow of a superintendent.

" Instructions," Ulyett continued even more bitterly, " are to handle the case with kid gloves. I would give half a year's pay to see the A.C. trying to pick a red-hot coal out of the fire and be able to tell him to be sure and handle it with kid gloves."

A little relieved by this outburst, to which Bobby had listened with extreme sympathy, Ulyett led the way outside and there selected a high-powered car from the police fleet. The only other comment he made was a sad little murmur:

" And me chasing off after dukes with my desk piled a foot high with cases needing immediate attention."

Bobby was too wise to utter a word of sympathy that might easily have meant the discharging upon his own head of the wrath boiling within Ulyett. But he tried his best to look as if he felt that never in the world's history had such a picture been presented of the good man struggling with undeserved affliction; and then he noticed a tall, thin youth with a brown-paper parcel under one arm, and a face that looked as an anvil must feel after a busy day in the smithy. The owner of it was looking round in a manner that proclaimed the puzzled stranger, and an idea struck Bobby. He went across to him:

" Mr. Higson from Weaver's, Brush Hill, I think ? " he observed.

" That's right," said Mr. Higson, and then looked startled. " How did you know ? " he asked.

" Oh, we know things here. Scotland Yard, this is," explained Bobby, with a wave of the hand that he hoped was suitably impressive.

Then he devoted a moment or two to telling Mr. Higson how eagerly they had been expecting him, how kind it was of him to come along so quickly, how important they were certain what he had to tell them would prove to be. Having thus got Mr. Higson purring—and it is wonderful how much information can come through a purr—Bobby took Higson up to Ulyett and explained who he was. The superintendent asked a few questions and then came to a sudden decision.

" Hop in," he said; " we'll treat you to a trip in the country, and you tell us if you see anyone you've met before. Wait here a minute, will you ? There's something I must see about."

He retired accordingly within the building, and Mr. Higson turned to Bobby.

" Wants me to identify a suspect ? " he asked. " I don't mind telling you now there was one customer Saturday night I noticed particular. Very likely I should have let you know before only for being "—Mr. Higson hesitated a moment—" temporarily indisposed."

" Just the sort of bad luck that often throws an investigation all out of gear," commented Bobby.

" I never saw the paper on Sunday," Mr. Higson continued, " never even heard there had been a murder in Brush Hill till last night when I saw it in the evening paper. I said at once: ' That's him,' and so, when I heard of you asking about it, I got the *corpus delecti*." He paused to watch the effect of this, and Bobby was quick to look properly impressed. " I've brought it along with me," he concluded.

" Smart of you," said Bobby admiringly, for he knew well how far a little harmless flattery goes. " *Corpus* in the brown paper parcel you have there ? Good. I'll take charge of it, shall I ? But we won't open it now. Important in these cases to preserve a perfectly open mind. Many a good case ruined because defending counsel has been able to suggest preconceived prejudice. So I won't even ask you what's in it, though I can guess all right. What we want you to do is to point out anyone you think you've seen before. If it's the man we expect, then we shall know we're on the right track. If it isn't, the whole blessed case will have to start again."

Mr. Higson nodded with grave approval, realising how important his testimony was going to be.

" My memory for faces is excellent," he announced. " A sort of gift it is with me," he explained modestly.

" Will it be all right with Mr. Weaver ? " Bobby asked. " Or would you like to ring him up and explain ? "

Mr. Higson looked at Bobby in a manner by the side of which an iceberg would have seemed a furnace.

" Him and me have parted," he said. " I couldn't reconcile it with my principles to go on working for a man who is Against the People."

" Is Mr. Weaver ? " asked Bobby, faintly surprised.

" Weaver," declared Mr. Higson, " is almost a—Fascist."

" But I thought," said Bobby, more puzzled still, " that you were a bit that way yourself ? "

Mr. Higson's voice was slow and solemn as he answered gravely :

" I am No. 4 in a Communist cell."

" Dear me," said Bobby. " Now in our cells we give them much higher numbers."

" Communist cells," explained Mr. Higson, entirely

unaware that this had been intended for a joke, "are limited to five members. Our slogan," he continued, "is 'C.S.C.S.'"

" Oh," said Bobby, puzzled. " Something about a co-op ? " he hazarded.

Mr. Higson surveyed Bobby with amused contempt.

" It means," he said, " Comrade Stalin Comes Soon."

" Jolly good," approved Bobby.

" I invented it myself," explained Mr. Higson, thawing visibly in the sunshine of this appreciation. " I dare say soon it'll be on the lips of every Comrade. And then," said Mr. Higson, growing grim all at once, " we'll give those Fascists what for."

" Changed your opinions a bit, haven't you ? " asked Bobby.

" My eyes have been opened," replied Mr. Higson, though this was only true metaphorically, since in cold fact they had been closed, both of them, for some time.

" Sudden conversion, eh ? " said Bobby.

" All true conversions are sudden," announced Mr. Higson. " You've heard of St. Paul ? "

Bobby admitted the fact.

" It's why," explained Mr. Higson, " I'm glad of the chance of seeing something of your methods. I consider it an opportunity to study police organisation at close quarters. In the Communistic State, the police force has a most important rôle to play."

" Bump 'em off good and plenty," suggested Bobby.

Further conversation was interrupted by the return of Ulyett, still morose. He instructed Bobby, who was at the wheel, to drive first to the Bloomsbury Hotel, where they were lucky enough to find Mr. Carton. He appeared very promptly in answer to the message sent in.

" I was coming round to see you," he said, before either of them had a chance to speak. " Irene says she told you I had shown her a pistol I have, a small automatic, and I remembered you were asking me about it and I told you I hadn't one. Well, that's right, but I meant over here. The one I showed her is the one belonging to the management —it was when she came to Nice for her holiday a year ago. I thought I had better explain."

Ulyett asked a few questions, agreed it was a misunderstanding that had needed clearing up, and, after a few more remarks, Carton retired again within the hotel and they drove away. Ulyett said:

" Think he was telling the truth ? "

" I thought it sounded all right," Bobby answered.

Higson, who had heard all this somewhat imperfectly, said:

" That one of the crooks you want me to identify ? I've seen him before, all right; could swear to him any time. But I can't quite remember. Something about a pistol ? Did he pledge ? Did he buy ? "

" Perhaps it'll come to you in time," suggested Bobby; and was ordered to drive on to Mayfair Square, where, however, the commissionaire, in answer to their inquiries, informed them that both Mr. Jacks and Mr. Wright were out. In answer to further inquiries as to when they were likely to be back, the commissionaire said that Mr. Wright had gone out early after being rung up on the 'phone, had come back in a great hurry, had been closeted with Mr. Jacks for a time, and then both men—" looking upset like," said the commissionaire—had departed in Mr. Wright's car. In the commissionaire's opinion something was up— definitely.

" Didn't say where they were going, I suppose ? " Bobby asked.

" They were looking at the map," the commissionaire answered, " and I heard Mr. Wright say something about finding the quickest route to Cheltenham."

" Cheltenham—good God ! " exclaimed Ulyett, startled

out of his self-possession, and the commissionaire looked quite offended.

" Cheltenham's a very fine town," he asserted. " I was born there myself."

" A haunt of the bourgeoisie," muttered Mr. Higson truculently from behind.

They drove away, and Ulyett told Bobby to make for the garage Denis Chenery owned. But when they got there they found that Denis also had departed for the day.

" Said he wouldn't be back till to-morrow," explained the foreman in charge. " Young lady came for him— excited like she seemed. Miss May her name is; she's been here before; boss sweet on her, if you ask me. They took a Bayard Twenty we've got on sale."

" Didn't say where they were going, did they ? " Bobby asked carelessly.

" No, only the boss told me to find him a map of the Cotswold country," answered the foreman, and Ulyett and Bobby looked at each other with a kind of wild surmise.

They drove away, taking the route for Cheltenham and making the best speed permitted by other traffic and a modified respect for the law. Once, on a clear, straight stretch of road, Bobby got up to eighty; but Ulyett remarked that he wished to reach Cheltenham quick but not dead, and Mr. Higson threw out a tentative suggestion about completing the journey by rail.

So Bobby overcame the temptation the next straight bit of road presented; and was not sorry when Ulyett remarked that they might stop for a few minutes at the next decent-looking pub they came to, so as to get a bite of something to eat.

" A quarter of an hour won't make any difference," he declared, and when they had finished their meal, and were standing in the doorway of the inn ready to leave, there went by at a high rate of speed a car of which, through trees that sheltered them from the road, they had a passing glimpse.

" See that ? See who that was ? " Ulyett asked, so far forgetting his dignity of superintendent as to seize Bobby excitedly by the arm.

Bobby, too, was staring after the vanished car a cloud of dust had so soon hidden from view. He did not answer immediately, for he almost thought there must be some mistake. But Mr. Higson spoke up:

" I know him—not the driver, but the gentleman sitting behind. It was Mr. Mullins. He's not a customer of ours, but he's well known in Brush Hill. Lives at a big house in Chesters Street—The Towers, I think it's called."

Ulyett was wiping his forehead, on which beads of perspiration were standing out.

" This," he said solemnly, " this is just sheer, unadulterated nightmare."

" Yes, sir," said Bobby, in full agreement, as usual.

CHAPTER XXVII

PURSUIT BEGINS

"Well, we had better push along after them," Ulyett said, rousing himself from his bewildered and uneasy abstraction. "Don't like it, Owen," he said to Bobby, who didn't like it either. "Don't half like it." He called to one of the inn staff standing near. "Main road to Cheltenham, isn't it?" he asked. "Go anywhere else?"

"Branches about a mile on," the man answered; "the right goes direct to Cheltenham, left takes you to the Cotswold country."

"They may be either place by now at the pace they were going—mile a minute or thereabouts," grumbled Ulyett. "Looks like trouble ahead to me."

They got into their car and started, and Higson said to Bobby:

"Was that him you wanted me to identify? Most respected gentleman; everyone in Brush Hill knows him."

"No, he was a bit unexpected," Bobby answered. "Not that he really should have been a surprise, but he was one all right."

"Was it him who was driving you meant, then?" Higson asked. "I didn't see him plain. Not a chance to recognise him."

"I knew him," said Bobby grimly. "Name of Wynne—Percy Augustus Wynne; and, if you don't like them, you can have others, as the political candidate said of his opinions. No, he was unexpected, too."

Ulyett had been plunged in deep and troubled thought. They had arrived now at the spot where the road branched, and he told Bobby to go on straight to Cheltenham.

" They may have information for us there," he said. " They'll have been rung up from our people by now and told to expect us. Six—that makes it we are six," he said, sternly regarding Bobby as though it were entirely his fault. " Poem, ' We are Six,' isn't there ? "

" I think it's ' Seven, in all, she said,' you mean, isn't it, sir ? " Bobby suggested cautiously.

" Well, you ought to know; Oxford and all," grunted Ulyett. " There's us, Denis Chenery and his girl, the duke on his own or not, the jeweller johnnies, and T. T. and his pal we've just seen; that's five, and the van makes six— six little nigger-boys—and soon there'll be less."

" Yes, sir," agreed Bobby.

" And what's going to happen," added Ulyett, " only the good Lord knows—if it isn't too much for him, too," added Ulyett, with a resigned sigh, evidently inclined to suppose that what baffled the Yard was likely to baffle Omniscience as well.

He sank again into his mood of uneasy abstraction, and Bobby drove on at a slower speed now that they were within a built-up area and there was more traffic about. Higson said plaintively in Bobby's ear:

" Couldn't you tell me what it's all about ? "

Bobby reflected that he only wished he was in a position to do so. Aloud he said:

" Oh, the whole thing will be plain enough when you understand."

Mr. Higson was plainly as deeply impressed by this as most people are by a platitude loudly announced. After a pause to think it over and allow it to sink deeper and deeper into his mind, he remarked suddenly:

" That Mr. Carton at the Bloomsbury Hotel."

Bobby looked round with some apprehension.

" Yes ? What about him ? Why ? " he asked, wondering
if Carton was to be the next to make an appearance in this
kind of universal hunt, possibly on a motor-cycle with Miss
Irene sitting behind.

Nothing would, in fact, in his present state of mind have
surprised him less, but Higson went on slowly:

" I've been thinking, and I've got it pretty clear now.
He was in about three weeks ago about an automatic pistol
we had in the window: licensed we are—I mean Mr.
Weaver is—for the sale of firearms," he added.

" Did he buy the pistol ? " Bobby asked, interested.

" No, only asked, and inquired about regulations,"
Higson answered. " What makes me remember him is along
of him talking about France, and what a lot less red tape
there is there—seemed to know a lot about France. But,"
added Higson with a modest pride, " I didn't let him go
without making a sale. Nice little brooch he took."

" Oh, yes," said Bobby. " Three straight horizontal gold
bars, crossed by a spray in emeralds and small diamonds;
cost seven guineas."

Higson fairly jumped.

" How did you know ? " he gasped.

Bobby only smiled—rather a good smile, he thought to himself, so full did he feel it had been of mystery and knowledge.

" Was you watching ? " Higson asked, awestruck.

" I mustn't explain our methods," said Bobby gravely,
' but it was plain enough from what you said yourself—a
simple case of deduction—just putting things together."

" Golly," said Mr. Higson, with all the reverence that
strange ejaculation demands.

" Elementary, my dear Higson," said Bobby, who, as befitted a B.A. (Oxon.), was well acquainted with the classics.

Higson collapsed, and only after some time recovered
sufficiently to say:

"You got the price wrong, though; it was 39s. 6d., reduced from seven guineas."

Bobby clicked his tongue and tried to look very upset.

"Was it, though?" he said. "Don't know how I came to make a bloomer like that. It just shows." He shook his head gravely at himself. "Bad slip-up," he declared. "Big reduction, wasn't it, seven guineas to 39s. 6d.?"

"Well, I don't say," answered Higson, with some reserve, "that we ever really expected to sell at seven guineas. Of course, we might have done. But we shouldn't have pressed it at that figure. Only when it had been in the window, even in a corner, at seven guineas, it was quite all right to mark it reduced from that when the new price-ticket was put on."

Bobby was spared by the exigencies of the traffic from passing any comment on this point of commercial ethics. A little later the traffic coagulated, as the amateur cook said of the scrambled eggs, and in the jam Bobby had to bring their car to a standstill. A little nervously, for his thoughts had not been comfortable after this revelation of Scotland Yard's efficiency and all pervading knowledge, Higson leaned nearer to Bobby and said in a low voice:

"Remember what I said about being No. 4 in a Communist cell and getting orders from Moscow? Well, in a manner of speaking——"

"Swank?" asked Bobby.

"Well—looking ahead," explained Higson. "About how to get even. The fact is, I've had enough of that sort of thing: fed up I am. I've really made up my mind to chuck politics."

"Sound man," approved Bobby.

"I shall vote," declared Higson, "for each lot in turn, so as to give 'em all a chance."

"That's the spirit," said Bobby. "Makes the British Constitution the envy of the world."

"After all," said Higson thoughtfully, "when it comes

to kicking the other fellow's ribs in, which is all these Fascists and Reds think about—well, a gorilla could beat 'em both at that game, couldn't he ? "

Bobby looked at Higson admiringly.

" Out of the mouths of pawnbrokers' assistants might the dictators of the world learn wisdom," he murmured. Aloud he said: " You're right. Funny thing that in the fourth decade of the twentieth century the gorilla should be an accepted ideal."

The traffic jam eased. They shot through, and presently drew up before the Cheltenham police station, where they were expected, as there had been a good deal of 'phoning going on between there and London.

Ulyett went in first alone and talked to the officer in charge, and then word came out for Bobby to join them. As it was he who had seen most of the various personalities concerned, it was desired that he should give as clear and complete a description of them as possible. This he did to the best of his ability, supplementing his words with those hasty pen-and-ink sketches for which he had a certain gift. The Cheltenham officer asked, too, about the numbers of the cars, a point on which London had not been very well informed. Bobby had a note both of that of Mr. Wright's car and of that of the Bayard Twenty believed to be driven by Denis Chenery, though it was, of course, possible that Mr. Wright was using a car other than his own, and possible, too, or even probable, that Denis's foreman had not been too anxious to be too accurate in describing his employer's car. There was no information concerning the number or description of any car the Duke of Westhaven might be using, or whether he was alone or with a companion or companions, and T. T. and Wynne had swept by too quickly, and their appearance had been too much of a surprise, for the number or make of their car to have been noticed.

" Comes to this," said Cheltenham resignedly; " you want us to issue instructions for a look-out to be kept for four cars, description doubtful, that may be anywhere in four counties, doing anything."

" Behaving suspiciously," corrected Ulyett.

" Most motorists do," said Cheltenham darkly, " most having enough on their consciences to make 'em. The furniture van ought to be an easier mark. Name of firm and register number——" He read them out, and Ulyett checked them and found them correct.

" Better concentrate on the van," he said. " Where that is, the rest of 'em will be hanging around."

" Where the carcase is——" said the Cheltenham man, for, as befitted Cheltenham, he was not without culture.

" And we've got to be the first carcase," said Ulyett, who was of the older school, " and how we're to do that, blessed if I know, when there's not a thing to tell us where to start."

The Cheltenham man tried to look, but not too pointedly, as if the Cheltenham force would have been fully equal to the task. Then he said:

" Perhaps you had better let me have make and number of your own car, so I can let 'em all know to be on the look-out and ready to help." He took a note of the required information and arranged that it should be sent out at once. " What it comes to," he repeated, " is that there's four cars out chasing round after this furniture van you think may have the Fellows necklace hidden in it, and you hunting round after the lot ? "

" That's right," said Ulyett, and looked all that he felt but that discipline and rank forbade him to utter.

" And the furniture van knowing nothing about it," continued the other. " Don't know that I should much care to be the fellow driving it. Four cars after him—and it. But they can't all be crooks, can they ? "

" Why not ? " asked Ulyett pessimistically.

" Well, anyhow," remarked the Cheltenham man, " there are two or three reports you had better see. We asked to be kept informed of anything unusual happening."

He went away for a moment or two and then came back with some papers and a map.

" Complaint from High Wood," he said. " High Wood's a village—here." He showed it on the map, on the eastern slope of the Cotswolds. " Two cars chasing each other through the village all out—hundred m.p.h., it says. Killed two hens and a lady's pet cat—lady very keen on having 'em traced, and is writing to the Home Secretary about it; has a friend who knows someone who met him at dinner last year. May be your affair, or may be two of the young gents from Oxford playing the fool, as seemingly is what they are mostly taught there."

" Yes, I've noticed that," agreed Ulyett. " So's the sergeant here."

" Yes, sir," agreed Bobby, prompt as ever in acquiescence. " Very successful, too, sir, very often." He added thoughtfully: " If the report says ' chasing,' it might mean either a race or—or chasing."

" If one lot had got the necklace and the others knew and were after 'em ? " said Ulyett uncomfortably. " Yes, it might mean that. I think we'll have to make for High Wood."

" Another report," continued Cheltenham, " from Stoneham—north, up Malvern way, lonely part—says shots were heard, several in succession; one report speaks of half a dozen, and a car being seen leaving the spot at a high rate of speed. Number not noted, but car thought to be a Bayard Twenty. Might be your affair again, or might just be a spot of poaching. Plenty of motorists carry a shot-gun, and bag a bird or a hare if they get the chance."

" Shots?" grumbled Ulyett uncomfortably. "Don't like

RJ

it—shots. Too suggestive. Have to give Stoneham a look round right away."

"Furniture van," continued the Cheltenham man, "reported from Devizes way. Noticed because it was making for the Wiltshire downs at a good rate of speed, and there aren't so many folk living that way, and what there are don't move often. But of course they do sometimes, and there's no details about the van."

"No, but," said Ulyett excitedly, "furniture van making for lonely country? That sounds our man. Have to be our first objective, and full speed, too."

"Van mentioned in a second report," Cheltenham continued. "Broke down on main London road and contents transferred to another returning empty. Normal incident. No details taken, and wouldn't have been reported but for general inquiry sent out. Empty van went off under towage. Nothing on record as to where either van came from or was going."

"Start," said Ulyett; "not much help, though."

Cheltenham continued:

"Mickleham—small place towards the Black Mountains—lonely part, very. Rather confused story just 'phoned in of empty car found deserted by roadside—bloodstains on the seat of car, on steering-wheel, and on road near. Might be an accident, of course."

Ulyett got to his feet.

"Wants looking into," he said resentfully, "and quick, too. Another place we had better get to first of all. Talk about a wild-goose chase—there's not even a wild goose, only a furniture van that may be anywhere in six counties, and four other cars all ahead of us and all of 'em most likely with better information. Nice game, ain't it?"

Cheltenham was sympathetic, and deeply thankful the game was not one in which Cheltenham was called upon to take a leading hand. Not theirs to hunt illusive vans chased themselves by a small fleet of cars of doubtful, or not doubtful, purpose.

But Cheltenham was zealous in promising to undertake the receipt and collation of all information received, and to send out further urgent requests that any even remotely relevant fact about vans or erratic motorists should be immediately reported. It was also arranged that Ulyett would ring up every hour to report from any available call-box, and that Cheltenham would act as a liaison between him and London, so that less time would be occupied in getting through.

" Good many lonely bits of country round here," Cheltenham said. " Especially south, Wiltshire way, and west, over by Wales—the Cotswolds, too. But a furniture van is big enough. We ought to be getting word soon of someone having seen it somewhere."

" The wrong one, most likely," grunted Ulyett, who was in a depressed mood.

" Several wrong ones most likely," agreed Cheltenham, whose mood was much more cheerful.

Further details of the organised search now to be under-taken were arranged, and then Ulyett observed that that was all so far as he could see to be done on that side, and he thought he would start off and skirmish round. He wanted to leave Higson behind now, but that young man, with unexpected spirit, begged to be allowed to accompany them, pointing out that it was not fair to drag him all the way from London just to dump him down in Cheltenham; and, besides, so far he hadn't had a chance to identify anyone, though ready, willing, and able so to do.

Ulyett agreed, therefore, to let him accompany them, and Bobby, in the driver's seat, asked which way he was to take.

Ulyett looked at him.

" Toss for it," he said morosely; " toss for it."

CHAPTER XXVIII

PURSUIT CONTINUED

Later, when the calm and warm autumnal day was drawing to a close, Bobby halted the car on one of the highest points of the Cotswolds.

Vague and contradictory reports had sent them to and fro, hither and thither, during the last few hours since they had set out from Cheltenham. They had disturbed an innocent smallholder busily loading up produce on a lorry reported to them as a van behaving suspiciously. They had interrupted the dispatch of his furniture by a lonely and artistic bungalow-dweller returning from a contemplative life in the country to the cocktails and chatter of Chelsea. They had followed for thirty miles at top speed a van conveying the possessions of a Glaswegian journalist ominously descending upon Bath. They had received all sorts and kinds of reports of strange cars strangely behaving, but nowhere had they found any reliable trace of those they sought or of the van they all pursued.

At the moment Bobby was by no means sure of their exact position, Ulyett had no idea which direction they ought to take next, and Higson was trying vainly to calculate how many miles they had already covered. He felt he would like to mention the total casually the next time young Bert next door boasted of the distances he covered at week-ends on his new motor-bike. Moreover, Bobby had just discovered and reported that their petrol was running short, and Ulyett, looking gloomily at the wide expanse of country lying beneath them—it was a celebrated viewpoint where they had halted—demanded:

" What's the use of running around this way when they may be anywhere, any of them, or scooting back to town by this time for all we know ? Better get back to Cheltenham and wait for reliable information. There's sure to be some sooner or later."

" Yes, sir," said Bobby. " I'm not sure we've enough petrol to take us that far. I suppose there ought to be a garage somewhere about."

They drove on more or less in the Cheltenham direction, and presently, as they started to descend the eastern slope of the hills, had a glimpse of a small house nestling so comfortably in an orchard among the trees that from the road it was only visible at rare intervals.

" Better ask there where the nearest garage is," Ulyett said, and accordingly Bobby alighted and made his way through the trees to the little hidden house, while Ulyett and Higson took the opportunity of the rest to smoke contemplative cigarettes together.

A middle-aged woman came out as the barking of a dog announced Bobby's approach. The nearest garage, it seemed, was on the Cheltenham way, about three miles north from the junction of the road they were following with the main road nearly at the foot of the hills. There wasn't, she remarked, much motor traffic about there. It was off the direct route for business purposes, and too rough and steep for tourists, though, as a matter of fact, two or three other cars had been by that afternoon. All in a great hurry, too, seemingly, she added.

To Bobby's further inquiries, she explained that she had not actually seen any of them; she had only had passing glimpses through the trees as they tore by.

" We're a bit shut-in," she remarked, " but in winter

it's a protection from the weather. The smoke over there you can't see from the house, only from here."

Bobby glanced in the direction she indicated, and saw in the distance, from some spot much further down the hill, a column of dark smoke rising in the still air. It did not interest him much, and the woman said with a faint suggestion of discomfort in her voice:

"Someone burning rubbish, but I don't know who it can be down there."

This neighbourly problem did not seem of importance to Bobby, and he asked next if any furniture van had been seen or heard of that day. The woman shook her head decisively. She hadn't seen such a thing for months.

"People don't move so much about here," she explained, "but it's funny you should ask. There's been a lady and gentleman here only an hour or two ago asking the very same thing."

It seemed that, like Bobby, they had left their car by the roadside and come to make the same inquiry as he had done. The good woman had not seen the car, but the description she gave of the two motorists convinced Bobby they were Denis Chenery and Hilda May.

"She was a queer one," the woman said. "Touched, I thought—in the head, I mean. When I told them, same as I have you, there hadn't been a furniture van in these parts for months except for the one that brought my niece's bits of things from London this afternoon, she sort of began—well, kind of joggle with her feet, as if she wanted to do a dance like on her own."

"But I thought you said," protested Bobby, "you hadn't seen a van lately."

The woman pointed out with some severity that he had asked if she had seen a van go by that way. She hadn't. The van that had brought her niece's "bits of things" hadn't gone by; it had stopped. Evidently it had never occurred to her that inquiries about a sought-for and missing van could apply to one that had actually been at her own house and about which and its errand there could be no mystery, since she herself was so well acquainted with both.

Further questioning revealed that Denis and Hilda had been gone only about half an hour. The van itself had left perhaps an hour earlier, though she wasn't sure. It was plain, in fact, that her calm and solitary existence had left her somewhat vague about times.

" Very obliging the gentlemen were that came with the van," she explained, " and helped me to get the things in and the big carpet down too. So I got them their tea with my raspberry jam and home-made scones, and they stopped on a bit smoking their pipes and saying how nice it was here and quiet; like Hampstead Heath, they said, on a week-day."

Bobby supposed all this explained why no report had been received concerning the van, and why no one had seen it. Snugly hidden behind the trees here, it could have remained unnoticed while whole troops of searchers passed by. Odd, Bobby told himself, to think of that peaceful scene, the " bits of things " amiably unloaded, the good woman serving tea, the quiet, unconcerned enjoyment of the country air, while on the hot and dusty roads their own car, and others, too, were rushing wildly to and fro, seeking and not finding, and in the van itself reposed, untouched and unnoticed, such a fortune in rare gems as few may ever even see.

" Can you tell me," Bobby asked, " which way the van went when it left here ? "

" Well, they asked me the quickest way to get to the main road," the woman answered, " and I told them the lane on the left would save them going round by the village, but it's that steep and twisty it wouldn't hardly be safe, not for a big thing like theirs."

" What did they say ? "

" The gentleman driving said there wasn't nowhere the van could get he couldn't take it," she replied, " so long as there was room for it to pass. Never had an accident yet, he said, and it had got so late with sitting over their tea they had better save time if they could. But there's been accidents down along that lane before to-day," she added, again looking a little uneasily towards that faint and distant column of smoke. " Burning rubbish," she repeated, " but I don't know who it can be."

Bobby that afternoon had seen several times smoke coming from autumnal fires where dead leaves and so on were being got rid of, and he did not pay much attention to this.

" Do you know which way the lady and gentleman went you told me about ? " he continued.

" They spoke of going the same way as the van," she answered. " I told the gentleman to be careful if they did, along of all those twists and turns, and he said he supposed they could follow where a furniture van had been before. A year ago," she added, " a car went over the bank near the foot of the lane and caught fire. We saw the smoke from here just like yon."

" We'll push along and see," Bobby promised her, and as he was going she called after him :

" Keep to the left; there's two turnings on the right that only lead to Middle Springs Farm, where there's no one living since Mr. Watson was sold up. That's why the lane is in worse state than it was, along of there being no one to look after it, and round the farm all boggy, too, with the springs overflowing along of so much rain as we've been having."

" The left—I'll remember," Bobby said, and, going back,

made his report to Ulyett, who had been on the point of coming to see what had become of him.

"Looks as if we're going to be too late," Ulyett commented. "Lady wasn't on the 'phone, I suppose? No. Ten to one Chenery and his girl will have got their claws on the necklace by now. We had better follow the way the van took and see if we can find out what's happened, and then ring up and get an alarm out as soon as we can find a call-box. Not one chance in a hundred, though, of picking up Chenery with the goods still on him. Ten to one he'll plant the thing somewhere and tell us he's just been taking his girl for a joy-ride."

"There'll be the evidence of the driver of the van and his mate," Bobby pointed out.

"Think so? Hope you're right," Ulyett mumbled, and subsided into a silence that Bobby did not dare to interrupt, fearful as were the thoughts with which it filled him.

The lane, they found, when they turned into it, more than justified the warnings they had received. At times it almost doubled back upon itself; and, apart from numerous hairpin bends, it was steep and often muddy, with a surface that seemed chiefly composed of a slithering mire. Bobby was a good driver, but he was thankful he hadn't a furniture van to manage. As it was, it took all his skill and care to keep their car on an even keel. He began to think but poorly of their chance of getting safely through; and as for the furniture van, he could only suppose that Providence had kindly provided a succession of miracles to save it from a catastrophe otherwise inevitable at every other yard or two.

The tracks the van had made in the lane's soft surface were plainly visible as they cautiously progressed, though Bobby had small time to notice them. Ulyett said:

"There's been another car before us and after the van —Chenery's, I suppose."

Bobby did not answer. He was perspiring gently, and had just managed to avoid sliding through a hedge and over a ten-foot bank into a field below. They came to a turning on the right, evidently the one leading to the derelict farm concerning which they had been warned. It had, in fact, entirely the air of being the proper continuation of the lane, and Bobby would certainly have followed it but for the warning received. Ulyett, who was standing on the footboard so as to have a clearer view of the tracks in the mud, said:

" The van went straight on all right, that's plain. But it looks as if Chenery, if it was him, turned off here, leads to an empty farm, you said ? "

" Yes, sir," answered Bobby, " considerable risk of getting bogged there, too, according to what that woman told me."

" Hope Chenery does get bogged," grunted Ulyett. " Give us a chance to catch up with the van first. Time we had a bit of luck, anyhow. Haven't had much in this show."

They drove on slowly and carefully, though the going was better now. Here and there the surface had been improved by the dumping of a load of stones or clinkers—possibly the work of the unfortunately bankrupt Mr. Watson, to whose farm this lane had apparently provided the most direct access.

They were getting close now to the column of smoke, by this time a little thinner, as if the fire from which it came were exhausting itself. Bobby, negotiating another, and, as it turned out, final hairpin bend came into a narrow but fairly straight and firm stretch of road, bordered on one side by a small wood and on the other by a hedge that a few yards further on showed itself broken through where some vehicle had gone over the edge of the bank just where the smoke was coming from.

" Something been happening," Ulyett muttered. " Get a move on her, Owen."

" Yes, sir," said Bobby, acquiescent as ever, but careful not to obey, since here even the deviation of an inch would be likely enough to send their own car somersaulting over the edge of the bank into the field below.

But the distance that separated them from that ominous gap in the hedge was not great, and Ulyett jumped down as Bobby slowed and ran to the spot.

" The van all right," he said, looking down at where it burned—or smouldered rather, for the flames had died down now and all that was left was a pile of glowing ashes. " What's become of the driver and his mate ? " he asked.

There was no sign of either of them, and, uneasily enough, Ulyett and Bobby looked at each other.

CHAPTER XXIX

THE SACKED DUKE

At this point the drop into the field beneath was about ten feet at an angle of some sixty degrees. The grass- and weed-grown surface of the bank showed clearly where the ponderous van had rolled down, to crash into flames at the bottom of the descent. Ulyett, looking down at the smouldering ashes, grumbled to Bobby:

" I suppose diamonds stand heat all right, don't they ? "

" I don't know, sir. I should think so," Bobby answered. He added: " You don't think they'll still be there, do you, sir, even if they were there to start with ? "

" Someone got away with them, you mean ? " Ulyett asked.

" I should think it's ten to one they're gone," Bobby answered. " Do you notice the tracks ahead, sir ? They're interesting."

There were plainly marked tracks in the soft surface of the lane that were not too difficult to read. For a few moments Ulyett and Bobby turned their attention to them. It seemed quite plain that a car coming in the opposite direction—from the lower end of the lane—had here met the van where there was barely room for the two vehicles to pass, and no room at all for either of them to turn. The van had drawn to the outside to give space to the car to get by. In consequence, it had overbalanced, whereon the car, instead of proceeding on its way, had backed for some distance till a comparatively free space under the trees had allowed it to turn and go back by the way it had come.

" If the vanmen had been injured, possibly taking them to hospital," observed Ulyett, " or going for help. All depends on who was in the car."

" Yes, sir," agreed Bobby. " It might be," he added cautiously, " that when the car and van met there was some excitement; that while the car driver and the vanmen were arguing what to do, somebody else from the car got down, walked round to the back of the van to see what things looked like there, took the opportunity to nip into the van and grab the necklace, and that then the accident happened—if it was an accident," he added. " Looks to me very much as if the van had been deliberately tippled over."

" All depends," repeated Ulyett, " on who was in the car. Young Chenery and his girl, if you ask me. Easy does for Chenery to keep the vanmen talking while the girl nips round behind. Then they edge the van over to give the vanmen something else to think about—perhaps they had got suspicious—and clear off with the necklace."

" Yes, sir," agreed Bobby, " only, if it was Denis Chenery, I don't quite see how they could have got here so soon, coming the opposite way, too. It was pretty plain they took the wrong turning higher up—the one that led to the empty farm."

" Might be a short cut through there somewhere," Ulyett suggested. " All I hope is, nothing worse has happened. Shan't be sorry to see those vanmen still alive. The diamonds gone for keeps most likely—nice snug hiding-place arranged for them, and there they'll stop for a year or two till there's a good chance to get 'em away—out East somewhere; Japan perhaps, or it might be South America. Better have a closer look."

He and Bobby accordingly scrambled down the steep

bank, leaving Higson to look after the car. What was left of the van showed no sign of having been disturbed, though to disturb it, considering the heat it was still giving out, would not have been easy. There was nothing to show that any struggle had occurred, or, indeed, that anything had happened beyond the fall of the van and its bursting into flames. Ulyett, with his hands in his pockets, stood looking at it discontentedly from as near as the heat permitted him to approach.

" Wish we had something to rake the ashes over with," he grumbled.

But Bobby had noticed, half hidden in long grass at a little distance, a crumpled ball of paper. He went across and picked it up. It consisted of the outer pages of the *Evening Announcer* containing the football results for the day of Mr. Jessop's murder. It had been used to wrap something in, something small and hard, for the paper was twisted and a little torn. Bobby showed it to Ulyett.

" Circumstantial evidence, sir," he said, " but pretty conclusive, I think."

" Means we were right," Ulyett agreed. " T. T. stuffed the necklace away in the van, and fussed us too much by the way he was raking out our chaps for anyone to notice what he was up to. Mightn't have come off so easily, though, if it hadn't been for the murder giving us something else to think about. Question is, who has got the thing now ? "

" Yes, sir," said Bobby. " There's someone coming."

A man was walking across the field to them. He was a cottager, working a small allotment of his own and doing odd jobs for neighbouring farmers as well. He had been on the scene before, attracted by the smoke, though he had not seen what actually happened. He took it for granted that Ulyett and Bobby were passing motorists attracted by the evidence of an accident. He agreed there was nothing to show that any injury to life or limb had occurred, and he added that the lane was dangerous and in his opinion ought to be closed for traffic, though it was little used since the farm up yonder had been vacant. To-day, though, an unusual number of cars had passed that way.

" There was two other gents," he said, " before you, wanting to know what had happened and if anyone had been hurt."

Ulyett at once asked about these other visitors. The cottager was quite willing to talk, and though he had not seen their car, since that had naturally remained in the lane above, out of sight, he was able to give of the men themselves a fairly good description.

" Tall, thin gentleman, one of them," he said, " and the other not very tall, but a big chap all the same—flat nose, and looked as if he had done a bit of boxing in his time."

Further details he added made it plain that it was Mr. Jacks and his manager, Obadiah Wright, whom he had seen.

" Was it them got the diamonds ? " Ulyett muttered. " Looks like we're a day behind the fair."

" Yes, sir," agreed Bobby, rather dismally. " Anyhow, they've got clear away."

" Have to get to a 'phone quick as we can," Ulyett said, " and send out word they were in this neighbourhood. Of course, with these blessed cars, they may be fifty miles away in any direction by now. I wish to the Lord," he said bitterly, " every inventor was smothered at birth."

From the bank above, Higson called down to them in a shrill, excited whisper. He was in the act of starting to clamber down the steep bank. He called to them :

" I've just seen him—plain I saw him, peeping out at me from behind the trees—the chap you want me to identify."

As he spoke, there rang out a swift succession of heavy pistol shots, rapid and dreadful in the quiet evening air. Higson screamed out aloud; he flung up his arms and screamed again, and down the steep bank he plunged head-long, to lie in a bleeding, unconscious heap at their feet.

For a moment, a fraction of a second, the sheer dread and unexpectedness of the thing held them motionless. Bobby always remembered the open-mouthed gape of the cottager as he stared uncomprehendingly upwards, like a man who had just seen a tree walking or heard an animal begin to talk.

" Look after him," shouted Ulyett, with a gesture at the prostrate Higson, and made a gallant rush at the steep bank.

But years had robbed him of some of his former agility, and had bestowed upon him instead a certain rotundity of form. His rush carried him half way up the bank, but there he slipped, stumbled, rolled down again. Bobby, who had bent down to assure himself that Higson was still alive, said to him quickly :

" Let me, sir, may I ? "

Without waiting for a reply, he charged up the bank and reached the lane above. A thin wisp of smoke still hung in the air under the trees just opposite, and Bobby plunged headlong in pursuit into the wood.

It was very quiet and still there beneath the trees, and very dark as well, for it was growing late now and here in the wood night had already come. The assassin, too, had had some moments' start, and Bobby was soon convinced that pursuit was hopeless. He pushed on, however, and came out presently on the other side of the trees. In front was an open field, beyond that again the main road, and from it came the sound of a motor-car growing fainter as he listened.

" Making off at about a hundred m.p.h.," Bobby muttered.

He hurried back, for it was plain there was no more to do, and found that Ulyett and the cottager between them had managed to get Higson up the bank, into the car.

" Have to get him to a doctor first of all," Ulyett grumbled. " Give the gunman a nice start, worse luck. We'll have the wood gone over in the morning, though, and we may find something to help. Pity it's nearly dark. Not that footprints are much good nowadays, with everyone wearing the same kind of shoe from the same multiple shops. We may find the pistol, though, or something useful."

" Yes, sir," agreed Bobby. " I suppose this means Higson was recognised, too, by whoever it was he recognised, and the idea was to stop his giving evidence. Is he badly hurt, do you think, sir ? "

" Hit twice," Ulyett answered; " the other shots must have missed. One hit in the back under the ribs and another in the shoulder. I should think it's a toss-up whether he pulls through or not." Slowly Ulyett added: " Jacks and Wright seen in the vicinity, and known to possess a pistol."

" Small calibre automatic their licence was for, I think, sir," Bobby reminded him. " I thought what we heard sounded more like a revolver, ·45."

Ulyett was looking at him doubtfully.

" Yes, I remember," he said. " I see what you mean. But then——" He lapsed into deep thought. " Oh, well," he said. " First thing is to get this poor chap to hospital or a doctor's, and then we can try to work it out."

Their cottager friend was able to direct them to a small local hospital only two or three miles distant. If they turned north along the main road at the foot of the lane and took the first turning they saw on their left, they would get there, he thought, in less than a quarter of an hour. They followed his directions accordingly, Bobby driving very carefully as he tried to strike the happy medium between the high speed desirable to get the injured man to the hospital as quickly as possible, and the necessity for avoiding

SJ

jolts and jars. Ulyett was holding Higson in as comfortable a position as possible, watching, carefully, too, to see that the hastily applied bandages did not slip. He said to Bobby:

" What about that parcel you said Higson brought along with him ? "

" The raincoat ? " Bobby asked. " At least, I suppose it's that. If it's anything else was pawned that night, it'll knock all my ideas of what happened on the head. Shall I look, sir ? "

" Yes, do," Ulyett said, lowering the unconscious Higson into the seat and supporting him there with cushions.

Bobby ripped open the parcel. As he expected, it contained a raincoat, nearly new. A ticket attached gave particulars showing when it had been pledged, and for how much. Putting his hand into one of the pockets, Ulyett brought out a rubber glove from which the thumb had been torn off.

" Look at that," he said.

Bobby looked at it gravely. He remembered the thumb-piece from such a glove caught in the trigger of the pistol that had dealt Jessop his death.

" Conclusive, sir, isn't it ? " he said.

" If Higson dies," Ulyett asked, " shall we be any further forward ? "

Bobby did not answer. A mistake, he supposed, not to have taken Higson's evidence in full while that had been possible. One could never be sure of the future. It had seemed better, of course, that Higson should make his identification without any name having been mentioned, so that no question of previous prejudice could arise. Now it was doubtful if any identification at all were going to be possible.

They reached the turning their cottager friend had warned them to look out for. Bobby turned into it, and almost at once they saw a car lying upset half in and half out of the ditch by the roadside.

"Another accident," Bobby said. "Not one of our lot this time, I suppose." And, almost before he had finished speaking, both he and Ulyett were staring blankly, in a kind of dazed bewilderment, as if this time quite unable to believe their own eyes.

For there in the field just beyond was a bundle—a shapeless bundle, a sack, a parcel, a what you will—performing apparently spontaneous gyrations, standing on one end one moment, the next prostrate again and rolling on the ground, then once more wriggling itself upright.

"Someone inside," Ulyett gasped. "What's up now?"

Bobby brought the car to a standstill. Both Ulyett and Bobby jumped out, Ulyett still holding the raincoat. Together they raced towards the still gyrating sack.

They reached it just as once more, after remaining on end for a moment or two, it had toppled over. Bobby had ready in his hand a pocket-knife he had opened as he ran. With it he ripped the thing open, and there appeared the head and shoulders of the Duke of Westhaven.

"I have been requiring assistance for some moments," he said with cold rebuke. His eye caught the coat Ulyett, who had just come up, was still holding in one hand. "Ah, my raincoat," he said, and incontinently fainted.

CHAPTER XXX

RENEWED PURSUIT

A T T H E C O T T A G E H O S P I T A L, which was only about a mile and a half further on, the duke and Higson received prompt attention. Higson's wounds were dangerous, it was said, but there was an excellent chance of recovery unless unexpected complications ensued. The duke's condition was diagnosed as due to more than a mere faint; shock was the convenient word used, rest and quiet the treatment ordered, and he was at once put to bed in a vacant cot, next, alas ! to the bed occupied by Higson; to Ulyett's shocked remonstrance, when he knew this, the inadequate excuse being tendered that the hospital had no other vacant bed, and that its only private ward was occupied by two jay-walkers suffering due penalty for obstructing the passage of a motorist to whom had been confided by his firm the task of demonstrating the merits of a new car model, by lowering the road record from Land's End to John o' Groat's.

" There's an appeal out in the papers for funds to provide another private ward," said cheerfully the young doctor who told Ulyett this. " Perhaps the old blighter you've trotted in will cough up the dough when we've got him toddling again."

" Better," suggested Bobby, " charge him a whacking fee —a bill duly delivered is worth a dozen appeals in the Press."

Ulyett rebuked sternly so uncalled-for an expression of opinion. Before this he had been busy at the 'phone, calling up the headquarters of every police force anywhere near so that now he hoped the whole country-side had become one huge watching eye. Every car was to be stopped, and its inmates questioned and detained if their identity and innocence were not clearly established. Pedestrians, too, were to be examined, since there was a possibility that cars might be abandoned. On railway stations and 'bus stops the closest watch was to be kept. Over an area of something like a hundred miles from side to side was to be spread, in fact, a kind of enormous drag-net, through which Ulyett observed with complacence only a very slippery fish indeed would have any chance of escaping.

" Yes, sir," agreed Bobby, though thinking to himself that the fish they had to deal with were slippery beyond compare.

" Only," added Ulyett, with a discontented grunt, " they all want to know what it's all about—as if," he grumbled, " anyone could tell what a nightmare was about. What do you think's been happening, Owen ? "

Fortunately, it was plain he expected no answer, and Bobby therefore, busy at the moment refilling their tank with petrol he had been able to obtain at the hospital, was spared the necessity of replying. It was quite dark now, and Ulyett had decided that they would spend the night at Cheltenham. But he wanted first to go back to the scene of the burning of the van and the shooting of Higson, to await there the police he had asked should be sent to keep ward and watch till daylight permitted a close search of the scene of the accident, of the ashes of the van in case they still concealed the necklace, and of the wood in which it was hoped might be found evidence of the identity of Higson's assailant.

The night was dark, only a few stars showing in a cloudy sky. The wind was rising, bringing with it a hint of rain, and Ulyett looked up in a very discontented way.

" Going to be a storm," he muttered. " Lots of heavy rain to wash out any footprints or tracks. Just our luck."

The dark, unlighted roads—for this was no " built-up " area—imposed care and a certain restraint of speed on Bobby. When they were near the spot where the lane down which they had followed the furniture van joined the main road, they saw the lights of a car drawn up by the roadside a little further on.

" Wonder who it is ? " Ulyett grunted. " None of those we want, I suppose, but we had better see."

Bobby halted accordingly, and, getting down, went across to where the strange car stood on a strip of grass by the roadside under the shadows of the overhanging trees of the little wood behind. By the light of the headlamps he could see a man who had evidently just completed the task of changing a tyre. Near him was a woman engaged in putting away the tools her companion had been using. Bobby, recognising them, exclaimed :

" Hullo, Mr. Chenery. Oh, and Miss May, too."

He had spoken loudly on purpose. Ulyett, who had been listening, got down at once and came to join them. Denis, wiping his hands on a rag, looked up and said :

" Oh, it's you chaps again, is it ? "

" I'll trouble you to explain——" began Ulyett in his most official voice, and then paused, not quite sure what exactly it was they were to explain.

" Well, if you want to know, and as I suppose you're on it, too," Denis answered, " we've been chasing around after the Fellows necklace. Jacks and Wright are after it, too. I expect you know ? They got a tip somehow it was packed away in a furniture van."

" What's your interest in the Fellows necklace ? " demanded Ulyett.

" Five thousand pounds reward for it, isn't there ? " Denis retorted. " Five thousand jolly good reasons for any-one to be interested in it, if you ask me. Enough for a good whack each for Miss May, for Miss Ellison, who tipped us off, and for me, too. Worth scooting round a bit for."

" The furniture van has been found overturned and burnt not far from here," Ulyett said. " No trace of the driver or his mate. A man who had given us information has been shot and dangerously wounded. The Duke of Westhaven has been assaulted—shockingly assaulted," added Ulyett, feeling that a duke deserved an adverb.

" What ? " said Denis, bewildered. " What's all that ? "

" What do you know about it ? " demanded Ulyett.

" Things been happening," Denis commented. " We've been out of it, though. An old girl way up on the hills told us the van we were hunting had been at her place. But she did us down for some reason. Told us the van had gone down a lane she showed us she said led to the high road. Instead, it led us to an empty farm and a bog, where I'm jolly sure no furniture van ever got through. We got stuck so badly I thought we were there for keeps. When we did get out, I wasn't going to risk going back the same way. We found a cart-track that looked good, but it led us right in among trees. We foundered on some stumps that finished my front near tyre for good and all. I've just been changing it."

Ulyett grunted. The story was reasonable enough, and to some extent the condition of the car confirmed it.

" If you knew where the Fellows necklace was, it was your duty to give information to the police," he said.

" Was it ? " asked Denis coolly. " For one thing, I didn't know. All I knew was something Miss Ellison thought something she heard Wright saying might possibly mean. Apparently he had a private detective bloke messing about trying to find out things. It was his business to say anything to you chaps if he wanted to, not mine. What I wanted was to get in ahead of him if I jolly well could."

" Mr. Wright," Ulyett pointed out, with rebuke in every tone, " is in lawful charge of the Fellows necklace."

" Then what," demanded Denis, " was he up to when he nearly did in Hilda ? I owe him for that," said Denis, with deep anger in his voice. " You said yourself another half-hour and Hilda . . ." He left the sentence unfinished, but there was no mistaking the deep emotion in his tone. " And then you expect me to sweat my innards out getting his necklace back for him. I meant to make him pay all right, if I could."

" You are charging Wright with the attack on Miss May ? " Ulyett asked. " Have you any evidence ? "

" Your job, isn't it ? " retorted Denis.

Ulyett turned to Bobby.

" Wasn't there a report you made ? " he asked.

" Yes, sir," Bobby answered, remembering the fragment of steel identified with Wright's pocket-knife and how Wright had forestalled questions thereon by spontaneously volunteering the information that he had lent it to Denis himself. " There was some evidence, but it was hardly thought sufficient to take action on. Miss May was unable to help us. There was one point that seemed to clear Wright. He was stated to have been at the Yard with Mr. Jacks, reporting to you, sir, the loss of the necklace."

" That's right," Ulyett answered. " So he was. Better check up on the times, though. It'll be on record. So far as I remember, Mr. Jacks came up alone first and Wright waited in the car outside. Wright only came up afterwards, to confirm some point or another Mr. Jacks wasn't quite sure about."

" That would probably give him time to get round to Miss May's flat, as far as that goes," observed Bobby. " Spoils his alibi, anyhow." He turned to Denis and said: " We have information that that day, or the day before, you called at the Mayfair Square shop and borrowed a certain article from Mr. Wright ? "

" Rot," asserted Denis, with swift emphasis. " Who told

you that? I was never at the Mayfair Square shop in my life, and the only thing I would borrow from Wright would be his walking-stick to break over his back, blast him."

" No good talking like that without evidence," declared Ulyett.

" I told Mr. Chenery I thought it was Mr. Wright," interposed Hilda, who had been listening quietly to all this. " I thought it was like his step. He has a quick, light step. I'm not sure."

" I believe he had some sort of cracked idea Hilda had the thing hidden in her flat," Denis said. " Like his cheek. He's crooked himself and so he thinks everyone else is. Crooks always do. And Jessop had been telling lies behind Hilda's back because she told him what she thought of him, the filthy old blackguard. Perhaps that's what put it into Wright's head," said Denis, grudgingly admitting a faint shadow of something resembling a possible excuse. " And I dare say they were all pretty well off their chumps —they were about done in if they didn't get the necklace back. Good thing, too. Wright ought to get ten years for what he did to Hilda."

" Denis," Hilda said quietly, " I told you I wasn't sure. And I would rather go through it all again than have to go into a police court and tell everyone, and have everyone asking questions."

" Yes," said Denis bitterly, " you want to let the brute off. Just like a girl."

" No, I don't," Hilda contradicted him with some heat; " only I don't want anyone sent to prison, that's all."

" Who burnt the van? And who got shot? " Denis asked Ulyett. " Wasn't Wright, was it? " he added hopefully.

" We don't know yet exactly what happened," Ulyett answered. " All we know for certain is what I told you."

" What about the necklace? "

" We have no information," answered Ulyett, " except

that we believe it may have been concealed in the van. Anyone may have it now for all we know. It may be anywhere; it might still be in what's left of the van among the ashes. Not likely, though."

" You bet it isn't likely," agreed Denis.

" And," continued Ulyett, " I must ask you to accompany us to Cheltenham. I shall want you to make a statement there."

" Thought that's what I had been doing," grumbled Denis. " Besides, I want to get back to London now this is a wash-out. How far's Cheltenham ? "

Bobby looked up from the map he had been studying by the light of the car lamps.

" I can't make out quite where we are," he said, " or where this road goes to."

" Straight on across the Wiltshire downs by Stonehenge," Denis answered. " At least, a chap in a Hotspur Seven said so. He stopped to see if he could help, and I asked him where this road went to, and that's what he said."

Ulyett had been looking at Denis's car. He remarked:

" At your garage your foreman told us you were driving a Bayard Twenty. It's a Hotspur, isn't it ? He gave us the wrong number, too."

" Must have got mixed somehow," answered Denis. " Good chap, George. Tactful and all that. Very. Can't think how he came to make such a bloomer."

" I can," said Ulyett severely, but Denis had turned his head.

" Someone pushing along in a hurry," he said.

That was evident, for now out of the night there came to them the roar of a car—of cars, it seemed, from the volume of sound—rushing with the wind behind as though it were the wind itself they raced. As they listened, as they stood, before they had time to do more than draw a step or two aside, a car came screaming at them from the night that split before its headlights, and then closed again, more darkly even than before. It fled on, the miles as naught before it, and after it there followed another at the same wild, frantic speed that, at every yard almost, played even chances with disaster. Nor was that all, for behind was still a third, travelling at a rate as wild and fierce, and adding to the clamour of their general passage the shrieking of its horn, in angry, unheeded summons. Then from the first car in this lunatic procession, as it went roaring by, those at the roadside saw a stabbing flash of light dart out, like a strong lamp turned on and off, and then another and another and another.

" What's that ? " Bobby exclaimed, though he knew.

" Shots," Denis said. " Pistol. He's potting at 'em."

" It was Wright in the first car," Bobby said. " He was driving. Our headlights showed him up a minute."

" Wynne and T. T. following," Ulyett said, not moving; " and a police car after them both. Wright was shooting— trying to do in their tyres, most likely. If he does, they'll somersault, the pace they're going. They'll scrag him if they catch him."

" Hilda, you stop here. I'll see what's happening," Denis exclaimed.

" I'm coming, too," Hilda said.

Denis was starting the car. Hilda leaped in by his side. He said something. He was plainly telling her to wait. She took no notice. He started the car and followed in the wake of the others.

" Don't we, too, sir ? " Bobby said to Ulyett, astonished at his senior's inaction.

" It was Wright firing," Ulyett said. " At their tyres. Silly trick."

" Yes, sir," said Bobby, almost dancing with impatience. " What do we do ? "

" I think I'm hit," Ulyett said, and sat down gently on the road.

CHAPTER XXXI

LOST

Bobby bent down anxiously over the stricken man.
He had been hit on the left thigh, where showed a gaping,
jagged wound from whose appearance Bobby guessed it
had been caused by a ricochet. Fortunately the artery had
not been cut, and, as Bobby was doing his best to bandage
the injury, Ulyett opened his eyes.

" What you doing ? " he demanded fiercely. " Get after
'em."

" Yes, sir," said Bobby, who, indeed, was near to weeping
as he thought of that wild chase continuing through the
dark night and he unable to take part in it. " Got to fix
you first, sir."

" Fix nothing," retorted Ulyett in the feeblest of whispers
that was ever intended for an intimidating roar. " I'm all
right. Get after 'em. Orders."

" Yes, sir," said Bobby, acquiescent as ever. " One
moment, sir, till I've finished this."

Ulyett jerked his injured thigh away, so undoing all
Bobby's work and starting the bleeding again.

" Orders," he gasped again. " Get after 'em."

Therewith he fainted, and to Bobby's relief he heard a
motor-cyclist approaching—if approaching is the right word
to use when scarcely had the noise of the engine become
audible when the thing itself was there, roaring by, throwing
the miles behind it, one and more to every passing minute.
The rider took no notice of Bobby's shout, possibly did not

hear it even. Unheeded equally was the signal Bobby made by flashing his headlights across the road. He roared on, a dark and huddled figure bending low over his handle-bars, and in a second or two was no more than a clamour dying into the distance.

Bobby was not much given to violent language—he heard so much of it in the execution of his duties that it bored him, as chocolates are said to bore the girl assistants in confectioners' shops—but the curse he threw after that cyclist now would have astonished the most lurid of the practitioners in the profanity genre. There were tears in his eyes—actual tears of rage and disappointment—as he set himself to the task of getting the now unconscious Ulyett, who weighed a good fifteen stones, into the car without starting his wound bleeding once again. He had lost quite enough blood as it was, and his life must come first, but Bobby's self-control almost broke down as he thought of what might be happening elsewhere.

" That motor-cyclist," he said to himself, " going all out like that—who was he ? "

With a feeling of deep thankfulness he became aware of another car approaching, though this time at a more normal speed and from the opposite direction. Bobby shouted, and again signalled by flashing his headlight up and down across the road, and the newcomer stopped.

" Accident ? " the driver asked. " Homicidal maniac on a motor-cycle just passed me. Was it him ? What's happened ? I'm a doctor."

" Thank God," said Bobby fervently. He explained briefly. The doctor looked at Ulyett's wound, asked a question or two, and pronounced it probably not serious. He rearranged Bobby's bandage, admitting that possibly, though only possibly, it might have been put on more clumsily, and he undertook to convey the wounded man to the hospital.

Together they got Ulyett as comfortably as possible into the car, and the injured man, opening his eyes when they had settled him, gave Bobby a baleful glare.

" Insubordination—report you—discipline board," he gasped, and then, in a kind of muffled roar: " Get after 'em," he said, and forthwith fainted again.

The doctor climbed into the driver's place, and for just one second Bobby hesitated. A detective-sergeant's pay leaves no great margin for luxuries, and Argus was but poorly supplied with eyes compared with those who in the receiver's office check expense lists. No C.I.D. man exists who is not convinced, and can prove by figures, that he is down pounds and pounds every year for what by rights a niggardly country should provide. Still, Bobby had an odd copper or two in the savings bank, and pay-day does ultimately come round, even though with incredible slowness, and, as the doctor was starting with his patient, Bobby said quickly:

" Oh, do you mind ? Would you tell the hospital people I'll give a guinea to their funds if they'll put Mr. Ulyett in the next bed to the shock patient they've just got ? "

" Friends ? " asked the doctor, and, without waiting for a reply, drove off, while Bobby was aware of a glow of pure philanthropy as he thought of Ulyett's nicely mingled awe, embarrassment, wonder, and delight at finding himself bedded next to a duke.

Then he forgot it as he made a leap into his car, started it, jammed a foot on the accelerator, vanished into the darkness, like the nightmare of a bullet shot from the maw of chaos and old night.

He supposed that after this long delay those he sought would be many miles away, and in which direction he had no idea. Not much chance of either finding them or overtaking them, he felt. Still, at the speed they had been using there would not have been much opportunity for taking side-turnings, and Denis Chenery had said that the road ran straight across the Wiltshire downs. Wright, driving the first car, might have known that, and have thought the lonely Wiltshire country—the lonely Marlborough Downs or the even lonelier Salisbury Plain—a good place in which to shake off his pursuers, or perhaps, Bobby thought uncomfortably, those pursuers might have been deliberately shepherding him that way. If Wynne's reputation were anything to go by, if it were true that he cared as little for his own life as for the lives of others, then there might be grim work done that night on the wide Wiltshire plain.

That must mean, then, that Wright and Jacks, and not Wynne and T. T., were in possession of the necklace. Presumably somehow they had got hold of it before the other two had found the van, and then Wynne and T. T. —T. T. probably dragged and coerced into the adventure by his reckless associate very much against his own will —had set out in pursuit. Naturally this pursuit and flight had soon drawn after it one of the cruising police cars warned to be on the look-out. The motor-cyclist Bobby was not sure about. He might be merely a youth enjoying the thrill of night-riding at speed, or he might be someone in a hurry for some reason of his own, in no way connected with these happenings. But if he were concerned in them, then Bobby supposed it would not be difficult to guess his identity.

Bobby pressed a little harder on the accelerator. It did not make much difference. The car was already travelling at a rate that would have set the joint hair of all concerned in its manufacture on end with mingled pride and terror and incredulity. There were times when the wheels seemed hardly to touch the ground, as though the car no longer ran upon the solid earth but went by long leaps through the air. A hare the headlights dazzled, and that tried to lollop along in front, was swept over as if it had been standing still; the dogs in the farms and cottages Bobby passed had hardly begun to bark before he was out of hearing; through the darkness he fled and was gone; the night opened before him and closed again in the same instant; a watcher from afar wondered whether the trail of light he made as he traversed higher ground was on earth or a meteor on the horizon; when he came to a hill, he devoured it as though it had been a level racing-track; with every yard or two he threw dice with disaster and with death; the wind itself seemed to follow him in vain, the gusts of rain to toil helplessly behind.

Marlborough he had left behind; Wansdyke he had crossed without knowing; now he had come into a great level plain, and he was no longer on the road that somehow, somewhere, he must have left, and he was altogether lost. He slackened speed, and, as if they had been waiting for the chance, the wind snarled at him in angry gusts, the rain dashed against the side of his car, and in the distance he thought that he heard thunder.

His headlights showed that he was on a mere track across a close-growing turf. He supposed that the track would lead somewhere—at any rate, he hoped so. It was very dark, lonely, quiet, save for the angry wind and the swift, pattering rain. On the wet turf his wheels had small grip, and more than once he skidded. Of those whom he pursued there was no sign; only the impenetrable night was there, and the wind, and the rain it flung against his windows. It seemed he was quite alone in this bare, unfenced land, primitive as when the Romans had known it, or those who were here before even man had won his kingdom from the animals.

His compass gave Bobby his direction. The track he was on seemed to be following a southerly course, and he decided to continue on it. But that was not easy, and he had not gone more than a few hundred yards before he had hopelessly lost it, and then quite suddenly he was in the midst of a flock of sheep that rose up all around him, vague bundles of dingy white the earth seemed to be spawning and that ambled slowly away to resume elsewhere their disturbed rest.

"Only hope," he muttered, "I don't get into some blessed hole or gully."

A flash of unexpected lightning—for he had heard no more thunder—threw the landscape into vivid momentary relief, and showed at a little distance what seemed a series of vast and upright stones, standing there as they had stood all through the passing of the troubled and uneasy centuries. Could it be Stonehenge, he wondered? If so, that would give him his position. He wondered if there were guardians of the place in permanent residence, and, if so, if they would possess a telephone. If it were Stonehenge, Amesbury and Salisbury would not be far, and anyhow there would be telephones there. Scotland Yard would want to know as soon as possible what had happened. Only then this might not be Stonehenge. He had a memory of having read of other such relics of the Dawn on Salisbury Plain that were to Stonehenge as a cathedral is to a parish church. The momentary glimpse the lightning had given had not been enough for recognition. He drove slowly and carefully in the direction of the stones; and then became aware of a light on his right hand, a light at first but a tiny flicker, almost as though someone were lighting a cigarette, then flaring up suddenly, becoming at once a pyramid of leaping flame that the wind fanned joyously, that the rain assailed in vain.

"Car overturned and caught fire," Bobby said to himself.

Instinctively he quickened speed, and almost at once his own car plunged deep into an abrupt hollow in the ground. Bobby jumped down. He saw that the two

TJ

off-wheels were fixed deep in a rut, so that there was no hope of extricating them without help. He began to run towards the fire. Then came a sharp crackle of pistol shots, and he could see figures outlined before the fire, distinct for a moment in its glow, and then vanishing again into the dark. From a distance he could hear the chug-chug of a motor-cycle thumping its way nearer across the turf.

Another shot rang out. Bobby reflected uncomfortably that Ulyett had had an automatic but that he himself was quite unarmed.

CHAPTER XXXII

ON WILTSHIRE DOWNS

FOR A MOMENT Bobby stood still. The flames from the burning car leaped higher, fanned by the wind, indifferent to the driving rain. He saw again dark figures running to and fro before it and behind. The light it cast round showed where, close by, there reared itself in the darkness, twelve feet into the air, a huge and upright stone that had watched there for ten thousand years, perhaps, but had seldom seen stranger happenings—a pagan stone that could well have thought this night that pagan times had come again. Near it lay another, enormous as itself, full length upon the earth, as though it at least had bowed beneath the passage of the years, and the wind blew more fiercely still and the rain came down more heavily.

Bobby grabbed a spanner from the tool-box. It would at least be better than nothing, he thought, since bullets were flying so freely. He ran forward and, catching his foot on a huddled form he had not seen, went headlong, shaking himself badly, and letting the spanner fly off into the darkness, irretrievably lost. The huddle he had fallen over emitted a squawk of terror, and Bobby, scrambling to his knees, seized it, not too gently.

" What's all this ? " he said. " Let's have a look at you."

" Oh, my God," wailed a faint voice Bobby recognised at once for T. T.'s. " Oh, it's the C.I.D., thank God," moaned T. T., who seldom before had thanked God for anything, and certainly never for the C.I.D.

" What's up ? " demanded Bobby. " Where's Wynne ? He was with you. Where's Wright and Jacks ? "

But at this moment another shot rang out, not very far away. T. T. screamed, jerked away from Bobby's grasp, flattened his body passionately against the earth, as though in his extremity of terror he would force himself for shelter to be one with it.

There was plainly nothing to be got out of him who was but a shivering jelly of panic. Bobby got to his feet and ran on, thankful for the darkness, that at any rate gave him some measure of security. He was careful to leave well to the side the circle of light cast by the fire, for he had the idea that to enter it would mean swift death.

Somewhere near by in the night he was sure hid Wynne, lurked Wright, each armed with a pistol, one with the necklace, both equally reckless and resolute. Nearer came the chug-chug of the motor-cyclist. The sound gave the direction, but no headlight showed. Probably the shooting had been heard and the headlight prudently extinguished. As cautiously, as silently as he might, so that he might take every advantage from the wind, the rain, the night, that were here his only help, Bobby ran on. A hand shot out of the darkness and caught him by the ankle. He went down with violence. Before he could recover from the shock of this second fall, a voice whispered :

" Look out, you fool. He's got a gun; he's done in Jacks already."

" You're Wright ? " Bobby asked.

" Yes. Wynne's there. Quite close. Keep quiet. He'll get us both if you don't mind." Bobby tried to rise, but Wright's heavy hand pressed him down again. With his mouth close to Bobby's ear, though indeed the wind, the pattering of the rain, muffled all other sounds, Wright went on : " You showed up against the fire. I saw you. If it had been him you would be dead by now. He's taking no chances. Got a gun ? "

" No," Bobby answered. " Have you ? "

" Empty," Wright answered. " No more ammunition."

" Can't lie here," Bobby muttered, " and let him get away."

" He won't," Wright answered grimly. " I've the necklace. I saw him and another fellow looking at it. I grabbed it. Like that. I started up and went off top speed. They followed—shooting. Edged us away from houses. We didn't dare stop. Knew they would shoot and grab and run. Only chance to shake them off, and we couldn't, or get to a town, and we couldn't." He added: " There's someone coming."

But, as he said this, the chug-chug of the motor-cycle bumping its way towards them across the short cropped turf, ceased abruptly.

" Who is it ? One of your pals ? " Wright muttered.

Bobby did not think so, and he said nothing, though he believed he could make a good guess at the identity of the new-comer.

" We can't stop here for ever," he muttered, after a brief pause.

" If you don't shut up, we will all right," retorted Wright grimly. " Listen."

Footsteps were drawing near—the slow and careful footsteps of some intent searcher.

" Oh, there you are, I see you now," a voice said loudly. " Look here, Wright, I don't want to hurt you. Why should I ? Hand over the necklace and we'll go fifty-fifty."

Wright made no answer, though Bobby could feel with what intensity his whole body stiffened, understood with what an agony of apprehension it grew rigid, could hear the muffled panting breaths Wright drew. A gust of wind blew with renewed violence; in a fresh squall the rain rushed by, soaking them as they lay who were soaked through already. Wynne cried, his voice a high-pitched scream to make it carry above the storm:

" All right, all right. Now you've asked for it and now you'll get it. I'll give you till I've counted three. One——" And Bobby knew rather than felt with what rigidity of purpose Wright held himself still.

" Two," counted Wynne, his voice screaming against the storm, and Bobby thought to himself:

" If he gets Wright, he'll get me next."

Both he and Wright had nearly ceased to breathe. Bobby wondered abstractedly how it was, when his face was sheltered by his arms as he lay, yet the rain was trickling down it; and then he realised that it was not rain, but sweat, and this puzzled him, for he felt very cold. He wondered who would be promoted to sergeant in his place. He wondered half a hundred other things; matter for more thought, indeed, passed through his mind than would, as a rule, have entered it in a week, with such a kaleidoscopic lightning-like speed was it working now.

" Three," Wynne shrieked, and a flash of light stabbed the night, and the sharp whip-like crack of an automatic.

There followed a burst of rich profanity, and Wright permitted himself to mutter into Bobby's ear:

" Knew he was bluffing or he would have spotted there were two of us. Bit hard to lie still, though."

Bobby fully agreed.

" We've got to do something. We can't stop like this," he repeated.

" If we don't, he'll get us soon as we try to move," Wright answered. " If we do, he'll get us soon as it's light."

This seemed likely enough to Bobby, and did not make him feel any more cheerful. He tried to think what to do and found his mind a blank.

" There was a motor-cycle coming," Wright whispered. " I heard it. Perhaps it's bringing help."

Bobby did not think so—not, at any rate, if his guess at the identity of the rider were correct. He found himself wondering what had happened. Probably Wright and Jacks in the first car had made the same error that he himself presumably had made, and had left the main road at the same spot, following the same track, to bring them here as it had brought him. Wynne and T. T. had followed. The police car in pursuit had most likely been out-distanced, and had probably proceeded along the main road. As for Denis and Hilda, they might be anywhere within fifty miles. Bobby thought the only chance was that the police car might give the alarm and that a search-party might be sent out to cover the Wiltshire Downs, somewhere whereon which he supposed they were, and so might find them in time to be of help. But this seemed to Bobby an extremely slender hope. He thought it more likely that by that time only a few dead bodies would be there to find, and this reflection gave him a curiously empty feeling in the pit of the stomach. Discovering again that he was very cold, and being obliged to smother at this moment a fit of sneezing, he reflected that, anyhow, he was perhaps going to be spared the discomfort of a bad cold in the head, or that rheumatic fever with which his landlady was constantly threatening him when he put on a fresh shirt without having let her previously air it. But this reflection did nothing to alleviate that uncomfortable feeling inside him. To Wright he whispered:

" Whose car is burning ? "

" Mine," Wright answered. " It overturned and caught fire."

" Where's Mr. Jacks ? " Bobby asked.

" Wynne got him while we were watching the fire. I fired back. It was the only shot I had left. He chased me round the fire. I dodged away, and it's so dark he couldn't see, only hear. He got so close I thought my best chance was to lie up. I saw Jacks crawling away. He wasn't dead then. Perhaps he is now. He was badly hit."

" Got to do something," Bobby muttered.

" Better keep quiet," Wright advised. " He's got a gun. You haven't. He'll use it."

" I know," said Bobby, who had small liking for the job before him. " Look here," he suggested, " you call him. He can't be far off. He's sure to hear. He'll think you want to make terms. As soon as he gets near, I'll rush him."

" Not me," said Wright frankly. " Not one chance in fifty to bring that off."

" You're scared," said Bobby. " So am I," he sighed, and wriggled away into the darkness.

" You're a fool," Wright whispered after him, and Bobby was quite of the same opinion.

When he had gone a little distance he got to his feet and shouted with the full force of his lungs:

" No gaps mind. Let every man keep in touch. Guns ready."

Then he dropped to the ground and lay still, awaiting results. There were none. Only he heard someone laughing lightly at a little distance. That meant his bluff, obvious enough for that matter, had been a failure. He lay still, listening intently. The rain was less violent now; the wind had fallen a little. He was making rubbing noises with his hand on the wet and slippery turf that he hoped would sound like footsteps, and he thought how lucky Ulyett was to be snug in bed in the hospital. But superintendents always had all the luck; that, in fact, was what it was to be a superintendent or any other kind of boss. Then the luck came to you as naturally as decorations to a staff officer. He got cautiously to his feet. At once a shot rang out, and Bobby screamed and pitched forward on his face. A figure Bobby knew for that of Wynne ran forward from out of the dark, shouting something incoherent. Bobby leaped from the ground in one movement and seized him. That bluff, at least, had worked. But he had leaped a little too soon. His grip was insecure. A moment of fierce struggling, a swift exchange of blows, then Wynne had wrenched himself free and leaped away again.

But he left his pistol behind. Bobby's first aim had been to grip that. A fierce exultation possessed him. He felt safe now, now that he had the other's weapon and so had rendered him comparatively harmless.

" All right, Wynne, all right, all right," he shouted into the darkness. " No hurry, but we'll pick you up when we've time to spare."

A furious curse answered him. Bobby, taking no notice, began to walk in the direction where Wright lay. He looked at the automatic and found all the clip had been fired except one shot.

" Hullo, Wright, where are you ? " he shouted.

He was feeling happy and excited. Death had been very near. He had felt the coldness of its breath upon his brow. Now it had passed and was far off again. He felt a little drunk.

" Hullo, Wright," he shouted. " All in order now. I've Wynne's little pet pistol and you've the necklace, so everything in the garden's lovely."

Wright gave an answering call. Bobby went to meet him. They were standing in the circle of glowing light made by the flames from the still burning car.

" We must find Jacks," Bobby said, more soberly. " I hope he's all right."

Once again the darkness behind them was rent by a darting fire, once again above the now quieter wind and rain rang out pistol shots in swift succession. One bullet came so close to Bobby he could feel the wind its passage made, and heard plainly its vicious snarl, a sound once known none ever forget again. Wright yelled and fell down flat. Bobby fired back, and the moment he had done so knew how foolish it had been. For he had fired by instinct, and at random, and it was the only shot the pistol held. Wildly he thought what a fool he had been not to guess that Wynne might have had a second pistol in reserve. A wild-looking figure, a heavy revolver in one hand, was standing just where the circle of light from the fire faded into the darkness of the night. But it was not Wynne who stood there.

" You've the necklace," the new-comer said hoarsely, a note of hurry, almost of panic, of wrought-up intensity of purpose, in his voice. " Give it me or I'll blow your brains out. Quick now. I'll dump your bodies in the fire there and no one will ever know. Hurry up."

The tone of half frantic menace in his voice was daunting in the extreme. It suggested that the speaker had no longer control of himself, that no longer did he fully realise what it was that he was doing. A hysteria of fear and panic had him in its grip. Against the bright light of the flames behind them both Bobby and Wright knew themselves clearly out-lined. The thought came to Bobby that it was a little hard thus to be snatched back from safety, much worse than if safety had not a moment before seemed won at last. He also thought he had been a fool to forget so entirely that approaching motor-cycle, chug-chugging its way towards them, and his guess at the identity of its rider. He noticed how the firelight gleamed dully on the barrel of the revolver, threatening them with so deadly an intention. Wright saw it, too, and suddenly his resolution cracked. This new threat was too much.

" All right, take it, take it," he yelled, and from his pocket he snatched the shining, glittering thing, source of all these woes, and flung it at the feet of the new-comer, who stooped and picked it up but still kept them under the menace of his pistol.

" All right, all right, all right," he muttered. He said: " All the same . . . or you'll tell . . . I let the duke go, but I can't let you."

There was an odd regret in his muttering voice that made the threat that it conveyed all the more intentional, the purpose so expressed seem all the more inevitable, inescapable. Wright screamed. The strain, so long continued, had been too much for him. He was nothing now but all one quivering fear. Bobby was conscious once again of that unpleasant sinking feeling in his stomach. He made a movement, or rather he began one, and instantly the other moved also, stepping nearer, as if he wished to be quite certain of his aim. He fired, but his bullet passed harmlessly, far to one side, for a clod of earth, thrown from a distance, struck him at that moment on the cheek and deflected his aim.

He swung round, firing again, at a figure that came rushing at him from the night, as though the darkness there had materialised into a man. Twice he fired at that onrushing figure, but twice he missed in the darkness and confusion, and then Bobby had him round the body, and the new-comer was upon them, too, and all three rolled upon the ground in a hopeless tangle till at last Bobby found himself uppermost.

" That you, Chenery ? " he said as the light from the burning car showed him the new-comer's features. " Much obliged. Not hit, are you ? "

" Tip of left ear shot away," said Denis ruefully. " What's up ? We got lost. Then we saw a fire—and shooting. What's Dickson been doing ? "

" Oh, lots of things," Bobby answered, fitting handcuffs to Dickson's wrists. " Sacking a duke and making it a general shooting-party all round. Also he'll be charged with the murder of Mr. Jessop."

CHAPTER XXXIII

THE DUKE LISTENS

NEXT MORNING a pale and washed-out Bobby appeared at the hospital sheltering both Superintendent Ulyett and the Duke of Westhaven. Bobby's report had gone in, and various high officials were coming down later in the day to have a look round for themselves, to consult with the local people, and to interview Ulyett, who was not yet, the doctors said, fit to be moved, and to be present when Dickson was brought before the magistrates, when a remand would be asked for. And in far-off California film magnates were already preparing to offer Miss Fay Fellows fresh contracts at the salary of her palmiest days, though only on condition that she wore in every picture the necklace of which all the world would now be talking, to see which all the world would soon be willing to pay those sixpences, shillings, and half-crowns that presently add up to so many millions. For there remains personality, and genius, and beauty, but greater than these is publicity, and with glad tears in his eyes Miss Fay Fellows's publicity agent acknowledged that, even if he had arranged the whole thing himself, it could hardly have been better done.

In the private room of the chairman of the hospital, in the chairman's own special arm-chair, in a dressing-gown provided by the resident medical officer, sat the duke, a little pale, a little wan, slightly displeased with a universe that allowed such incidents to happen even to the best people. On the table by his side lay a cheque he had just signed, his contribution to the hospital funds in recognition of services received. The cheque was for one guinea, but the hospital authorities did not know that yet, and were still optimistic. Opposite to him sat Bobby, summoned to the ducal presence, a presence somewhat more nervously apprehensive than usual with one accustomed from youth to find a world suitably washed and ironed for his acceptance.

" Not," he said darkly, " that I am surprised to hear—after yesterday—that Dickson is a murderer. When one considers——"

" —the way he treated you, sir," Bobby completed the sentence—tactless for once, even consciously tactless in fact. " It was a bit thick."

" It is a subject that need not be referred to again," said the duke coldly. " I shall be interested to know if there is any valid reason why Dickson was not arrested earlier. At the moment the delay appears to me inexcusable."

" Have to wait for proof," explained Bobby. " Got to be sure of your ground before you send your case to the Public Prosecutor's office. They want it complete, trimmings and all, so all counsel have to do is to reel it off. And till we got hold of Higson to identify Dickson as the man who pawned the raincoat the night of the murder, the case wasn't cast iron. Now there's something extra, now we've found in it rubber gloves fitting the thumb-piece torn off by the trigger guard of the pistol that shot Jessop."

" Why did Dickson pawn the coat ? " the duke asked, forgetting for the moment his own grievances. " What made you suspect him in the first place ? "

" Well, sir," Bobby answered slowly, " as to why he pawned the coat, that was largely a case of panic and guilty conscience. He had shot Jessop—panic, too—he had discovered the necklace he did it for was only imitation, he had thrown it away, he was scared, excited, nervy to a degree, and he showed it plainly enough to make a policeman who saw him wonder what the matter was. Our men keep an eye on people in the streets who seem excited and upset. Dickson saw he was being watched; that upset him still more; he knew if he was stopped and questioned it was all up. He tried to dodge up a street turning; he saw the constable start to follow him. Close by there was the door of a pawnbroker's shop—as you know, pawnbrokers generally choose a corner for their shops."

" Do they ? " said the duke, interested. " Why ? "

" So that people can slip in without being seen," explained Bobby, thinking to himself how little dukes and such-like know of the commonplaces of everyday life. " That's what Dickson did. He had to have some excuse for going in, so he pawned his raincoat and asked if they would let him out through the shop into the main street, so that he wouldn't have so far to go to the tube station— he said he wanted the money to pay his fare back to town. He may have thought that getting rid of the coat would help, too; be a kind of disguise. He forgot about the rubber gloves—perhaps he never even noticed that the thumb had been torn off one of them."

" I thought," the duke said, looking puzzled, " there was a complete—alibi, I understand it is called."

" No guilty man can have a complete alibi," Bobby answered. " That is impossible. But Dickson managed to suggest one—he didn't prove an alibi; he suggested one. As soon as he got back to town he bought some whisky, drank some—he probably needed it—and spilt some on his person and clothing so that he smelt of it pretty thoroughly, and then he got himself run in for being drunk and disorderly. If he had spent the afternoon and evening getting drunk in the West End he couldn't have been committing a murder at Brush Hill. The weak point, of course, was where he got the drink, so he staged his act outside the Cut and Come Again, because he knew the people there always deny anyone has had anything to drink from them except ginger beer and cold tea."

"Why cold tea?" asked the duke, interested again. "A curious drink, surely."

"I only meant," explained Bobby gravely, "cold tea as a generic name for non-intoxicating beverages."

"Oh, I understand," said the duke.

"So he hoped," Bobby continued, "their denial of his having been at the club would be taken as merely routine—as it nearly was. Also, as it happened, we had independent evidence he had been seen there earlier in the day and had announced his intention of having a week-end soak. Perhaps preparing his alibi already."

"What made you suspect him in the first place?"

"We didn't," Bobby answered. "There was Mr. Chenery. There was Mr. Jacks, the dead man's partner. There was his manager, Mr. Wright. We had soon discovered things were not quite as they should be in the business. There was Wynne, a bad character who was plainly mixed up in it somehow. There was even Mr. Patterson, the American gentleman whose cigar was by the dead body—and who hadn't gone back to New York. Then there was a croupier from Monte Carlo we found had been on the spot that night. It was only by degrees things began to point towards Dickson. For one thing, he had lost a brand-new raincoat that night. Left it in a 'bus. An odd thing to lose in rainy weather. Sometimes clothing is got rid of because there is blood on it. That wasn't the reason in this case, but it did just cross my mind as a possibility. Then next day he had it again, and he was rather careful to explain it had been returned direct by the finder, not from the Baker Street Lost Property Office. I wondered in a vague way if that was because inquiries can be made from the Baker Street office. It's not impossible, of course, for an article left in a 'bus to be returned direct to the owner, but ninety-nine times in a hundred it goes to Baker Street. Then it seemed probable the whole thing began with the rumours circulating in the Cut and Come Again, started by Wynne's drunken boasting, about the big deal T. T. was to be asked to put through. Dickson was a member of the Cut and Come Again. The pistol used was one originally belonging to Mr. Chenery, but his story was that he had given it to Miss May for protection when she was in charge of the duchess's jewels, and apparently she put it away in a drawer in the room she used in the Park Lane flat and forgot it and left it there. Dickson used that room, too, of course, when he took over her job, and so might have come across the pistol there. The cigar, too, he had access to—in fact, he seemed to fill the conditions every time. Then, too, he was connected with the duchess, and it was clear that in some odd way you yourself, sir, and the duchess were concerned. We knew you had inspected the necklace, apparently with a view to purchase."

" I received a 'phone message," said the duke, "from Plymouth, apparently from Patterson. He said he was willing to buy the Fellows necklace for £30,000. He didn't wish to act personally, as the price would probably be increased for him, but he had an idea that from me a much smaller offer than £30,000 would be accepted for the—er——"

" For the prestige of having you as a customer and on the chance of getting the custom of the duchess away from the people she generally dealt with ? "

" Exactly," said the duke. " Quite natural ; quite reasonable. I called to see it and I offered £25,000. The offer was not accepted. Indeed, a certain discourteous surprise was most unnecessarily expressed."

Bobby tried to look sympathetic, though he wished he had been there to see the faces of the partners when a visit from which they had probably hoped much resulted in such an offer. He also reflected that his grace of Westhaven had contemplated making a very nice little middleman's profit.

" In fact," continued the duke, frowning at the memory, " I was weak enough, as I gathered I had really been mistaken about the value of the necklace, to let them think I had merely made a kind of preliminary suggestion, and might reconsider it."

Bobby thought that explained why the partners had paid so little heed to the warnings Miss May had given them.

" I communicated with Patterson when I heard he was in Paris," the duke went on, " and he entirely repudiated the 'phone message. I could not understand it."

" Probably Wynne or T. T. preparing the ground. T. T. is always great on that; part of his regular plan always, preparing the ground," observed Bobby. " Of course, an American accent is easily put on."

" Patterson's is extremely marked," agreed the duke. " but I don't see why my name should have been used."

" The calculation," Bobby explained, " was evidently that Jessop would only part with the necklace for cash or on cast-iron guarantees—or what he took to be such. If he could be induced to think he was dealing with the Duchess of Westhaven, he would think that cast iron all right. The whole thing is pure T. T. all over. He thought it out, you can bet anything, and then brought in Wynne to do the actual work. Wynne has special qualifications. He is both plausible and a gunman. The plausible crook generally doesn't like violence, and the gunman isn't often plausible. Wynne's both; uses his tongue and a gun. But no one's perfect, and Wynne lets his tongue wag when he's in drink. It did this time, till half the crooks in London knew T. T. had something big on, and that zero time was Saturday evening."

" I still fail to see," said the duke resentfully, " why my name should have been made use of in this fashion."

" Not only your name, sir," said Bobby. " Hastley Court

Uj

and your London flat as well. I expect what suggested the plan to T. T. was, first, the fact that the duchess is known to be interested in jewellery and precious stones generally, and occasionally to carry out deals in them; and, secondly, the fact that her former secretary was now in the employ of Mr. Jessop. The first thing done was to get you, sir, to show yourself interested in the necklace but hesitating at the price. Luckily for the conspirators, you did let the firm think you might reconsider your offer. The next step was to get a hint round to Jessop that the duchess was interested, which of course was true enough in a way. Jessop sent Miss May to show her the necklace. Naturally the duchess suspected nothing, and looked at the thing and talked about it and how much she would like it if only you, sir, didn't think it too expensive. Next thing was a 'phone message to Jessop in her name to say she was still thinking of buying, and could the necklace be shown her again, only on the quiet, as she didn't wish her husband to know. For that reason Miss Hilda May wasn't to be told or brought along, as she was known at Hastley Court by all the staff—by you yourself, sir, too, of course—and her appearance there would be noticed. In the same way, the day chosen was the day of a big garden-party at Hastley Court, so that one or two strangers extra wouldn't attract any attention. Instead of Miss May, Mr. Jessop took Mr. Wright, the firm's manager, with him. They were to pretend to be guests—very likely they were not the only gate-crashers that afternoon."

" I have long suspected it," said the duke moodily. " It adds enormously to the expense. But what can one do ? One can't possibly know all the people who have to be invited, and those who are will forget their invitation cards. Besides bribery—half a crown to the lodgekeeper and so on. It's most difficult."

Leaving this problem unconsidered, since it was not his, Bobby went on:

" Wright and Jessop waited in the car-park. Wynne found them, and introduced himself as the duchess's secretary. Up till then Dickson knew nothing of what was going on. It was his busy day, indeed; no time for conspiring so far as he was concerned; his absence for more than a minute or two would certainly have been noticed. Wynne took Jessop into the house, into a small empty room where a woman called Magotty Meg was waiting. Wynne had managed that by telling one of your staff that one of the guests, an elderly lady, had found the heat and excitement too much for her, and could she be given some quiet place where she could rest alone for half an hour. Naturally your people wouldn't suspect anything; quite possibly a ten-shilling note changed hands, and there was this woman established in a room at Hastley Court as if she belonged there."

" I-I-I-never," said the duke, stuttering his indignation, " heard of such insolence in my life."

" Oh, there's worse to come," said Bobby cheerfully.

The duke looked his entire conviction that that was not possible.

" Next thing," Bobby explained, " was to get the use of your Park Lane flat. That wasn't difficult. Easy to find out when you and the duchess and the servants were at Hastley Court. I believe when you and the duchess are not at the flat there is only one woman in charge."

" There is no reason," the duke pointed out, " to pay servants for doing nothing."

" Of course not," agreed Bobby. " She was got out of the way by a gift of two theatre tickets—good seats; stalls —for a matinée, and during her absence Wynne, a bit of an expert in these things, climbed the fire-escape as a workman, got into the flat, changed his clothes again, let in the woman whose job it was to personate the duchess, and, when Jessop arrived by appointment, admitted him.

The absence of servants was explained to Jessop by the necessity of keeping the business secret for the time being —it was always impressed on Jessop that you yourself, sir, were not to know anything about it till the transaction was completed, when the idea was it would be too late for you to object. I take it Jessop never suspected anything. If he had ever seen the duchess, it was only at a distance. The woman personating her was made up to resemble her— I'm told the duchess has a distinctive style of dressing."

" I am glad to say," remarked the duke, " she ignores modern fashion crazes."

" So I was told," Bobby went on. " Made Meg's job a whole lot easier. Anyhow, Jessop was taken in all right. The ground had been so carefully prepared, almost any-one would have been. You yourself, sir, had been roped in to show an interest in the necklace. Miss May, who knew the duchess well, had reported how anxious she was to buy if only your consent could be got. Everyone knows the duchess is a connoisseur in all kinds of precious stones. Jessop had seen the same woman in a private room at Hastley Court, and now apparently in full possession at your Park Lane flat, and with what seemed a good reason for a certain show of secrecy—that for the time it was all to be kept from your own knowledge. Jessop probably argued that, once the necklace had been handed over and a payment made on account, it was quite safe. At the worst, he had only to fear the return of the necklace, when he would be the first payment to the good."

" Was a payment made ? " the duke asked.

" Five thousand pounds," Bobby answered. " That was the amount found in French and Swiss currency in Jessop's flat. Probably some plausible tale was told to explain the use of foreign money. Really, of course, the object was to prevent its being traced. I rather think Jessop was told that it was money deposited abroad during the 1930 crisis.

The Stock Exchange advised many clients to take their money out of British securities at that time, you remember."

The duke looked a little startled.

" As a matter of fact," he admitted, " certain funds . . . it seemed prudent . I believe some were in the duchess's name . . . one had advice. . . ."

" Quite so, sir," agreed Bobby. " After all, *dulce et decorum est* doesn't mean cash, does it ? " And, before the duke had quite taken this in, he hurried on with his story. " I think it all fitted in quite nicely with Jessop's own plans. The firm was in low water and he himself in difficulties. The reserve price for the necklace was £50,000. At the interview with the sham duchess, £65,000 was mentioned. It's fairly certain Jessop intended to give a lower figure to his partner. I think he intended to report the price he had accepted as £55,000—five thousand more than the limit—and keep the £10,000 extra for himself. It was quite possible for him to do that, as the whole thing was to be kept secret ; his supposed client, the sham duchess, always stressing that, on the ground that you were not to know anything about it till it was too late for you to interfere."

" As I understand it," the duke said, " Mr. Jessop was being deceived by a gang of rogues impersonating the duchess and her secretary, Mr. Dickson, and actually having the audacity, the insolence, to make use of Hastley Court and our London flat ? "

" Yes, sir ; awful cheek," agreed Bobby. " It's cheek that does it," he added thoughtfully, quoting a maxim that is no doubt the first in the Golden Book of the Wisdom of the World.

" But if Dickson was innocent of all this, knew nothing about it," the duke asked, " why is he accused of the murder ? "

" That's another story," Bobby answered.

CHAPTER XXXIV

AND LAST

"To make that part clear," Bobby continued, "I'll have to go back a bit. You know the *Upper Ten*? High-class shilling weekly; goes in for photos of ' leading personalities.' Jessop knew the duchess was supposed to be at the races the day of the sham interview. It was put to him as part of the plan to keep you, sir, from getting to know too soon what was on. He would be told the plan was for her to show herself at the races, then drive up by herself to town, and then go back and show herself at the races again as if she had never been away. All that to keep Jessop from smelling a rat, as he might have done otherwise if he had heard of her being at the races that day. But it just happened that the *Upper Ten* put under her photo the exact time when it was taken—at the finish of the three o'clock. Well, that made it plain she couldn't also have been at Park Lane at three, when Jessop thought he saw her there. Naturally he got the wind up. Perhaps he had really been a little uncomfortable before about all the secrecy. Apparently he didn't notice the *Upper Ten* photo for a time. The firm takes in some of the smart weeklies for customers to look at—the dentist and doctor idea, you know. It was only by chance Jessop happened to notice that photo Saturday morning. But it showed him at once there was crooked work somewhere, though he didn't dare say too much for fear of his own little crooked game coming out—didn't dare say a word to his partner or manager, for instance. In his first excitement he rang us up and said he had been swindled out of the Fellows necklace, though even then he rang up, not from his own place, but from the Cut and Come Again. But then he thought better of it and refused to tell us any more. Of course, our people said they couldn't do much unless he gave full details. Whereon he rang off. But we had information T. T. was bringing off a big deal that same night. So it was decided someone should go along to Brush Hill and see if they could find out what was really on, and the super took on the job himself. Keen on bringing in T. T. if possible. There wasn't much time to arrange anything, and it's a bit of a job to get near T. T. when he has a big deal on. He takes precautions; puts scouts out. The best that could be thought of was the old furniture-van dodge and a faked accident. It didn't work too well. T. T. got his warning, though he only had time to bluff us by pushing the necklace away in a locker in the van. He meant, if it was found, to say we put it there ourselves in an attempt to plant it on him. He has the cheek of the devil."

"How did Dickson know all this?" interrupted the duke.

"He didn't, not then," answered Bobby. "He can only have tumbled to what was going on much later. Probably he knew of the rumours in the Cut and Come Again. At first he wouldn't pay them much attention. You remember Jessop didn't 'phone from his own place when the photo in the *Upper Ten* showed him there was something very wrong. Most likely he was afraid of being overheard. His first impulse was to rush round to the Cut and Come Again. He knew a lot of talk had been going on there. He would hope to find out something—to get T. T.'s address for one thing. He may have meant to tackle Wynne, too, if he could find him, as the originator of the stories. Jessop didn't know Dickson, but Dickson knew him by sight. He saw how excited Jessop was; probably heard Jessop had been asking about T. T. and Wynne. He began to put things together. He knew Jessop had been at Hastley Court; he knew about the lady who had been taken ill and was allowed to sit by herself in a quiet room to recover, and of whose identity no one seemed sure; he knew the duchess was fond of carrying out deals in jewellery. So he thought he would visit Brush Hill, too, and, by way of precaution, he took with him a small automatic Denis Chenery had given Miss May and she had put away in a drawer and never thought of again. Also he provided himself with rubber gloves by way of extra precaution—precautions can cut both ways, though. If you're straight, you don't need 'em. And to screw himself up he drank rather a lot of whisky. He may even have had already some idea of establishing an alibi by showing himself at the Cut and Come Again. Drink affects almost everyone differently, you know. A glass of beer will knock some people off their legs. Whisky doesn't affect Dickson's legs. It does affect his judgment, his self-control; releases all his impulses, so to say. He was in that state, his mind, as it were, hanging on a hair trigger, when he got to Brush Hill. At first he was headed off by T. T.'s scouts. He waited, the whisky working on him all the time. He was smoking one of Mr. Patterson's cigars, probably with some sort of subconscious idea of soothing himself down a bit. As it happened, he left the cigar behind him, together with his pistol he used. Next thing was that T. T.'s scouts cleared off, ' according to plan,' as soon as they had warned T. T. Dickson wouldn't understand that, of course. He would just realise the coast was clear, and he climbed in by the study window where he had seen T. T. and Wynne talking. At a guess he meant to claim a share of the booty, but he found the room empty, and when he looked in the safe he saw what he thought was the Fellows necklace. Actually it was a replica made for film purposes T. T. had bought up on the chance, I suppose, of its being useful some day. It seems that, while he was looking at it, Jessop appeared. He may have seen Dickson climb in and followed him. Probably Dickson saw himself cornered. It was dark, and he may have taken Jessop for one of T. T.'s bodyguard. Or he may just have lost his head, what with the whisky and being caught in the act and so on, and fired more or less at random. Most likely all he was conscious of was that he had the Fellows necklace and he meant to keep it. All that is certain is that the automatic went off and Jessop was hit—fatally. I should be quite willing to believe Dickson never meant to kill, only to make sure of getting away safely. Very likely it was a shock to him to realise what he had done. He dropped cigar and pistol and bolted, and, once outside, it must have been a still greater shock to him to realise that all he had was a worthless imitation. He threw it away. When, a few minutes later, as he was hurrying away in a state of great panic and excitement, he saw a uniformed policeman looking at him rather closely, he could think of nothing better to do than to dodge into a pawnbroker's. Now the pawnbroker's assistant has identified him, and we have found the rubber gloves he wore in the pocket of the coat he pawned."

" Is that the raincoat I saw in your possession ? " the duke asked. " I remember I saw you had one I thought was mine."

" His was given him by the duchess," Bobby answered. " I expect it came from the same shop as yours, and looked much the same."

" Is all this why Dickson tried to shoot the—er—person you speak of as assistant to a pawnbroker ? "

" Yes," agreed Bobby. " Higson. As soon as he saw Higson with us, he realised what that meant, lost his head again, tried to silence him. ' Suppress his evidence ' idea. Silly. We knew too much by that time. It was a great piece of luck, though, that Jessop put in his pocket that copy of the *Upper Ten*. It looked as if there must be some reason for his having it; his last words were something about ' duke '—and there was a snap of the duchess in the paper. I brooded over that photo for hours, but the only thing I could see distinctive was that it did give the actual time when it was taken—and that didn't dawn on me for long enough. Even then, at first it didn't seem much help. Only other things turned up—a woman named Magotty Meg, for instance, we began to think might have been used if personation had taken place. You see, sir, it was certain you and the duchess were in it somehow, but it was certain you couldn't be knowingly, so that suggested conspiracy, and that suggested personation. At first we thought Dickson was in that part, too. But we couldn't bring him in. There was no trace of any connection with either T. T. or Wynne. He had a clear alibi both for the Hastley Court business and for the Park Lane breaking in. So he was rather falling out of the picture till he brought himself in again by dropping hints about Chenery. Funny thing. No criminal can ever leave well alone. Against nature, I suppose."

" Do you mean Dickson will be tried—hanged ? " the duke asked, for once a little human emotion piercing the starched frigidity of his manner.

" Well, sir," answered Bobby slowly, and in fact proving himself to be a good prophet, " there was no premeditation: he might even pretend he was only at Brush Hill to recover the necklace for its rightful owner. I expect something of the sort was in his mind when he persuaded you to come hunting the necklace with him—display of innocent intention. Then, when he saw Higson, he lost his head again. But they may even reduce the main charge to manslaughter. He'll probably get off with a term of penal servitude."

" I am glad to hear it," said the duke.

" But all that," continued Bobby, resuming his narrative, " didn't help us much to find out what had become of the necklace. Then we found T. T. was talking a lot about moving, and was nosing round trying to find out where the furniture van we used came from. Till then we had assumed Wynne had the necklace. T. T.'s inquiries made us guess it might have been hidden in the van. If it hadn't been for the murder happening, and giving us plenty to think about, we should have spotted that at once; first thing we should have thought of," declared Bobby with more confidence than he really felt. " Only then again, but for the murder, and for the way we kept T. T. under close observation, he would soon have found a chance to get hold of the thing again. As it was, in the excitement he didn't even notice where the van came from. Other people began to get the same idea. I think you yourself, sir—— ? "

" Dickson," said the duke with dignity, " put certain suggestions before me. They seemed reasonable. I had no idea they were the result of guilty knowledge. I authorised him to take steps. I considered it was wholly proper to attempt to recover the necklace, though I did not wish attention to be drawn to efforts that might be entirely misconceived."

Bobby was also privately of the belief that his grace had not been wholly indifferent to the prospect of pocketing a fat reward. Even to the wealthiest, £5,000 is £5,000, and the duke was far from enjoying a reputation for indifference to such considerations. Even the suggestion of buying the necklace he had only accepted when he believed there was a sure market in view.

" Everyone seems to have got the idea at the same moment," Bobby continued. " Wright had a silly idea in his head that Miss May had the necklace. After his little effort at housebreaking failed, he went to a private inquiry agent, who seems to have kept an eye on Dickson as well. He found out Dickson was inquiring about furniture vans— Dickson tried to pump me once or twice—and reported to

Wright, who guessed what that meant. He told Jacks, and they started off almost as soon as you and Dickson. That brought in Mr. Chenery and Miss May, and by that time Wynne and T. T. were on the same idea. So there were the whole lot of us, careering through the Cotswolds after the most illusive furniture van known to history, and it all the time parked in an orchard, with its crew tucking into raspberry jam and home-made scones. We were afraid at one time they were going to turn up casualties, too, but they've reported safe from the pub they walked to after the accident Wynne and T. T. engineered. I don't suppose they've any idea yet that a £100,000 necklace was hidden in their van all the time they were using it. I take it, sir, you were not with Dickson when he shot Higson ? "

" He left me in the car while he got down by a wood where we stopped," explained the duke. " We could see smoke on the further side of the trees, and we had seen a car come out of a turning just ahead at a very high rate of speed. Dickson said he would go and see what was happening. He was away some time, and when he returned I told him I had heard shots and asked him what they meant. He seemed excited. He wouldn't give a plain answer. When I pressed him, he grew insolent. I informed him I should request the local police to investigate. He replied with an expression of extreme vulgarity, and hit me violently over the head with some hard implement. On recovering my senses I found myself in the—er—circumstances of which you are already aware. I should wish you clearly to understand that I desire no reference to be made at any time or in any way to—er—those circumstances."

" No, sir," said Bobby; " that's quite understood."

" So many subversive and revolutionary interests in these days," the duke reminded him, " are only too anxious for any opportunity to throw an appearance of ridicule or discredit in any form on the established institutions of the country."

Bobby regarded with more awe even than before that special established institution of the country at the moment speaking to him.

" Very regrettable tendency of these days," he murmured, shaking his head sadly. " The *Daily Trumpet*, for instance."

The duke scowled.

" A paper that should not be permitted to appear," he pronounced.

" Or the *Weekly Red*," observed Bobby thoughtfully.

The duke shivered.

" Distinctly—Bolshevist," he said, shuddering a little as he pronounced that word of dread and shame and horror.

" You may be sure I shall be careful, sir," Bobby assured him earnestly. " And I'm sure Mr. Chenery will be, too, as one of the family."

" Mr. Chenery—Denis ? " asked the duke. " He doesn't know . . . know . . . ? "

There was a certain uneasiness in his tone as he spoke, but Bobby's voice was bland as cream and honey.

" As one of the family," he explained, " Mr. Chenery was naturally anxious to know if the head of it was safe. He was present, in fact, last night while my report was being made."

" Inexcusable," said the duke—and how he said it !

" I wouldn't attempt to excuse it," Bobby murmured truthfully. " He was exceedingly interested. I understand he is writing a film play."

" A—a what ? " said the duke, who had risen to his feet like destiny personified, but now sat down again as if his legs had suddenly given way, rather like a dictator coming suddenly upon an inscription carved deep in marble of a resolution he was just going to break.

" A film play," repeated Bobby. " You know, sir, one of those things they show in cinemas."

" You say," almost gasped the duke, " Denis is—— ? "

" Yes, sir," said Bobby confidently, because, after all, what is true of practically everyone in the country was probably true of Denis as well—no reason to assume the morbid eccentricity abstention would indicate. " He seemed to think the unfortunate affair of last night would be most effective on the screen."

The duke was quite speechless now. Bobby continued dreamily:

" I understood he had an idea the Hollywood people would think it funny—British duke in a sack. A vulgar lot," he said, with a reproving frown.

" Funny ? " repeated the duke, quite bewildered. " Did you say—funny ? "

" Oh, they think anything funny over there, in the States," said Bobby regretfully. " A most perverted sense of humour."

" I shall see that it is stopped at once," declared the duke, striving to recover his normal poise.

" Very necessary, sir," agreed Bobby. " I believe "— after all, in a credulous age, one can believe anything; why not ?—" I believe the *Weekly Red* is already consider- ing making certain offers—they might be afraid of the *Crimson Banner* getting hold of the story first."

The duke had become very pale. His voice was small and weak as he protested:

" But Denis—Denis Chenery. He's one of the family, in the line of succession."

" Far off," observed Bobby. " Thing of the future; thing of the present is that he's hard up. Wants to get married. Keen on it for some reason. Don't know why. It's Miss Hilda May. She's been talking to him about the film idea."

There was an awful silence. The duke was wiping his forehead. Bobby was telling his conscience once again that everybody is writing a film play. Therefore Denis was writing one. And, if so, it was quite certain that he and Hilda were talking about it. His conscience was not satisfied but it was silenced, which is just as good.

" The garage hardly pays," Bobby went on. " That's why money might tempt him—easy money, lots of it. Films. Cinema. Articles in the Bolshevik Press. All that sort of thing."

" It must not be allowed," said the duke, just like that.

" No, sir," said Bobby.

" I shall——" said the duke, and paused.

" Yes, sir, I should," agreed Bobby.

" Only what ? " asked the duke.

Bobby somewhat ostentatiously rubbed his nose, scratched his head, gave other signs of doubt.

" Denis owes a duty to his family," declared the duke.

" He owes cash to his creditors," said Bobby. " No doubt if he had an allowance from the estate . . . settled   . as prospective heir . . . twelve or fifteen hundred a year . . ."

" Eh ? " said the duke, utterly astonished at so novel a notion.

" Give you the whip hand of him, you see, sir," explained Bobby. " Stop it any moment. If a film was put on——" The duke shuddered. " If an article appeared——" The duke shivered. " Make you perfectly safe——" The duke sighed.

After a long pause, he said :

" I will instruct my lawyers."

" Yes, sir," said Bobby.

" And I'm obliged to you for—er—warning me."

" Not at all, sir," said Bobby politely. " After all, Mr. Chenery saved my life last night at some risk to his own."

" Did what ? " asked the duke, evidently trying to bring this remark into some kind of relation with what had gone before.

" Saved my life," repeated Bobby. " I'll let him know what you say, shall I ? You see, sir, if once the cinema people get a contract——"

" Quite so," said the duke, forgetting suspicion in panic. "Tell him at once—tell him I wish to see him immediately."

" Yes, sir," said Bobby, and retired.

" And that," he thought to himself with satisfaction, " is as pretty a piece of blackmail as any C.I.D. man ever put through."

THE END